T0267606

this is
me trying

this
is
me
trying

RACQUEL MARIE

FEIWEL AND FRIENDS
NEW YORK

A Feiwel and Friends Book
An imprint of Macmillan Publishing Group, LLC
120 Broadway, New York, NY 10271 • fiercereads.com

Our books may be purchased in bulk for promotional, educational, or business use. Please
contact your local bookseller or the Macmillan Corporate and Premium Sales Department at
(800) 221-7945 ext. 5442 or by email at MacmillanSpecialMarkets@macmillan.com.

Library of Congress Cataloging-in-Publication Data

Names: Marie, Racquel, author.
Title: This is me trying / Racquel Marie.
Description: First edition. | New York : Feiwel & Friends, 2024. |
    Audience: Ages 14–18. | Audience: Grades 10–12. | Summary: Growing up,
    Bryce, Beatriz, and Santiago were inseparable, but after the dissolution
    of their friendship and Bryce's suicide, Beatriz and Santiago attempt to
    reconcile and navigate love, mental illness, and forgiveness.
Identifiers: LCCN 2023028808 | ISBN 9781250891389 (hardcover)
Subjects: CYAC: Grief—Fiction. | Friendship—Fiction. | Mental illness—
    Fiction. | Forgiveness—Fiction. | LCGFT: Novels.
Classification: LCC PZ7.1.M3713 Th 2024 | DDC [Fic]—dc23
LC record available at lccn.loc.gov/2023028808

First edition, 2024
Book design by Abby Granata
Feiwel and Friends logo designed by Filomena Tuosto
Printed in the United States of America

ISBN 978-1-250-89138-9
1 3 5 7 9 10 8 6 4 2

AUTHOR'S NOTE

This book largely follows the aftermath of a teenage boy's death by suicide. The method is never disclosed. These characters also deal with obsessive-compulsive disorder, anxiety, panic attacks, depression, grief, and morbid ideation. I have tried my best to write about each of these subjects with care, and I encourage you to extend that same care to yourself when deciding whether to proceed with reading.

For a more specific list of content warnings, please visit **racquelmariebooks.com**.

Resources, if you need someone to talk to:

- **The 988 Suicide & Crisis Lifeline**: Call 1-800-273-TALK (8255) or text 988. Visit their website at 988lifeline.org.

- **The Trevor Project, for LGBTQ+ youth**: Call 1-866-488-7386 or text START to 678-678. Visit their website at thetrevorproject.org.

Much love,
Racquel

For me,
then, now, and later

chapter one

BEATRIZ

I'm unnaturally talented at pretending to be asleep.

Generally, it's a pretty useless skill to have. But when the nightmares and subsequent insomnia took the reins a few years back, I began wasting nights away watching the stars instead of the insides of my eyelids. Usually, I slipped back into my room by the time Mom was up. As was inevitable with her work schedule, she finally caught me one morning.

Her on the ground. Me on the roof. The look on her face that said she thought my gaze was set in a different direction than the sky. After that, I knew something had to change.

From then on, she woke me up. Or at least believed she did. It didn't matter if I spent the night whispering to the stars, sketching constellations, or toying with the unusable key dangling around my neck. By the time sunrise rolled around, I made sure my ass was in bed. Eyes shut, breathing heavy, limbs askew, the picture of safe and sound.

Today is no exception.

Mom raps lightly on the door. "Abejita? Time to get up."

I force myself to yawn as she pokes her head in. "Morning."

Lottie scampers through the cracked door, a chipper bad omen despite her old age. The black cat leaps onto my bed with ease and receives my pets more enthusiastically than Mom's. I thank my long nails for that.

"So what'll it be today? We've got toast with that strawberry jam from the farmer's market, huevos con frijoles, or cinnamon granola." Mom pulls her thick, dark hair into a ponytail and tries to smile. First-day breakfasts are a staple of hers even if domesticity isn't.

"I can just grab a banana on my way out." I free myself from the sheets, and Lottie curls up in the warm impression my body left behind.

"Are you sure?" Mom asks. "I could make pancakes! We've got plenty of maple syrup and probably some chocolate chips lying around somewhere." Try as I might, I can't ignore the way her hands shake at her sides.

Dammit. "Actually, I'd love some eggs."

"Con frijoles?"

"Just eggs. Thanks."

She's already humming as she goes downstairs. I wait for the click of the stovetop flame before I lock myself in the bathroom.

Avoiding my reflection, I splash my face with water. Gentle cleanser to wash. Toner applied with a reusable pad. Moisturizer with SPF 50. Pea-sized squirt of each of my dermatologist-prescribed creams. It's only when my face is glistening that I can bear to meet my eyes in the mirror.

Acne scars line my cheeks and jaw, dotting a few spaces on my forehead. I run a hand over my scalp, the light fuzz of hair growing back too quickly. I'll have to buzz it again soon. And re-shave the ends of my brows while I'm at it. I categorize the things I see objectively: the bags under my eyes, the bump on the side of my chapped mouth, the pores around the dorsal hump making up most of my nose. I repeat them in my head as I apply makeup. I repeat them until I forget what my face looks like as a whole, remembering it only in parts.

Eye shadow primer, base color, blend the crease contour, pack that shade beneath my lower lash line, pick a shimmery lid pigment. Clean up the fallout.

Eyeliner, falsies, two coats of mascara. Face primer, foundation, concealer. Light powder, contour, highlight. Sharp brow pencil in a color three shades darker than my natural ones. Line and fill my lips with black, add gloss on top. I consider blush but decide against it. Five spritzes of setting spray. And I'm done.

Mom hears me before she sees me, the thick platforms of my boots echoing against the aged wood floors. I tuck my necklace under my shirt as she slides a plate of eggs onto the counter. "So," she starts. "Candace called."

She and Mom still talk on occasion when they run into each other at the store or during parent-teacher conferences. Mom always invites her for dinner to chat over enough wine to lubricate their minds, but the goal seems vague. Bonding over broken children and dead first loves only gets you so far. Their first and only big talk did enough, so it's a relief Candace never takes up the offer. "That's nice."

"She asked if you could drive Whitney and Olive to school today."

"Whitney has a car," I reply between steaming bites.

"Something's wrong with the engine. Tomorrow she'll ride with the Richards kids." Mom plays with the new bracelet on her wrist. It's dainty and silver and sports small circular charms that tinkle when she moves her hands, which she does about as often as she blinks. She's worn nothing but long sleeves since she got it last week, but fabric can't muffle the fairylike sound.

I don't drive Whitney around anymore, not since last fall. But explaining that to Mom is actually less appealing than just doing the favor. My fork whines against my now empty plate. I wasn't even hungry. "Fine. I'll do it."

"Thank you." She stands and kisses my forehead, laughing a little as my spiky layer of hair tickles her mouth. I leave with her smile impressed on my mind.

Whitney and Olive are waiting on the porch when I pull up to their house, just two streets down from mine. Whitney already texted me five times this morning, but I put my phone on Do Not Disturb before she could send a sixth.

"At this rate, we're going to miss graduation," Whitney groans as she climbs into the passenger seat. Olive slips into the back and flinches at their sister's tone as they buckle in. I'd flinch if Whitney spoke to me any other way.

"School bus will be passing by in fifteen if you'd prefer that," I reply as I pull away from the curb.

"Bite me."

"Thanks for the ride," Olive interjects. They fiddle with the strap of their baggy purple overalls when I meet their eyes in the rear-view mirror.

It confuses me how Olive and Whitney can have such similar faces but still look nothing alike. Maybe it's just the only child in me talking. They share brown skin, thick black hair, round faces with high cheekbones, and upturned eyes so richly brown that they're basically black. Whitney's hair falls in calculated curls over her exposed shoulders. Olive's hair is bluntly cut at their chin.

"You don't need to thank me," I say, and adjust my mirror so they're out of sight.

"Especially not when she's late," Whitney adds as she picks at the ends of her hair. I wish I could say it was heat-damaged, but she's definitely still using the same protective spray I bought her in tenth grade. "Ignoring timely texts is rude."

"You texted, and I quote, 'Beatriz, if I'm late on the first day of school because you're too busy applying your goth clown costume, I will sue you.'"

Olive stifles a laugh in the back seat. Whitney just touches up her lip gloss using her front camera. It's also a brand I recommended. "Don't be cute. You haven't answered any of my texts for weeks."

"My cuteness is out of my hands," I say as we pull up to school. A perk of finally being seniors is getting to use this lot instead of parking on the street. Our student population of less than four hundred means fewer cars, but it also means a smaller campus to find parking.

Whitney shoos Olive away as we head through the front chain-link gates. The pair may be siblings, but Olive is a junior. It likely goes against some code of conduct in Whitney's mind to be seen with them in public.

A few people cast uncomfortable looks our way when it's just the two of us. If we were in any other town, it'd be because I, as she so gracefully put it, am in my goth clown costume, while she, as I'll so gracefully put it, looks like an amalgamation of all of fast fashion's greatest hits since last fall. But we're not in any other town. So even though it unsettles people and reminds them of things no one likes to think about, nobody questions why Beatriz Dougherty and Whitney Ocampo are walking into school together.

"So are you waiting to tell me something or are you just looking for an excuse to hang out?" I finally ask Whitney once we reach the front office.

From behind her receptionist desk, Kim hands me my schedule. She doesn't need to be reminded who I am. "How are we today, my dear?" she asks before Whitney can sass me.

"Just peachy," I say.

"That's good, that's really good," Kim says, like I just told her I cured cancer over the summer. "Oh, and Whitney, dear, here you go." She hands over her schedule too.

"Thanks, Kim. How are your kids?" Whitney asks. I resist the urge to roll my eyes.

"Oh, they're doing just great now that Amy is settled at U of A," she coos. Then her face shifts, because of course it does. "But *truly*, how are you, my dears? This has got to be rough for you two, being back here for your final year."

She says this like we haven't been back at school before. Like we haven't been back for more than two years, haven't hit milestones and celebrated birthdays and holidays. Didn't already attend the funeral and every bullshit memorial service the school and neighborhood committee insisted on hosting. Like these halls are a unique reminder. Like just breathing isn't enough of one.

"Feelin' like a rock star," I say.

Whitney kicks me where Kim can't see. "We're great, thank you. We'll see you around." She practically drags me out of the office, nails biting into the mesh of my sleeves.

"If you're going to bruise me this badly, at least take me out to dinner first."

"She was just being polite. You don't have to be a bitch."

"What was I supposed to say? 'Thanks, Kim. You're right, this is shit. Let's chat *all* about Bryce! Who should go first, me or Whitney? You want the girlfriend's or the stepsister's side of things—'"

Whitney puts a finger to my lips, a smudge of my black lipstick inking her. She has to stretch on her tiptoes to reach me, a reminder that there's over a foot of height difference between us. "It's *me*, okay? I get it." Her eyes lower to my chest. A cocky remark is on the tip of my lips before I realize what she's actually staring at.

The golden key is out from under my shirt. It normally hangs against my heart, hidden. In the spur of the moment, my hands must have reached for it.

Whitney's eyes go soft. "You still wear it."

I quickly conceal the key again. "Let's go."

We head to our new lockers, stopping at mine first because I'm closer to the front of the alphabet. I turn the dial as Whitney reads off the combination for me.

"Aren't the Richards clones waiting for you?" I ask.

"You know, it's pretty rude to refer to twins that way."

As I pop open my locker, I'm hit with a wave of stale air. "The only time I hung out with y'all, Abby told me that I look like the type of corpse even a necrophiliac wouldn't fuck."

Whitney rolls her eyes. "That wasn't the only time you hung out with us, and you can't blame Dustin or even Abby for that. She was high for the first time and profusely apologized literally the next day."

"By telling me any necrophiliac would *gladly* fuck me."

"You're missing the point."

"Which is?"

She huffs and pulls out her phone, making a noise between a squeak and a gasp.

"What? Are Abby and Courtney kicking you out of the group Halloween costume?"

"No, I just—I think we should talk about the elephant in the room."

Metal hinges groan as I shut my locker. "What elephant?"

Whitney bites her lip and stares at me. Suddenly, I'm scared this conversation is headed somewhere dangerous. Because while there are a lot of things we don't talk about, there are some things we *really* don't talk about.

I hike my bag onto my shoulder. "Actually, I've got to get to homeroom. Last thing I need is to be stuck with a seat in the front and give people ideas about talking to me." I turn as Whitney calls my name.

My chin slams into someone's face—hard. Were I not over six feet tall and well accustomed to wearing platform boots, I'd have fallen backward onto Whitney from the impact. As it is, I barely catch myself on the wall of lockers.

I press a hand against my throbbing chin and open my eyes, expecting to see Rick or one of the other basketball guys. But instead, I see a ghost.

"Santiago." My voice is miles away. It's a child's, a preteen's. It's something only I've heard, whispered and cried against wet shower tiles or open starry sky, where no one can ask me to repeat my confessions.

Santiago's hand is pressed against his nose, a mop of brown waves falling out of a loose ponytail and onto his face. But I can still see his eyes—dark and wide and confused. Painfully familiar.

Whitney throws her hands into the air. "Welcome home!"

chapter two

SANTIAGO

Fuck.

Admittedly, it took me a second to recognize her. In my un-
biased defense, the last time I saw Bea, she was fourteen, had long
blond hair, and was still rocking mismatched combinations of
neon colors anyone with a less cool mom would've been dissuaded
from leaving the house in. Technically speaking, I guess, the last
time I saw her she was wearing a color palette more comparable
to today's look while screaming through tears at me, but Bryce's
funeral was an anomaly in more ways than one. So, frankly, I think
my shock is understandable.

It's less understandable that I say nothing as she stares at me.
The horror on my childhood best friend's face tells me there's no
way Whitney let her know I was moving back to town to help my
abuelo and, despite my best and most delusional wishes, she is not
pleased to find this out. She says my name once—more statement
than question—before practically running away, her feet clamoring

against the linoleum floors in what can only be described as stilt-like torture devices disguised as shoes.

The first words I manage to get out of my mouth, minutes later, eloquently represent my current mental state.

"She's *tall*," I say as Whitney leads me to my homeroom. She's taking me the long way around the science buildings to avoid any voyeurs. "And goth. Like, really goth."

"You're practically the same height," Whitney says. I don't argue that in those shoes, Bea was taller. My bruised nose can testify. "And I warned you that she looked different. You look different too."

I glance down at my outfit, dark cuffed jeans and a band shirt from a show Eric dragged me to back in California. Reminders of Eric don't elicit fond memories, but I slept in this morning and the shirt had already been out of my moving boxes, sitting at the foot of my bed. Reminiscing never gets me anywhere, and yet.

I push my hair out of my face. I need to invest in better hair ties. "*You* look the same."

Whitney rolls her eyes and, as if to prove me wrong, hikes up her seasonally inappropriate halter top. Yeah, okay, fair. Late puberty hit us all. "I can't believe you didn't tell her you were coming back," she says, the edge in her tone coming straight from her stepmother's mouth. "Seriously, what the fuck were you thinking?"

There's nothing she could say to me that I haven't already said to myself in chronic bouts of self-loathing, but I spare both of us any attempt at a defense. I *wasn't* thinking is the truth, or at least half of it. The other half is that thinking gets me about as far as reminiscing, which is to say I've spent most of the past few years with my brain numbly submerged in the present.

Honestly, Whitney replying with the utmost optimism to my

out-of-the-blue message a few weeks ago about moving back for senior year was more than I deserve. The look of horror Bea gave me before stumbling off was far more apt.

We pause on an empty path carved into grass, the rest of the school a galaxy away. "I didn't know what to say to her," I admit and lie. "We haven't talked since the funeral."

Whitney's face softens. Once, I worshipped that face and the ground she walked on. Once, she was just a hot girl I knew because Bryce's mom married her dad. Now we're members of an unfortunate club, also brought together because of Bryce and a church.

We keep walking, only shifting direction in conversation. "So, how long has she been . . ." I pause, careful with my words in a way I so often am not. ". . . Like that?"

Whitney stares at me like I asked her what my own name is. "Since Bryce."

"Oh" is all I manage. We turn a corner and join a crowd of students milling around, hugging and yelping in first-day-back excitement.

I feel a surge of nostalgia as I instantly recognize face after face. Kids from first grade, kids who carpooled with me when Pa was touring the East Coast, kids whose parents watched us on field trips to museums a few towns over, and kids who didn't bat an eye when I disappeared before freshman year to help chase Pa's dreams of stardom in California, only popping back months later for half of a funeral.

"Holy shit," someone calls from my right. Whitney laughs, pushing me on before I can see who's speaking. Then a tall, dark-skinned Black guy is hugging me. As soon as he's done, a petite, pale white girl does the same.

"Dustin!" I say excitedly, then, "and Courtney!"

"Honestly, I thought Whitney was bullshitting when she said you were coming back," Dustin says, slapping me on the shoulder so hard that I struggle not to wince. "But here you are, Santiago Espinosa in the fucking flesh."

"Here I am." I do a slow spin with my arms raised. Dustin wolf whistles. At the back of my mind, I realize what a whiplash this is. I should be thinking about Bea right now, but I relish feeling wanted here in a way I never expected to be again.

"Alrighty, calm down," Courtney says to Dustin, pulling his arm around her as she snuggles into his chest.

"You two?" I point between them. They give each other obnoxiously sweet, scrunched-up faces as they nod. Last I saw Dustin Richards, he was barely Whitney's height and his gums were so swollen from his braces that you could hardly find his teeth in his mouth. Last I saw Courtney Johnson, she was the epitome of a Horse Girl despite never having ridden or touched one.

Even though our graduating class is a whopping ninety-seven students, the four of us don't all have homeroom together. Luckily, Courtney and I do, so while Whitney and Dustin head off, Whitney moaning about how much trouble she's going to be in with Abby—Dustin's twin sister and another familiar name—for ditching her this morning, Courtney and I head to class.

It's almost comical how quickly everyone notices that 1.) I am new here, and then 2.) I am, in fact, not new here, but 3.) I am someone from their childhood who has miraculously reappeared.

Courtney and I take random seats while I try to pretend I can't hear the whispers around us.

"You're like a celebrity," she says, chuckling as she pulls a notebook out of her bag. She tucks a strand of strawberry blond hair out of her face while she writes, in startlingly perfect cursive, *Homeroom Notes—Week One, Day One.*

"Am not," I reply, torn between flattery and shame. I know they're not just staring because of my return.

The final bell rings and the last of our classmates shuffle in. I'm so busy watching the door for a certain face that I nearly miss when the teacher says my name for roll call, but the ensuing chattering draws my attention. "Here!" I say, confirming what everyone has already known since I stepped through the door: Santiago Espinosa is back.

chapter three

BEATRIZ

Santiago Espinosa is back.

I toss out the ice pack Nurse Cav gave me for my poorly faked cramps. She's familiar enough with how bad my real ones get. I missed homeroom, but she sent a note to my class, so no one's worrying about my absence. Not that anyone would worry regardless. Or, more accurately, the only person who would worry already knows why I'd choose to wallow in the rank scent of Nurse Cav's homemade tuna-salad breakfast instead of sit through a winding speech about the impending magic of senior year.

I snuck a peek at her schedule this morning. She's right on track for first-period calculus when I yank her away from turning a corner.

"Ow!" Whitney whines, rubbing her arm while we move from the merging halls. "I have class *that* way."

I pull my phone out of my pocket and make a show of unlocking it and tapping on the screen.

"What are you doing?"

"Just checking." I call Whitney's phone and hang up as soon as it starts ringing. "Yup, looks like it works."

"Congrats?"

"I just don't see how I managed to miss the call where you told me Santiago was moving back."

"God, you are so dramatic." Whitney rolls her eyes. "Is this little performance necessary? I thought you *knew*. I tried texting you so we could talk about it, but you, as per usual, left me on read."

"Yeah, because you just kept cryptically asking how I was doing!" I defend, hearing the weakness of my argument as it leaves my mouth.

"There's nothing cryptic about checking in on you! And I also asked to hang out."

"Going to the mall with you and Abby or strawberry-picking with your family who hates me wasn't exactly enticing."

Whitney sidesteps a passing group of juniors. "My family doesn't hate you."

I refuse to let this speed bump of a lie halt me. "A call would've been nice."

"Again, *I thought you knew*." She shakes her head. "In what world would Santiago reach out to me and not you?"

The same world where a boy we all loved is dead.

I resist the urge to rub my eyes, remembering the makeup seconds before disaster. I've grown so used to the layers, I forget they aren't my own skin.

"Look, I'm sorry." She reaches for my hand, but I pull away. I try not to notice the hurt on her face. "He only told me like two weeks ago that he was coming back. I freaked at first too! It brought so much to the surface. Seeing him again, without Bryce, after all these years? Part of me thought it wasn't real." She sighs, her voice losing the confident tone she lacquers it with these days.

I want, in a rare moment of easing my repression, to hug her. I want to wipe away the film of tears threatening to spill from her dark eyes. But I know where that intimacy leads. So instead, I cross my arms to pin them down.

The bell rings, and Whitney looks up. "I have to get to class." She waves down the hall where Abby is messing with the ends of one of her many braids, pretending not to be unsuccessfully eavesdropping.

"Fine," I say, straightening. "Just tell me one thing. Did she know?" I nod toward Abby. "Did Dustin and Courtney? All of your so-called friends?"

"They're not 'so-called' just because they aren't you, Bryce, and Santiago," she says, but not as cruelly as I wish she would've.

I nod once, lips pressed tight. That was enough of an answer for me.

Bryce Dawson's death didn't come with a handbook or tutorial. Losing someone rarely does, but teenage suicide comes with its own unique baggage. Baggage that this town's roughly four thousand residents and inability to keep anything a secret for long were ill prepared to interrogate. Word spread faster than wildfire when Candace found Bryce. The conversations about mental health awareness, however, died out faster than any flames I've ever seen.

What our town saw was this: Bryce was a happy kid.

He pulled pranks, he loved astronomy, he carved little pockets into the soles of his shoes to hide notes we'd pass in class and coins from states he wanted to visit. He wore a key to Santiago's house around his neck like it was made from real gold. He didn't throw a fit when his mom remarried Whitney and Olive's dad only a year after cancer ate through his own father. His favorite color was a soft orange just a touch less saturated than his hair, and when people asked what type of music he liked, he asked them to answer first and then based his response off theirs. He had friends, he had family, he had me.

By the time he died at the end of ninth grade, he didn't have Santiago anymore.

I'm making my way to my car after school when I hear Santiago calling my name. This would be inevitable even if we didn't have calculus, PE, and English together. He managed to avoid me just fine from states away. But in this town, I know I can't accomplish the same.

Regardless, I slip my earbuds in and keep walking. I flinch when I feel his hand brush my shoulder.

"Sorry." Santiago pulls back. I turn around without meaning to. "I was calling your name."

The first word he's said to me in years is an apology, just not the one I was looking for.

My words are just as pathetic. "I couldn't hear you over my music."

He lifts my earbuds' cord from where it dangles down my body, plugged into nothing. He cocks an eyebrow.

I snatch the cord back.

"Sorry I didn't recognize you earlier," he starts, missing the mark again. "You just—Well, you look pretty, uh, different? I mean, it's not bad! The piercings are cool! I had a teammate with that nose-bridge one back in California. I've been meaning to look up its name, what are they called—"

"What do you want?" I snap.

"I'm just . . ." He pauses. "I'm saying hi, I guess."

I don't even justify that with a response beyond turning to leave.

He chases after me. "And you know, again, I wanted to say sorry I didn't recognize you. And sorry for bumping into you, although if we're getting technical, you sort of bumped into me." He chuckles awkwardly, and I feel a slight thrill at his discomfort. "I wanted to talk to you earlier, but you kept leaving class so quickly and I couldn't find you at lunch."

I reach my car, unlocking the driver's side manually and shoving my bag over the seat into the back. I get in behind the wheel and reach for the door.

"Whoa! Wait," he says, leaning down.

I stick my key in the ignition. "Why?"

"You don't seem . . . You're not . . ."

I decide to help him. "I'm not pissing my pants in excitement over your return?"

He balks. "I know it's been a while and it's a weird surprise, but I was thinking . . . I don't know." Even with the voice drop, he sounds like a little kid.

Disgustingly, I think of his ninth birthday. His older cousin blew out his candles before Santi could finish making a wish. When he was twelve and didn't ask Whitney to the sixth-grade dance before Tommy Larkin did. When his dad missed our elementary school graduation despite promising to come, the chance to tour across New Hampshire dive bars taking priority.

I squint up from my seat to properly look at him. He's tanner now, all that beach sun bringing forth a warm glow. The familiar milky birthmark on his collarbone peeks out from his loose shirt. His dark hair curls where it brushes his shoulders, longer than I've ever seen him wear it.

For a second, he's familiar. My first and best friend, the one whose family Mom and I spent countless Noche Buenas with, who bought the glow-in-the-dark stars that still decorate my room, who wore a golden key to my front door around his neck every day. Someone I considered a permanent fixture in my life—as one does when they're a naive child.

But that boy got in a fight with Bryce, moved away, and didn't look back. Whoever he was when he returned for the funeral hopped into his dad's truck in the middle of my breakdown and decided I wasn't worth talking to anymore.

This time it's my decision.

"I don't know what you were thinking either." I slam my car door and drive away.

I wait at the top of the stairs for hours, leg bouncing. Lottie bats at me for a bit but gives up when I don't play back. There isn't even homework yet to distract me, and I turned off my phone when the first text from Whitney came in. It wasn't until I unlocked the front door that I realized I was probably meant to give her and Olive a ride after school too. Mom will definitely be getting a call from Candace.

Concern over what that conversation will look like melts away when Mom gets home. Tattooed arms crowded with grocery bags, she kicks the door shut behind her. When I stand, her eyes dart up to me.

One preoccupied arm bends to press a hand to her heart. "You scared me! What are you doing up there?"

"Did you know?"

"Know what?"

"That Santiago was moving back?"

She drops a bag. "Santi is back?" Her face looks like a mirror. "You really didn't know."

I descend to collect the fallen groceries and relieve her of half the bags. Now that we're on even ground, we make our way to the kitchen.

She sighs when she's unburdened. "Candace said Whitney had something she'd been meaning to tell you. I thought it would be about—" Mom cuts herself off. We have an unspoken rule in this house. I don't talk about my dad and she doesn't talk about Bryce. We leave our dead loves untouched.

The thing is, when Bryce's dad died, I felt something. I won't say it was relief. But it was close. Maybe just hopeful thinking tacked on with guilt, like most things I feel.

Santiago's mom bailed early and his dad was absent enough that he wasn't a stranger to grief in his own way. Whitney and Olive's mom remained in constant communication, even when her temporary trip back to the Philippines to take care of her own mother turned into a permanent return to their home country. But I know the distance ached.

Still, I craved a more paralleled understanding. Bryce and I had both lost our fathers now. This was it.

But at Bryce's father's funeral, at the same church we'd be in about a year later for Candace to marry Whitney and Olive's dad, and about four years after that for Bryce's own funeral, I didn't recognize myself in Bryce's eyes. I entered this world missing a piece of myself. Bryce had that piece carved out, watched the knife go in and remove it bit by bit. The diagnosis, the surgery, the jump to chemo. As his father withered away, so did Bryce.

It wasn't the first time I tried and failed to find solidarity in convergent evolution. I'm staring at my first attempt.

"Why didn't Santiago tell you he was coming back?" Mom asks.

I soften the truth for her, make it more digestible. "We don't really talk anymore. I shouldn't be surprised."

She looks concerned, like she wants to say more. It's her default expression. "You're okay though, right?" I wonder if she hears the question the way I do.

"I always am."

chapter four

SANTIAGO

After school, I piled into a diner booth with Whitney and all of her—or I guess *our*—friends. We occupied the same peeling pleather seats Bryce and I used to picture taking our first girl-friends to on a double date, back when he and Bea were still only a whisper of an idea. If I squinted, the vision almost looked right. Me and Whitney, Dustin and Courtney, Abby leaning away from Rick Bruno, who used to target Bryce and me in middle school dodgeball but apparently passes the vibe check now. Other seniors bordered our group, names and faces I'd thought I'd left behind, two very noticeable ones missing.

I got the generic questions I expected: what California was like, if I missed Greensville and Vermont as a whole, if the beach was truly better than the lakeshores everyone here flocks to during the closest thing we get to summer heat. I got a few I hadn't anticipated—if I had dated anyone, if I was currently dating any-one, if my number had changed and if so, what was it.

I let the high of social acceptance power my bike ride home, ignoring the uncomfortable ache of nostalgia that the emerging streetlights bring forth. The temptation to close my eyes, listen to the whir of my bike spokes, and pretend to hear another set beside me is almost enough to send me crashing to the pavement, but I quit playing pretend months ago.

"There's my roommate!" Abuelo shakily carries a mug of tea over to his lumpy orange chair, falling into the cushions with a huff as I lock the front door behind me. "How was the first day?"

I drop my backpack by the sofa across from him. "I thought you were going to be at the senior center while I was at school."

He gives me a pointed look over his mug. "Santi, it's five o'clock."

"You're not supposed to be home alone. That's sorta the whole point of me being here."

When Pa and I got the call in June that Abuelo had taken a bad spill, my first feeling was betrayal; that June was here to rob me again. Though I had seen very little of him since Pa and I moved to SoCal—couch surfing until we found a place to rent with some of his bandmates—I'd performed every annoying OCD ritual that popped into my mind to keep Abuelo safe from a distance. Luckily, he hadn't been badly hurt and, after three hours on the floor, managed to get up and call for help. A bruise spread across his side like an expanding galaxy, but there was no internal damage to anything but his ego. Living alone when he was well into his late seventies was a questionable call; his eyesight had already earned him a failed license renewal, and his bones weren't getting any stronger. Espinosa men are known to be stubborn though, case in point that Pa couldn't move back home to small-town Vermont when he was sure his band was finally going to get their big break—the same one that drove us out to California three years ago. They'd played across the LA dive-bar scene long enough that it seemed inevitable they were on the precipice of something, and even his dad's wavering health couldn't stand in the way of what he clearly felt was his destiny.

So I volunteered. Pa tried to talk me out of it—it wasn't a secret to anyone why I wouldn't want to move back to the home-town cradling the grave of my best friend—but I made up my mind, for more reasons than one. Like I said, stubborn men.

"Psh." Abuelo takes a long sip, steam crawling over the wrinkled terrain of his face. "Here I thought you came back just because you wanted a good spot in my will."

My fingers find a stretch of dry skin on my palm and pull at it. "Not funny."

He waves me off, death a planned trip for him already.

It's just bad balance. They're just worried about him falling again. He was fine the first time. He's fine. You're fine.

"So, how was today?" Abuelo asks. "I take it you weren't sitting in the library these past few hours getting a head start on the year."

I recount the day for him, pointedly carving around the most notable moments. Maybe I'd get away with it if my eyes didn't drift to one of the framed photos on the wall of me, Bryce, Bea, and Whitney at our seventh-grade formal, all of us mid-laugh as the camera's flash bounces off our exposed teeth.

I switch hands quickly and pick at the opposite palm to even the tingly sensation left behind by the removed skin.

"You feeling okay?" Abuelo asks, staring down at my fingers.

I make my hands limp creatures in my lap and look away from the memories decorating the room. "You mentioned that you still see Señorita Delgado around. That she gives you rides home from the center when Billy is busy or there aren't any volunteers."

"Questions are better answered when they're actually asked."

I bite the inside of my cheek twice in the same spot. "I saw Beatriz today and she looked different, that's all. I just wasn't sure if you knew how she was doing." After Bryce, Abuelo tried giving me updates on Bea, but when I did nothing more than hum in response, he got the hint and stopped. I still can't decide which hurt more—hearing about her life without me and Bryce in it, or giving my imagination creative freedom.

Abuelo sets his mug down as carefully as he can manage. I watch a trickle of tea splash against the lip and slip down the side, a warm tear that his fingers narrowly escape. "If you want to know how she's doing, you should ask her yourself. Maybe you should've asked her a few weeks ago."

I grew up on Vermont temperatures, even if Southern California softened my tolerance, but the look in Bea's eyes when she saw me was cold enough to freeze. I deserve every degree of it, and worse.

Abuelo claps. "All right, come help with dinner or we'll be eating burnt beans. Why they can't print recipe instructions in a bigger font, I'll never understand."

Before bed, I plug my phone in. Playing social media catch-up on my classmates all night killed my battery, as did trying to find signs of Bea existing online anymore, but I forgot how far the outlet is from my pillow. Readjusting to the bedroom I spent most of my life in is taking longer than expected. I'm strong enough to re-arrange the furniture now, but I'm still waiting for my childhood self to grant me permission to change anything.

I brush my fingers over the aging Superman poster above my dresser, a lump behind it that's obvious to my eyes and maybe no one else's. Carefully, I slide my hand between the paper and the wall until it hits metal. I run my touch over the shape, feeling each familiar groove of the key. I've been home for two days now and I still haven't built up the courage to pull it out and actually look at it.

My phone dings, so I release the key and let social media do what it does best: distract me. Follower requests have been procreating all day as I've slowly added people on the accounts I created in LA and kept deliberately separate from my life here. But below the latest notifications sits a new text.

Eric: Did you really move back to Vermont?

I suffocate the screen against the dresser. Shutting off the lights, I crawl into my cramped bed, where the threadbare blue flannel comforter feels too warm against my skin.

All the childhood mementos—posters and photos and plushies and busted board game boxes and empty DVD cases and cracked-spine yearbooks and key necklaces—forge this room into a time capsule of my life. I'm submerged in what used to define me. And somehow, ignoring a friend is the thing that makes me feel most like myself.

chapter five

PE lockers being assigned saved me from it yesterday, but today Santiago stands a foot to my left as Coach Simmons takes attendance. As kids, we thrilled over being seated together alphabetically. Inseparable Dougherty and Espinosa. Today, I feel like kicking something.

We aren't dressing for exercises yet, but Coach Simmons still makes us stand on the blacktop while she gives us the typical speech. Mile runs on Tuesdays, twenty-minute runs on Fridays, a weekly sports unit on the remaining days. I can feel my physicals being educated already. With our snowfall, we'll probably spend most of the year corralled in the gym.

Once dismissed, I head for the bench tucked into a scrap of shade beside the girls' locker room. Summer is easily giving way to fall, but the direct afternoon sun still burns in this outfit. Predictably, Santiago starts following me until he's intercepted by the other uncomfortably familiar face in this class.

Olive's smile rivals the sunshine. "You're back," they say to him. Their giddiness emphasizes their youth, but that could just be my cynicism talking. They were always happy to be involved in our antics. It's hard to stop seeing them that way, even if all of us have grown up.

Almost all of us.

Santiago's face goes shamelessly goofy as he pulls Olive into a hug. "You're so big now," he says. His eyes show that he's found the shame, but for the wrong reasons. "I mean—sorry, it's just . . . you're, like, older."

Olive tucks a strand of their short hair behind an ear decorated with clay mushrooms. Whitney teased them for their funky jewelry creations once upon a time, but last I heard, their Etsy business is doing quite well. "I, uh, saw you yesterday. Here. In class, I mean." Laughter breaks up their stumbling words. "You were chatting with some people, so it didn't seem like a good time to say hi."

"It's always a good time to say hi to me," Santiago replies. I can't help scoffing.

He glances over. Olive follows his gaze and gives me a little wave.

"Look at all of us," Olive says, like ending up in a class with someone you know at this school is anything but expected.

"How come Beatriz and I are the only seniors?" Santiago asks, and I feel the slightest indignation that he's recognized everyone else quickly enough to realize this.

"PE is only for three years," Olive says, pointing to themself. "This is my third year."

Santiago takes a step closer to me. It takes effort not to recoil, but I do indulge my eyebrows in lifting slightly. "So why are we here?" he asks.

I look back and forth between the two of them. Then I lean into the building and force my eyes elsewhere. It's awkward and drags the lax conversation to an uncomfortable pause. I relish it, this brief respite in which I can feel them both remember it's unpleasant to talk to me now.

Olive cuts through the silence, always the antidote to apathy. "Well, what did you do for PE in California?"

"I only took it for a semester," Santiago says. We hardly talked during that first year after he moved. Bryce was still alive but fuming over their fight for months past what seemed reasonable. So every small attempt at conversation with Santi felt like a betrayal, a siding with the enemy.

Regardless, I practically mouth his next words alongside him. "And then I started a badminton team," he says, the cadence of the phrase the same as it was during the few phone calls the two of us had managed to make. As far as Bryce knew, our contact died as soon as Santiago moved. Theirs died only a week prior.

"Oh, those credits probably didn't fully transfer over," Olive says, far too pleased to have solved this mystery.

Santiago nods, satisfied. But then he looks at me again. His return is still so bizarre, like a bad dream. He surprises me by not asking why I'm here a second time, and I feel a flash of gratitude like a needle prick.

Olive's friends shout for them from across the field, waving plastic discs that Coach Simmons must have given them.

"Want to join?" Olive asks us.

"I'd rather deal with starting a fifth year of PE," I say without meaning to. Looking away doesn't stop me from noticing Olive's hurt. Better that than them catch my crumb of admission.

Santiago tries to take it in stride though. "You used to love—"

"Don't." My voice doesn't sound like it came from me. "You don't get to disappear for years and do this. Stop pretending this is fine."

I don't touch a lot of things. Dead dad, my and Whitney's history, Candace's feelings toward me, Bryce in those final months, Bryce when no one but me was listening. Keeping my hands clean of it all is a full-time job. But Santiago's homecoming is a fresh wound and there's a momentary satisfaction in ripping off this bandage and letting the blood pour out. Every time I imagined his return, I thought I'd scream at him before anything else, listing all the things he did wrong. It's so much easier to be righteous in your fantasies.

The relief from lashing out fades, swiftly replaced by embarrassment. No one is meant to see that I'm still capable of bleeding.

"I'll leave you two to talk," Olive says, flustered in a way that makes me angrier. Bryce was their brother and here they are, welcoming Santiago back with open arms.

Santiago doesn't meet my eyes. It seems like we're both invested in acting like I didn't just say what I did. "No, I'll come with you."

He follows Olive, joining the chorus of our classmates enjoying the last of the summer sun. Alone in the shade, I decide I'm glad he didn't stay.

★ ★ ★

After school, I find Whitney leaning against my car. The bottom of her shoe is pressed into the dust coating the driver's door.

"I'll call you an Uber," I say as I walk over. "Nearest one should only be a few cities away."

"Abby already said she'd give me a ride," she replies, pushing off the car. "She gave us one yesterday."

I take my sweet time looking up from the footprint she left on the aging metal. "I was really worried for a second there that you were going to tell me something I cared about."

Whitney rolls her eyes as I brush past her to unlock my door.

"I just want to know how long it's going to last this time."

"How long what's going to last?" I ask.

"You being mad at me, pretending that we're done." Someone calls her name in the distance, but she doesn't look. "Last record was, what, a handful of months after the accident?"

"Don't call it that," I snap, annoyed. "Cars have to actually crash for it to be an accident." It was just us, spinning out, narrowly avoiding something disastrous.

I don't want to think about it.

"And I'm not pretending anything," I continue. "You didn't make sure I knew about Santiago. It's fine. We're not friends. We're not anything."

"You're really playing that card?"

It's the only one I have left. "You should go catch Abby if you don't want to walk home." She doesn't move. "Whitney. Go."

She lets out a frustrated sigh. "Fine. Whatever. Keep pushing me away. Just don't forget to hold it against me for listening." And then she's gone.

On the drive home, I count the broken streetlights. I list all the lipsticks I own by memory. I sing the alphabet in Spanish, backward.

I'm nearly home, but it doesn't matter.

I pull over, hoping no one feels like driving down Maple Way at this hour. It's bullshit, really. That Santiago's return didn't do this, that the mention of Bryce more than once over the past two days didn't do this. That Whitney, acting blameless and catty and guilt-tripping me after *she's* the one who left me out in the dark and brought up something she knows I don't like to think about—even if she doesn't know why—did this.

I roll down the windows and breathe. Deep, long, fast. My dress is loose, which works in my favor. But the air is stifling, especially in all black, and it's like every sensation is both heightened and numbed.

My heels rubbing against the rough lining of my shoes. The oily sheen building beneath the foundation on my forehead. The trickle of sweat falling down my neck. I push the door open and lean outside, head bent. I try to focus on the cracks in the pavement. Watch the ants dart in and out of them. The light dancing off the broken glass in the gutter across the street.

Instead my brain flashes to Whitney, arms crossed and shaking her head, pitying me. The worst part is, I can't even tell if this memory is from today or then. I see Santiago driving away with the terrible promise of never moving back and I see him breaking that promise and I see Mom and her concerned breakfasts and exhausted smiles and I see Bryce and a year later I see a long stretch of highway and both times, I don't see the danger.

Finally, after minutes or hours, I heave up whatever I ate at lunch. It's green slime now, webbing from my lips with spittle. I cough until it comes out dry.

I catch my breath, close the door, and start the car again. When Mom asks how my day went, I'll tell her what she needs to hear.

chapter six

SANTIAGO

The first few weeks of school slip by, along with every oppor-tunity to talk to Bea for more than a handful of worsening seconds. She's never at our neighboring lockers in the morning, she's first to leave her seat when our shared classes end, and she spends PE either beating nearly everyone in runs or giving a lackluster attempt at participating in group activities. It's worse than if she yelled at me like she did at the funeral, because I could work with her hating me—and certainly deserve as much. Instead, she seems to feel nothing at all about my existence, which, I suppose, I deserve even more.

Today, I decide to focus on more solvable issues, like figuring out how the hell to use a sticker gun without marking my forehead as a clearance item.

"Having trouble?" Dustin laughs from where he's placing pumpkins at the front of the store. I'd been helping him, but the arrangements kept looking off—the spacing and alignments feeling wrong, not messy or disorganized but *wrong*—and there's no real way to tell someone that seeing that made me feel like Pa's plane ride here for Thanksgiving next month would crash or Abuelo would crack his skull against the shower tile tonight.

"Wait." I smack the side of the sticker gun and try to use it again on a box of plastic cutlery. When the bright yellow oval successfully glides onto the cardboard, we let out a unified cheer.

Abuelo insisted I didn't need to get a job, especially since I'm playing mediocre caretaker as it is, but it still felt necessary. Pa's band hasn't exactly made it big, meaning there's little he sent back to Vermont with me besides old graphic tees and well-wishes. Which doesn't bode well for my college fund.

Dustin's family still owns the main grocery store in town, and he happily offered me a position when he heard I was looking, which saved me the effort of applying to the same library that Bryce and I once got kicked out of when we couldn't stop laughing over snow-warped comic books, or the restaurant that Bea and her mom used to take me to for my birthday if Abuelo was working and Pa wasn't around. The thrift store is apparently desperate for applications too, but I think I'd have lost it if I walked in and found any of Bryce's old things—astronomy pun shirts or shoes with those goofy pockets he'd cut into the soles. An intentionally lost and miraculously found key to my house.

I've yet to venture through town beyond going to school, work, and Dustin's house, but every time I get a glimpse of something from my past that I have to recontextualize in the present, I'm forced to reckon with the fact that this place doesn't exist in amber. Eric asked me once if I was homesick—a question I had to answer carefully given what he didn't know. In the end, I said no and meant it. Because by the time he was asking, Bea hated me and Bryce was dead, having hated me in life, and I figured you can't be homesick for a place that doesn't exist anymore.

I look through the glass storefront, watch the way the sun is lazily tugged higher into the sky through the morning clouds, and wonder how it is, then, that I'm homesick for a place I'm already at.

The quiet wraps Dustin and me in companionable silence as we finish opening. Clearance stickers applied, bathroom stocked, fresh produce checked over, doors opened. Eventually, I run out of excuses and rejoin him by the pumpkins. According to the psychologist I saw a few times the summer after Bryce's death—and only met because she was dating Pa's bassist—exposure therapy could help me. She told me I had OCD and complicated bereavement, so I told Pa I didn't want to see her anymore, and Pa's bassist told her roughly the same thing after deciding he wanted his bachelorhood back, whisking her out of my life before I had to properly contend with her diagnoses.

"You can keep stickering everything in stock if you'd rather not help me." Dustin huffs as he lifts another pumpkin from the shipping crate and drops it onto the display table. With the amount we've got here, you'd think this was the only place in town to buy pumpkins, and you'd be correct.

I hip-check him and, despite myself, adjust one of his pumpkins so it looks *right*. An incoming text distracts him long enough that I can shift a few more without him noticing, and by the time he slips his phone back into his pocket, my brain doesn't feel so fuzzy. I know it's only a temporary reprieve, but I take what I can get these days.

"Things good with the missus?" I gamble when I notice his grin.

He rolls his eyes, but his face doesn't lose any joy. "Yeah, yeah, we're good."

"How'd the two of you come to be, anyway?" I ask as he pulls out the last pumpkin. "You guys never really hung out when we were younger."

"Did you and I really hang out?" Dustin asks jokingly. We had the same teachers, went to each other's birthday parties, and he'd play games of PIG with Bryce and me during middle school PE, but we were never close.

"Fair point," I concede.

We move toward the registers. "Courtney and I took biology together freshman year and—"

"You realized you had *chemistry?*" I say, and wiggle my eyebrows. He feigns annoyance.

"We've been together for, like, I don't know, a year and a half now?"

"Don't act like you don't know the exact time."

"Fine. Not including the pauses, a year, seven months, and two weeks. Tell Rick I told you that, and I'll kick your ass."

I hold my hands up in surrender, chuckling. "Hey, your secret is safe with me. You two seem good together. You and Courtney, not you and Rick." I'm not ashamed to say it's a test.

"I think I'm a little out of Rick's league," he replies. "As for me and Courtney . . ." He pauses to tug at the jammed cash drawer, the muscles in his arms bulging and going taut. I busy myself with adjusting a flyer on the side of the conveyer belt advertising a sale on ground beef. "We can be a little intense. We don't always work, but when we do . . ." Now it's his turn to wiggle his eyebrows before leaving to greet the first customer of the day.

When he comes back, his face has lost the mischief it held before. "While we're asking about relationships, what's with you and Beatriz? I thought she might rejoin us at lunch when you returned, but I haven't seen y'all together at all."

"'Rejoin'?" I ask, jumping on the information. "She used to sit with you guys?"

"I mean, barely. Just a few times last year."

"So she had friends? Like, you were her friend?"

The look of pity he gives me twists my gut. "We chatted, I guess. And partnered on a history project." Averting his eyes, he pokes at the register keys. "But I wouldn't call us friends, really. I think Whitney tried to make her feel included, but it didn't last." He clears his throat. "What about you two?"

I opened this Pandora's box, I guess. "We just grew apart," I say, and hope he'll leave it at that.

"Before or after Bryce . . . ?"

No one finishes that sentence around here. "Bryce and I weren't really talking before he died." I'm surprised my voice doesn't catch on the word. "Same with me and Beatriz, especially after. Life just got in the way." It's not a complete lie, but it certainly strays from the truth.

"So Whitney is the only one you told about coming back?"

Who else was I going to tell? I want to ask.

Over the years, Whitney and I exchanged the average birthday and holiday messages, but we'd otherwise mutually let our semblance of a friendship rest. I didn't even know she'd come out as a lesbian or that Olive was non-binary until I moved back here, facts that have me reconsidering nudging my bisexuality back into the hometown closet like I'd planned.

It'd be easy to blame the distance on Bryce lingering between us at all times, the shared loss making it awkward to say anything that a boy we loved would never live to hear, no matter how mundane. But Whitney and I were never really close friends at the end of the day. She was Bryce's pretty stepsister, the fourth corner of our friend group who we inherited in sixth grade. By the time we made it to the end of middle school and I was packing up my life, she'd already started breaking free of us and hanging out with Abby.

Bea and Bryce were choices. We talked about their relationship and my crush on Whitney like we weren't just children. Bea and I lent and borrowed family members to fill out each other's houses, her mom covering for my absent parents, my abuelo covering for her estranged grandparents. Bryce was my best friend at sleepovers, shitty basketball games, indoor poolside naps where we reeked of chlorine and our mouths were sticky from watermelon Candace had packed for us, Mother's Days eating lunch where no one else could see me. It's not easy to forget that Bea was beside us in every one of those memories, but I tried to anyway. It made what I was doing easier—or so I tried to convince myself. I'm a good liar, but not that good.

I realize I haven't spoken for a while and expect Dustin to press on, but he drops it, giving me a sad, knowing smile. Ironic, given what he doesn't know. What nobody but Bryce ever will.

Years that I was gone, and not just from the state. When I first left, the fight with Bryce fueled my desire for a clean break, but for months all I was met with were jagged edges that shredded my heart. The second time I left—straight from the funeral without saying a single goodbye—I looked around at my new life in California, rough cuts and all, and I didn't look back.

chapter seven

BEATRIZ

It's practically a rite of passage to leave your Good Samaritan volunteer hours for senior year. Our guidance counselor's insistence it'll look good on college apps makes no difference for early completion. But college and group activities are equally unmotivating for me. Procrastination is why I'm in my car, parked outside of the senior center.

I file my nails while waiting, coffin-style since I can't pet Lottie when they're full stiletto. A knock on the passenger window sends my nail file flying into the windshield.

"Perdóname." Santiago's abuelo's muffled voice carries through the closed doors.

I jump out of the car before he can even step off the curb. Offering my hand, I help him into the passenger seat. He watches me, amused, as I get back behind the wheel.

"Beatriz," Señor Espinosa says, leaning comfortingly into the Spanish pronunciation that most people don't favor, but I do. It almost makes me smile, it sounds so much like home. "I didn't know I'd be seeing a familiar face when they told me someone volunteered for the driving program." I glance at my reflection where thick wings expand from my eyes. "Though I do see it on your mom every day."

My hair is blond and my skin is white like my late Irish American dad's. Mom's hair is dark and her skin is brown like the maternal Colombian grandparents I've never known. But my facial features were copied and pasted off her. Even with the different coloring, there is no denying our relation. Wide-set brown eyes, bump on the bridge of the nose, puffy upper lip and thinner lower one. My makeup doesn't hide our similarities, but that's not what it's there to do.

"She's happy to have the extra shifts," I reply neutrally. Mom's been a receptionist at our town's best attempt at a hospital since she moved here with me at eighteen years old, but she's only been doubling at the attached senior center for the past few months.

Señor Espinosa always took a paternal liking to her. Her story generally drives people to extreme kindness or extreme judgment. Born in Colombia, raised in the US. Knocked up at seventeen, couch surfed various friends' houses after being kicked out, planned to run away with my dad until he was acquainted with a drunk semitruck driver. A friend of a friend hooked her up with the receptionist job and a temporary place to stay once she became a legal adult. So she ditched New Hampshire and ended up here. Nowadays, our mortgage—and whatever college savings are out there in some pristine bank with my name stamped on them—are handled by my dad's parents.

"It's very sweet of you to volunteer," Señor Espinosa says, unable to let us sit in silence. His grandson a closely fallen apple,

I avoided him all these years for a reason. Though he may as well have been my grandfather too, once upon a time.

"Just doing my Good Samaritan hours like everyone else."

"Only one person signed up to offer rides for the center." He gives me a pointed look. "Santi is decorating the gym for Homecoming with Whitney." His eyes stay on me, and it's almost endearing that he thinks I'd let my emotions show. Whatever Santiago does now is none of my business. He made sure of that.

I pull up to his house. It's harder to hide my emotions about this.

"Not much has changed. Even have Santi in that same tiny bed, pobrecito," Señor Espinosa says, slowly unbuckling his seat belt.

I haven't set foot inside since Santiago moved away a little over three years ago. Bryce's neck once bore a key to that front door, but it was lost to the trees bordering his house after he chucked it during that bullshit fight with Santiago.

I get out to help Señor Espinosa walk up the yard. He doesn't commend me for this beyond grinning. The front door swings open as he pulls an overcrowded key chain from his pocket.

"I got home and you weren't he—" Santiago's panicked voice cuts off when he sees me. "Oh. Hey."

I wait for my heart to slow down. "Hi."

Señor Espinosa's grin doesn't disappear until he does into the house. "Thank you, Good Samaritan!"

And then it's just me and Santiago.

I mean to leave, but my eyes snag on the wall behind him. I spot myself in a familiar collage of framed photos and catch a whiff of Señor Espinosa's favorite lemon wood polish.

And then it's me, Bryce, and Santiago arranging photos on the floor, deciding what'll look best where. Bryce insisting to Santi's abuelo that he's old enough to help with hammering, claiming his dad taught him how before passing, then slamming his thumb not half an hour later. If I squint, I can almost see the small dent he left behind. He was so much more concerned about it than his pain.

Santiago leans into my line of vision. "Did you want to come in?"

I snap back to now. "Why would I want that?"

"The yearning glare you were giving the living room sort of implied an interest."

I scoff and step off the porch.

"Are you going to Homecoming?" His question carries, following me to my car even as he stays planted inside.

I face him and catalog his appearance. Baggy gray sweats and faded black T-shirt, some '80s band logo screaming that it's a hand-me-down from his father. His waves are messy but not from a nap. I recognize the signs of anxiety-induced hair tugging. I've had to find new coping methods myself.

"You never texted me back." My voice isn't loud, but the words themselves have enough volume. "No calls, no emails. Not even a DM or follow request. Over two years. He died and you left me all alone." Santiago looks down at his feet. "But you told Whitney about coming home."

It's a childish admission of hurt, hardly even the point. I never competed in my friendships with Bryce and Santiago. You don't set the sun against the moon, compare apples to oranges. But Whitney was something else, and he reached out to her.

"I didn't think you'd want to hear from me," he says. It's even more pathetic than my jealousy.

I get in my car and drive away, and he lets me.

* * *

As I'm washing the dishes after dinner, Mom enters the kitchen with a stack of envelopes. "These are for you." She tosses them casually onto the counter but watches me intently as I dry my hands and pick them up.

"Why do colleges even bother with print mail anymore?" I carry them over to the recycling bin.

Mom's hand reaches out. "You don't want to look at them first? I saw some good schools."

I flip through the papers quickly, then recognize one from a few weeks ago. "Why are they sending doubles?"

Mom sips her tea, avoiding eye contact.

I check them all. "Mom."

She sighs, setting the mug down. "I wasn't sure you'd seen them."

"So you fished them out of the trash?" I let judgment seep into the question.

"Abejita, I just want to make sure you're considering all of your options."

"I *am*," I say, exhausted by the repeated conversation.

Community college and beauty school. I suggested it once last fall, when the optimism I tried to ignore was given a moment to run rampant in my heart. Before Mom's dreams immediately shut mine down. *With your grades, with your drive, you could do so much more.* My silence was taken as agreement, but I can see the skepticism about my obedience has kicked in.

"Just . . . keep thinking it over."

It's unspoken, hanging there between us in the very DNA of

our relationship. She didn't get college. If her parents hadn't thrown her out for being a pregnant teen, if my dad's parents hadn't been too riddled with grief to consider us until I was a toddler and Mom had already been struggling to care for me for a year in Greensville, if society gave even one fuck about young, single mothers, if I didn't exist at all—maybe she could've furthered her education.

I scoop the papers into my arms. I won't throw them away again. Our dreams are mutually exclusive, and only one of us deserves to see theirs come to fruition.

I can do this for her. I know all too well how to bury my feelings in places she'll never find them.

chapter eight

SANTIAGO

I didn't go to a whole lot of school dances in California. Eric and the badminton team were a little above all of that—their words, not mine—and admitting that I found dances sort of thrilling felt exposing. I was meant to be camouflaging, not drawing attention to myself. So everyone here being super excited for the annual Halloween-themed Homecoming is like a treat packaged up nicely just for me.

Abuelo was right that I wouldn't fit into any of his old suits, but luckily Pa left one behind that he used to wear when the band got booked for weddings. The sleeves are a bit short and the pants strain around my thighs, but it's fine, because with the cheap glasses I found in the pharmacy aisle at the grocery store and the Superman T-shirt I usually sleep in, I feel like the perfect Clark Kent.

I email the group pics we just took to Abuelo, who refuses to get a cell phone, while Whitney and Abby pose in front of Rick's fireplace. They're wearing matching flowy fairy dresses, peach for

Whitney and lavender for Abby. They hug unabashedly and kiss each other's cheeks while Candace snaps photo after photo on her iPad. It's nice to see Whitney find a friend like this. Growing up, she'd sometimes watch me and Bea and Bryce with this yearning sort of gleam in her eyes, like even though she was always with us, she knew there was something we shared that she didn't.

"Hot, right?" Rick asks, sidling up beside me as I watch the girls force themselves into a giggling fit for candids.

"Your wig is fucked up," I reply, and he adjusts the heavy piece of hair meant to resemble Elvis's. I look around for Dustin and Courtney—dressed as the Joker and Harley Quinn—and spot them taking selfies by the huge stairwell that serves as one of many reminders that Rick is richer than I remembered.

"Little Ocampo cleans up surprisingly nice too," Rick adds, redirecting his gaze onto Olive, where they lean against a painting-covered wall while looking at their phone. Apparently it was Candace's idea for them to come with us—none of their friends were interested—and Whitney tolerated it in exchange for Candace paying for her new ethereal dress and shoes.

Olive's dress, on the other hand, is black, long-sleeved, and tight against their curvy frame. They complete the look with a large witch's hat I recognize from Whitney's first Halloween here. Olive looks good, inarguably, but not particularly comfortable. Rick's staring likely isn't helping, so I put my height to use and take a subtle step between the two of them to block his view.

When Candace's iPad runs out of storage, she sets us free. Whitney and Abby dart back to the kitchen where they left their purses while snacking, and Candace turns to face me for the first time all evening. She drove separately from her kids, and by the time she got here, Whitney was already insisting we were late and needed to take photos quickly.

Candace's light eyes go a little hard, pale cheeks a little red, as she takes me in. "You're all grown up."

I smile tightly at the accusation. Candace scared me as a kid, in a very conventionally maternal way. If Bea's mom was the Cool Mom, the one who took us for ice cream after school and let us stay in pajamas past noon during sleepovers, Candace was her foil. At Bryce's house, we washed dishes, woke up early enough to help cook breakfast, and always did our homework before we were allowed to play. Neither was better than the other, though without a real mom myself, I don't know how much weight my opinion even carries.

The last time I saw Candace was at her son's funeral, about nine months after he stopped calling me his best friend and made it abundantly clear it was a habit he never intended on picking back up, and she looked at me then with just as much apathy as she does now.

The girls return, bags in hand, shouting for everyone to get in the car before we miss even more of the dance. For a moment, I see fondness in Candace's eyes as they track her stepdaughter badgering her other stepchild to haul ass. I heard Whitney call Candace "Mom" earlier, something she didn't do as a kid, and it struck me that I'd never considered whether anyone after Bryce ever would.

We pack ourselves into Whitney's recently repaired car, her and Abby up front, Courtney and Dustin in the way back, and me, Olive, and Rick in the middle.

Olive gets in first, their dress riding up as they bend over.

"Nice," Rick whispers.

I step ahead of him and start scooting in after Olive.

"Whoa, what are you doing?" he asks me. "Olive should sit in the middle. You can go around."

"I get carsick, so I need to see through the windshield." I click my seat belt before he can get another word out.

The drive is as fast as any in this small town, and then we're walking into the gym decorated in purple flashing lights and the cheap, fake spiderwebs we've been selling at the grocery store. We spent all of Friday after school getting it ready, and I still can't look at it without thinking of Bea, who loved Halloween before she started looking like someone who celebrates it year-round.

The group stays together long enough for us to find a table and abandon our purses, jackets, and, in Rick's case, capes. But after half an hour of getting ourselves settled, Whitney and Abby are whisked away by Annabeth Coleman and Maggie Oliver, also dressed as fairies, celebrating the accidentally shared costume over selfies. Dustin and Courtney rush off to dance, leaving me, Rick, and Olive.

"Shall we, Little Lady?" Rick asks Olive, faux accent and all.

"I'm not really a dancer," they say, then disappear into the crowd. Rick watches with a set jaw.

Whitney has referred to Olive as her sibling, with they/them pronouns, plenty of times in front of Rick. "They're not a lady," I say.

He rolls his eyes in a flash of disco light. "It's an impression."

"Not an excuse."

"Whatever." He sneaks an engraved flask that probably costs two months' worth of my grocery-store salary out of his pocket. "Liquid courage?" His fair cheeks are already flushed.

"Pass," I say, never having been one for drinking. Most of my battle with OCD is over control, and alcohol doesn't promise a whole lot of that. I smoked weed once during tenth grade, the first time Eric invited me over and only a handful of months after Bryce's death, but the ramped-up anxiety and intrusive thoughts were enough to scare me off that too.

Rick scoffs as I head for the punch table. The bowls are completely uncovered, so I give my cup a whiff before I take a sip. Sugar clings to the roof of my mouth, the drink so sickly sweet that I can practically feel it dyeing my tongue red.

Most of the school turned out for the celebration, so the dance floor is clogged. Growing up, we watched teenagers flock from the trick-or-treating streets to the school for Halloween Homecoming, our bellies full of candy and jealousy. Everything looks so much cooler when you're a child being told you're not old enough for it yet. At the time, I would've traded anything to be here, but now I'd trade anything to go back.

In eighth grade, Bryce, Bea, Whitney, and I did throw ourselves a private Halloween Homecoming in Whitney and Bryce's living room that Candace filled with the same spooky décor currently hanging around the gym. We bobbed for apples in the big plastic tub they used to wash their old dog in, a disgusting anecdote to consider now. But Candace wasn't one for candy and sweets, so we took what we could get and gorged ourselves on wet apples as we danced to music playing from what was probably the same iPad that Candace used for photos tonight. Whitney dared Bryce to climb on top of the sofa, and the few glorious seconds of him doing the sprinkler on the thin piece of wood supporting the back cushions before toppling over and spraining his wrist are seared into the core fibers of my memory. I can still feel the apple juice sticking to my cheeks, pulling the skin around my mouth taut with every laugh that scored our whole journey to the ER. Bryce didn't cry once, even rated his pain so low that the doctors assumed he was fine and Candace had overreacted by bringing him in. Just as prominent in my memory is the moment we found out how bad the sprain actually was—a fully torn ligament—and all Bryce could do was chuckle and say he must have a high pain tolerance.

The crowd cheers as a new song comes on, and I remember where I am. My gaze drifts over the bodies, snagging momentarily on Whitney and Abby twirling together while Courtney tries to grind on Dustin. I should join them, try to be normal for a night.

But out of the corner of my eye, I see Rick's bright white suit making a beeline for Olive hiding in the shadows. Their arms are crossed tight in front of their chest, and anyone could see that the smile they offer Rick is as empty as the guy's heart.

Man, fuck this.

I grab a fresh cup of punch and sloppily dance my way over to them. Olive laughs at my shitty moves, which honestly take effort after years of dancing with Abuelo during chores, causing Rick to turn. Just in time for me to—totally accidentally and not remotely on purpose—stumble and spill red all over his chest.

"Fuck!" he yells, jumping away from me. The gym is loud enough that only a few people notice. Olive hides a laugh behind their hand.

"Shit, man. My bad." I step forward like I mean to help, but Rick storms away, cursing as he leaves for the bathroom.

"Thanks," Olive says as we watch him go.

"For what?" I smile over the lip of my cup and offer them the remainder of the one I spilled on Rick. They smile back at me as they accept it.

Whitney and Abby emerge from the dancing mob. "Power went out on our street," Whitney tells Olive, her bright pink nails tapping away on her phone screen. "Mom texted as they were leaving for the church candy drive, so we should be careful on our way home. And bundle up."

Olive sighs. "The Brexlers and their Halloween light-show extravaganza?"

"What else?"

Abuelo stayed home to pass out candy. Alone, in the dark, on a porch full of loose and uneven bricks. "Hey Whit, is it just your street?"

She shrugs. "Your house should be fine. We're still on the other side of town." We always hang out at Dustin and Abby's or Rick's, so I haven't seen Whitney and Olive's new place since I've been back. I don't know if I even want to.

I deal with one crisis at a time and step aside to call Abuelo on the landline, but it just rings before going to voicemail. His hearing isn't great, and with the chaos of the night, I doubt he'd be able to hear the phone if it was working anyway.

Or maybe he did hear it, and then tripped over nothing on the way to answer. Reaching for help in the pitch-black, slowly chilling house. Miraculously finding the phone only to struggle to dial without light as his hands and body begin to freeze.

I shouldn't have left him alone.

My fingers drum a heavy, repetitive beat on the plastic cup in my hand. "I'm going to go check on my abuelo." After taking a quick glance at Olive, who is helping Abby get a piece of glitter out of her eye, I lean closer to Whitney. "Look after Olive, yeah? Rick was being weird."

Whitney sighs, unsurprised exhaustion on her face. "He asked them out over the summer and they said no. I thought he'd given it up, but I guess he just got better at hiding it. I'll talk to him."

I know I need to leave, need to make sure my abuelo isn't dying on the floor with a cracked-open skull, but a more realistic danger nips at me. "Why even hang out with Rick?"

Whitney bites her lip. "Slim pickings?"

She got dropped here at age eleven as one of the only Asian kids, and now she and her sibling are some of the only relatively out queer kids too. I can't fault her for wanting to keep her enemies close, but one of these days, there's going to be collateral damage.

Abuelo is still alive, wrapped in a blanket on one of the two wicker porch chairs, smiling at everyone who stops by our fully powered house. I lie that I forgot something at home to explain my presence, mumbling when he asks me what it was, but seeing him here—breathing and grinning—was well worth the walk.

He tosses a piece of chicle at me as I pull my bike out of the garage, so I at least have something to chew on as I ride back to the dance.

Relaxed now, I can take in the evening. Costumed kids dragging their shed coats and trailing parents begging them to put them back on litter the roads, dipping in and out of the shadows wedged between halos of streetlamps. I've always loved Halloween here, savored the inevitability of running into a crush or showing up at a classmate's house unintentionally, thrilled at the freedom of being set free past sundown. Everything that annoyed Whitney and Bryce about living in a small town—a funny attitude to share since only Whitney had ever lived elsewhere—endeared me to the experience.

Nostalgia has me taking the long way back to school, winding through the streets with the kind of muscle memory that used to serve me well but now just serves me guilt as I realize where I am.

I cling to the brief moment when my childhood memories super-impose over my eyesight, until reality comes barreling into view.

Bryce's old house sits on the same street as Bea's, a big place that Candace was nearly forced to sell after their family finances took a massive hit from Bryce's dad's short but intense cancer and subsequent death. Turns out dying is almost as expensive as living.

The house is empty, a FOR SALE sign on its last legs in the over-grown lawn and a padlock over the door that Bea's key necklace once opened. The passing years show in the chipped paint and foggy windows. According to Dustin—my trusty source for answering questions I don't have the right to ask anyone else—another fam-ily lived here for a few months after Bryce's family moved out. It took a while for the property to sell at first, not just because it was haunted by what happened in the upstairs bedroom decorated with glow-in-the-dark stars, but because of a series of break-ins that followed Bryce's death. Dustin said it became a target for bored high schoolers, a common dare to see who would step inside the hallowed grounds, each venture leaving the place marginally more trashed until Candace's once pristine home was unrecogniz-able. Whitney tried to track the origins of a rumor about Bryce's vengeful ghost roaming the halls, but she never got any further than lecturing some guys on the basketball team who used to tease him in PE.

The lights are off, which doesn't strike me as odd until I realize so are the entire street's.

Those glow-in-the-dark stars on Bryce's walls were a gift from me to him and Bea, because of his love of astronomy and because of her fear of a room without light.

I ride down the block just to see, promising myself I won't even stop, let alone knock and check in on her. I pass a few groups on the sidewalk, but most have stuck to the brighter neighbor-hoods. It's quiet except for Mr. and Mrs. Brexler arguing on the phone with the power company over which of their decorations was responsible for the blackout.

I look one yard past theirs and see it, the choppy picket fence and half-tended-to garden. The last I saw of Bryce was during our fight, so we didn't say proper goodbyes before I left, but the closest thing I had to one with Bea happened here. Abuelo drove Pa and I to the airport directly after.

Now Bea's house is as pitch-black as her wardrobe, her car in the driveway.

I don't even register knocking until a voice barks from inside, "No candy!"

"You're going to get egged with that attitude."

Bea's door swings open, and the face I find waiting behind it is its own Halloween ghost.

"What are you doing here?" she asks. Her eyebrow piercings border shaved skin where the ends are usually drawn, a septum ring grazes unpainted lips, and nasallang studs and chain hang free of foundation smudges.

The words fall out of my mouth. "You're not wearing any makeup."

Her barer brow bones dip down. "That's not a Sherlock Holmes costume, and yet."

Clearing my throat clears most of my thoughts, but I still can't stop staring. I'm more and less acquainted with her face like this, an almost uncanny-valley replication of the Bea I grew up with, but there's something missing, and it's not the makeup. "You weren't at Homecoming." Her expression remains neutral to the point of boredom. "And I was in the neighborhood."

Her hand is still gripping the half-open door. "Okay?"

"Plus, the Brexlers' power outage. If you were home alone, you know, with Halloween being a big night at the hospital and all, I just wanted to make sure you were okay," I say, words jumbled in an irrational order. Her face still doesn't budge. "Because it's dark."

She snorts, finally relaxing into her stance. "The Brexlers knock out the power constantly. And I'm not afraid of the dark anymore." She backs farther into the house as if to prove a point, the shadows lapping at her until only her pale face remains visible, a haunting relic. "You weren't here to see it, but I did grow up."

Her declaration is punctuated by the door gently closing, somehow more embarrassing than if she'd slammed it. Humiliatingly, I wait a minute before I leave, wishing that the promise of Halloween was true. Right now, I'd like to be anyone but me.

chapter nine

The walls melt into shadows, inky night bleeding in through the cracks between the curtains and windows.

I light candles. I leave flashlights spaced out across the house. I try the sky but it's cloudy, starless.

I hold Lottie, invisible, in my lap. I close my eyes to create my own obscurity, yield some control over it. I beg myself not to choke on the abyss.

It doesn't matter. Though it isn't unusual for me, I don't sleep all night.

Mom comes home from her long Halloween shift in the morning. Miraculously, nothing in the house signifies that I didn't spend the night at Whitney's like I told her I would. She texted as soon as she heard about the power outage and the lie fell easily from my fingertips. By the time she walked through the front door, the lights were back on, and as far as she knew, I'd arrived home shortly before their return.

On the other hand, everything about Mom screams that she didn't spend the night alone. The long shift seems true, she wouldn't lie about that. But she's home later than she'd usually be after one. Fresh coffee and laundry detergent I wouldn't find in our cupboards perfume the air around her.

For now, I'm willing to allow her secrets of her own.

A few days later, there's a break in the showers serving as November's opening number. I take advantage of the dry sky and lean against the hood of my car outside the senior center. This time, when Señor Espinosa exits the building and smiles at me, I'm unfazed.

I help him into the passenger seat and then we're on our way in silence. But I only give it a few moments before he—

"Santiago won't be home when you drop me off," he says casually, like he's observing the fiery trees going bald. "He's getting a bite with friends."

I hold my tongue. For all his grandson's faults, I actually like Señor Espinosa. Even when Santiago was gone, with the clear intention to never return or respond, his abuelo tried to do well by my mom and me. I was granted my space, but I know he and Mom chatted when they ran into each other between the hospital and senior center. I always found it morbid that they're so close. The buildings, that is.

When we get to the house, I help him up the yard again. As I turn to leave, he beckons me inside. "I know the hospital is collecting donations for a clothing drive, and I have some of my Santiago's old stuff that your mom said I could leave with you."

I shut the front door behind me, sighing at Mom's meddling. While he wanders toward what was Santiago Sr.'s room, I stay in the foyer. I don't want to step a single foot farther into this museum than I have to.

But there are a few boxes sitting out here, the closest of which has yearbooks I don't recognize peeking through the poorly closed cardboard.

I grant myself one additional step and slip my hand inside. Our yearbooks are always dull. Plain black things with GREENS-VILLE PUBLIC COMMUNITY HIGH SCHOOL typed out in white. But this book is thrice as thick with solid hardcover binding. A collage of filtered photos decorates the front. I scan them, but don't see him.

Carefully, I open the book topping the pile and flip to the freshmen section. The alphabet carries me to *E*, and there he is. Here, Santiago looks the way I remember him. Hair unruly and short atop a scrawny build, grin goofy and wide. Then I turn to the front, where signatures should be.

A few messy scrawls wish him a great summer in a spectrum of color. The biggest message is in bright red, the thick words dominating the page.

Had fun chatting in English! Glad we got the team started! —Eric

The name rings a quiet bell, but Santiago never shared many specifics about his life in LA during our spotty communication behind Bryce's back. Vague allusions to plenty of friends and lots of badminton were the only things he'd really mentioned. But these entries are hollow, and this is the only one referencing the team. I mean to put the yearbook back where I found it and walk away, but the temptation is too great.

I grab the next one and don't even bother checking for his photo or cameo on the cover. The signatures are all as generic as the last's, but there's definitely more. Most notable is *Badminton King Santiago!!! Thanks for all the fun games and practices, we'll make it to regionals next year! —your favorite co-captain, Eric*

"Still looking for one more bag!" Señor Espinosa shouts from the other room.

"No worries!" I shout back, quickly trading yearbooks. Eleventh grade, last year.

Santiago jumps out on the cover. He's in a group of people I presume are the badminton team. They're cheering around a comically large trophy.

I'm ready to be struck by the amount of friends he made, ready to be spiteful of the intimacy in their messages. Prepared to face my replacements. But I'm struck by something else instead.

This book is empty. Not a single person signed it.

chapter ten

SANTIAGO

My bike isn't precisely built for the rainier weather November brings forth, so I start snagging rides to school with Dustin and Abby or Whitney and Olive, a different pair of siblings chauffeuring me depending on the day. It gives me the chance to catch up with everyone in calmer, closer environments, less through talking and more through observation.

Abby and Whitney are always texting, so Whitney fidgets when she drives, antsy to check her phone at the few stop signs between my house and school. Olive is quieter around Whitney than they are in PE among their friends. Several times, I've caught them reading astronomy books in the car, only realizing they all used to be Bryce's when, one morning, Olive set a particularly dense-looking hardcover on the dash for a second to fix their hair, and I spotted his signature scrawled across the pages' edges. BRYCE, blocky and sloppy and unapologetic. He never imagined a time he wouldn't own it.

The rides with Dustin and Abby are a gamble. Abby is reliable;

she hates driving but constantly corrects Dustin on his without glancing up from her screen, and she gets her nails done every other Tuesday from a woman who lives on the outskirts of town, always excited to show me the new color and design. But Dustin, I'm learning, has less consistency in his morning moods.

His playlists change when he and Courtney are fighting—or rather, they change when they aren't fighting, given that's the rarer occasion. Since Homecoming, they've been especially out of sync, something I had to pry out of Dustin during one of our shifts a few days post-dance.

We were checking the sell-by dates in the bakery section, tossing expired breads in the trash and stale ones into the clearance bins. Having not returned to the dance myself, I'd asked how the rest of the night had gone. Mine had been spent passing out candy with Abuelo, followed by a thirty-minute search for a horror movie that he fell asleep two minutes into. I woke up the next morning to a stiff neck from crashing on the sofa and my phone full of missed texts from the group chat, but none from Bea.

Dustin avoided the subject, only coming around when I asked if he was upset with me for leaving early.

"What? No, of course not," he said, letting a moment of panic break through the exhaustion coating his eyes. "It's just Courtney drama. Nothing new."

It was new to me, having only heard allusions to their messier moments until then. It's a good thing I've become a decent liar in the past few years, because when he told me that Courtney made the two of them leave the dance after Rick and I separately had, because "it would be weird to stick with the group when there's only one guy left," the devil on my shoulder begged me to tell him to break up with her. Jealousy is a fair, normal emotion, but feeling it because your boyfriend is spending time at a fully crowded dance with his sister, a lesbian, and a junior he barely talks to definitely pushes the boundaries of my empathy. I've never been in a relationship though, so I don't know if anyone is exactly vying for my advice.

I was saved from the conversation by my phone ringing just like it is now, the same name crossing my screen both times.

"Watch out," Whitney says over the table, drawing me away from Eric's call and my memories of the recent past. "Dennings is on the prowl." She tilts her head toward the math teacher on cafeteria duty strutting between rows of tables with his eyes scanning every student for signs of phone usage.

"Thanks," I tell her as I stick my phone back in my pocket, guessing that Eric dialed me on his way to school, figuring it would be my lunch hour with the time difference. Him putting that much thought into reaching out makes my stomach sour for rejecting it again. The guilt hasn't quite toppled into regret, though it's an inevitable aftertaste.

We all held out as long as we could, but the elements inevitably humbled us with the reminder that we live in Vermont, so the entire school is back to lunching in the stuffy indoor caf, the fluorescent lighting jarring against the faded-white walls. It's hard to even hear yourself think in here, though given the thoughts my brain tends to favor, that might actually be a perk of the location.

I tune back in to the conversation as best I can.

"No," Whitney says definitively to Dustin. "I am not wasting another Friday night watching our basketball team lose a scrimmage against themselves." Her glare shifts from Dustin to Rick, where he sits tables away with the rest of his team. Since Homecoming, he's been keeping his distance.

"Do you have a better idea?" Abby asks. "Or are you just going to complain about everyone's suggestions?"

Whitney squints over her Tupperware of fried rice sprinkled with tocino, a staple of her dad's cooking. "You're sassing me."

"And you love it," Abby says sweetly.

Dustin and I exchange a look of mutual *Are we third-wheeling right now?*

"What about the diner?" I try. Whitney and Abby release each other from eye-footsie to offer me patronizing smiles. "Or not."

"After the first day back, that's more of a sophomore thing to do," Whitney explains with the gentle disposition of a preschool teacher.

But I missed that, I want to say. When everyone nods their heads in agreement, even Dustin, I know it's not worth arguing.

"What did you do for fun with your friends in California?" Abby asks, and all eyes shift my way as I'm reminded of the role I played in missing those diner days.

"Uh, nothing special," I say. Eric's basement, Eric's car, parties at random people's houses, badminton practice, the beach, the park, the mall. "We just . . . hung out."

"You must miss them," Abby says. "I'd probably miss y'all if I moved across the country."

"Flattering," Whitney notes. Abby bumps her. Their small battle veers the conversation away from me, and though I'm sure it's mostly fueled by whatever game of flirtation they've begun playing, Whitney's eyes do catch mine once they subside, an apology in them.

After school, I do a walk-through of the store to put back any misplaced inventory, which is a nicer way of saying a tornado of middle schoolers just passed through and I have it on good authority from my own youth that they left the candy aisle in a state of disarray.

I'm restocking the sour gummies when I hear a gasp. As I turn around, I'm overcome with warmth, even if part of me had been actively avoiding this particular encounter since I made my return to town.

Bea's mom's eyes shine as she takes me in, face devoid of any of the disdain her daughter now holds for me. "Look at you all grown up, Santi." Her first words to me don't deviate much from Candace's, but there's an entirely different emotion behind them.

We hug, though the arrangement is unfamiliar. She used to wrap me tightly in her tattooed arms, holding me close in a way I'd rarely experienced from Pa and can't remember ever experiencing from my own mom before she bailed. Now, I swallow her whole, bending down so she doesn't have to stretch. I wonder how Bea feels every time they hug, if she notices the same blatant passage of time.

"I was hoping I'd run into you," Señorita Delgado says when I let go first, refusing to be the last one holding on. Her hands return to her shopping cart. "Bea told me about you moving back, but I can't believe your abuelo didn't mention it earlier."

I laugh awkwardly, wanting to know exactly how Bea phrased my return. "I would've stopped by, but . . ." I catch myself before I tattle on Bea to her own mom, though I'm sure she's familiar with her daughter's attitude toward me and even surer I've earned it. "It's nice to see you."

She smiles knowingly. "Well, you should come over for dinner sometime. Your abuelo has bingo on Tuesday, yeah? It would be perfect, and I can send you home with leftovers for him. Or he could join us another night when he's free!"

"Oh, um. That's really nice of you." I repeatedly wipe my damp palms on my apron. "But I don't think Bea would like that very much."

Señorita Delgado clicks her tongue and tilts her head. "You're a good friend for looking out for her feelings, even now."

It takes a great deal of effort not to tug at my collar. "I'm really not, and haven't been for a long time," I admit, painfully aware that I should be saying this to a different member of the Dougherty/Delgado family. "I just don't want to upset her anymore."

She smiles at me, the same look from the birthdays Pa missed and the Mother's Day dances she and Bea would sit out on, opting to spend the night watching movies with me and Abuelo instead. I want another hug suddenly, despite knowing I don't deserve one.

"Let me talk to her," she says.

chapter eleven

"Absolutely not."

Mom ambushes me with the plan as I'm trying to get out the door. I'm already running late because Lottie wouldn't eat her delicious breakfast of fish mush and brown pebbles. Turns out the only person in this house more stubborn than me is my cat.

"Santiago used to be like a son to me," she pleads. Her tender eyes track me as I dart around the room on the hunt for my car keys. "I want him to know this home is still open to him."

"Seems like false advertising," I say. "I can name at least one member of the family who feels otherwise." Lottie meows from the sofa. I point at her. "I'm counting that as her cosigning my veto."

"I think my vote outweighs yours," Mom says.

"Why?" I ask, then regret the implication. Neither of us is paying this house's mortgage, sure, but I know where I rank.

Mom doesn't reply, only lifts her hand. My keys dangle from her fingers.

I walk over and reach for them, but she pulls back at the last second. I sigh and wait.

"You don't bring Whitney around here anymore. You're always in your room, never out with friends. Not even to study or work on a project." She places the keys in my hand. "It's just dinner."

I make a fist around the metal, barely feeling the dulled edges against my skin.

I considered hunting him down to yell at him the first chance I got. Upon further consideration, I realized Santiago might throw a parade if he thought I was actively seeking him out. I settle for glaring at him in calculus. And at lunch. And when I pass him in the halls. By the time we make it to PE, I'm disappointed we aren't playing dodgeball.

After a riveting game of street hockey inside the gym, Coach Simmons asks me to put the equipment away in the supply closet. It's notoriously easy to get locked in, which means that at least once a year, a couple is caught hooking up inside. Despite my refusal to participate beyond what is required to not tank my grade, Coach Simmons has taken to liking and trusting me. Apparently running fast is endearing to gym teachers.

I'm struggling to push the two garbage bins that've been repurposed as hockey-stick holders when Coach Simmons barks out another order. "Espinosa!" Santiago startles out of his giggly conversation with Olive. "Help Dougherty with the gear."

Shockingly, he looks less excited by this request than I am. He extracts himself from his group of juniors to follow me out. I leave one bin for him, figuring it would diminish my impending rant if I ended up tripping from trying to push both.

My mouth opens right as the gym door closes behind us. "Dinner with my mom *and* helping me put away hockey sticks. You sure know how to woo a girl."

"Technically I didn't volunteer for either of those."

I dare a look over my shoulder. "You realize me giving your abuelo a few rides home for volunteer credit is not the same thing as you hanging out with my mom."

"Look, I know, but *she* invited *me*."

"Oh and god forbid you say no." I roll my eyes even though I've already faced forward again. I know he can sense it. "Wouldn't dare tarnish the perfect little reputation you're remaking for yourself."

He steps past me to open the supply closet, propping the door with his foot. "You've gotten more sarcastic with age."

"Apparently you've gotten more clueless." I start to roll the bin past him but pause in the doorway. "Is this an apology?" I ask, gesturing between us. "All of this shit you've been doing since you came back? Because if so, I don't want it. It's about two and a half years too late."

"Can't I just want to be your friend again?" he asks, exhausted for someone who has put in very little effort. "You do remember that we were friends not so long ago, yeah?"

"Oh, so now *I'm* the one who forgot we were friends?" I push on, but the wheels of the trash can snag on something, toppling both it and me over. The ground kisses my chin as I fall onto my stomach.

"Shit, are you okay?" Santiago rushes after me.

"No! Don't clo—"

My words are cut off by the slammed door.

"Great," I say. Then notice his hand around mine. I smack it away.

"Sorry," he says as I sit up and start silently collecting the fallen hockey sticks. The skin on my chin burns. I hope it's one of those familiar wounds you can feel but not see.

Slowly, he passes me a hockey stick. I stare at it. "It's not an olive branch," he tries. I relent and take it. His eyes track me, hands motionless at his sides.

"Can you stop doing that?" I snap.

"What?"

"Apologizing for everything except the thing that matters." I stop wrestling with the hockey sticks gathered in my arms. "If you have a speech, now's the time to give it. There was plenty of time to come up with good excuses, so I want to hear the most creative ones first."

"I—" His mouth flaps uselessly. "I don't know where to start."

"With the most creative ones. Didn't you hear me?"

A frustrated sigh escapes him. Seeing him flash his sharp edges shouldn't give me so much satisfaction, but this is a mess and it deserves to be treated as such. "I'm sorry for ignoring you all these years."

I laugh. "Seriously? That's the best you can do?"

His hands make a mess of his hair. "Look, it was complicated—"

"Oh! It was *complicated*," I shout, somehow still laughing. "You decided I wasn't worth any of your time anymore. What's so complicated about that?"

"I wasn't supposed to—"

"What? Be there for your grieving friend? Answer a single fucking text? Guess you replied to everyone else's messages and calls over the years, seeing how they're falling all over you, but some of us weren't so lucky to be graced by your glorious friendshi—"

"*I was told to leave you alone!*" he shouts, loud enough that I startle and knock over a bucket of tennis balls behind me. "Shit, shit, I'm sorry." Dropping to all fours, he scrambles to clean the mess. His hands shake; the balls slip like sand through his fingers and spread across the floor. "I'm—I'm sorry for yelling."

Carefully, I join him. We collect the balls in silence, the only noise gentle thuds as they hit the bottom of the bucket. That and the echo of his confusing outburst. When everything's been reorganized, he sits back.

"Do you remember our conversation at the funeral?" he asks quietly. The funeral he left early. The last time I saw him. Bagged eyes, life sucked out of him. We barely spoke, but most of that day after I broke down is a blur. I shake my head. "You were crying and shaking and I tried to help and you just . . . you started screaming at me."

His voice is almost drowned out by the pounding of my heart. Joining in the duet is the jingle of my earrings as I shake my head again. I was having a panic attack. Not the first nor the last, but by far the worst. I'd hidden them so well that only Bryce knew, which made it even worse, realizing it was a secret that belonged only to me again. "I just wanted to be alone, but I didn't tell you to *go*."

"'You weren't here then, so you don't have to be here now,'" he says. Though his pitch doesn't change, there's a shift in his tone. I know I'm being quoted. "'You should've been here and you weren't. You cared more about a pointless fight over keys than about your friendship. He needed you and I needed you, but you didn't care, so guess what, you're not needed here anymore.'"

My lips make a small, wet noise as I open them to say something. But my voice doesn't engage.

"My phrasing might be a bit off," he says. "It's been a few years."

"I didn't—I don't—" The words I'm trying to speak trip over the words clogging my thoughts. Mentally, I rewrite history. Though I have no problem casting myself as the villain of my own life, this narrative is too convoluted for me to reprise that role just yet. "He died. I was upset." I sound hollow. "It didn't mean anything."

"Yeah, it meant absolutely nothing to me." Santiago rubs at his eye so hard I'm scared it might pop out. "My childhood best friend—who I hadn't spoken to in almost a year—died." The implied guilt is loud enough it might as well be explicit.

"Well, you certainly took it all to heart, didn't you?" The fight has already left me, but I'm a feral cat on the best of days, so I take a swing anyway.

"Yeah. I did."

I was the victim here, and here alone. I gave myself this, nothing more. "I reached out," I try. "A lot." Communication had already been scarce. But once Bryce died, so did the last of those rare talks.

"I'm not saying I was right for it." He picks up a tennis ball and plucks at the worn, graying fibers. "I was hurting. He died for me too." The tennis ball rolls to the ground.

It was different teeters on the edge of my lips. But moons and suns, apples and oranges. And honestly, I may never understand the full depth of what we all were to each other. I just know my side, my pain.

"I never got to tell him sorry." Santiago's voice catches. Watching him take a moment to catch his breath is too difficult. My eyes find the ceiling. "But I can tell you." Another pause. "I'm sorry."

Seeing him still feels like a dream. Any moment, someone will wake me up and it'll mean I finally got some sleep. Yesterday, I would've sacrificed him being here for just that, one night where dreaming wouldn't be Russian roulette. But today, he's giving me what I thought I wanted for so long.

He picks at his cuticles, replicating the rips on both hands so they match. "Do you want me around?"

"Am I giving mixed signals?" I ask drily. It's easier than admitting my uncertainty.

"Bea, I'm serious." It's so earnestly the Santiago I remember, I'm suddenly compelled to cry. Or hug him. Or both. And I hate it. "I know I'm not your favorite person in the world for a lot of reasons, all of them valid." He leaves out that once upon a time, he *was* my favorite person in the world. A shared position. "So it's fine if you don't want me around you or your mom—really. If all I'm doing is hurting you and bringing up the past, I'll give you your space. All of it."

Bringing up the past. Like it's something so easily buried. A casket, an urn.

My eyes stay trained on the laces of my running shoes. This uniform doesn't protect me. I might as well be a preteen or kid again. I might as well be someone who never thought she'd hear Santiago say words like these to her.

"But—" His voice comes quickly, a knife through the thick silence. "But, if maybe you were open to the possibility of being friends again, you wouldn't have to decide right now. Maybe we could just see how it goes, you and me talking. And I'm fine with you being like . . ." He motions limply at me. "Like *this* to me. I'm not picky—I can grow without water or sunshine."

He's looking at the ground. Which means he can't see my heart clawing its way up my throat.

I swallow painfully. "I don't think I can have dinner with you and my mom." It's easier than admitting I don't deserve to.

He nods fast, so eager to make sure I know that this is fine. It's okay.

If I let him believe I want him gone, this time he won't come back. He won't question me twice. I will have my days of solitary confinement. I will be alone.

"But—" Now my voice is the quick one, my teeth catching on my lip. His eyes skyrocket off the floor to find mine. "But you should have dinner with her."

"Yeah?" he asks. It would be so easy to cut out the hope. It would be the hardest thing in the world.

"Yeah," I say.

"Okay."

The door swings open, nearly knocking Santiago over. We spring up as Coach Simmons looks between us, annoyance furrowing her brows. "Locking yourselves in the supply closet to ditch class? Detention after school, both of you."

★ ★ ★

We don't sit together in detention. We don't leave together either. But as I'm getting into my car, he calls my name.

He jogs up and hands his phone over. For some reason, I take it. It's a years-old model in a plain black case covered in stickers, most of them peeling from age and browning at the edges. HE/HIM/HIS, a blocky palm tree that seems like some kind of logo, a badminton birdie, a gradient sunset that's just innocuous enough to be a discreet bisexual flag.

"So I guess what they say about friend groups growing up to all be queer is true," I note. By the time we hit middle school, the two of us had already danced around the subject with each other. But his eyes were so heart-shaped for Whitney—and I'd already attached myself to Bryce—that it sort of got placed on the back burner.

He smiles. "You too?"

"Queer or pan," I say, using the labels in equal measure for myself. "The four of us are really populating that acronym." His brow dips, but I know he knows this already. "You, me, Whitney, and Olive."

"Oh, right," he says, but his face hasn't relaxed. "Thinking of a different group of four."

Without asking permission, I click on the home screen and am faced with a photo of Santiago and Bryce in their middle-school-graduation best.

"You think he'd have made it a group of five?" he asks, a little hopeful.

I'm unwilling to play my least favorite game, even with the person best equipped to play it. Especially when locking eyes with a reminder that Bryce's future will always be just that—a game of speculation. A sad wish that'll never come true.

I clear my throat and loosely lift Santiago's phone. "So what am I doing with this?"

"I don't have your number anymore," he admits. "I didn't know if you had mine."

I swallow. "How'd you lose it?" I only deleted his a few months ago.

"Switched phones last year, decided not to transfer the contacts." At least he has the decency to look ashamed. "I DMed Whitney on Instagram when I reached out. We didn't follow each other before that, if that means anything." I must make a face. "I'll stop fishing for brownie points."

"Why do you need my number?" I ask, making him work for this. If I have to, so should he.

"You've driven my abuelo home a few times," he says. "If anything happens, I'd like to be able to reach each other."

"Passcode?" I ask.

"Zero one zero one," he says. January first. His birthday.

"Hackers must love you." I open his contacts and type my number in, leaving my name simple, BEATRIZ. "Please tell me you grew out of the emojis." The contact saves and I move back to the full list, met with a world of colorful little hearts and creatures attached to every name. "Never mind."

He takes the phone and texts me.

it's Santi

"Weird. I just got a spam text," I say. His eyes twitch into a roll as he sticks his phone back in his pocket. It's then that I notice his bike where he left it propped up against a fence a few feet away. "You are *not* still riding that old thing around. In this weather?" Today is the first day in two weeks that it hasn't rained, and snow is just around the corner.

"Are you kidding me?" He pats the worn seat and I'm surprised it doesn't fall apart from that act alone. "Why wouldn't I be? This baby cost us an entire afternoon of washing cars."

"Yeah, and most of Bryce's Christmas money." I freeze with my hand on my open door. One afternoon of neutrality with Santiago, and the gears keeping my mouth shut for years have apparently been thoroughly greased.

"What are you talking about?"

I shut my eyes and take a deep breath. They open to his

hurt-puppy gaze. "I wasn't supposed to tell you." The back of my neck itches, but I don't relieve myself. One burden at a time. "Bryce paid for the bike."

Me, Bryce, and Santiago stationed outside the senior center with the deal of the summer. Two-dollar car washes for anyone willing to trust three sunbaked twelve-year-olds. Whitney and Olive were on their annual trip to the Philippines to visit their mom. If Whitney had been with us, we'd have probably charged fairer prices for our labor.

"He slipped his cash into the stack before you could count it. I promised him I wouldn't tell you." My mouth isn't seventeen right now. "I thought he would tell you himself one day."

"Oh." Santiago blinks rapidly.

We look at the bike through the same eyes, watching this transform from something funny to something sad. The bike is ancient, years past its prime. But here it is, still existing. Still, in some way, alive.

I give him a ride home.

chapter twelve

SANTIAGO

As promised, a few days later, I'm sitting in Bea's kitchen for the first time since I was fourteen. And, also as promised, Bea isn't sitting here. At least one of us was telling the truth in that closet.

"This tastes amazing, Señorita Delgado," I say while shoveling the deconstructed empanada into my mouth. I'm not as starved for homemade Colombian food now that I'm back with Abuelo, but I'm still making up for lost time.

"You can just call me Magda, Santiago," she tells me, like she has for as long as I've known her. I take the napkin she offers and wipe the ají dribbling down my chin.

"Gracias," I tell her. Then add, "Magda."

She smiles, warm and motherly, and it reminds me of growing up here, secretly wishing Magda could be my mom. Pa had me pretty young—getting my mom pregnant when he was only cracking his twenties—but Magda had Bea when she was about my age. I've always known this, but when you're a kid, everyone above eighteen and below eighty sort of just blends together. I see her youth now though, in a way I didn't back then, and it makes me feel like a kid and an adult all at once.

The aging black cat that had no interest in me when I walked in is now batting at my leg. I bend down to offer her my hand, and she stares at it for a beat before firmly pressing her forehead into it.

Magda smiles. "That's Lottie. Bea picked her out from the shelter last year."

"She finally convinced you?" I ask. Bea wanted a pet desperately when we were younger—a big dog, to be exact—but Magda always shut it down, a rarity in this household. As kids, it was easy to blame her for killing the fun. I wonder if letting us believe that was easier than admitting she couldn't handle another mouth to feed.

Magda's smile softens. "I thought she could use a friend."

Lottie scampers off toward the stairs.

"Actually, that reminds me," Magda says, quickly scooting out her chair and then rushing over to the coffee table to grab a stack of books. "I found some old albums you might like to see." Magda loved film photography when we were kids, always taking pictures twice—once on her phone and once on a camera. I don't see many new photos lining the walls, or at least I didn't on my quick glance when I walked in, but maybe the hobby got too expensive. Or maybe she just stopped having things to photograph.

She places the pile in front of me, four variously colored scrapbooks and photo albums bursting at the seams.

I wipe my greasy hands on a fresh napkin, but still hesitate to touch any of them even as Magda nods me on. Eventually, she takes the seat next to me and grabs the scuffed dark green book with fading gold paint spelling out *Good Times* in cursive on the cover.

She cracks the book open, and with it, my chest.

My fingers graze the first photo. It's of me, Bea, and Bryce on Halloween in fourth grade, all of our smiles a bit too wide and stiff. Bea and Bryce were Spider-Man and Spider-Gwen, respectively, both of their costumes made with Magda and Candace's joint efforts. At the time, we were aware of three total superheroes, only knowing about Spider-Gwen because we googled "girl spider-man" when Rick told Bea the month before that she couldn't be him for Halloween, so I was relegated to a thrift-store Superman find held together by Magda's mending.

"The three of you were something, huh?" she asks, only seeing best friends and not the memories behind one of their eyes.

"Yeah," I reply numbly, then turn the page.

Bea's seventh-grade yearbook photo stares back at me. Choppy bangs hang over her forehead and kiss the tops of her eyebrows, and she's grinning especially big since she'd just gotten her braces off the week before. She must be shit at wearing her retainer these days, because her old gap is fighting its way back to the center of her smile—a blessing, if you ask me.

This photo is far too nostalgic. Seventh grade was a complicated enough time; hormones flooding my body, uncertainty about why the locker rooms made me feel so weird, Whitney and I dancing around the idea of dating—a hilarious concept to think about now. But it wasn't made any simpler by the way Bea and Bryce started acting from this point in our lives onward, like a real, solid couple.

"She never lets me look at these things with her," Magda says, almost to herself. I'm not sure how to respond, or even if I should, until she glances up at me, waiting.

I whisper my fingers over the corner of the photo, realizing Bea wasn't much older than she was here when Bryce died.

"Does she ever . . . ," I start, unsure where I'm going. "Does she ever look like this anymore?"

Magda tilts her head to consider and then, instead of answering me, proposes her own question. "You want to know how I reacted the first time Beatriz dressed the way she does now?"

"You let her express herself?" I try. Magda's always been cool—supportive and empathetic where people like Candace were judgmental or stern. Where people like my mom were absent. I think it's because of how she became a mom—not receiving that kindness making her more inclined to give it to others. Not to mention the tattoos snaking up and down her arms, the undercut that, from the looks of things, she is just now growing out, and the assortment of piercings decorating her ears.

She smiles sadly, almost embarrassed, and pushes the photo album away from us. I clench my fingers so I won't reach for it again. I didn't allow myself to look at pictures of Bea for years, and I'm suddenly starved for the sight of her again, for any piece of the person I let myself lose.

"After Bryce, you know, Bea was—she was just so quiet." Goose bumps prickle my arms. "She cried at first, a lot, but she wouldn't talk about it with me. I thought, given her father, we could relate." Bea's dad, a ghost that's been haunting her since birth. "I think Whitney tried too, but they've always had a relationship I've never quite understood." That makes two of us. "She had the whole summer to feel whatever she needed to feel, but when school picked up again, she walked down from her room covered head to toe in black, lace and studs and leather, all of it stolen from my closet. She shaved her entire head without me knowing. Even after Bryce . . ." Her words drift off. "I didn't notice my daughter taking buzz-cutters from my bathroom."

Abuelo asked Pa to watch me like a hawk those first few months, his constant concern carrying loudly over the phone when the two of them thought I couldn't hear.

"I want to say I showed understanding for my daughter's grief, but I didn't. I was the parental cliché and yelled at her. I told her she wasn't allowed to leave the house until she changed her makeup, put on something bright and cheery, and grew all her hair back." She pauses to laugh at this, but it's without humor. "I was scared. I wanted my daughter to be the way she'd always been, or I guess the way I always thought she'd been." A heavy sigh. "I didn't want her to live with the pain I do."

I feel like I should say something, even if the first thought that comes to mind is *Bryce dying by suicide in his childhood bedroom isn't the same thing as Bea's dad dying in a car accident*, but my mouth feels cemented shut. I fight through it. "I'm sure you did your best."

"I didn't at first," Magda says. "She went back to her room and came down half an hour later in a pair of normal jeans, a yellow T-shirt, and a beanie covering her head. She did exactly what I told her to, looked exactly like the daughter I wanted back. But she was also a complete stranger."

When I saw her on Halloween, it was precisely as though preteen Bea got taller and older and grew into those big eyes and teeth of hers, but somehow she still looked fake, like someone had photoshopped her into what they thought she'd be at seventeen. Her face was the same, but she didn't look at all like the person I knew.

Magda smiles small. "So, I took her to the thrift store instead of school. I bought her whatever she wanted. And then we went to the mall and I had her sit with one of those makeup artists to show her the basics." She motions to her own face, blurry black eyeliner and a few coats of clumpy mascara from what I can tell. "Lord knows I wasn't helping her in that department."

Even though all of this sounds more like the Magda I knew in my childhood than her original reaction did, I'm surprised. "What changed your mind?"

She shrugs easily. "I know what estranged parenthood looks like, and I didn't want that for us."

"Do you miss her though?" I ask, hoping Magda gives me the answer that'll relieve me of my guilt. I miss the sunshine, I miss when I wasn't responsible for so much of the rain.

"Of course I do." I wait for her to go on, to tell me she stopped expecting to see the old Bea ever again, but she doesn't.

She pulls the albums back, flipping one open to a photo of me, Bryce, Whitney, and Bea on some field trip. The four of us wrapped up in one another, three faces scrunched in discomfort from the direct sunlight. Only Bea is smiling, eyes completely closed in bliss.

After working at the grocery store for a few weeks, I still haven't detected a strong pattern for what days will be busy and what days will be so slow that Dustin and I end up volleying expired oranges back and forth in the fruit section until one bursts on my shoe, forcing me to walk around smelling like moldy citrus for a week. We learned our lesson that time, but this slow shift with his mom has me missing the chaos. Curse him and Courtney for taking Saturday to get spiced cider at that cozy place an hour north of here. If their bickering during lunch this week was any indication, the trip will either do them some good or end in nuclear war. I make a mental note to text him and see how he's feeling when I get off work.

I'm at the register again today, placing bets with myself on whether the next person who walks through the door will be someone I've known since elementary or middle school. As the door opens, my brain scrambles. If it's someone from elementary school, something bad will happen tomorrow.

I shake my head, blinking away the thought viciously even though I've learned that that only makes them come back tenfold. At least the bargain was vague, generously allowing something only marginally bad to enter my brain, but I still feel relief when I realize it's Olive. We met the summer in between.

"I didn't know you were working today," Olive says, briefly stopping to admire one of the finger-painted turkeys hanging in the window—courtesy of Dustin's little cousin—before walking over to me.

"I didn't know you knew I worked here," I admit.

"You've lived here longer than I have," they say. "You know the town loves to whisper."

"And what are they whispering about me?" I say back, belatedly realizing that my voice has taken on a flirtatious lilt. I remind myself this is Bryce's sibling. "Actually, I'd rather not know. But can I help you with anything?"

They lift a piece of crisp stationery with a large, curly blue C at the top. "Candace sent me to pick up some stuff for Thanksgiving. She's convinced that all the good cans of cranberry sauce will be gone after the countdown hits less than ten days."

"Sounds like Candace."

"Yeah." Olive laughs, then tucks the list into the pocket of their long coat, a lime-green garment that reminds me of cartoon frogs.

"But since you're here, there's actually something else you might be able to help me with? I'm taking extra science classes this year—bio *and* physics—so I can do an astronomy course online when I'm a senior. I thought it would look good for college apps if I actually had experience on paper in my major."

My fingers find the lip of the counter where the register sits, and pick at some of the peeling paint. "You want to major in astronomy?"

Olive nods, gnawing their lip. "But I've been struggling a bit with physics. I know you're taking bio right now, unlike most of the other seniors, but Whitney told me that's because you took physics last year, so I was hoping you might be able to help me with some of my homework? Or with studying?"

I'm still processing their major—which was supposed to be Bryce's. Because Bryce was supposed to go to college, and Olive was supposed to be the younger one, the one that didn't do anything until their older brother and sister did. But now Olive is talking about college applications and majors and senior-level classes, and Bryce died with a ninth-grade education.

"If you're too busy or just uninterested, that's totally fine," Olive says, taking a slight step away from me. I cram the infinitely growing list of things that Bryce will never get to do into the bottom of my chest. The fuller the list becomes, the emptier I feel.

"No, no, I'm super down to help," I correct quickly. "Just shoot me a text whenever you need me."

Olive relaxes into their coat, a warm smile spreading across their round face. "Great. Thanks, Santiago."

"Let me know if you struggle to find anything on the list," I say as they head for the aisles.

"I'm pretty familiar with the place, but thanks." I watch them strut off, confident in a way I rarely see them at school.

Bryce will never shop for his mom again.

Bryce will never tutor his sibling in science.

Bryce will never—

I find a bit of raised paint, mentally promise to tell Dustin's mom I'll repaint the counters during my next shift, and rip as hard as I can.

chapter thirteen

BEATRIZ

For the first time since she moved here, Whitney and I don't have any classes together. It's made avoiding her at school easier than usual. But the streets were always fair game, and it was only a matter of time until this happened.

She and Abby slow when they spot me taking Lottie for a walk. It's the first day of Thanksgiving break and despite the chill, they're sharing a cup of ice cream. Whatever flavor it is, it's pink and covered in tiny marshmallows that look like Lottie in the little white winter coat Mom sewed her.

Eventually we're right in front of each other, both pretending like we didn't see it coming.

"Small towns, huh?" I offer with a fake smile. Whitney's face doesn't budge.

"I don't think I've ever seen a cat in a coat and harness before," Abby says, delighted.

Her past non-sober comments aside, I don't dislike Abby. She and Dustin are two sides of the same overly friendly coin, but I think I'd like her more if she and Whitney weren't so close. "Can I pet them?"

"By all means."

Lottie takes to the head scratches easily. She has far fewer socialization problems than her owner. With Abby crouched down beside her, I can almost squint enough that it looks like it's just me and Whitney here.

"How have you been?" Whitney attempts with a forced smile, emulating Candace in her obligation to be polite.

"Better than ever."

She blows out an annoyed breath. A civil Whitney is a fraudulent one, and I've always preferred she hate me than play pretend. "We should keep walking. We're going to go watch a movie at Abby's. Santiago is meeting us there."

I suppress a laugh. "Is this the part where you want me to be jealous, or am I meant to fish for an invite you're already waiting to give me?" Abby lets go of Lottie, joining us back at human level. Her gaze flickers between us.

"Fuck off, Bea." Whitney brushes past me. "And don't come to the party."

"What party?" The way her shoulders tense, it was the wrong thing to ask.

"Thanks for letting me pet them," Abby inserts, with the first real smile this conversation has seen, before chasing after Whitney.

I watch them unapologetically, hoping they hold hands, hoping they don't. Ultimately, their hands graze, and they disappear in the distance. I stand here, completely still.

Thanksgiving with my grandparents is a newer tradition. I've never met my abuela and abuelo and doubt I ever will. There's always been tension between my mom and her parents for how they responded to her pregnancy—i.e., me. My dad's parents were equally unsupportive, but by the time I turned two, checks started arriving. At first, Mom sent them back as quickly as they arrived. She didn't want their money or pity.

But it wasn't about that. It was about my dad, and him not being here. And I think Mom let it go on because she understood that grief, the desire to do something—anything—to make it go away.

Every time a new check arrived, she'd look at me, and for a moment, I swore she let herself mourn me. Pictured me as the kid in the ground and her as the parent left to carry on. I think the image came easier than either of us would like to admit.

Then the moment would pass, she'd place the check in her purse, and I wouldn't see her for a few hours.

I don't know if it's the money or the grief or the desire to give me some semblance of an extended family that drives us to the restaurant to meet my grandparents for Thanksgiving dinner.

For all her annoyances about college and friends lately, Mom never asks me to dress differently for my grandparents, so I don't. I pair a black corset with a long-sleeved dress that droops down my legs like a fairy costume. Whitney once said this outfit makes me look like a bored Renaissance-fair attendee, which is why I keep wearing it.

The restaurant is half an hour outside of town, but Mom doesn't complain. We're the least inconvenienced party here considering they're driving in from the edge of New Hampshire. It's the type of place that uses valet and takes our coats. When we step inside, my grandparents, Eileen and Neil Dougherty, are already seated. The only family I've ever known who share my last name.

"Oh darling, look at you," Eileen coos, taking me in. I let her hug me. "Growing so much."

I added my highest platform boots last minute. Eileen almost cried when she saw my height for the first time. Apparently my dad was rather tall.

She lets me go and steps aside to greet Mom. Neil stands to pull out the seat next to him. "Please, please sit." He doesn't try to hug me, never has, and I like him better for it. "Thirsty?" I nod.

While Neil pours water for Mom and me, Eileen runs through the usual questions. She asks Mom about work, the house, the neighborhood. She *tsks* when she inquires about my other grandparents and Mom says she still hasn't heard from them since my fifteenth birthday. Last year Eileen offered to pay them a visit, hoping to build a bridge on our behalf. Not that we would've accepted anyway, but they traded New Hampshire for Florida a few summers ago. At least according to the distant cousins Mom still has occasional contact with.

I down my water fast, never letting more than a few moments pass without it touching my lips. Neil keeps refilling it, but when the jug and my glass are empty, Eileen turns to me.

"So, Beatrice—"

"Beatriz," Mom corrects because she knows I won't. She started the nickname of Bea like bee. But she's firm that Beatriz is *Bay-uh-treece*.

"Of course, I'm sorry," Eileen says sincerely to her. Then to me, "Beatriz, how has senior year been going for you? College applications should be done by now, yes?"

I reach for my drink and remember it's empty. "It's been good," I lie.

"Do you know where you and your friends are interested in going?" Eileen asks, dragging her finger over the foggy condensation on her glass.

"We're considering our options still." I avoid Mom's gaze.

"Her friend Santiago is mainly looking at schools in California," Mom says. Dinner between the two of them must have been informative, because I didn't know that. I don't know much about him in general now, though.

"Oh, *Santiago*," Eileen says, pronouncing his name fine. I shift in my seat. "Is this *just* a friend, or a boyfriend?"

"We're not dating," I say.

"They grew up together," Mom inserts. "He recently moved back to town, so they've been reconnecting." I nod along with the fib, hoping to satiate Eileen.

"And what about you, Magda? Are you dating anyone?" Eileen asks.

Mom chokes on her water, droplets clinging to her chin as she places her glass down on the table. "Me? Oh no, no, I—no."

I watch her fingers slowly slide toward the bracelet on her wrist, tucking it under her sleeve. The key under my shirt burns.

Eileen passes Mom a thick cloth napkin. It looks more expensive than my entire outfit. And these boots weren't cheap. "Well, darling, you know you're allowed to move on and date if you'd like. Don't let us stop you, if that's a concern. We know he'd want you to be happy." Her hand finds Mom's on the table. "You two were lovely together, but it was still just a high school relationship."

"I need to use the restroom," I say, and excuse myself.

This place is far too nice for me to have a meltdown unnoticed. I book it to the bathroom and run my shaking hands under cold water until they go numb. The goal isn't pain—I just need something to ground me until my body slows down. But my heartbeat kicks right back up again when I open the door to rejoin dinner and find Neil standing outside.

"Fuck, shit, I mean—" I take a breath. "Sorry, I—you scared me."

"Apologies, sweetheart, I just wanted to check on you." He holds his hands behind his back, like he's stopping himself from giving me a hug. I forgot to look in the mirror to see if I'd started crying, but I've been wearing waterproof lately.

"All good here," I say, barely resisting the urge to offer a thumbs-up. "Just drank my water too fast."

He smiles politely. I wonder if he ever gave that face to my dad when he was hurt or heartbroken or struggling with school. Or whatever it was that painted his days. The only details I really know about my dad surround my birth and his death.

"Your grandma Eileen has a tendency to meddle," Neil says. I try not to jolt at him calling her what she is to me. "She regrets not being more involved when you were younger, and just wants your mom to know that we won't go anywhere if she decided to start dating again."

"That's, uh, nice of her."

"She's not encouraging your mom to replace your father though," he says, scratching his chin. Eileen always says my dad was the spitting image of Neil, so I try to find some of my face in his. But his lips are too thin, the shape more pointed than mine. His nose doesn't bend and stretch. Supposedly his hair was blond once, but it's gone gray now.

"I know," I say. If not for me, my parents probably would've broken up. If not for me, maybe my dad wouldn't have been on that road at all and they'd have both gone on to live happy, fulfilled lives. "I don't have any problem with my mom dating someone new."

He tilts his head. "Does she know that?"

Over his shoulder, I see our food arriving. "We should get back." And because he is my grandfather, and he seems to want to be a good one, he lets me leave without answering his question.

On the drive home, our to-go boxes warm my thighs through my dress. Mom talks about Eileen and how age has made her gentler, kinder. Mom's glad we do this; she wants me to have a family and it's better late than never, maybe she can call up some of her extended relatives and see if they'd like to meet me someti—

"I like your bracelet," I say.

One hand remains on the wheel and the other adjusts the piece of jewelry drooping from her wrist.

"Thank you," she says, and we're quiet the rest of the way home.

That night, I submit seven college applications. Some in-state. Some out of state. I use Mom's credit card and leave a sticky note on her bedroom door about the fees. When I get emails back confirming my applications have been received, I erase the messages and sit outside my window. The sky is full of stars tonight, but it's never looked darker.

chapter fourteen

SANTIAGO

Thanksgivings in California were generally spent fighting my dad's bandmates for pieces of greasy, discounted, presliced turkey or cold servings of watery mashed potatoes. Most of their families had also been left behind in Vermont, so holidays were a group activity, always resulting in more band practice by the end. This year, Abuelo and I prepared a turkey together, bringing the plentiful leftovers to the senior center. Pa was supposed to fly in for the actual holiday, but flights were wildly expensive, so we settled on him coming the day after and staying through the weekend.

Abuelo and I, without licenses or cars, are relying on one of his younger friends at the center—younger being late sixties—to give us a ride to the airport. Since early this morning, I've had my shoes laced and ready, knee bouncing as I sit on my bed as I try to distract myself with everyone's posts from yesterday. As I scroll past the dozenth photo of unseasoned turkey, Abuelo pokes his head through my open door.

"Is Billy here?" I ask, shoving my phone into my pocket and hopping up. The expression on his face and the landline pressed to his shoulder catch up to me, and my stomach bottoms out. "What's wrong? Is Pa okay?" The plane crashed and burst into an explosion of flames and Pa is dead in the middle of—

"Yes, yes, he's fine." Abuelo nods quickly, forcing his somber look into a pitiful smile. "He wants to talk to you."

I grab the hunk of plastic from Abuelo, shoving it against my ear hard enough to bruise. "Pa? What's going on? Why aren't you on your plane right now?"

His pause is loud and nostalgic. "Tito, I'm so sorry." I close my eyes. The older I get, the more I hear my voice in his. "We got booked for a last-minute party. We need the money and exposure."

"So you're not coming." It isn't a question.

"You know how it is," Pa says. Weirdly enough, my brain flashes to my mom, a jumbled kaleidoscope of pale arms and blond hair, all vague snapshots from childhood, all of her turning away from me. "We need to get back into it, and give it our all this time."

This time. The first time was my whole childhood, trying to make it big in the middle of Southern Nowhere, Vermont. The second time was the move, the California coast sprawling with possibility. Then Pa missing gigs to fly back with me for the funeral, to make sure I was eating, to watch me as I watched the TV, aware of my empty, blank stare even as I was incapable of doing anything about it, begging his bassist to ask his psychologist girlfriend to see me. It was a blip in our relationship, bittersweet in more ways than one. I didn't know my dad was capable of fatherhood like that, but I was too removed from myself to really appreciate it, and now it's gone.

Bryce died and so did I and then I blinked and Pa was back to constant rehearsals and penny-paying shows and somehow years passed without any change in their fame. I was playing badminton and lying and ignoring Bea's desperate messages and going to Eric's to do homework and hating myself and cooking my own dinners. If this third time is marked by my absence, it started long before I moved back home.

"Will you at least be here for Noche Buena? Or my birthday?"

He clears his throat, and I hear someone distantly call our name, reminding me of another thing we share. I've never fully had one to myself—a name or a dad. "I'm going to try. But look, I have to go. We need to start setting up for the venue. Thank your abuelo for calling me, okay? Love you, Tito."

"Yeah. Love you too," I say numbly. He hangs up, but I don't remove the phone from my ear just yet.

If Pa had boarded his plane, he'd already be in the air and landing in about an hour. Abuelo called and Pa didn't, both of them knowing this. Knowing he wasn't coming.

I trade the landline for my cell and read through the busy group chat thread with me, Whitney, Abby, Dustin, and Courtney. They discreetly transitioned to this one after everything at Homecoming, though Rick still sends the occasional meme to the old chat he's in.

Tonight's hot topic is the eighteenth birthday party Whitney's hosting a month early to throw off her parents' suspicions. Candace and Phil are out of town this weekend, celebrating some anniversary in New York, so the timing is perfect. The group's all sending fit checks and updates about their attempts to snag alcohol from their houses, given that it's impossible to get away with a fake in a town where everyone knows everyone.

Just then, a text comes in, separate from the chat.

Whitney: have fun with your dad!!!

I told her I couldn't come to the party, anticipating this week-end being father-son, father-son bonding time for the Espinosa men. From my room, I can hear Abuelo already snoring over a backing of telenovela reruns. I rub my thumb against the side of my pointer finger for four minutes before replying.

Santiago: change of plans! I'll be there in an hour

The first birthday Whitney spent in Greensville, she was turning twelve and didn't know anyone in our grade well yet, so the guest list began and ended with me, Bea, and Bryce. She wanted something formal and dainty, living up to Candace's dream-daughter expectations, so we all got dressed up for a tea party in the dining room with the fine china Candace never uses outside of holidays. The tea was gross and bitter, and I had to eat twelve of the dry finger sandwiches Candace prepared to even begin to feel full, but I was hanging out with my best friends and a pretty girl, so I was happy.

Bryce decided to spice things up and suggested a game of backyard hide-and-seek over the final piece of chocolate cake. Bea acknowledged that it wasn't his cake to wager a game on, but Whitney seemed apathetic about the technicality, just desperate enough to impress her new brother and his friends to let it slide. How quickly her confidence grew over the years to come.

We all ended up soaked, shivering in our fancy shirts and dresses, streaked with dirt from the muddy December snow. It wasn't even until we were chilled down to the bone that we real-ized there was no way to use hide-and-seek as a decider for who got the cake. We were all winners, we were all losers, and we didn't mind one bit.

Candace yelled loud enough to shake the house when she found us outside, and quickly made everyone change into spare pajamas Bryce and Whitney had so she could wash our clothes before we went home. But as we all huddled on the sofa, freshly wrapped in warm PJ's and blankets while Whitney split the last slice of cake into four pieces, we were content. Whitney said it was the best birthday she'd ever had.

This party is nothing like that one.

Dustin hands me a red Solo cup sloshing with something that smells sharp and promises a brutal hangover. I found him immediately upon arriving and have clung to his side since, barely able to navigate this unfamiliar house.

I sniff the drink and grimace. "Dude, what the fuck is this?"

He laughs and takes a pained sip of his own cup. "Badly mixed jungle juice."

"I can smell the jungle, all right."

Courtney stumbles over, already tipsy, and latches onto Dustin's side. She eyes me up and down with a sly smile. "You look cute tonight."

"So do the two of you." I motion to the couple with my full cup.

Courtney downs the rest of Dustin's drink and her face pinches in displeasure, likely from me and the beverage. "We need to find you a girlfriend," she slurs, her bobblehead flopping toward Dustin. "Doesn't Santiago need a girlfriend?"

I eye Dustin subtly, but he keeps his gaze down. "I think I'm good."

"You *are*," she coos, pawing at my shoulder across her boyfriend.

My next glance to Dustin isn't subtle at all, and neither is his discomfort. "Too good to be standing here with us two all night."

It dawns on me that I'm in the middle of some type of fight. "I should go find the birthday girl," I tell them, excusing myself before they can reply. Even over the music, I can hear the rumble of their argument picking back up as I head into the living room.

I haven't seen Whitney since I got here, the house packed wall-to-wall with what must be our entire school and a few from neighboring towns. Suddenly, a hand grips my shoulder and yanks me forward.

"Santiago!" Rick cheers, breathing hot, rank air into my face. I cough without meaning to. "*Mi hermano*," he singsongs in an exaggerated accent. It's a wonder that he's allegedly failed Spanish twice. "Where have you been, my guy?"

I peel his hand away, grateful for the intoxication loosening his grip. I may be bigger than I was when we were kids, even bigger than him now, but I've never been a fighter and doubt I could get him off me if he was sober. "Just . . . around."

He smacks me on the back, laughing. "This fucking guy, am I right?" His question is simultaneously to no one and everyone, but he stumbles back into the crowd before I can get another word out. I think I hear him mumble something about Olive though, so I pull out my phone and type as I walk.

Santiago: Not sure if you're home, but Rick is on the prowl and drunk off his ass

Their reply comes immediately.

Olive: spending the night at a friend's to avoid the party chaos. thanks for looking out <3

Satisfied, I look up from my screen and make eye contact with Bryce.

I nearly drop my drink.

What must be his freshman year photo hangs above the stairwell. I know it's a trick of the light, but I swear his smile deepens the longer I stare at it, though it's hardly there to start.

Some junior I vaguely recognize from PE rushes down the steps, screaming about the song playing in the living room being *her* song. In her scramble, she bumps into Bryce, and I watch, helpless, as he crashes to the ground.

Over the music and chatter, no one but me hears the glass break. My arms shove everyone out of the way as I rescue shattered Bryce from the floor and carry him to the nearest upstairs bedroom.

I'm genuinely shocked no one is hooking up inside this room that screams *Candace* from the pastel floral bedding to the soft beige walls. Even the lamp on the side dresser is cushioned by a lace doily that matches the trim along the comforter and pillowcases.

Bryce and I sit on the bed, and I neatly stack the three glass shards resting atop his face until they look *right*. Only then can I take a moment to breathe. This may be one of the final pictures Bryce ever took, which makes me never want to risk a glance at the walls again, just in case there's a more recent one out there. The idea of a piece of him existing that I'll never perceive is almost, if I squint, the same thing as having future memories waiting on the horizon.

My fingers graze the photo, trace the shape of his face and hair that won't ever change, and I wonder what he'd make of who I've become.

When someone's spouse dies, you call them a widow. When someone's parents die, you call them an orphan.

What do I call myself? What name do I put to my losses?

Voices break through the noise outside, muffled through the shared wall that I'm assuming leads to a bathroom. Running water further distorts the words, but when I catch familiar names, I get up to hear better.

"I'm surprised I haven't seen Beatriz."

"Really? She doesn't come to these types of things."

"Yeah, but she and Whitney still seem cool with each other, at least sometimes."

"I do *not* get that."

"What?"

"Being friends with the girl who let her stepbrother die."

"What do you mean?"

"There's no way she didn't know he was going through something. If you're really that close with someone, you'd see it coming."

I leave a broken Bryce behind for the hallway, but everyone's already gone. The bathroom is empty, unlike my head. The overheard words echo, the outright disgust toward someone who claimed to love Bryce but couldn't save him.

All the times I typed up a text, all the times I deleted it. All the distance I maintained between us that wasn't physical. All the things I could've said but didn't.

I bump into Courtney as I descend the stairs, and jungle juice sloshes over the rim of her overfilled cup.

"Sorry, Court," I apologize distantly.

She pats my face with her dry hand. "Don't worry about it."

She shoves her cup into my grip as I help her to the bathroom, making sure she's safely inside with the door locked before I walk away. I text the group chat that she's in there and Abby replies immediately that she'll go check on her.

At the top of the stairs, I realize I'm still holding her drink and the gnawing sensation in my gut hasn't gone away.

"Fuck it," I say to absolutely no one, then take an endless sip.

chapter fifteen

BEATRIZ

I'm halfway through the last calc proof in my Thanksgiving-break homework when my phone starts ringing with a video call from an unsaved number. I looked at the text from last week enough times to recognize it.

I answer and leave the phone face up on my desk while I continue working. "What?"

"I miss *youuuuuu*," Santiago slurs. My pencil stalls. "Are you *maaad* at me? Because you should be. I'm a *liaarrrr*."

I pick up my phone. Too close to the camera, Santiago's shadowed face takes up the whole screen. "Are you drunk?"

"Come to the *partyyyyy*!" He sways in and out of view, blue and purple fairy lights illuminating him in flashes. Why does that look like Olive's room?

Oh. Whitney's words from earlier this week suddenly make sense.

"I wasn't invited!" I shout back. More accurately, I was asked not to come.

"Right! Right!" A single pointed finger comes into frame. "Because you and Whitney aren't friends. Because *none* of us are friends!"

"Exactly," I say at normal volume. The phone continues spinning. "Look, are you going to be okay? Should I call Dustin or something?"

"I love Dustin!" he shouts.

"Yeah, Dustin's great."

"And he got cuter," he whispers, apparently sober enough not to out himself. "But you did too! Don't worry! We all got cuter." He hiccups as his expression goes solemn. "Well, not *all* of us." The phone flips through the air before landing on the ground. A beat later, he picks it up. "I tripped," he laughs.

I scratch my head. My nails are longer than my hair. Both are longer than my patience. "Santi, is anyone around you sober enough to drive you home?"

"Pft!" he raspberries into the microphone. "No."

I press my fingers to my temples and notice he isn't surrounded by the fairy lights anymore. "Where are you?"

He swivels his head. "Whitney's house."

I am going to hide every bottle of alcohol in existence from him for the rest of our lives. "Yes, I know you're at Whitney's house." I leave my phone on my desk while I start lacing up my boots. "What part of it?"

The speakers crackle. "Uhhh, I'm in a hallway."

"Did you walk upstairs to get there?" I grab my keys and throw my leather jacket on. Even after years of having a shaved head, I still move to pull my hair out from under the collar.

He gasps. "How did you know?"

I pop a beanie on as I clomp downstairs and meet the cool

outside air. My fingers swiftly lock the door behind me. "Lucky guess." My phone is dying, but Mom stole my car charger last week. "Santi, I have to hang up, but stay where you are. I'll see you in a few minutes."

"I love when you do that," he sighs.

I slide into my front seat and start the car. "Do what?"

"Call me Santi."

I freeze halfway to buckling my seat belt. In the moment of stillness, I notice how quickly my heart's begun to beat. "I'll be there soon."

Whitney's party is in full-blown chaos when I get there. Red Solo cups litter the lawn like bread crumbs to lead back the few stragglers braving the cold. As if the music isn't enough of a North Star. Or the smell.

If it were any other house, I'm sure the cops would've been called by now. But it's Whitney. She's the golden girl whose brother died *so, so tragically*. These neighbors won't steal her moment of joy. They also won't acknowledge Bryce's death beyond this kindness.

I roll my eyes as I open the front door.

My search is fruitless at first. After he doesn't answer my calls, I search for Santiago upstairs. I kick a half-undressed Sarah Bruno and Wells Green out of Olive's room and lock the door from the inside. Olive can get in through their attached bathroom later. Even though I know Bryce's family moved for several reasons more valid than this one, I'm glad I didn't have to find my classmates fumbling around in his old bedroom.

My lack of luck continues downstairs. In the kitchen, Dustin has one arm hooked around Courtney and waves at me with the other. It's not like he's cheering for my entrance, but Courtney's expression when she sees me is as if I started making out with her boyfriend right in front of her. If only she knew.

I push my way over to them. "Have you seen Santiago?"

Now that I'm closer, I can tell Dustin is tipsy. "Not for, like, an hour." He shrugs sloppily, messing up Courtney's hair.

She pats the cowlick down. "I thought Whitney didn't invite you."

"Security was tight, but I snuck my way in." I gaze pointedly at Kennedy Fisher chugging a Natty Light, then shooting the empty can at the sink beside us. She misses, and it clatters to the floor.

"Well, this has been fun," I say. Courtney's smile is sharpening by the second, and it's harder to act unfazed within these particular walls. "I've got over six feet of drunk teenage boy to go find."

I excuse myself to resume the search. Staying in one place too long lowers my chances of finding Santiago and increases my chances of running into Whitney.

And then she appears like magic from across the living room, her body wrapped in a tight red halter top and black boyfriend jeans. Whitney presses the golden heart locket Candace gifted her at the wedding to her chest as she tips her head forward and tosses it back to take a shot.

Laughter filters through her puckered lips. If I snapshotted the moment, you'd never guess Whitney had been sad before. One of the worst things that can happen to a person happened to her, and here she is.

To grieve is to live, yet it seems impossible that you can do both. She disproves this impossibility every day, and I hate her for it.

Before she can see me, I tug open the sliding-glass door to the backyard.

My phone dies as I pull up Santiago's now-saved contact. "Shit."

It's freezing, so there's almost no one out here other than a few people smoking weed and tobacco alike. It's hard to get a breath of fresh air, so I walk farther into the yard.

I sit on one of the lounge chairs cast in shadow. It hits me that being here—at a party where I'm looking for my friend and avoiding someone I share a complicated history with and watching my peers indulge in inebriation—is the closest I've come to being a normal teenager in years. It makes my lungs squeeze.

"That's not a party face."

My heart does a backflip. "*Jesus*, Santiago. Are you trying to kill me?"

He sits up in a chair three down from mine. With the light spilling from the house, I can just make out his face. "No more funerals," he whispers.

I walk over and offer a hand. "Let's go, buddy."

He laughs. "I thought we weren't friends."

"You were a much happier drunk twenty minutes ago."

He tilts his head back, gazing past me. "The stars are so bright tonight."

"They always look like that."

"Not in LA," he says. "Too much pollution."

Objectively, they are beautiful. Sparkling diamonds against black velvet, more bursts of shimmering light out there than grains of sand on all the Earth. I never forgot the look on nine-year-old Bryce's face when he told me that fact, his awe at the vastness of existence.

Candidly, without Bryce's secondhand fascination for astronomy, I doubt my eyes would drift up as often as they now do. After his death, I think I inherited a version of that obsession. Or maybe the sky just means something different in grief, my roof the closest place to where so many people claim he is now.

"They sold his telescope first," I say, grateful for the dark. "Olive wanted it, but Candace said she could get them a new one."

Santiago sighs. I can't tell if he's sobered up or if the momentary dip into our grief we're allowing ourselves is balancing him out. "They sold the house too," he says softly. I sit down on the chair beside him. "I can't even pretend he's here. He never was."

"I know," I say, surprised at how I don't choke on the words. Of all the things Bryce won't ever experience, in this moment, never setting foot on this property feels like the saddest. "I tried, at the old house before they moved. I couldn't even get past the foyer." My hand wanders to the key tucked under my shirt, going cold against my skin.

Santiago lazily turns his head toward me. "I'm sorry I made you come."

"Couldn't let you wander the streets drunk and have someone else pick up my mom's stray."

He tries to smile. "I meant making you come *here*."

I swallow. "I've been before. It's fine." And then, because I get it, "You had to see it for yourself."

"My dad was supposed to fly in tonight," he admits. "But he bailed." A long exhale streams from his mouth, clouding the air. "Thought I'd distract myself with a party."

I shut my eyes against the confession. His dad was the parent who stayed, but only in the loosest sense of the word. He was always too busy chasing his own life. Always forgetting his son was supposed to be part of it.

Parents and their lost dreams. Children and their inability to compensate for them.

I stand and re-offer my hand. "Let's get you home."

He takes the help. "Do you think Abuelo will be mad?"

I hear the want in the question. A concerned parent enraged by love and a desire to protect their kid. If Mom had been home when I left, she'd probably have thrown a parade. Somehow, it all comes from the same place.

We maneuver out the side gate to avoid the rest of the party. Tension leaves my body as I leave the property. But I turn around for the slightest moment as we reach the end of the driveway, just long enough to meet Whitney's gaze.

She watches us from the balcony. Her eyes move to my and Santiago's joined hands before she slips back into her party and we slip back into the shadows.

Señor Espinosa tries to take Santiago off me at the front door, but I already managed to drag him up the yard, so I insist on finishing the job. As I drop Santiago onto his bed, Señor Espinosa places a glass of water on the nightstand. I steal glances at the familiar home the entire journey in and out of it.

On the porch, a wrinkled hand reaches for my arm.

"I didn't even know he'd left." Señor Espinosa sighs, rubbing at his temple. "Thank you for bringing him back."

"Happy to help." I think it's a lie until the words leave my lips reeking of honesty.

"Will I see you at the holiday dinner next week?" he asks me, an abrupt shift of topic.

The senior center holds one annually; a nondenominational dinner for all the folks living there and in the community who'd like a nice meal with friendly company. I doubt he knows I've volunteered for it every year, even after I stopped attending with him and Santiago. I always stay out of the way and leave before the food is actually served.

"Maybe," I say. "I could use the hours."

"Well, you don't get Good Samaritan hours for *this*," he accuses, nodding his head toward Santiago's room. "You don't fool me."

This man, so convinced of my goodness. I wonder if, when he looks at me, he sees who I was as a kid.

"I'm not fooling anyone," I say, almost wishing it were true.

chapter sixteen

SANTIAGO

I find her on the first day back from Thanksgiving break, sitting on one of the benches lining the hallway outside the cafeteria with a lumpy sporkful of yogurt on its way into her mouth.

"Is this seat taken?" I ask, nodding to the empty space beside her.

"Yes," Bea says, popping the spork into her mouth and taking a moment to swallow. "I'm very popular these days."

I don't realize I'm smiling until I notice the faintest hint of one mirrored on her lips, come and gone in a flash.

"Is there something you needed?" she asks.

"Yeah." Awkwardness worms its way between us, or maybe that's just on my end. "I'm sorry for the other night. For calling you to pick me up from Whitney's." It feels weird, referring to that house as Whitney's and not Bryce's, even if I know he never lived there. "I shouldn't have put you in that position."

"You know you already apologized, right? And you didn't ask me to come get you."

The water I guzzled in the middle of the night probably helped dampen the hangover, but the shame that hit me when I woke in the morning—clashing with the headache induced by Abuelo's cumbia music blasting at a punishing volume from the other room—was an entirely different beast.

I didn't black out at any point, which is good news for my brain's health and bad news for my ego. Me calling Bea in desperation, moaning to her in the backyard about my grief, her lugging me all the way to my bed. It's been running through my head in the days since, the embarrassment throbbing rhythmically. At least my OCD got to demonstrate its range, allowing me to experience obsessive thoughts of humiliation alongside compulsions to aggressively brush the same patch of teeth until my gums sting or mop the grocery store floor in repetitive swipes until Dustin steals the stick to use as a microphone while lip-synching to the radio. A small part of me kept insisting if I did these things *right*, somehow everything would be fine come Monday.

I try not to indulge the need to run my thumbnail over the pad of my pointer finger in a calming cadence. "Felt like it was worth reiterating."

She stares at me for a beat longer, then tilts her head toward the space beside her. "It's school property. Just as much your right to sit here as mine." I take the invitation and try not to show how greatly I cherish it. "But . . . why did you call me?"

I could make something up, crack a cheap joke about her being near the top of my contacts list. A few other options come to mind, all of them saving me from fully putting myself out there. I couldn't find Abby, who was playing designated driver and would've taken me home, I was mad that Bea kept holding me at arm's length even after we'd cleared a bit of the air—albeit with my lies—I was upset at my dad and wanted Bryce and she was the next best thing.

In the end, I do something I haven't done much of in the past few years, or even much of lately. I tell the truth. "I missed you."

Her face betrays nothing as she nods, shifting her gaze down to her food. I poke at my lunch tray with my spork until there are four rows of four punctures, perfectly aligned on the bottom of one section.

"You want my blueberries?" she says, startling me. She scoops an even amount onto her spork, then holds it above my tray, waiting for my response.

"Sure," I say an uncomfortable amount of time after. Almost every conversation we've had since I got back has been loaded with something—guilt, anger, dishonesty, betrayal, confusion, alcohol. This gesture is so small, so inconsequential and unrelated to anything in our history. I don't even like blueberries that much.

I tilt my tray toward her. "Want my raspberries?"

She shrugs and takes them, and it's ridiculous, that this makes me more hopeful about the future of our friendship than anything else.

Billy drives Abuelo and me to the center early to help with cooking, the ground hidden by too much snow for my bike and my fear of rejection too surface-level to ask Bea for a ride.

While I wait for her in the lobby, I tap my foot on the ground, sort of shifting it each time. Then I notice my foot landing perfectly perpendicular to the lines in the carpet's design. When I try to repeat the movement, my foot doesn't end up in the right spot. I do it again, then realize I've been establishing a new pattern, now incomplete as well. Okay, once more in the perpendicular spot. Okay, three more times at an angle. No, not right. One more and—

"Hey."

I look up and find Bea, close enough that I should've detected her. She's peeling off a black scarf, revealing a charcoal-gray sweater under a thick leather jacket. Her jeans are ripped—and black, obviously—but she's got dark purple leggings beneath them, covering her skin and probably saving her from the biting air outside. Her makeup is just as intense as usual, but her face looks different, and I try to sort out the reason why before it's obvious I'm searching for something.

Her cheeks, I realize. They're delightfully rosy, flushed with the cold.

"Hi," I say as I shift my foot again, unable to help myself. We both look down at it, a question in her eyes, but I'm too pleased over it landing in the right spot to worry. I step back, freeing myself from the space.

"Oh! Beatriz!" Kim rushes over, and I'm reminded of how Greensville it is that our school receptionist is also the event planner for the senior center. Everyone knows everyone, everyone does everything. "You must be our other volunteer."

"That's me," Bea says.

"So nice to see friends making good use of their free time." Kim presses a hand over her heart as she glances between us.

"Or classmates doing their school-mandated volunteer hours," Bea corrects.

Kim's smile falters, but she powers through. "Well, my dears, the napkins and utensils are in those baskets over there." She points toward the desk that she or Magda normally resides behind, the decorations endearingly matching the ones Kim has in the front office at school. "Just head into the dining hall and start placing them by each chair. Someone is still pulling the extra plates out from storage, so we'll have those for you shortly." She leaves us in a flurry of energy, shouting after someone carrying a sack of potatoes in the opposite direction of the kitchen.

Bea takes the basket full of napkins, so I grab the utensils and follow her into the dining hall. I almost comment on my surprise at her knowing her way around—the center has changed a bit since I lived here—but it feels like the exact type of pointless observation that screams *I forget that you had a life here after I left.*

"So," I start. "We're *classmates.*"

"Do we not go to the same school?" she asks, folding a light blue napkin into a triangle. I gently place a fork and knife on top of it. She smiles to herself as she slides the fork to the left.

I fill the now empty space by the knife with a spoon. "Pardon my manners."

"Apologize to Candace, not me," Bea says, moving down the table. "She's the one who taught us that shit." Her long fingers gracefully fold another napkin. My hands feel clumsy in comparison as I follow suit with a set of utensils.

"But that's what we are to you?" I dare to ask, pushing the subject even though I should just take what I can get. "Classmates?"

"Yup," she says, but her eyes don't leave her task.

I press a hand to my chest in jest to hide the actual wound. "Not even *acquaintances?*"

"Not if you keep misplacing the utensils," she says, correcting my spoon and fork arrangement again.

We shift across the table, an easy rhythm to the movements. The muffled sounds of people preparing food in the neighboring kitchen and Kim shouting for help with the autumnal vases and fake flowers keep us company as we work.

By the time we make it to the third table, I build up the courage. "What if we play catch-up?" I offer.

"I'm not sure I'm familiar with that game," she says, which isn't a *no*.

The girl I formerly knew like the back of my hand—one for her and one for Bryce—is essentially a stranger to me now. Once upon a time, we were close enough that our bones could've fused and neither of us would've minded, or even noticed. Now, we're standing far enough apart that it feels almost painfully symbolic. History remains, that's half the problem, but there's a gap in our timelines and I'd like to at least see if we can reach across it. The gap has grown, but so have we.

"I ask something about you or your life, even if it's something I knew before," I say, then softly add, "and we try to catch up on what's changed."

She finally looks up from the napkin she's been fiddling with. I've managed this long without focusing too closely on the way they're sitting, my eyes more glued to Bea than the work, but now it's impossible not to spot the unaligned layers in this recent fold.

With her gaze still on me, she fixes the wrinkles. "What do you want to know?"

"What's your favorite color?"

Her darkly painted lips crack into a grin, letting the smallest laugh of disbelief escape before she can lock herself back up. "That's a little too personal, don't you think?"

I wave at her outfit. "And a little too obvious."

She throws a napkin at me, but I catch it easily. "Don't rumple the linens," I tsk. "Now look who's forgetting Candace's lessons." She positions her arm like she's going to throw another, and though I'm sure we've never had a textile fight before, the moment feels so familiar in its ease. "Fine, fine. What are your post–high school plans?"

"Purple," she replies.

"Sorry?"

"My favorite color," she says, then taps at the single purple earring on her left ear, tucked deeply into the curved cartilage. "It's purple."

My face pulls into a smile. "Look at us, getting to know each other better already."

She rolls her eyes, but it doesn't hide the amusement in them. "My mom told my grandparents that you're applying to schools in California." She must have actually been paying attention when Candace was drilling manners into us over dinners at Bryce's for all those years, because she's perfected her casual, small-talk tone. Bryce and I were usually competing to see whose posh accent was more convincing. "That true?"

Her words catch up on the tail end of the memory. "Wait, you don't have grandparents."

"My mom and dad didn't both spontaneously erupt out of holes in the ground one day."

"Come on, you know what I mean." I rest my basket on the table. "You don't have grandparents the way I don't have a mom." I remind myself of the point of this game. "But I guess things are different for you now?"

She ignores my digging and takes her own turn. "Speaking of family, how's your dad?"

Pa hasn't called since Thanksgiving, and I'll probably hear

from the heavens before I hear from my mom. "Back to colleges, please."

Her mouth tilts into an entertained smirk. I consider the tables turned, but she does relent without pushing, once again demonstrating manners I've yet to possess. "Fine. College, California. Go."

"I applied mainly to SoCal schools, yeah. The UC hype sort of pulls you in when you live there, and I'll still get in-state tuition since my dad is a California resident." At least one good thing is coming out of him not being here. "But I applied to a few colleges on the East Coast too. All of them for good old reliable engineering."

Now it's her turn to pause. "Excuse me?"

"Oh yeah, I forgot to mention that I'm smart now." When I left, I wasn't pulling bad grades, but I certainly wasn't where I'm at now.

"Or did you just come up with a better bribe than when Bryce offered Mrs. Heather his cafeteria chocolate milk for a whole year if she automatically passed him on every math test?" It's obvious the words are out of her mouth before she can stop them, her brain speeding down memory lane fast enough to leave her breathless. It's interesting, though, the way she looks a little surprised every time she brings up Bryce, which she does more often than I ever have since he died.

"He was a clever little fifth grader, huh?" I offer as a lifesaving buoy, tossing myself into the bittersweet depths of remembering with her. A beat passes before her gaze refocuses, and I wonder how long it's been since she brought up a memory like that completely of her own volition, no bike or stars or heated conversation in a supply closet drawing it out.

"So, um. School," she says.

"Right, yeah," I say, navigating back to the catch-up. "Swapping out physical books for audiobooks and retaking my notes for better retention helped a lot, but the biggest thing was going to tutoring to realign my wonky base for mathematics. Everything sort of fell into place after that."

"Sounds like school was the problem, then, not you." She flaps a napkin out and tucks it to her chest to fold it.

I point a fork at her. "Careful, that sounded like a compliment." I drop to a hush. "*Friends* like to give those."

"At best, it sounded like *a defense*," she whispers back mockingly, knocking the fork away. "But it was mostly an indictment of our education system."

I step forward to drop the fork on top of her freshly folded napkin. When she looks up, I realize I'm standing close enough that I can see the fine lines in her foundation, the texture of her imperfect skin, her pupils where they hide in her impossibly dark irises.

"I'll take what I can get," I say, the words hushed by accident this time. And then I step away first.

Hours later, I catch Bea as she's wrapping her scarf back around her neck.

"You're not staying for the dinner?" I motion to the crowded dining hall, loud with chatter and eating. "Abuelo was hoping he could get your thoughts on his cursed new practice of dipping turkey in ají. He loves it and I hate it, so we need another Colombian to settle the score, and I'm scared Magda will side with him just because of parental solidarity."

"What makes you think I won't side with him out of anti-Santiago solidarity?"

"Here I was thinking my *classmate* would do me a solid."

She rolls her eyes and tugs her jacket zipper, struggling to get it to budge.

"Need help with that?" I offer. "One favor in exchange for your vote."

"I'll manage just fine on my own." Finally, it gives, but her thumbnail gets caught in the track, drawing a string of curses out of her mouth.

"All that work you did to make Candace proud tonight, down the drain."

"Candace's pride in me was already a lost cause," she says with a touch of pained sincerity. "Give your abuelo my best. And thanks for the game."

She turns to leave, but halfway through the door, she pivots back around. Cold seeps in around her, slowly crawling toward me until it kisses my cheeks and exposed neck. When she opens her mouth, I can see her breath fog the air. "My mom wants me to at least get my bachelors after high school. Computer science or premed or engineering. Something smart. The more stable, the better."

I consider this. "So what are *your* post–high school plans?"

"I just told you."

"No," I say. "You told me what your mom's plans are."

She shivers. "Your plans are all about your parents, too," she says, not unkindly.

The two of us, the products of broken and misplaced dreams. It's not unusual for kids to pick up shattered pieces and try to make something good from the destruction. Sometimes it's the only way to make sense of what the shards once were.

chapter seventeen

BEATRIZ

When I get home from the center, I need a long, hot shower.
In the foyer, Lottie licks at the clumps of snow I couldn't stomp
off my shoes. She trails behind me as I walk through the house,
meowing for a dinner I'd bet Eileen and Neil's bank accounts that
Mom already fed her.

The living room windows reveal Mom's shadowy figure on the
back porch, facing away from me. Laughter streams from her hidden mouth alongside smoke from a cigarette in her raised hand.
She only indulges the old habit once or twice a year. I'd smell it on
her otherwise.

I watch her through my own translucent reflection in the glass.
It's just watery and vague enough in this light that I can pretend
the projection is real. She's the daughter sneaking a smoke and
flirting on the phone while Mom isn't home.

After another drag, she pulls the cigarette away. Moonlight
sparkles against her bracelet where it sits on her fully exposed wrist.

I go upstairs and try to wash the day off me.

"Hey, how was the event?" Mom stands in my doorway half an hour later, leaning into the frame. "I didn't hear you come home."

"I jumped straight into the shower," I lie. It's harder to pull off without my makeup on, but Mom likes believing me. "Tonight was nice. Good chance to get more volunteer hours in."

"How many of those do you need, by the way?" She picks at her dark hair, focusing on a split end.

"A lot," I say vaguely.

"Hmm." She yanks the broken hair, then flicks her fingers so it drifts to the floor. "Well, I'm really glad you got out of the house and went. Spending time with Santiago is good for you. Both of you." Her eyes crinkle with contentment.

I make a noncommittal noise so I don't think about his laughter and how hearing it again cracked open something I feel ill-equipped to hold closed. "Well, I'm wiped. Think I'm going to crash."

I expect her to interrogate my exhaustion, but she just smiles. "There are leftovers in the fridge if you end up getting hungry. Night, Abejita." She blows me kisses and closes the door.

Despite the chill, I pry open my window and maneuver onto the roof. Once, this was the most perilous journey known to me and my friends. It scares me, just a bit, how easily I navigate it now.

I tug my lumpy winter pajamas closer to my body and take a deep inhale. Slowly, I release it. The air almost looks like smoke. I bet if Mom was watching me from below my window, it might fool her too.

★ ★ ★

Señor Espinosa is already waiting outside when I pull up to the center after school. He stands on a small patch of concrete cleared of snow, bundled in a wool coat and cream sweater I think his late wife made a lifetime ago.

I get out quickly, glad for the traction on my boots. "Why aren't you inside?"

He closes his eyes and breathes in the crisp day. "Don't deny an old man a breath of fresh winter air."

I offer him my arm and slowly move us toward my car. Someone carved a path from the front door to the street, though the snow on the ground is mostly slush.

"I can't believe they let you just stand outside like that," I say as I start the ignition. "You're like Santiago with that bike . . ."

Señor Espinosa smiles. "This isn't my first winter in Vermont, mija. It isn't his either."

"Then you should probably act like it," I snap, barely stopping myself from pointing out that it's still technically fall. The moment passes. "Sorry."

"Good Samaritans don't often talk back to their elders," he notes without malice. "You've earned it, though."

After our last few encounters, I assumed Santiago would try to talk to me today. At lunch, I sat on the same bench I usually do. I didn't intentionally leave an open space beside me. It just so happened to be there.

In calculus, we had a pop quiz. In PE, we were divided into teams for dodgeball. I got out immediately, on purpose, and he was the last man standing. In English, we were asked to peer-review

122

essays. He swapped with Will Sanders. After school, I saw him leave with Whitney and Olive.

It shouldn't bother me, and it doesn't. I'd developed a routine of solitude, is all. Santiago's return changed it and I'm still fine-tuning my new expectations.

Señor Espinosa clears his throat as I turn onto his street. "Kim mentioned that you've completed your required volunteer hours. With the dinner and all the driving, you're the first one in your class to finish."

I stop the car outside his house. I got Kim's email this morning. "Well, I can still give you rides home."

He clicks his tongue. "It's okay. My friend Billy lives just a few blocks away and said he can start taking me back."

"Oh."

"You should be happy," he laughs. "No more driving this viejo around. More free time to spend with your friends." His gaze unsubtly slides to the house.

"Let me help you out."

Wary of the snow, we make our way to the porch. Once again, the door swings open to Santiago.

"You need shoes with better traction," Santiago scolds, then offers his abuelo a hand.

Señor Espinosa nods his head toward me. "You sound like her."

Santiago gives me a smile as we watch his abuelo shuffle away. "Kids these days."

I think of Mom smoking on the back porch in the freezing cold. "Tell me about it."

"By the way, uh, I'm sorry I didn't get to talk to you at school today," Santiago rushes to say before I can depart. "I swear the day was conspiring against me; like, I was going to find you at lunch but then Olive and Dustin were asking for help with physics and it ended up taking *way* longer than expected to get them to stop making 'mitochondria is the powerhouse of the cell' jokes."

"That's biology."

"So you understand my struggle." He pauses to let out a laugh. "Actually, how are you doing in physics? You could join our little study group if you want, though I doubt you'll need it, and it would probably be—why are you smiling like that?"

I touch my mouth. My cold fingers come away with the smallest hint of dark purple lipstick. But they also hit my teeth.

"I don't need help," I say. I should have left while he was talking. I should have said the day was working in my favor by keeping him away.

"Of course you don't," he says, admiration seeping into the words. "No worries."

I'm in that supply closet all over again, acting against my own best interests. Or maybe for them. It's so hard to know the right or wrong thing to do here.

"But, um, if you need another set of hands." I lift mine up pathetically. The tips that looked pale moments ago have gone pink where they peek out of my fingerless gloves, restricted veins expanding to allow blood flow to return.

"I'll let you know."

"I should—" I glance at my car on the street. "Bye."

He smiles, and feeling comes back into my hands. "Talk to you tomorrow."

The sentiment keeps me warm on the ride home, but I don't stop shivering.

chapter eighteen

SANTIAGO

December snow hasn't relented since it arrived, so we're in
the gym for PE more often than outside of it, since zero isn't a hard
number to beat. Basketball, Hula-Hoops, jump rope, and yoga are
our usual options, and though my fingers have twitched once or
twice for a badminton racket, as embarrassing as that sentiment is,
I think playing would just make me sad and guilty. More so than
usual.

Bea's jump rope hangs limply between her hands, but she's at
least borderline participating, with me, no less. "Forty-seven, forty-
eight, forty-ni—"

I trip, narrowly catching myself before I face-plant. "Damn."

"New record for you," she says flatly, then pretends to adjust
her grip on her unused rope when Coach Simmons walks by.
"You'll get to fifty someday."

"Maybe in my dreams," I say, sighing wistfully. "All right, your
turn."

"You know, I really prefer counting over jumping," she says, glancing down at her chest. "A sports bra can only do so much for a person."

I look away from her with difficulty, pretending to be fascinated by a bit of my rope that's fraying out of the braid. "Fine, but at least give me a fun game to play while jumping. One of those songs you used to sing for us when we were in elementary school."

"I don't remember them."

I give her a look, and it's impressive that I last a solid three seconds before worrying I'm pushing my luck with whatever tenuous friendship she's offering me. The brief risk works though, with her impatiently waving her hand for me to continue. I start jumping at the same time she starts singing, my feet serving as drums for the song as they hit the glossy wooden floor.

"Ice cream soda with a cherry on top, who's your . . ."

"Boyfriend, girlfriend, or partner," I fill in quickly and quietly.

"I forgot, is it A, B, C, D, E, F, G, H, I . . ."

In the corner of my eye, I notice Olive and friends with their Hula-Hoops frozen around their waists, cheering me on.

"L, M, N . . ."

At O, everyone in the group except for Olive drops their hoops, the sound loud enough to startle me into stumbling.

"Would you look at that," Bea deadpans. "Looks like you're going to date someone whose name starts with an O."

Olive ducks their head, pushing their giggling friends to the other side of the gym.

"I did kiss a guy named Owen at a party last year," I admit. "He didn't seem like the committing kind, though."

"Brutal assessment for a sixteen-year-old."

I grin. "He was seventeen."

Bea scoffs, toeing at her rope. "That the only broken heart you left behind on the lesser coast?"

I whistle at the dig, though my loyalties do ultimately lie with the East Coast. "Hooked up with a couple of people here and there, but nothing serious." It's the most literal use of the word *couple*, but I hope Bea registers it more casually. Owen and, before that, a random girl at a party sophomore year, both of whom were only talking to me because Eric felt like scheming to distract from his own boyfriend drama.

I don't reciprocate the prodding because I've witnessed Bea speak to approximately five people other than me since I've been back.

After PE, I meet her in the hall to walk to next period, dreading braving the cold even though it's a shortcut between here and English. Just as she leaves the locker room, Dustin rounds the corner and jogs over.

"Still on for studying for the gov final later?" he asks me. "Anything less than a B and I lose my A."

"Yeah, I'm down," I say, pointlessly adjusting my backpack on my shoulder while Bea watches us.

"You're a lifesaver." Dustin presses his hands into a prayer, spinning around to walk backward toward his next class. "Welcome to join us, Beatriz."

"No, that's—" I start.

"Sure," Bea interrupts. "See you after school."

Dustin nods, smiling, then leaves as Bea continues in the opposite direction.

I chase after her outside. "You want to study with Dustin?"

She glances over her shoulder, strutting confidently through the white-gray haze of the day in platform boots that're all black except for their shiny, bloodred buckles. I wonder what her shoe budget is. "Is there something wrong with that?"

"Of course not," I say. "But you don't like people."

"I don't," she agrees. "But I do like passing tests."

I haven't been to Dustin's in a few weeks, and before moving, had only been a handful of times for birthday parties or school projects. He and Abby live in a nice house, almost barnlike with the red and white wood. All the bedrooms except for Dustin's are upstairs—his is in the basement—leaving the ground floor available for a big, open-plan living room and kitchen, the wide space made cozier with warm pastels and polished knickknacks decorating every surface.

His parents are working at the store, and Abby is holiday shopping with Whitney and Courtney, but Courtney has already video-called him twice since we got here to "check in." Each time, his smile gets a little more strained, voice a little more fragile, as she asks him to show her proof of what he's been working on.

After an hour of silently making index cards, Bea stands. "I'm going to use the bathroom."

I start sliding off the sofa. "I can show you, it's just down—"

"Oh, I know." She leaves the room as Dustin reenters it, a tray of snacks in hand, and they nod in passing.

"Bea's been over before?" I ask, watching as he freezes slightly. Bryce and I would get invited to Dustin's parties as kids, but he and Abby celebrated their shared birthday separately, and Bea never really hung out with anyone but our group of four back then.

"Uh, yeah. Remember? I told you about us being partners for a project last year."

"Right." I shake my head, remembering for the dozenth time that they were all people while I was gone.

We quiz each other with the completed index cards, turning it into a competition that Bea dominates. By the time we go through the entire stack enough times to avoid missing a single answer, we're exhausted.

"Okay, I have an idea." Dustin drops his head onto the sofa cushion beside him, arm dangling toward the ground. "Low-stakes, rapid-fire questions to keep our brains pumping while we take a break."

I groan and roll over on the rug. "My brain is pumped enough."

"Best meal in the cafeteria?" Dustin asks, ignoring me. "I vote the potato wedges."

"Potato wedges," I agree.

"Nothing in the caf tastes good," Bea says. We give her a look, and she rolls her eyes. "Whatever, potato wedges."

"See, don't you just *feel* your brain pumping?" Dustin says, flexing his hands. Bea tries not to smile, but the afternoon has weakened her resolve.

"All right, uh, best teacher?" I ask next.

"Easily Mrs. Ridley," Dustin says. "Wait. High school only, or are we talking middle and elementary too?"

"Eh, one for each," I answer.

Bea ticks them off on her hand. "Ms. Young, Mr. Zhao, Coach Simmons."

I sit up. "Our PE teacher?"

She shrugs. "I'm her favorite."

Dustin agrees with Ms. Young and Mr. Zhao but sticks with Mrs. Ridley for high school.

I sink into the comfort of shared childhoods, the ease in which the conversation flows. Favorite middle school play. Favorite street name. Favorite house on the main road.

Shrek, Wimberly, the light-orange one with the yellow roof that always has Christmas lights up until June.

They aren't my answers, but they're the first that come to mind, and I wonder if he'd have changed them by now.

"Dream superpower?" Dustin asks.

Bea clears her throat, and with it, the comfortable energy of the room. "Necromancy."

Dustin watches her carefully, eyes darting to his phone where it lights up with another unanswered text from Courtney, then quietly adds, "Invisibility."

They look at me, faces open. "Time control," I admit.

We share a collective sigh, the air suspended for just a moment, before Dustin sits up to message Courtney back, Bea grabs the cards to go through them again on her own, mechanically mouthing the right answers, and I sit there, watching them leave their dreams behind for reality.

chapter nineteen

BEATRIZ

Finals season sweeps through school like the latest cold front. It's inescapable, creeping into our bones and conversations as invasively as the glacial air outside. Stick season ended quickly this year, giving way to winter with less of a fight than usual. But the look on Mom's face every time I tell her I'm going to Santiago's or the library to study with him and Dustin, sometimes even Olive, is enough to melt the snow coating the town.

Friday before finals week, Mom opens my door right as I shut my window. I freeze despite the heated room hugging my chilled skin.

"Did you fall asleep with the window open?" she asks like she's prompting me.

"No," I say, because it's a bad lie, even gifted. "I just wanted some air, but it's too cold out."

Mom scans my face. Without makeup, my cheeks must be flushed from the hours sitting on the roof. I'm lucky I took my coat off immediately. I'm lucky I've given her fewer reasons to worry about me lately. "Well, speaking of cold, the school just sent out a message. First snow day of the year." I get a delightful twinge of childish glee from the news, even as she adds, "Your teachers should be emailing you work for the day."

Both pieces of news are expected. Vermont gets more average annual snowfall than any other state. But in the digital age, they're not going to let us off as easy as they did the generations past.

Mom goes downstairs to do some administrative tasks from home before a coworker with "better" snow tires can come pick her up. Given that both our cars are perfectly equipped for this climate, I assume this coworker is familiar with that bracelet of hers.

My phone dings from somewhere on my bed. I rustle around in the sheets until I find it.

Santiago: I've never loved Vermont more than right now

Beatriz: You need to raise your standards

He's calling me.

I stare at the screen. He saw me without makeup on Halloween. And a million times before that, before I ever started wearing it. It's fine.

I count to three. And again. Then I answer.

Santiago is lying in bed. A gray fleece hugs his arms and baggy red flannel pants squeeze his legs. They don't reach his ankles. Half his hair hangs in his eyes and the other half stands up in a cowlick. "Happy snow day," he sings.

"Southern California made you soft," I reply, sitting up. Lottie jumps into my lap.

"I've been living in a seasonless state for three years—let me have this. Today is a glorious day, and I'm calling to ask how you plan to celebrate it."

I scratch Lottie's neck under her collar and she purrs into the phone. "Doing classwork. Studying."

He boos and I laugh without meaning to. But also without meaning not to. I worked so hard to develop a certain level of control over myself and my body, and yet here I am.

"Well, I have very exciting plans," he says, then lowers his voice to a whisper. "Abuelo is making me *hot chocolate*."

"How glamorous."

"I can bring you a cup."

"You and what car?"

"Hey, I'm saving the environment one bike ride at a time."

"You are not riding that death trap in this weather," I say, aware of the edge my voice has taken on.

"Come on, it's not even that bad out." He looks through his bedroom window. All the harsh morning sun reflects off the snow-covered ground and casts onto him ghoulishly. "The journey will be character building."

"You're quite the character already," I say. He drops the window curtain and flops back into bed. "Stay off the roads, okay? Please."

It wasn't snowing when the accident almost happened. Whitney and me in the car, momentarily sure it was the end. It wasn't snowing when my dad was hit and killed either. Which almost makes both situations worse. We know snowy roads are dangerous, and so we prepare for them.

No one prepares for a sunny day. A boy dying on an early June evening. We forget that the universe doesn't play by our rules of logic. Real life doesn't care about setting or theme or foreshadowing. Sometimes bad things just happen.

"I'll have to bring you a cup when it's safe, then," Santiago says. But there's something in his tone, an acknowledgement of my unspoken thoughts. Safe doesn't really exist.

chapter twenty

SANTIAGO

I invite Olive over to study for their physics final after my weekend shift, bummed that Dustin has to work and can't join us. Though I have a handful of tests I should be preparing for myself, Olive's needs are a welcome distraction from the fear that my own grades won't be enough to impress the colleges and dozens of scholarships I applied to last month.

"Break down what the formulas are for, if that helps with memorization," I suggest, using a pencil to tap at the velocity formula. "Velocity, velocity. Speed with a direction," I sing.

"That's not very catchy." Olive mouths the song over a few times, their lips shiny with a gloss they've reapplied three times in the past fifteen minutes. "But I'm willing to try whatever. This semester has been kicking my ass." Hearing them curse still sounds foreign, but I try not to show it, smiling instead at how harshly they're judging the B+ they've held all term. "If I ace this test, I will erect a statue in your name." Their eyes stay trained on their paper while mine drift to their earrings, two large clay snowmen bobbling with their every pen stroke.

"You don't want to do that when you grow up?" I ask, then point to their jewelry.

Olive blushes, shrugging. "I love creating, but I do it for me."

"So who's astronomy for?"

Their bashfulness falters. "You know who."

As they turn back to the formula sheet, I want to argue with their aspirations. Olive has a bright future ahead of them no matter what path they choose, but their plans shouldn't be dictated by their brother's incomplete dreams. Bryce's wishes aren't a guideline for the rest of our lives.

My mouth stays shut though, because somehow, being a hypocrite on top of being a liar is where I draw the line.

chapter twenty-one

BEATRIZ

We make it through finals. I turn in a crappy watercolor painting of Lottie for art class that Mrs. Manos calls inspired. My focus on calculus and physics when studying serves me well. Dustin and our note cards are in my mind throughout the entire government exam. Though the sound of shoes squeaking against the gymnasium floor has been stuck in my head since, I ace the timed sprints in PE and do unnecessary extra-credit push-ups and sit-ups. Santiago gets the highest amount of sit-ups, but I win at push-ups. And I barely make it under the maximum word count, but my English paper exploring thematic ties between *Romeo and Juliet* and *King Lear* is the first on Mrs. Ridley's desk.

I stare at my flawless report card when it arrives a week into winter break. Mom cheers, going off about how good this will be for me when colleges start admissions. Numbly, I want to ask why this can't be good for me now, just for the sake of being good. But I don't. It's the holidays, and I'd like to give her as many gifts as possible.

I feel less selfless as we stand in Candace's doorway on Christmas morning.

"Oh, this looks delicious, Magdalena," Candace says, taking the tray of empanadas from Mom. "I'll set this in the kitchen with the rest of the food. Come in, come in!"

I try not to laugh at Mom's mismatched socks as she leaves her boots in the foyer. Mine take longer to unbuckle, so I'm left behind as well.

Mom and I used to jump around on the holidays. Most we spent with the Espinosas. A few with the Dawsons, who became the Ocampos when Candace married Whitney and Olive's dad, Phil. After Bryce, we just dropped off food. An offering to a family whose grief would linger long after the funeral casseroles stopped coming.

I hang my scarf and coat once I get my shoes off. Usually, Whitney would be front and center to greet guests. But the only face I see is Phil's as he heads for the bathroom, avoiding eye contact with me.

He took us camping once when we were kids. Only once, because it turned out that none of us other than Whitney were built for life in the wilderness.

Bryce burned the sausages. Santiago's attempt at tent-building resulted in mine and Whitney's collapsing halfway through the night. I took the cake, though. The pretty, three-pronged leaves I collected for Mom's scrapbooking earned me arms covered in poison-ivy oil.

Whitney salvaged the remaining food. Whitney fixed our tent without waking Phil. Whitney made me scrub my skin raw with soap, water, and rubbing alcohol before the rash could develop.

Her adolescent fortitude was awe-worthy. Whitney had her

shit together before the rest of us could even use that word. It was the first but not last time I was jealous of her. I wanted to be the one who fixed things, not the one who needed fixing.

Bryce, Santiago, and I whined as Whitney tended the weak fire that chilly night. We couldn't understand why we didn't just pack more blankets. Then Phil turned to us and said one of the only things he ever has to me: "You kids want to know the difference between a campfire and a blanket? One provides warmth, one just protects it."

I got up and started stacking the logs. An hour and countless handfuls of kindling later, fire blazing and skin toasted, I realized my hands were littered with cuts and splinters. I was so focused on the fire, so numb from the cold, I hadn't even noticed all the ways I'd been hurt in the process of helping everyone else.

Now, I'm staring down at my hands when I sense someone behind me. I smell her perfume before she speaks.

"I'm surprised you're here," Whitney says. I turn around and find her in her Christmas best, a red turtleneck and black corduroy skirt. Her black loafers have golden buckles that shine in tandem with her dainty locket and sparkling headband.

"I had a lot of options," I say. "It's so hard being popular around the holidays."

She doesn't take the bait. "I thought you'd be with Santiago. He stopped sitting with us to eat lunch with you every day, so." An equally transparent comment about her and Abby is fighting its way to my mouth before we're interrupted.

"Girls!" Candace calls from the other room. Calls, never shouts. "Can you clean the dishes for me?"

If I didn't grow up around her, I'd wonder what dishes need cleaning before the eating has even begun. But I already know. They cost a fortune and are only used a few times a year. She dusts them weekly but still insists they're washed before proper use. This actually used to be my and Bryce's task on the holidays I spent here.

Whitney and I rinse Candace's fine china in silence. Were it not for the running water, we'd probably be quiet enough to hear what Candace and Mom are talking about over tea a room away.

Olive pops their head in to the kitchen. "Need any help?"

Whitney dries off the plate I just washed. "Mom only asked us girls to help with cleaning."

Olive laughs. "I can take over the drying, then."

Whitney tosses her hair over her shoulder as she wordlessly leaves. I wonder if my defense mechanisms look as calculated as hers. Maybe we're both just walking clichés, two sides of the same scratched-up coin.

"Hey," Olive says as they join me. I pass them a plate and they pick up Whitney's discarded red towel covered in white evergreens. "Thanks for bringing food over."

"My mom cooked it."

"Still." They're probably sucking up, but I've tasted Candace's cooking. There has to be genuine gratitude in there as well. "You know, I realized that you and I don't talk very much. I've been spending more time with Santiago, but I'm sorry I haven't really with you, outside of those few group study sessions."

I could almost laugh if I wasn't working overtime not to cry. Olive used to chase us down the street on their scooter when we went on bike rides. They crashed our movie nights and begged to join sleepovers at my house. Bryce always invited them. I never minded.

"Don't apologize to me," I say once I get a grip. "Please." If anyone owes someone an apology here, it's me. Even knowing this, I can't bring myself to give one. I wouldn't even know where to start.

Olive nods, letting the topic settle. Then they shift gears.

"So you and Santiago have been hanging out a lot too, huh?" They aren't nearly as good as their sister at feigning disinterest. Though Whitney's grip on the skill is clearly dwindling these days.

"Am I talking to you or your PE friends right now?" I ask, since it's clear they're all harboring crushes. Then I catch sight of their face. Oh. Oh no.

Their cheeks are a crimson I didn't think possible. "Sorry, I'm not trying to steal him if the two of you—"

"We aren't dating."

"Really?"

"*Obviously*. I mean, he's—Bryce was his—" Whatever this rumor is, it needs to end right here and right now. The worst part is that I watched them as they implied it. They weren't judging me or Santiago for it. My hands twitch for my key necklace.

"Cool." They wipe at the same dry dish they've been working on for the past five minutes. "So . . . do you think he'd go out with me?"

I wish I'd stayed home. "You should be asking him that."

"But you're his best friend."

I laugh. "No, I'm not."

"You used to be."

"Emphasis on the past tense there." And that I wasn't his only one.

"Then what are you now?"

A blobby, shadowy version of myself stares back at me from the polished surface of a newly rinsed plate. Something moves behind it.

I turn to find Whitney watching us from the doorway. She's waiting for an answer as much as Olive is. As much as I am.

I set the plate on the counter. "I should go see if my mom is ready to leave." I face Olive but want Whitney to hear. "Ask him out if you want. He thinks you're cute."

Having given my Christmas gift to the pair who lost their brother because of me, I walk away.

chapter twenty-two

SANTIAGO

I can't exactly call Pa not coming home for Noche Buena another broken promise, since he didn't exactly make any guarantees he'd come in the first place. He shoots a text telling me I have a gift in the mail, which is apparently supposed to fill the 6' 5" absence in the house.

Abuelo and I exchanged presents last night, following the tradition that Noche Buena is more of a holiday to us than Christmas itself. I gave him a poetry book in Spanish from the library's annual used-book sale and fur-lined loafers I found brand-new at the thrift store, the grip on the soles vastly superior to his current pair's. In turn, he gave me new winter pajama pants that actually fit and a check for thirty dollars to spend on whatever I'd like. I got Pa a pack of vintage Vermont postcards and decide to use one to send him some snail mail, spending Christmas morning writing it up.

I swing open the door to make the trek through the cold to the mailbox, but find my gift waiting for me on the porch, the cardboard box already soggy from snow.

I plop the package onto a towel in my room, abandoning the postcard for now. I'd shake the box experimentally if I wasn't worried about the entire thing disintegrating. Pa must have shipped it himself since there's no company name on the label. I key open the tape and peer inside.

It's a photo album, the front frame occupied by a black-and-white picture of a random couple swinging a toddler by the hands between them, made of a stiff brown material that's leathery, but a little too factory-made to be the real thing. Printed on the cover in off-white ink is one word. MEMORIES.

I open the book, and it's empty.

On the back is a sticky note, the message warped from the wet box. Holding it up to the light and squinting, I barely manage to make out some of the words near the bottom.

all the good times. —Pa

My hands flip through the endless blank pages. My eyes try to fill them with memories, inserting Pa into them the way I managed to insert Bryce into all these years I've lived without him. Some days, pretending was so easy that I almost convinced myself I could wake up the next day and have the life I always wanted, as long as I didn't stare at it too closely. Pa caring and involved, Abuelo safe and healthy no matter what, Bea in my life guilt-free, and, more than anything else, Bryce alive. But I stare at the house key in my hand—my makeshift knife—then glance up at the wall where another key hides behind a poster, and remember where pretending got me.

Billy invited folks over to his place for a casual Christmas dinner, with plans to swing by the center after to visit everyone who can't leave. He reextends the invitation to me when he picks Abuelo up, but I don't want to be surrounded by people who will just ask about my family or lack thereof. There are only two people I want to talk about today with, and only one of them is somewhat available, according to her text.

Billy and Abuelo wait in the car while I knock on Bea's front door.

"Feliz Navidad," I say when she appears.

"You're letting all the cold in," she says, waving Billy and Abuelo off as she ushers me in and makes her way back upstairs. I trail behind her like a second shadow, the first one being Lottie. "All right, let's hear it."

I choose to hover in her open doorway as she dives back onto her bed. "Hear what?"

"Your dad did something." She focuses on Lottie as she says it, scratching her chin until purrs overwhelm the silence. "Or, more likely, nothing."

I crouch on the floor, using the wall as a backrest. "No-show for another holiday, but he did send me this." I dig around in my backpack, still cluttered with papers from last semester, and yank out the photo album. Bea flexes her hands and I toss it to her, startling Lottie off the bed and past me, down the hall. "Sorry!" I call after her.

Bea's long fingers comb their way through the book. "You look hot here." She lifts up an empty page. "I think it's the hair."

"Just for that, there's going to be an entire section dedicated to your bangs era."

"Some of our foreheads aren't made to be hidden."

I try to give her a smile, but my heart isn't in it.

She stares at me for a minute, unrelenting. "Come on," she says finally, with an air of acceptance, grabbing a thick coat off her desk chair and nodding to the window. I crawl over her bed and out onto the small roof landing after her. We only climbed up here once as kids, the ensuing lecture from Magda enough to discourage a repeat offense. Bryce nearly fell off the edge that first time, a life almost cut tragically and senselessly short. We considered ourselves so lucky.

But here we are again.

"Am I allowed to be mad at him?" I ask, using a gloved hand to poke at a small chunk of snow, then clear my throat. "My dad, I mean."

"I don't know," Bea says, honest words puffing into the air. "Who gets to decide that?"

I glance over, but her eyes are trained on the stars. "What do you mean?"

"Some people would say no, you can't be mad at him. He had you young and stuck around when your mom didn't, but he still had dreams to follow. You aren't the only thing that ever happened to him."

I swallow. I've made that argument enough times in my own head and wonder if Bea has done the same. "And what would other people say?"

She tugs on the hood of her coat, sheltering her bare head in a puffy cave that casts shadows across her face. "You want your dad around, and he barely ever is. It's hard to be mad at anyone but him for that."

"I can be mad at the universe, then, I guess. Or God or whatever."

"Yeah, keep it simple. People are too complicated."

I laugh, at odds with how I've felt all day. "Fair point."

She bumps me once, lightly so as to not kill both of us. "I have an idea."

We spend the rest of the night combing through those same photo albums Magda showed me when I came over for dinner, except this time, pictures are coming home with me. I feel bad peeling myself out of their pages, even though there are a lot of doubles and Bea insists. The hours slip by as we transfer memories from one book to another, shedding light on the life I tried so desperately to run away from.

Bea silently passes me a photo from a box she's digging through, a blurry and aged shot taken at my sixth birthday, a rare one that my mom was still around for. There she is, right beside Pa, an off year when he wasn't touring during the holidays, both of them wiping frosting off my face while Magda cuts cake slices and Bryce's hand pokes in from off camera, nothing to identify him but a smear of orange hair in the corner.

How can something as simple as a photo hold so much grief and joy in equal measure? It's a gift, but it's also a reminder of everything I've lost.

I turn to Bea, and she's smiling at a picture of us at our fifth-grade spring concert, me in a too-big button-up and her in a bright yellow dress stained with grass. *That smile*, I think to myself, despite all I've done and hidden, *I haven't lost that yet.*

chapter twenty-three

BEATRIZ

The first time I got my period, I didn't realize what was happening. I'd been in health classes and sex ed and had a mom who was always very open about her horrendous monthly pain. Still, I was confused by the brown stain stretched across my underwear when I came home from a day spent watching movies at Bryce's house. At first, I thought maybe I'd spilled something. But the logic wasn't there. So I mustered up the courage to waltz into my mom's room and tell her what I thought was the truth: I'd shit myself.

My mom has seen every injury and accident you can imagine as an emergency room receptionist, so she didn't laugh or tease or make me feel lesser. But when I handed over the ruined fabric, her face took on a shade of disappointment. Years out, I still wonder if it was her beating herself up for not preparing me to recognize this inevitable aspect of growing up.

She directed me to the shower to rinse off, then presented me with a basket when I came out. Pads, tampons, menstrual cups, pain meds, heating devices of all shapes and sizes, chocolate. Her speech was brief and to the point: I got my period. I was going to have it for a while, though my regularity remained to be seen. It was normal and natural and something almost everyone with a uterus deals with at some point, in some way.

I was grateful in that moment to have a mom who knew it was better to tell me the truth about something that would pain me for years to come than to sugarcoat. But every time I get my period, I don't think about that conversation. I think about Bryce's funeral a year later.

Mom's glassy eyes, tears glazing her cheeks, staring at the closed casket. When she looked down at me, she had the same expression on her face as when I'd wandered into her room, but this time there was no speech. No care package. No preparation.

"How do I look?" Mom glides into my room on the same pair of black heels I've seen her wear to every formal occasion for the past decade. There's still a scuff on one from Bryce when they danced at Candace and Phil's wedding. As she spins in her outfit, I lose sight of the mark.

The dress is new though, a tight but modest purple number with off-the-shoulder sleeves. It flaunts her legs and tattooed arms in equal measure.

"You look really pretty." I shut my book. The dense paragraph explaining the universe's directional favoring was making my thoughts go fuzzy, but that could also just be my cramps nudging their way back to center stage as my afternoon dosage of prescribed pain meds wears off.

She smiles, scrunching her face into her shoulder. It ages her the way the dress does, in reverse. She's so young. Thirty-four and on her way to a New Year's party with work friends. "Thank you," she sings. "Do you have time to do my makeup before heading over to Whitney's?"

I nod, grateful I didn't build my lie around a specific time. If she knew I didn't have plans, she'd stay home.

Mom hops onto my bathroom counter. She isn't short, at least where general standards apply, but it does surprise me when we're up close like this, how much taller than her I've grown.

"Did you already take medicine?" she asks as I collect supplies and rub at my abdomen. Our cycles are synced, but she's on birth control, so I suffer alone. I tried the pill for a few months last year to help with the cramps, but it didn't agree with my brain.

"Earlier," I say. "I'll take more later."

"Don't forget." She tugs at her dress's hem. "You don't want to be miserable all night." God forbid.

I skip foundation and just spot-correct Mom's face with concealer. Fill in her brows so the arch is more defined. Line her eyes with a warm brown gel, then smoke it out. No false lashes, she says even my lightest pairs feel too heavy. Soft contour on her temples and cheeks, a muddy pink gloss to even out her lip color.

When I finish, she gasps at her reflection. She does this every time I do her makeup. I applied a full face on myself earlier to back up my lie; wings that cover my entire lids and stretch past where my eyebrows would end if I'd drawn the tips on. Glitter falls down my cheeks in a cheap imitation of tears.

"You're so good at this," she whispers, cupping my face. She then whisks past me, off to find her clutch, her perfume and compliment slowly dissipating.

When I get a call from Santiago as the clock creeps toward the eleventh hour, I experience brief déjà vu.

"If you're fucked up at Whitney's again, please tell me it's at least off something classier than jungle juice this time." Before he can respond beyond laughing, I squeeze it in. "Happy birthday."

"You're about an hour early," he says, sounding clear and sober. "But you did always want to be first."

Bryce and I made a competition out of it. Since he died, this is the first time I've said the words to Santiago. I don't think unanswered texts count. "You don't sound drunk."

"Probably because I'm not. My dad was supposed to come into town to celebrate, but the band got booked last-minute." He sighs, and I wonder how badly he wishes it were a scream. "Just me and Abuelo now, though he conked out about thirty minutes ago with a party hat on his head. It's quite the sight."

I shift the heating pad on my stomach and shut my book. "You Espinosas really know how to ring in the holidays, huh?"

"Yeah, we try." He blows out air, almost like a party noisemaker. "So what's your itinerary look like? Face masks with Lottie?"

"My mom thinks I'm at Whitney's, so I'm staying home until I can see on her location that she's headed back here. Then I'll take a quick trip down the street, fuck up my makeup a bit, and come back fifteen minutes after her."

"Fucking up your makeup will raise suspicion," he says. "It's always perfect." I don't know how to respond to this observation, so I don't. "But how would you feel about leaving the house for real? To validate your lie, of course."

"Of course."

"It's not my birthday yet, so I have no authority," he says, quieting. "You can pick the destination."

I'll bash LA all I want, but we do have our own delicate sheen of light pollution in Greensville. Outside of town are long stretches of road completely free of it, opening up the sky.

On a trip back from visiting cousins in Massachusetts a few months before he died, Bryce told me about a rest area his family stopped at. He swore he'd never seen so many stars.

When I suggested we go again, this time with blankets and food and a plan, his face shifted. He'd already been. All the good he was going to get out of that place had been felt. There was nothing more to experience.

It isn't as painful as the memory, but a wave of hurt rushes over my abdomen. Twenty minutes into the drive to this mystical spot, I realize I never took more pain meds.

"Dustin just texted that Rick has already thrown up twice," Santiago reports from the passenger seat. "So the Richards' party is already going better than Whitney's hypothetical one. You're not worried your mom will say something about the nonexistent celebration to Candace?"

"I told her it wasn't Candace-approved. She wouldn't rat on Whitney."

"Yeah, guess she's too cool for that."

"No, it's because she'd worry about killing my social life." My words go strained at the end of the sentence as another cramp nips at me. I look at the time on the dash. If we turned back now to get my medicine, we'd barely be out of the neighborhood when midnight/Santiago's birthday strikes. I suck it up.

But then the car shudders, and every rotation of the tires

becomes a roller coaster. I panic from memory for only a second. This isn't last year. We aren't spinning out. I'm fine.

We bounce as I pull over. I turn off the ignition. The engine and my anxiety sputter out.

Santi's eyes shoot sideways. "I'm not a car scientist, but this doesn't seem good."

The back right tire is shot, a collection of rusty nails stuck in its surface like a botched piercing job. I let out a groan, clenching my hands as I round the car with my phone's flashlight. I already know what I'll find in the trunk. Nothing.

"I never drive out this far," I say. "I didn't think I'd need to keep a spare."

"Makes sense." I want to bite at his agreement just to give myself something to sink my teeth into. He checks his phone. "No service. Can't call for a tow."

I open my mouth to reply, then double over. Forehead pressed to icy metal, I breathe through the hurricane of a cramp, moments away from yanking my uterus out of my body with my bare hands.

"What's wrong?" Santiago asks. He places a hand on my back and I flinch from the comfort, even though there's a ridiculous amount of layers between our skins. "Sorry, sorry." He pulls away. "What hurts?"

"My stomach."

"Do you need to go to the hospital?"

"No," I say through clenched teeth.

"What if it's your appendix bursting?"

"Kinda hard for it to burst when it's not in my body anymore."

"Wait, what? When did you get an appendectomy?"

"When do you think?" Halfway through sophomore year. I'd

sat with the pain for days, convinced they were just my usual menstrual cramps. By the time Mom dragged me to the hospital, the organ was ready to make confetti of itself inside me. Candace left flowers for Mom and me on the porch when we got home. They'd already wilted.

"Sorry," Santiago says, though I'm unsure what exactly for. "Why are you acting like you know what's going on?"

I sigh. "They're period cramps."

He doesn't even try to hide his smile. "Oh, let me just leave you here in the middle of nowhere, then. Would hate to be in the presence of something so malevolent."

I groan at another slice through my abdomen. "Does sarcasm seem helpful right now?" Jesus, my uterus is being ripped open from the inside. I might not even need to remove it, it might simply combust on its own. Appendicitis 2.0.

"I'm just amused that the girl who made me stand guard outside the bathroom when she had to change her pad at school for the first time in eighth grade is suddenly shy over her period with me."

I flip him off from my curled position. "I'm not being *shy*."

"Are your cramps normally this bad?"

I nod in lieu of answering.

"Do you have Advil or anything?"

I shake my head and find my voice. "I have prescription pain meds at home, but I took my first dose late and forgot the second."

He sighs. I know guilt when I hear it. "We didn't have to do this tonight."

It's his birthday celebration, his eve as much as the new year's. But he's hardly cracked a smile all evening. If I checked his phone at midnight, maybe even tomorrow afternoon, I doubt I'd find more than a sentence or two from his dad waiting there. If that.

But I can't say this, so I say nothing.

Santiago looks down the dimly lit road, not another car in sight. At least there isn't much snow either. It didn't stick last night. "There should be cell service at the gas station we passed about a mile back, or at least a phone we can borrow. And maybe they'll have something to hold you over until we get a tow."

"We don't need a tow." I tilt my head to the side to watch him, my body still draped over the trunk. "If we can just get a spare at the gas station, I can fix it, and you can drive us back."

He purses his lips and makes a little noise. "I can't exactly drive."

"What do you mean by *exactly*?"

"Like . . . at all?"

"Santiago!"

"*What?*"

I pull at my thick beanie. "Why don't you know how to drive?"

"If I tell you it's internally homophobic to ask me that, will you hate me more than you already do right now?"

"It certainly won't help." Another wave of pain, and I dig my fingers into my puffer. "God, just leave me here to freeze and get eaten by wolves."

"I'm sure you'd make a delicious icy treat, but I have another solution." He shifts his jacket a bit, then crouches in front of me. "Get on my back."

"Very funny."

He raises his eyebrows, an impatiently amused look on his face.

"Am I going to have to bruise your ego and remind you that we're the same size?"

"No, but you might bruise me with some of your jewelry." He

steps close enough to flick one of the chains on my belt. Close enough to feel his radiating warmth. I refuse to be distracted from my pain. "Bea, let me try. I'm stronger than you think."

Because we're sort of out of options, I let him.

I use the back bumper to get a little boost. He wobbles forward as I leap on, nearly pitching us into the asphalt, but he catches himself and stabilizes in time.

"This is a terrible idea," I moan, sputtering as a stray piece of his hair gets caught in my lip gloss.

"Oh yeah, spit on my head while I'm trying to be helpful." He adjusts his hands on my calves and starts toward the gas station.

"I bet you only make it a quarter of the way before you need me to hop off."

His grip is gentle but firm. I let myself feel like deadweight. I let myself be held, and I try not to cry.

He laughs, not noticing. I'm both grateful and resentful for it. "Just for that, I might never let you down."

After making it nearly the whole trek, Santiago requests I dismount. The gas station is a beacon of hope in sight by now, so I manage on my own. I'm proud I only stop once when a particularly brutal cramp chomps into me. Teasing him helps with the pain.

Because the service is especially active on New Year's Eve to prevent drunk driving, our ride and tow will be here within an hour. We gather meds and a haul of snacks for the wait.

"Happy Halloween to *you*." The aging cashier waggles his thin eyebrows. It's not an unusual comment for me to receive. Wearing my floppy skeleton sweater under my puffer and black cargo pants with orange zippers makes it especially warranted. "What's a pretty girl like you doing here on a night like this?"

Convinced I'm hallucinating this parody of a man, I look to Santiago. His mouth curdles in equal parts amusement and horror but neither of us speaks, which makes me want to laugh even more.

The guy's eyes dart between us as he scans the items. He clears his throat, embarrassed. "That'll be eighteen fifty even."

I drop a twenty on the counter while Santiago is still scrambling in his pockets. "Consider this your birthday present."

We carry our provisions outside despite the temperature. We already tolerated the cold on the walk over and I doubt we could handle being in the same space as the cashier without losing our shit. As is, we're cracking up before the door even closes all the way behind us.

I drop onto the pavement and immediately wash painkillers down with enough scalding, bland coffee to mask the chalkiness.

"Better?" Santiago licks a hot chip–stained finger.

"It's not that fast acting, but sitting down helps." I set aside the coffee in favor of warm water. "The bumpy ride added to the nausea."

He rolls his eyes. "Go ahead and knock me down a star rating." I pluck the chip from his fingers and pop it into my mouth. He hands me the bag and takes out his phone. "Minutes till midnight."

"And there goes my attempt at a special birthday for you."

"She says as she eats my chips."

I forcefully hand the bag back to him. He grins, the red dust giving the illusion of lipstick. Despite our difference in appearance, me being well aware of where we are, and the fact that he's smiling, for a second I can convince myself I'm looking at my reflection in the mirror. A bit of smudged lipstick on my own face. So I do what I'd do if this were true and gently wipe it off. Even gentler, he lets me.

"Hey, you two!" The cashier leans out the door, greasy hair flopping into his face. My hand drops from Santi's mouth. "Fifty seconds to midnight!" The cashier puckers his cracking lips. "Halloween, you want to make my year?"

I don't know why I do it instead of telling him to fuck off. My favorite game to play as a kid was always house.

I bury my head into Santiago's shoulder. "The position is filled!"

The cashier scoffs and waves me off, slipping back behind the counter.

"Aw, but he seemed so nice," Santiago says, his words rumbling against me.

"He'd get over me if he knew me."

"Doubtful."

I can sit up now. If I sit up now, this wasn't a moment. It was a moment in time, but nothing more.

I don't move my head. "Thirty seconds now?"

"I'd wager." Santi speaks softer, not moving a muscle.

We count silently in our heads, ticking the clock down. The pulse at his neck thrums against my scalp. My lungs tighten. Something flutters in my stomach.

Bryce's favorite game was always any variation of chicken. He loved a gamble, a risk. He'd put it all on the line every time.

Santiago and I hated it. The anxiety was too much to bear, so we always lost. Even when playing each other, we'd jump ship at the same time. So many signs, for all of us.

"Ten," I whisper.

"Nine," he replies.

I tilt my head up. The neon lights shine against his hair, the fluorescents unworldly enough that I can lie to myself about this being real. *Eight.* In this light, this far away from our hometown and lives, I can almost pretend this is a dream. *Seven.* Or like he's just someone beautiful on New Year's. *Six.* Someone I could kiss and walk away from—*five*—never needing or wanting more than that. *Four.*

I can't have much, but I could have this. *Three.* Only this. *Two.* And the excuse of the night and someone else suggesting it.

"One," he says. One time. That's all I'll take.

I lean in.

"Wait."

His voice jolts me back.

In his eyes, I see my actual reflection.

I blink rapidly. What the fuck am I doing? What are *we* doing?

The moment shatters and I return to my head. I'm me. I'm Bea and this is Santiago and Bryce was our best friend and he's dead.

"Bea?"

My eyes have gone blurry. They strain to refocus, especially on him.

He bites his lip. "I need to tell you something."

"Please don't," I say. "We don't need to talk about it, it was just—"

"It's not about us."

My face goes hot, even in this frigid air. I need someone to save me from my thoughts. One night away from that fucking town and here I am pretending to be someone else. God, *what* am I doing?

"It's something I should have told you months ago, but I didn't know how. And I think now that we're . . . I don't know, becoming friends again?" He pauses, and we both know why. My eyes glance down at his mouth before I can stop them. "I just—I need you to know this."

Whatever it is, I don't want it. "Santiago, please—"

"I told all my friends in California that Bryce was still alive."

My head shakes of its own volition. My key shifts against my chest. "I don't understand."

"I lied," he says, grinding his teeth between words. "I'd told people about you and Bryce when I first moved, and then when I came back from the funeral after freshman year, I just didn't say anything about it, and then sophomore year started and they kept asking about you guys and if I visited over summer and I just—I pretended like Bryce was alive and then they found out he wasn't and that's why I was so eager to leave and why I don't talk to anyone from California anymore. Because they hate me, and so should you."

"You pretended Bryce was alive?" I blink rapidly as it catches up with me. "You pretended. You pretended he was alive." I meet his eyes, and whatever expression I'm making, he flinches at it. "You."

"I didn't want it to be real." It comes out like a whisper.

I should scream or cry or something. I used to be so vibrant in my feelings, their saturation always turned up high. But this dampens me. It freezes over everything that'd begun to thaw. "You got all my texts and calls. You knew I was here, how I felt. You could pretend, or you could face it with me."

"It wasn't that simple." He doesn't sound like he believes himself.

That speech in the supply closet. The blame I'd accepted after everything that already burdens me. My words at the funeral were his excuse, and I took it, so desperate for salvation from my self-imposed loneliness. Right now, I don't even know which one of us I hate more. But one thing is certain, Bryce was right to throw that key away.

I stand and brush the night off me. The air stings, the only proof I can still feel anything. "Don't talk to me ever again."

chapter twenty-four

SANTIAGO

When I made the decision to come home, I promised myself there were two secrets I'd always keep from Bea. Half of this was me being selfish, hoping to shelter us from my lowest moments, though my brain does a fine job of dismantling that shelter every chance it gets. The other half, though, the other half was for her.

I thought I was doing her a favor, but that was before she looked at me the way she did on the edge of a new year. In that moment, I would've wished on the entire galaxy to be anyone else, someone who deserved it, but the unfortunate reality is that I was and always will be me.

She was leaning in and I was leaning in and I couldn't lie anymore, not even because of her or me, but because of Bryce and the look and request he gave me the last time he saw me.

I already feel like a failure, so fifty percent isn't too bad, all things considered.

★ ★ ★

Dustin drives us to school on the first day back from winter break. I'd like to say it's because I feel bad that we've barely seen each other outside of work lately and I miss my friend, but the reality is that I needed a ride. Since New Year's, Bea and I haven't spoken.

The tow came, bad '90s pop blasting the entire time it took to get us and Bea's car back to Greensville. When the driver dropped me off at my house, Bea mumbled a happy birthday, and it's been silence since.

The tables have turned, the last three texts in our thread all coming from my phone, all unanswered. I can't tell if it makes me a good or bad friend for not listening to the newest request to never speak to her again.

"So your holidays were nice?" Dustin asks as we pull into the student lot. Abby got a ride with Whitney this morning.

"Yeah, mostly laid around watching movies with my abuelo." It's a half truth, all I'm good for these days. "What about you?"

"Pretty much the same."

"I didn't know you and my abuelo were close like that."

He chuckles and we get out of the car, his face souring as we spot Rick.

"You all right?" I ask.

"Not as long as I keep seeing him around. After getting supremely fucked up at our house on New Year's, he tried to ask Whitney to put in a good word with Olive again."

"What is Rick's obsession with them?" I ask. Olive is cute and sweet, but Rick's insistence doesn't seem to have anything to do with Olive themself.

Dustin shakes his head. "He doesn't like rejection. Honestly, I feel like we let too much shit with him slide over the years. It was just easier, you know? Having him as a friend than the other way around."

In my memories of Rick tormenting Bryce and me as middle schoolers, targeting us in dodgeball and, once, tossing our PE clothes in the showers so we had nothing to change into, I suddenly see Dustin too. One of the only Black kids in school, just as much a victim of the bullshit as us, realistically way more.

"Fuck that guy," I say.

"Amen."

Bea and I don't have class together until third period calculus, but she shows up right as the bell rings, so I don't get the chance to talk to her. The seating chart isn't alphabetical, so we're on opposite sides of the room, and with the advantage of being by the door, she manages to dart out when class ends before I can even finish packing up my notes.

I sigh on my way to lunch, not even bothering to search for her, and when I drop down at my old table, Whitney smiles.

"To what do we owe the pleasure?" she teases.

I try to return the smile, but it feels as rubbery as the mac and cheese the caf is serving today. We're joined by a few additional people, so I don't have to contribute much to the conversation, everyone talking about their break, what they got for the holidays, their respective experiences at Dustin and Abby's New Year's party.

"I didn't ask, how did your New Year's go?" Whitney says. She texted me a little after midnight for my birthday, but it came in while I was riding in the world's most uncomfortable tow, so I forgot to reply.

"Your dad came up, right?" Dustin asks between bites of mac.

"Yeah," I lie. "It was the perfect birthday."

chapter twenty-five

BEATRIZ

I've slipped up before—that summer between sophomore and junior year leading into the fall—but I know how to course correct. We survived that almost-accident. I can survive this one.

I spend the rest of break doing homework, taking Lottie on icy walks in neighborhoods where I won't run into anyone I once called a friend, and dodging Mom's questions about how Santiago is doing. The truth would only make her worry about us both.

When we get back to school, I make things right again. PE was always going to be tricky, so I feign cramps and ask to go to the nurse's office. I only leave for last period because we have essays due in English. I arrive as the bell rings, like I did with calc, but Ridley doesn't bat an eye. The things people in this town let me get away with.

Santiago's gaze is heavy as I pass him. The alphabet chopped us apart for once, so I sit at the end of one row and he sits at the start of its neighboring one. Ridley, still clinging to the past in a way I can almost respect, asks us to turn in hard copies of our essays at her desk.

Everyone shuffles their way over. A few kids already have theirs out while others dig through their bags. I fall into the latter.

When I stand, Santiago is on his way back from Ridley's desk. His eyes hold a question. I thought I knew the answer. I stand corrected.

He sits. I turn in my work. When I walk by him again, I take a page out of his book and pretend he doesn't exist.

The roof is still my sanctuary. Winter makes it a dangerous one though, a frustrating oxymoron. So I do my best to watch the stars from behind glass, hand wrapped around my key. I'd open the window and stare from my bed if it wouldn't waste Mom's warmth. This house is doing everything it can to provide me shelter, but the thing actually keeping me inside is self-preservation. Realizing I still have any left chills me all the same.

chapter twenty-six

SANTIAGO

It's September in January and I'm back to having friends. Sitting with Whitney and all of them again reminds me of trying on the clothes I'd left in Vermont when I first moved back. There were things I swore still fit, shirts and pants that in the confines of my room felt totally fine, but proved difficult to navigate actual life in when worn to school or work. All stiff, restricted movement. Anyone could've looked at me and not seen the discomfort, but that doesn't mean it wasn't there.

On the bright side, Rick is unofficially out of the group as basketball season takes over and saves us the effort of banishing him in any formal capacity. Unfortunately, two weeks into term, after Dustin darts off to talk to Mrs. Ridley before school about his essay revision, the seal of mutual silence is broken as Rick chases me down the parking lot, shouting my name.

"Just the man I was looking for," Rick says, slapping me on the back hard enough that it feels intentional. "Been a minute. How've you been?"

I shrug him off. "I'm all right."

"Nice, nice. So what are you doing this weekend?"

"Probably just my homework."

"Look at you, Mr. Studious," he says, nudging me, slightly too hard again.

I rub my shoulder. "Yeah, well, I need to go to my locker—"

"Before you do that, I wanted to tell you about a little get-together I'm throwing this weekend."

"Can't make it."

"Well, I kinda need you there."

I keep trying to head toward the main hall, the chilling air as uncomfortable as this conversation. "Why?"

"You and Olive are cool, right? Like, if you come to my party, Olive will too?"

I blink at him. "They already said they weren't interested in you, and Whitney—"

"Whitney is *so* dramatic and blew Homecoming way out of proportion. Which, by the way, you still owe me for."

I realize I'm not getting out of this. I shove my gloved hands into my coat pockets. "How so?"

His brows furrow. "I was *this* close to getting with Olive that night until you spilled your drink all over me."

I scoff. "Right."

"Look, don't be such a pussy," he says, and I almost laugh at the lack of creativity. "I'm not *that* guy. Do you see anyone else asking Olive out? It's a compliment."

I clench my jaw. "It's not. It's fucking weird and embarrassing. Let it go."

"Oh, I get it." His face shifts to a condescending pout, and he steps close enough that his breath clouds my vision. "You have a little crush, don't you?"

You're taller, you're stronger, you're not the little kid you used to be. I run over the facts like mantras in my mind, but none of them stick because even though Rick is looking up at me, I still feel like I'm in middle school again, staring at my shoes and waiting for his bullshit to be over.

But the mindset reminds me of Bryce, and how maybe if he were here, he'd be better at this than me by now. Braver, stronger, more protective. Am I just projecting on the blank canvas that is his unreachable future? Probably, but it at least inspires me to pull my gaze off the ground where I dropped it and step closer. Rick rests below my chin.

"Let. It. Go."

"Oh, sorry." He bumps my chest and it takes effort not to stumble backward. "Wouldn't want to insult your real girlfriend."

I flinch, and he catches it.

"Yeah, I've seen the way you've been staring down Miss Doom and Gloom. Say whatever you want about me being weird, but at least I'm not the one horny for my dead friend's girlfriend."

It isn't snowing, but the stark white of the day is hypnotic and confusing, blending this moment with a million others, the most prominent ones being New Year's and the last time I saw Bryce, both of them gutting me with the same sick hollowness. It doesn't matter if Rick is a piece of shit, if the people pausing to watch this ordeal instead of going into the comforting warmth of the school are just nosy assholes interested in the latest drama of Bryce's fucked-up friends, it doesn't matter that Bea and I aren't even talking anymore, because right now, I feel alone and awful enough that I can't convince myself I don't deserve this.

"Did you always have a thing for her?" He tilts his head, jutting his chin out to the side. "You *did*, didn't you? I bet you were happy when that loser killed himse—"

Something blurs past me.

Rick is down, one hand pressed to the concrete, the other to his mouth.

Bea stands over him, clutching her crimson fist, nails splintered with their jaggedly snapped-off tips littering the icy parking lot.

She looks up at me, eyes bright and wide and in shock as her palm drips blood. "Fuck. That hurt."

Bea sits on the bench outside of the principal's office with her left hand and its accompanying ice pack cradled to her chest, melting. I sit down beside her, offering the fresh one I got from the nurse's office once I remembered how high they keep the indoor heating. "Figured that might be liquefied by now."

She switches them out, exposing her mangled hand in the process. It looks worse already, the glaring red crescent moons sliced into her palm blooming bruises to match the ones decorating her knuckles. "I should've worn gloves today," she says, her quiet voice loud in the empty hall. "I can't believe I punched him."

"I wanted to." I look down at my unmarred hands. "I don't know why I didn't."

She adjusts her ice pack.

"Did you hear what he said?"

"No, I just punched him 'cause I was in a bad mood."

I snort.

"Olive doesn't deserve all of that," Bea says. "No one does."

I take a second. "And the rest of it?"

She sighs. This is our first conversation since New Year's, and it takes effort not to look at her mouth. I can't believe what almost happened. I've known Bea basically my whole life, and now part of me wants to know what it would've been like to kiss her. The other part hates me for even considering the idea.

"People broke into the old house," she says suddenly.

"Dustin told me." The series of break-ins trashing the place enough that it did the impossible and made a house a kid died in even harder to sell. A kid who is reason enough for me to ignore my curiosities about Bea.

"Rick started it."

My blood goes cold. "What?" I ask. Her right hand clenches tight, and for a second, I worry she'll snap those nails too. "Does Whitney know?"

Bea shakes her head. "I told her I had something on Rick if she ever needed it. I wanted to give her some protection. But also wanted to protect her from it." She blows out a breath, leaning against the wall. "I'm surprised she never guessed it was him with the way he used to treat you and Bryce and half this town. I think she just hates seeing things for what they are."

"How'd you find out?"

"I saw him leaving once, in the middle of the night. I never saw anyone before that."

"What were you doing there?"

She sighs again, resigned to honesty, too pained to lie. "Trying to find your key in the backyard." Before I can ask, she answers. "I never did."

Principal Jefferys steps outside before I can decide how to respond to this admission. "Kim tells me the two of you attacked Mr. Bruno?"

"No, no, I—"

"I punched him," Bea interrupts, standing. "He and Santiago were just talking. I escalated it."

"I see," Principal Jefferys says with a sour twist of his thin lips. "Mr. Espinosa, you should get to class, then. But we're going to have to call your mother, Miss Dougherty. Follow me."

He slips back into his office and Bea moves to follow, but my hand reaches for her before I can stop myself. "What are you doing?"

She shrugs, knocking me off her shoulder. "I hit Rick. You didn't."

"Well, you barely beat me to it, so."

This earns me another smile, one wide enough I'm surprised her dark lipstick doesn't crack. "Maybe next time." And then, as quickly as her smile came and went, so does she.

chapter twenty-seven

BEATRIZ

"Beatrice, this is a very serious matter," Jefferys says. It's almost funny that his scolding voice sounds so similar to his fake grief voice. He gave a speech to the school after Bryce died. It wasn't moving.

"I'm aware." It never feels worth the effort to correct my name.

"So you're aware that punching another student is unacceptable behavior?" he asks. I want to be a smart-ass so badly right now. But Mom wants me to graduate.

"Sir, I know my actions were . . . distasteful," I say. He looks like he's trying not to roll his eyes. "But Rick was being incredibly distasteful himself." Technically, punching Rick doesn't negate the firm stance I took a few weeks ago to never speak to Santiago again. If I'm being especially technical, though, talking to him in the hallway does.

Jefferys clears his throat. "Yes, well, I will be speaking to him about this matter as well. But whatever he did or said does not excuse your actions, which are grounds for suspension, if not expulsion."

"For punching *one* guy? This is rid—"

The door flies open and Whitney storms in, looking more disheveled than she'd ever normally allow. To the public eye, at least. I've seen her far more unkempt.

"Miss Ocampo, you cannot just waltz in here in the middle of an important meeting, especially when you should be in class right now," Jefferys scolds.

Whitney takes a breath as she approaches the desk. "I know, sir, and I'm so sorry to interrupt, but I think I can shed important light on today's events."

Jefferys looks at me. I look at Whitney.

She takes my neighboring seat. "Rick brought up my brother. The one who . . ."

Jefferys softens. "Yes, of course I know all about Bryce."

Whitney smiles gently. It's an act, but I'm one of the only people who could ever see that. Jefferys didn't know shit about Bryce, but few people did.

"The thing is, sir," Whitney continues, "Rick bringing up Bryce right now, of all times, hit hard for Beatriz. For all of us, really. You see, it was his half birthday this week."

I hold my face still. Nostalgic laughter bubbles up my throat, but I swallow it down with the reminder that this is a joke he doesn't get to make anymore. We shouldn't be able to either.

Jefferys looks back and forth between us. "His *half* birthday?"

Whitney nods vigorously. "Bryce loved his half birthday so much. It was a really special day for him."

"I see." Jefferys adjusts his collar. "Well, of course I empathize with your loss, young ladies. But that doesn't change that what Beatrice did was against school policy."

"What if we talk it over with Rick and his family?" Whitney asks.

"'We'?" I question, wondering when this became a team effort.

Whitney ignores me, still playing lawyer. "If his family accepts an apology, will that settle things?"

Jefferys rubs at his temples and groans. "Beatrice will be suspended for the rest of the week and attend after-school detention for two weeks, starting Monday. I want to be formally notified of Rick's acceptance. If his family wants to press charges, I have no power there."

Whitney clasps her hands together. "Oh, thank you so much, sir. I know Bryce would've really appreciated this."

They both turn to me, a reminder of who this is about. "Yeah, um, thank you, sir."

He nods, dismissing us. Once we're clear of his office and the front desk area, I whirl on Whitney. "What the fuck was that?"

"*That* was me saving your ass," she says. Her arms are crossed, hip popped, and whatever act of gracious innocence she was putting on for Jefferys is blessedly gone. "You can thank me in your valedictorian speech."

"You can't just throw Bryce's memory around like that."

She laughs. "Are you kidding me? You know better than I do how often he used his 'half birthday' as an excuse to get out of things." Ditching, eating cupcakes during classes where teachers normally forbid snacks, buying extravagant things he didn't need with money he didn't have. Bryce's half birthday was every day and for some reason no one ever questioned him on it. His real half

birthday was months ago and I'm only now realizing I didn't com-
memorate it, which makes me want to punch something again.
"He's probably pissed we haven't played that card in years."

I want to say that he isn't pissed about anything anymore. But
I can't say that to her, even angry. "It's not our card to play."

"Funny, here I was expecting a 'thank-you.'" She scoffs and
grabs my bandaged hand. "Jeez, you really need to learn how to
punch with long nails."

I snatch my tender hand back and it hurts worse than her taking it did. "I don't need you waltzing in to save me."

"But you can waltz in to save Santiago?"

The hallway's silence is interrupted by distant footsteps. Then
a door shuts, and it's just us again.

"That was different," I argue, because I don't want to think
about how quickly my anger over his New Year's confession didn't
matter when he was in trouble. How swiftly being by his side felt
more right than standing in the distance, watching him suffer
alone. The irony, it never ends.

"Why can't you just accept the favor?" Whitney shakes her
head. "Why is it suddenly a problem for us to help each other? Or
is it only a problem for someone to help you?"

We're not having this conversation today. Certainly not in this
hallway, and certainly not when my palm is still pulsing with pain.
"Thank you," I say between my teeth, then push past her. Hoping
to leave with the last word. Caring about that more than anything
else.

chapter twenty-eight

SANTIAGO

Kim sent me to class when I tried waiting outside of Principal Jefferys's office for Bea, so I don't learn about her suspension from Whitney until lunch. Abby also overheard someone in first period say that Rick's parents picked him up to take him to the hospital, ignoring that Bea is probably more injured than he is. I tried to plead Bea's case after school, but an hour of waiting left me with nothing but a request from Kim to go home, since Principal Jefferys wasn't interested in any further discussion.

So now I'm here, walking home in rain-soaked clothes that weigh on me as heavily as the guilt, when a car behind me honks.

I flinch, shielding my eyes as I look for the culprit.

Bea slows her car to a crawl, taking a comically long time to crank her window down by hand.

"It's raining," she says.

"Oh, so that's why I'm drenched in water."

She stretches across the passenger seat and yanks up the lock. "Get in."

I tug the door open and literally slip inside. Bea fiddles with her ancient dashboard, adjusting the heater until it blasts me with air that may as well be magic with how good it feels on my freezing skin, then throws a towel at me from the back seat. "You look like a wet dog."

I ignore her and rub rain from my eyes. "Your punishment is bullshit."

"One week of suspension is nothing." She flashes me a wry look. "And I've done detention before."

I clear my throat when I notice she's steering with only one hand. "You shouldn't have held your fist the way you did when you punched Rick."

"We're giving fighting advice now?"

"You don't know if I've been in a fight before."

Skepticism is painted on her skin as smoothly as her makeup.

"You need to press your fingers down instead of in," I go on. "Your nails should be parallel to your palm instead of perpendicular."

We're paused at a stop sign, but after the obligatory few seconds, she lifts her uninjured right hand off the steering wheel instead of driving on.

"May I?" I ask. She offers me her fist in answer.

The cold is leeched from my flesh as I hug her hand in mine. Her skin is far softer than it looks, molding to my adjustments like warmed clay. I smooth my thumb over the topography of her bent fingers, a gentle act that manages to both intentionally correct their posture and unintentionally inflict me with goose bumps. Touching her has never been more natural and foreign than in this moment.

"This feels awkward," she says, and I drop her hand immediately. She looks at me in confusion before I realize what she meant.

"Oh." I clear my throat. "Yeah, well, it'll feel better than tearing your palm to shreds. Everything else stays the same: Hit with your knuckles and never tuck your thumb in, or you're going to have more to worry about than your nails."

She punches her thigh a few times, softly, then slightly harder. "How do you even know this?"

"Friend from California."

The car goes still in harsh contrast to the rain battering down on the roof, the hollow tin sound overwhelming the space between us.

"Explain it to me," she says, and it sounds a little like begging.

"I was trying to survive."

She shakes her head, frustrated but trying. "That's not good enough."

"He died hating me," I say instead, because it's the closest to the truth I can get. "My best friend died alone, hating me. He didn't call me, he didn't send a text or a letter or any cry for help. I didn't even know he was—he didn't reach out. But neither did I." I face her, because if I'm going to admit my cowardice, I can at least be brave about it. "What was I supposed to do with that?"

She opens her mouth, then closes it, a wet noise the only thing she can say in response without hurting me. But maybe I deserve to be hurt.

"He didn't hate you," she says like an exhale.

"I'm not going to argue about this with you."

"And I'm not going to listen to your self-pitying bullshit."

"Did he say a single good thing about me after our fight? Mention that he missed me or that I would've loved a show you were watching or brought up an inside joke of ours?" I ask, and her silence answers the questions. "He threw away the key, Bea. Far enough that you couldn't find it either." I want to ask how many times she searched for it, compare it with how many times I wish I could've.

"It was just a key. It didn't mean—"

"Then why are you still wearing yours?"

She looks down at her treasonous hand where it rests against her collarbone, a released fist now digging into the thick fabric of her sweater for the slightest hint of that metallic outline underneath. Her hand drops and she shakes her head, denying the moment. "How did your friends find out you were lying about Bryce?"

Bryce wasn't supposed to die, and after he did, I spent the summer in a shell, one that deflected all messages from Bea and Whitney and Abuelo. No one else reached out.

And then the first thing Eric asked me when we came back for sophomore year was if I'd visited those best friends of mine I'd mentioned who still lived in Vermont. I didn't mean to lie, it just sort of happened when I opened my mouth and said yes. He asked what we did, so I told him all about our summer—how we rode our bikes around at sunset, broke into the public pool after dark and swam until we were chased off by the opening staff, went to a drive-in movie out of town because Bryce got his permit and fuck the rules about only driving family, we *were* his family. Bea's favorite thing to play growing up was house, Bryce's was chicken. I'd never been great at either, too bad of a pretender, but suddenly, I was an expert.

After badminton practice, if I was on my phone reading a text from Pa that he'd be home late and I'd need to figure out dinner on my own, I went along with Eric's assumptions that I was texting Bryce. When the team discussed Homecoming, calling it cliché and boring, I agreed, and laughed along with them teasing that I just didn't want to go because I couldn't take Whitney. At this point, I didn't know she was gay, but the lie about me still having a crush on her was so far removed from her or me or reality.

Sometimes, the texts I was reading after practice actually were from Bea, something simple like *hey* or *how have you been?* The lies tasted the worst on those days, a smile on my face for my peers as I deleted the messages.

Now here she is, begging me to give her enough of a reason not to hate me, and I can't. "It was a party near the end of junior year, after our last game. Everyone was smoking and asking questions in this lazy version of high truth-or-dare in my friend Eric's basement. He asked if I could kiss anyone in the world right then and there, who would it be, and I said Bryce, for more than one reason." It's an admission and it isn't, and Bea lets me get away with it because we both know what the biggest reason is. "I told them you guys didn't have social media, which was a lie that'd always been built to break. When I was in the bathroom, someone finally found Bryce's old Instagram and read the comments on the last post." A photo of him and Bea on Valentine's Day, their faces squished together and grinning in this combination of appeasement for the person behind the camera—presumably Magda—and sincere joy. "It wasn't hard for them to figure it out from there."

The disgusted looks, the harsh questions, how swiftly the news sobered up the room. By the next day, plenty of people knew, because even if my school was big and I was small and no one cared about gossip the way they do here, everyone loves a spectacle in the shape of a teenage boy. The last week of school should've been the loneliest I'd been in California, but in a way, it was actually the freest.

Bea shakes her head once again. "You didn't need to ignore me though."

A million more lies flood my thoughts, ways to maintain the fucked-up facade sheltering her from the crushing truth. But this is a rare moment in which I can be honest without telling her everything, so I do just that. "I'm sorry."

Outside the window, she looks at my house, a destination we arrived to sometime over the past few minutes without me noticing. I make a second realization swiftly after. "Did you drive back to school to pick me up?"

She unlocks the car, then reaches behind her seat to pull out an old umbrella I recognize from childhood. "Stop walking through storms alone."

I finish my journey home with her gifted protection.

chapter twenty-nine

My timing on Saturday morning is perfect. I thought I'd have to actually knock on Rick's door and risk someone in his family answering, but he's already outside getting the mail. When he sees me, his eyes narrow and his chest puffs up. It doesn't hide the bruise along his jaw peeking out of his turtleneck.

"What the fuck are you doing here?" he asks.

I wait until I'm close enough to see the individual colors of the mark I've left on him. Echoes of purple remain but it's mostly yellow and green now. Sickly, and also a reminder that I'm a pretty shit puncher.

"I'm supposed to apologize," I say. My hands rest in my pockets where he can't see them shake.

"Go on."

"I said I was supposed to. I didn't say I'm here to actually do it."

He looks me up and down. I'm not wearing anything special. Black sweater, black boyfriend jeans. Chain belt. Thick trench coat that skims the tops of my platform boots. Black beanie. My face is painted to a T, my eyebrows sharp and dark. Mom asked if it was too cold out for me to walk the few blocks between our houses. She's otherwise left the matter of me punching someone untouched.

"Are you trying to apologize in other ways?"

I could've shown up in a hazmat suit and he'd still take it suggestively. "Not unless it'd be via a second punch."

He takes the rejection like a champ, which is to say that his face gets red from anger instead of just the chill. "Well then, maybe I'll have to press charges . . ." He lets the threat hang in the air but I don't flinch. It's a privilege, I know.

"Or you could punch me back," I offer.

"Are you fucking with me?"

"Nope." I motion to my face. Even take a step forward. "All yours."

"I'm not gonna punch a fucking girl." He shakes his head with disgust. This guy who'd probably have no issue assaulting me in other ways suddenly wants to play at having morals. "You're crazy."

I don't refute that. "Fine. How about I won't tell everyone that you're the person who kept breaking into Bryce and Whitney's old house?"

He scoffs but doesn't deny it. "No one would believe you. And who would even care?"

"Statute of limitation laws, for one," I reply, pretending as if I didn't google that last night. "Candace for two." His eyes don't light up with recognition. I forget she didn't help raise everyone in this town. "Bryce's mom."

"You have no proof."

"Maybe not," I allow. "But I hear your dad is interested in running for mayor. Bad look if his golden son broke into the dead kid's house and won't leave his younger sibling alone."

We both know enough about the world to recognize that he could get away with it, easy. But we also know he wants all talk of him being punched in the face gone, and fast.

"I won't say anything to anyone if this—" I motion between us, even indulging myself by waving at his face "—ends here. No pressed charges. No further complaints."

"You're a fucking bitch, you know that right?" he says.

I do. And I know we have a deal, so I walk away. I have something else to do today.

I go home for my car and drive this time.

I knock on Santiago's door without a heads-up text. It gives me a chance to back out.

My chest aches when he appears, already smiling at seeing me. Even as I invite the cold in. "Hey. I didn't know you were coming over."

"Can we talk?"

We go through the awkward formalities of him offering me a drink and a seat in a place I used to consider a second home. Five minutes later I'm perched on the edge of his sofa with a cup of cold water in my thawing hands.

"I need to tell you something," I say before I can think better of it.

"Okay." He sets down his glass.

"I slept with Dustin."

He opens his mouth, then shuts it. Then does it twice more. And a fourth time. "When?"

"Last year."

He releases a breath, and his relief is almost endearing. "Okay."

"'Okay'?"

The words don't come from his lips as quickly as they usually do. "I mean, I don't know what to say? He's a good guy."

My posture is held so stiffly, I'm worried I might strain something. "I went over to his house to do a project last year. March, it was in March." I clear my throat, easing myself into the memory. "The same week we got assigned partners, Dustin and Courtney got in this big fight at lunch. She kissed a guy from South Ridge High at some party Rick threw for the basketball team. Word was that they were done for good." I watch Santiago's expression. Other than flinching at the mention of Bryce's birth month, he stays neutral. "So when I came over after school, I asked if Dustin wanted to sleep with me."

"And . . . he said yes?"

I find it in me to crack a smile. "Shocking, I know."

"That's not what I meant," he defends quickly, neutrality giving way to fluster. I can tell he's on the precipice of mentioning he almost kissed me himself a few weeks ago, just to prove a point. "I'm surprised he thought he and Courtney were really done enough to sleep with someone else. Every time they fight, it seems like he's accepted it as some inevitable, never-ending pattern between them."

"I don't know how he felt, but *I* knew it wasn't over," I say. "I thought he was going to kick me out right after. Make an excuse about his parents coming home or having plans." I fiddle with my injured hand in my lap. My nails are going to take a while to grow back. "Instead, he lent me a sweatshirt and asked if I was hungry. We had some mediocre butter pasta and finished the project. Then I left, ready for everyone to be talking about it on Monday." I pause to sip the water.

"You wanted that?" Santiago asks, a little horrified.

My fingers dance up and down my cup. "Everyone in this town already knows all about me and my life. At least this was something I'd chosen." Sympathy crosses his face. "But nothing happened. Dustin said hi to me in class, and that's it. By the end of the week, he and Courtney were back together." The sympathy hasn't faded. "Stop that."

"Stop what?"

"Looking at me like I got my heart broken," I say. "I didn't think anything would come from me and Dustin—to the contrary. I'd hinged everything on him being a complete douche about the whole thing. I should've slept with Rick."

"Please never say that again."

I can't help a second smile. "If he told Courtney or Rick, I never would have heard the end of it. Me, Dustin, and now you are the only ones that know."

"You never told Whitney?"

I set down the cup. "Why would I?"

"Because people usually tell a friend about their first time," he says earnestly. "And Whitney is the closest thing you had to one of those."

It feels like Pandora's box. Or a field of land mines. Or my life. "It wasn't my first time."

"I—Bryce?"

"Freshman year." I feel an awful lot like a parent telling their kid Santa isn't real, and I'm not sure why. Maybe all of this is just easier when packaged in similes. "After you left."

I doubt he means to do it, but his eyes dart to the walls. Specifically, they dart to the last photo of all three of us. It was a few weeks before he moved, a few days before their fight. All our fourteen-year-old faces are tearstained and acne-pocked. We are so young and unaware of what will come next. But we'd already been through so much.

"I'm glad you trust me enough to share this, but why are you?" he asks finally, cautiously.

It isn't the same thing, I know. But I can't tell him everything, so I tell him this. "I did things to survive it too."

"It's not the same, Bea," Santiago whispers. "He was gone. You didn't do anything wrong."

Then why did it always feel wrong? Not just with Dustin.

I chew my lip and Santiago's eyes follow the movement, stay there for a second.

"You're really not mad?" Once, years ago, I wondered who Santiago would side with if Bryce and I ever broke up. No matter how I cut it, I couldn't imagine any of us without one another. And then the two of them did the unimaginable instead, and it cracked every other painful possibility open.

"No," he says, and his eyes leave my mouth. It sounds true, but I know what brilliant liars we both can be.

A car beeps outside and we startle.

Santiago walks me to the door and I cast myself back into the cold. Billy and Señor Espinosa wave from the end of the driveway.

"So, I'll pick you up on Monday?"

I can tell he doesn't understand how I've forgiven him for what he did, the lies and abandonment. Truthfully, I don't understand it either. I've withheld so much forgiveness for myself, I think I just need to put it somewhere. Why not give it to him?

"Yeah," he says, like he'd forgive me for everything I've done too.

chapter thirty

SANTIAGO

Bea and I slip back into our normalcy, or whatever we've got going on that constitutes normalcy. Riding to school, chatting in PE while we do the inane indoor activities Coach Simmons concocts, studying after her detention, and pretending like all the time we spend together doesn't make us friends. Lunch is also back on the regular schedule, but today, there's something new about it: She's not sitting alone.

"Come on, don't be shy!" Courtney says when she notices me stalling.

Bea widens her eyes in a plea. "Yes, join *us*, Santiago."

Dustin and Courtney sit on one end of the bench with a perfect space left for me beside Bea. I take it, wishing I could ask her what's going on without being overheard. I've also obviously seen Dustin since Bea told me about them having sex, but the three of us weren't together any of those times, so now it's difficult to look at my friends without immediately picturing them both naked.

"So, how's it going?" I ask, playing along with whatever this is and dimly wondering why Whitney isn't part of it.

"Courtney was just telling us about her day," Bea says, giving herself a cavity with all the sweetness she forces into her words.

"Yeah, where was I?" Courtney asks Dustin.

"Math class," Dustin says. His eyes meet mine in apology.

"Right! I swear Mr. Fisher has a stick up his ass when it comes to assignments. I missed, like, two days of homework last semester, and he dropped my participation score by half a grade. We're only a few weeks into the new term, but I already have so much homework I feel like I should just kill myself instead." She laughs.

A rock sinks to the bottom of my stomach.

Courtney is a lot of things, but when she realizes what she just said, her face freezes. "Oh. Oh my god, I'm so sorry."

Bea makes a noise, something between an exhale and a laugh, and stands. "Well, this was a fun experiment." She swings her backpack over her shoulder, leaving her lunch tray behind as she walks off.

"Please tell her I didn't mean anything by it," Courtney pleads, sincere enough that I almost bite my tongue.

"What about me?" I ask.

Her guilt bleeds into confusion. "What do you mean?" Dustin places a hand on her leg, and she reads between the lines on his face. "Oh, Santiago, of course I'm sorry to you too. But Beatrice was his girlfriend. It's different."

"How?" I ask without meaning to. Even Dustin's face changes shape. "Whatever." I don't even grab my lunch as I run after Bea.

I track her tall form easily, dressed in all black against the harsh white-gray of the sky as she heads for the main halls. By the time I catch up, she's sitting in a ball under her locker.

"I'm fine, okay?" Bea says.

"I didn't ask," I reply. She smiles.

While I sit down, she tugs her legs closer to her chest. "Dustin stopped to ask a question about English and then they just didn't leave," she says, and I hear her regret opening her world enough to allow this. "I tried before. Sitting with them at lunch. I really tried."

"I've heard." The way everyone tells it, she's been a recluse for years, but Dustin did mention the weird period of time during junior year that Bea sat with Whitney's group, though it sounds like it was months before Bea slept with him, and ended abruptly.

"It just—" she starts, pausing to sigh. "It never felt right without Bryce."

The badminton team was a conversational crutch for me and Eric, material to chat about in the locker room, during water breaks, between classes, over music and video games in someone's basement. It was easy to lie when the only things we ever really talked about existed on the surface, everything else buried deep in that ocean of grief. It was easy to be friends with people who weren't Bryce when I wasn't really me either.

"Whitney gets it though," I say, thinking of the handful of texts from her in my phone, rain-checked invitations to study or hang out that've accrued since Bea and I picked back up again. "She lost him too."

Bea nods slowly at this. "But I don't know how she does it." She glances down the hall, toward the rest of the school, everyone so far away that we might as well be in another galaxy.

Images of laughing at lunch tables, smiling in classes, and kissing near-strangers all flash through my mind. Last year, I almost went a full day without thinking of Bryce, and then I saw this goofy orange astronaut shirt at a garage sale down the street from our apartment and cried for the first time in months. "It should make us stronger, right? You survive the worst thing imaginable. Everything else should be easy by comparison."

"He died, so nothing else matters. That's how it should be," Bea says. "Instead, he died and everything else." The sentence feels incomplete, and yet nothing has better captured the feeling. So we sit with it, grief bouncing off the empty halls.

The next week, I'm not sure how to broach the subject despite having hours to brainstorm between when I got the text this morning and now. PE would normally be a land mine in this situation, but most of our class is using the weight room, with only a few people like Bea and I occupying the gym to shoot hoops. I already chickened out at lunch, so now seems like as good a time as any.

"Olive asked me out," I say, passing the basketball to Bea. Her quick three-pointer goes in with a swoosh, no hesitation or reaction. "They texted me this morning asking if I wanted to go to the diner sometime this week. As a date." They also thanked me for dealing with Rick, even though I'm not the one who punched him.

"About time." Bea motions for me to get the ball. I oblige and swap spots with her.

"What do you mean?" I shoot and miss, the ball spiraling off the hoop.

"That's *H*," she notes, and waits for me to chase after the stray shot. I stay put, staring her down as best I can for an answer. It's hard when her face is currently decked out in massive red wings dripping silver glitter and her brows are nonexistent, freshly and fully shaved off for once. "They asked for my blessing at Christmas."

I go after the ball. "And you gave it to them?"

"They offered me a handsome dowry."

I pass to her, and she dribbles between her hands, then under her legs, putting on a show, though I doubt she even realizes she's doing it.

"I don't know if I should go," I confess right as she takes a side shot. The ball goes wide, which earns me a glare that I admittedly cherish.

She stares for an additional handful of seconds as the ball—which is far closer to her than me, I might add—drifts across the gym before going after it. "Why?" She passes to me.

I dribble twice. "I feel like I'm betraying him, somehow."

Bea pulls at the neck of her uniform, and I wonder if she's also thinking about New Year's, how if siblings are off-limits, so are girlfriends. If Bryce and I hadn't been fighting when he died, I think I'd still consider us friends right now. So what does that make him and Bea?

We go on playing in silence, only talking to note how many letters I'm gathering. I make it to *H-O-R-S*. I used to beat Bryce at PIG all the time, but Bea always beat us both.

It's her shot. She considers the hoop, not looking at me, before speaking. "You should go on the date."

"Why?"

"Because you've clearly had a crush on Olive since you moved back."

"I have not."

She gives me a look.

"*I have not*," I insist, and mean it. "Thinking they're attractive doesn't mean I have feelings for them. I think you're attractive."

She rolls the ball between her hands. "And you obviously don't have feelings for me."

"Certainly not many positive ones right now."

I'm not sure what game we're playing, but it doesn't feel like HORSE anymore.

She sets up her shot, positioning her arms and crouching slightly. "If I make this, you'll go on the date."

I want her to chuck the ball at the bleachers or drop it in place. I want her to drastically miss, with no way for me to deny it wasn't an accident. "Okay."

She dribbles once and takes a deep breath. Meanwhile, I'm holding mine.

The ball sails in, nothing but net. The snap of the white yarn is a period to this conversation. I didn't get *E* yet, I haven't lost that game, but I feel like I've lost the one that mattered.

I allow myself one glance at Bea, but her mask is back on, eyes trained on the ball where it bounces softly below the net until it finally settles and rolls away in one definitive direction.

I've made plenty of mistakes in my life, enough for me to consider guilt more of a baseline emotion than anything else. But what I'm doing right now seems wrong on several levels, and I'm trying not to be eaten alive by the feeling before I can even eat.

Olive slips into one side of the booth and I slide into the space across from them, nodding to our waiter, Courtney's cousin Jimmy, as he hands us the worn plastic menus.

I look around while Olive scans the menu that hasn't changed in two decades. The place is packed with customers, not for the quality of the food but the legacy of it. The thin film of grease coating every inch of the interior is comprised of my childhood, memories that would be just as difficult to scrub away as the stains.

After drinks, we both order grilled cheese with a side of tomato soup, copying Bryce's regular order minus the two slices of apple pie he'd tack on.

"So . . . ," Olive starts, playing with their milkshake's straw. I take a sip of my root beer as a social crutch. "Are you excited about graduating?"

I swallow the soda, noting how flat it is. "Yeah, I won't hear from anywhere for a few more months, but it'll be weird leaving again after just coming back."

"You didn't apply locally?" they ask. I already know Whitney only applied on the East Coast.

"I did, but I think I'd rather go somewhere in SoCal. Like UCSD, maybe? Wherever gives me the best financial aid, I guess."

"Oh." Their brows droop.

"Did you . . . think I was going to go to school nearby?" I ask, feeling weirdly unfaithful, as if we're months into a relationship and I'm betraying them by having plans outside of their expectations.

"I guess I just figured since you barely moved back home, you'd want to stick around."

It's my turn to toy with my straw. "I came to help out with my abuelo. Otherwise, I would've stayed in California." The freak who lied about his dead friend being alive. Would Bea and I have ever started talking again?

Olive nods, and if I hadn't spent the past several months with a girl who hides every emotion behind three layers of a different one, it'd be harder for me to pick up on the volume of their silence. "What?" I ask.

They give a little shrug, making their floppy cardigan bounce.

I hadn't noticed the sunflowers on it matching their homemade earrings. "Didn't you miss this place?" They sound like when we were kids and Whitney would say they couldn't join us on a trip to the park or an errand run to the grocery store, though their disappointment couldn't last long before Bryce would veto Whitney and tell Olive to hop on his handlebars.

"Of course I missed it." It's harder to add the next part, even though it's painfully, gut-wrenchingly true. "I missed Bryce too."

Olive's response is quick. "You never reached out after he died."

Jimmy drops our bowls onto the table, red soup sloshing over the ceramic brims like thick blood, and then he's off to grab us napkins.

I stare at the crimson droplets that made their way onto my hands. "I'm sorry," I say to Olive, though I may as well make it the only thing I say to anyone ever again at this rate.

"You were his best friend."

Yeah, I want to say, *emphasis on* was. "I didn't know what to do."

Like a sped-up projector, images of those years blur by me as they so often have lately, the truth and the lies and the lack of stars, always wondering whether or not Bryce could see me and, if so, if he forgave me. If he accepted my attempt to make amends in the fucked-up way I'd chosen to.

Olive grabs half of their sandwich, dips it into the soup, and chews with the clear intention to speak when finished. "I didn't mean to bring all of this up." Shyness reenters their voice and face, or maybe that's just the anger and hurt leaving them. "Having you back here reminds me of those first few months without him."

I slept over a lot right after Bryce's dad died, always keeping Bryce company and making sure he was laughing in spite of his loss. The sleepovers lessened after Candace and Phil's wedding increased the house's population, but I suddenly remember one during the early stages of their marriage.

I woke up to Bryce slipping out of bed to use the bathroom. He was gone awhile, so I peered through his cracked-open door, just in time to see him escorting a nightmare-rattled Olive down the hall from their room to their parents'.

I had distant cousins and friends, Bea's mom and Bryce's parents and Abuelo, but I never had that. A hand in the dark, free of judgment or annoyance. In a way, I resented Olive for having it and still wanting to be older, one of us. I always and never was a kid who needed protecting.

I look back at Olive to compare this teenage version of themself to the childhood one, only to find they've been talking this whole time, and I've missed almost all of it.

"—and that's why I was so surprised when you said yes."

"Right," I laugh, determining how I'm going to play this. "Because . . . ?"

They smile at their lap. "Because I thought you knew about my crush on you, but you always liked Whitney when we were kids, and then I thought you and Bea were dating, and I didn't want to step on anyone's toes. But you and Whitney are obviously never going to happen, and knowing you and Bea aren't either, I thought: There's nothing to lose!"

I laugh fakely along with their sentiment. Just because Bea said I should do this doesn't mean I should've. Because watching Olive, seconds ago aching with memory, now celebrate this gain, reminds me of something you learn the hard way when you grieve: There is always something left to lose.

Olive and I met at the diner, Phil their driver and Dustin mine, but Dustin got caught up at work, so I end up doing the pathetic thing, hating myself for it even as I make the call.

"So, how was it?" Bea asks as I rush into the warmth of her car from the icy parking lot.

"It was . . . interesting." I buckle my seat belt and remove my gloves, practically shoving my hands into the vents. "We talked about Bryce."

"Lively topic for a first-date conversation."

I rub my palms together. "Did you and Olive talk much after Bryce died?"

Bea's jacket hood paints shadows onto her already sculpted cheekbones. "Not really. They had Whitney. They didn't need me."

I wonder if that's how she weighs relationships these days, by their practicality and function, by whatever objective positives or negatives she believes she brings to people's lives. "Thank you for coming to get me."

Bea looks up from where she was busying herself with the heater settings, like she hears the confession in my gratitude. The need I have.

When it's clear I won't push us into New Year's territory with my inappropriately timed yearning, she focuses on driving. "So are you going out with them again?"

For a terrible second, I want to lie and say yes, just to see what it does to her face.

"Nah, I don't think we work well in that way," I say truthfully. "I don't know how I'm going to break it to them."

Bea's hands still, but she doesn't look up. "Olive will be fine. They've been through worse."

chapter thirty-one

If I hadn't been awake most of the night, I'd be convinced someone ran me over with a bus while I was unconscious. I chalk up my perpetual exhaustion to my lack of sleep and the life I've lived, but today my runny nose, burning cheeks, and watery eyes tell me that something else is at play.

Mom left right after "waking me up" to cover both her and a coworker's shifts all day. Her ignorance about my current state of being saves me the trouble of convincing her not to stay home.

My bed is drenched in sweat, so I gather up whatever blankets are still dry and a ruana that hasn't fit since my growth spurt and wobble downstairs to the sofa. Once I'm relatively comfortable, I pull my phone from my waistband and tap on Santiago's name.

He answers on the second ring. "Santiago Espinosa's office, this is Santiago speaking."

"You're going to have to fire me as your personal driver."

"Why does your voice sound so gravelly and hot?"

I produce something between a laugh and a cough. "Are you implying that my voice isn't normally gravelly and hot?"

"That's exactly what I'm implying." It sounds like he moves the phone to his other ear, hair tickling the microphone. "You sick?"

"Yeah, sick of driving you around," I say as my words grow strained by a coughing fit that racks my lungs.

"Wow, and I thought you sounded hot before."

"I want you to know I'm using my last bit of strength to flip you off."

"I'm honored," he says. I touch my mouth and realize I'm smiling. "Guess I'll have to sit alone at lunch, see what all the hype is about."

I want to remind him he has other friends, but it'd be too much of an admission. "Try to survive one day without me, and I'll try to survive this flu."

"Ask Magda for extra honey in your tea."

I snuggle deep into the cushions, sleepier from the idea of warm tea. "Maybe when she gets home tonight."

"Wait, no one's there to take care of you?"

I cover the phone when another storm of coughs passes through. "I'll be fine. I'm a big girl."

"I don't see what your height has to do with you being bedridden and alone."

"I promise I'm good."

We hang up and I manage to get what could be seconds or hours of mediocre sleep, tossing and turning at the mercy of hot and cold flashes, when someone starts knocking on the front door.

It blends in with the pounding in my head, so I ignore it at first. It's not like I could get up and answer anyway. But after a moment of quiet, the knocking intensifies. If someone is about to break in and find me in Kermit pajama pants and a crop-top ruana, so be it.

My phone starts ringing. In my half-conscious fever-dream state, I have a Sherlock moment and realize there might be a correlation between that and the knocking.

Groaning, I stretch an arm out from under my pile of blankets. My fingers graze my phone on the coffee table over and over, the slipperiness of the screen matching the slipperiness of my sweaty hands. Finally, I grasp it and drag it back to my chest.

Five missed calls from Santiago. Hmm, maybe a correlation after all.

I call him back, practically prying my eyes open with the hand that isn't holding my phone.

"Most people answer the door when someone's knocking," Santiago says.

"Hi, Santi, yeah I'm feeling fantastic, thanks for asking."

"All right, I'm opening the door, smart-ass."

He hangs up as I hear the front door unlock. Sunlight bursts into the room behind him, cuffed jeans and a blue sweater hugging his frame. I study him as he strides over and dumps plastic bags onto the coffee table, kneeling before me with a tenseness that wasn't present on the phone. He presses the back of his freezing hand against my forehead. "You're really hot."

"You've been flirting with me a lot this morning." I attempt a wink but I'm pretty sure I just blink.

He ignores me, which I distantly know I'll be grateful for when I'm not feeling so out of it. "How long has your fever been this bad?"

I try to shrug under the blankets but it goes about as well

as the winking. "I probably would've slept through it if someone hadn't broken into my house."

"Keep sassing me and I'll eat your sopa de pollo," he says, but his tone is as gentle as his touch. He feels my face again and I find myself leaning into it, a relief for my aching body.

"I don't mind sharing," I say sleepily, feeling my consciousness fading again. "Why aren't you at school?"

To my disappointment, he stops patting my face. His attention shifts to tucking my blankets in tighter, stopping only for a second to smile at the ruana. His fingers glide over the wool. It's getting impossible to keep my eyes open.

"How'd you get in?" I try instead.

"Get some rest, Bea," he whispers.

The last thing I see before passing out is a key in his hand.

Religion's cashmere sleeves never quite fit me. Instead of a soft embrace, I often felt stifled by Catholicism, found myself picking at stray threads and pulling at the stitching. As a child, I recall watching peace wash over Mom's face the few times she swept us into a church. I wanted that for myself. Instead I squirmed, wondered why the pews were so rigid in a place meant to be comforting. I suspect my baptism was an appeal to my mom's already estranged parents more than anything else, but the notion of being prepared for an afterlife I'm not sure I believe in always leaves me feeling conflicted.

Regardless, I imagine I've muddied that ticket beyond recognition. Which is okay with me, generally speaking. If there is someone out there who deliberately planned my life thus far, I've got feedback for them.

All this being said, on the sofa, I dream of a kind of heaven. We're all stars making up a single constellation in the sky. Me, Santiago, Whitney, and Bryce. The latter brilliant and bold in all his glory.

Except I remember what he told me once: Stars burn brightest right before they burn out. And, almost like I make it come true by remembering, he flashes until everything goes white, and then he's gone.

The rest of us can't stay here. So we do the only thing we can. We fall.

Spiraling down to Earth, dropping from whatever graces we once considered permanent. Our crash is silent and quick, but unimaginably painful.

And then there we lie, husks of our former selves. Our twinkle has gone out, and I don't think it can ever come back.

I wake up to the sound of humming, my eyes peeling open like wet paper. Everything is blurry for a few seconds, but the dark room slowly comes into view. Yellow light bleeds in from the kitchen alongside the delicious scent of spiced meat.

Groggily, I manage my way into a sitting position and take inventory of my body. My head isn't pounding anymore, but soft pain still pulses like an unassuming heartbeat. My fever must have broken, because I'm sticky with sweat and feel only the warmth of the blankets wrapped around me. My lungs don't shake when I inhale.

The glass of water on the table is empty, so I free myself from my cocoon and stand on unsteady feet. Carefully, I teeter my way to the kitchen, where the brightness pains me.

"Hey, let me help you." Santiago's voice gets louder as he gets closer. He blocks out the light, sheltering me in shadow, and takes hold of my shoulders. We get me to a stool and I drop down onto it, practically lying on the tile counter.

I don't know where he found a thermometer, but he slips it into my mouth and waits, watching my lips so intently that I'm scared I might be blushing. I lightly scratch my chin and check under my nail to confirm there's no makeup there, nothing to hide behind.

After the longest minute of my life, he plucks the device out. "Good, you're not as hot as you were before." I open my mouth. "Don't make another bad joke."

"It was going to be good, I promise."

He smiles. "Don't make promises you can't keep."

A timer goes off behind him and he leaves me long enough to grab a bowl of soup. "Eat."

I take the spoon and blow on the liquid before cautiously slurping it. "How long was I out?"

He leans his forearms on the counter. Sometime while I was asleep, he traded his sweater for a T-shirt. I don't remember his arms being this distracting. "Awhile. It's about five now. Magda said she'd be here in an hour or so after dropping my abuelo off. I'll wait with you until then."

I eat another spoonful. "You called my mom?"

He shrugs, the shirt lifting to reveal a sliver of stomach. "Wanted her to know you weren't feeling okay."

I watch pieces of chicken swim after carrots in my bowl. "Thanks for ruining your perfect attendance for me." Bryce wanted to win an award for that in fourth grade but lost by October when his dad took him to an overnight observatory upstate.

"Anything for a classmate." Through the haze of soup steam between us, Santiago looks ghostly. Which reminds me.

"You kept your key."

He swallows. Makes a sort of helpless shrug.

Mine is upstairs on my bedpost, growing cold without me. "Can I see it?"

He pulls the familiar key out of his back pocket and rests it on the counter. "Bryce threw his away. Yours is to a house no one even lives in anymore. It doesn't seem fair for me, of all of us, to still have the only functional one."

I touch it. The metal is warm from his body. "I'm glad you do."

His throat bobs. "Yeah?"

New Year's. The almost-accident. Dustin. I'm playing a dangerous game. I blame it on anything but myself. I'm not supposed to want like this anymore. "Yeah."

chapter thirty-two

SANTIAGO

I text Pa as I wait for Bea at her locker, typing with one hand and using the other to twirl the gift I perfectly stumbled upon earlier. She had to help her mom bring a bunch of festive goodies to the hospital, so Billy dropped me off this morning.

"Please tell me that isn't for me." Her voice startles me as my text goes through. Hot-pink eyebrows arch over her red-rimmed eyes, crimson eye shadow and mascara giving her a sickly appearance, though she's long recovered from whatever bug she had last week. I don't know why the look still makes my chest flutter.

"Happy Valentine's Day."

Bea takes the limp, wet rose from my hand. "Wow. It's beautiful," she deadpans.

"Peeled it off the parking lot concrete just for you," I coo. "I saw Dylan Abbott run over it first, but I think that gives it a little something special."

"I'm honored." She chucks the rose into her locker, where it lands flaccidly. "For safe-keeping," she singsongs, and slams the door. "I gotta go ask Mr. Duval something about my physics homework. I'm going to try to finish it during art."

I tsk. "No respect for the humanities."

"Says the aspirational STEM major. See you in calc?"

I nod, a little uncertain of where I'm going with ten minutes left until first bell, before making eye contact down the hall.

Olive stands in a circle with their friends, an excited exchange of gifts happening, though their attention is on me now. They smile, and it lifts the red heart painted on their cheek.

We've texted a few times since our date, mostly about innocuous stuff like the party Candace is planning for Bryce's upcoming birthday—which I've been doing my best to avoid thinking about—or if I need a ride to school. It's sweet of them to offer considering it's Whitney who would actually be picking me up, but I've consistently declined in favor of Bea.

As they leave their friends to approach me, chased by a chorus of *ooh*s and *aah*s, I remind myself what fucking day it is.

Olive's outstretched hands somehow make contact with mine, leaving a bundle of red tissue paper in my palms. "Open it." I listen to them, unearthing a small clay bird painted oddly familiar shades of blue and orange. "It's a little bird, almost like a birdie. Like from badminton?"

I turn the creature over in my hands and finally recognize my old team colors. Olive must've scrolled down on my Instagram. "Thank you," I finally manage, focusing my eyes on the small bird instead of Olive.

They clear their throat. "So, did you have any plans tonight?"

I wish I didn't have to do this.

"Um, Olive, I'm really grateful for the gift." I lift the bird and my gaze. "And I had fun the other night. But I think we might be better off as friends."

"Oh." Olive's brow furrows, but they don't look upset, just confused. "Did I do something wrong? I know bringing up Bryce and all of that might have been a lot, bu—"

"No, no, you're so good." I move to put the bird in my jacket pocket, and my thumbnail grazes the top of my other hand. I try to do it again but hit my knuckle instead. Okay, hit the knuckle again. Okay now the hand. I can feel the spot, but I keep missing it and tallying up new ones. Finally, I touch my nail to the back of my hand, dragging it lightly over and over until pink rises to the surface, and Olive's words from the other night are a distant memory.

"Are you okay?"

I look up at Olive's concerned face and see Bryce there, somehow. The key I've taken to wearing again burns straight through my shirt.

"Yeah, I just . . . I need to go call my dad." Finally, I get the bird into my pocket. "We're okay though, right? We can still be friends?"

"Of course," Olive says, and I almost believe them.

Pa doesn't answer my call before class, or the one I make during lunch in a bathroom stall, or the two more I make while walking to Bea's car after school while she drops something off at her locker. When a fifth goes to voicemail, I wait for the beep this time.

"Hey, Pa, it's me. Just calling to see how you're doing. Probably just busy today, serenading couples and whatnot." An unconvincing laugh halts my rambling. "So just, uh, shoot me a message whenever you're free. No rush, it's all good here. Okay, yeah, bye."

As I hang up, a hand touches my shoulder.

"Hey, stranger," Whitney says, swinging a bundle of fabric roses tied together with red ribbons in her hand. "Happy Valentine's Day."

"Hey, Whit," I say, eyes back on my phone as I type out another text to Pa. He's at practice or sleeping off a late-night show. Maybe he's on a date. He's not dead just because he isn't answering my calls or texts. That's not how this works.

"Hello?" Whitney's hand cuts through my vision, blocking my screen. "Are you listening? Do you want to come to dinner with us tonight?"

"Um—" I try to run back her offer, but I can't hear anything besides the memory of Abuelo calling to tell me Bryce died. I wonder who would call if Pa did.

A horn honks, and I look up to see Bea waiting in her car, flashing Whitney a quick glance.

"Sorry, I gotta go," I tell Whitney, shoving my phone into my pocket and trying not to focus too much on how my shoes crunch the parking lot snow so I don't need to replicate it as I make my way to Bea. "Have fun!"

Abuelo and I cook sancocho in honor of Abuela, filling the house with the scent of her favorite meal. She passed when I was too young to understand what I was losing, the closest person to a mom I'd probably ever have in my own family, but the older I get, the weirder it feels that I even knew her at all.

I'm serving Abuelo seconds when my phone starts ringing from where I left it on the table. "Who's calling?" I shout from the kitchen, nearly dropping Abuelo's bowl. "Is it Pa?"

"I don't have my glasses," he groans. "Alo? This is Santi's abuelo speaking."

I rush into the room, forgetting Abuelo's food. "Dámelo." He obliges, and I don't even check before slamming the phone to my ear. "Dad?"

"Um, no. Hey."

I step away and check the screen to confirm. "Hey, Eric," I say over the sound of my pounding heartbeat.

"Are you—Have you been getting my calls and texts? No one's heard from you for a while."

Eric is the only one who has called or texted, so I don't know which of us he thinks he's fooling. "I'm fine. Good luck with the team. I gotta go." I hang up in the middle of him speaking, leaving the echo of his interrupted apology ringing in my ears long into the night. When I wake up the next day, it's to a text from Pa.

All good here junior <3

chapter thirty-three

BEATRIZ

Mom clears her throat across the dining room table. "Is that Santiago?"

I look up from the texts I've apparently been smiling at.

Santiago: *did you know your initials spell out BAD*

Santiago: *much to think about,,,*

I lock my phone and set it aside. "Did I cook it all the way?" I ask instead of answering. The pasta is leftover from Valentine's Day. She had "plans" with "coworkers," so I took a crack at making a meal. I went a few minutes over the box time to be safe, but I think I passed some threshold. The texture isn't great.

"You did perfect, honey." Her hand finds that bracelet under her sleeve again. "So, um, Eileen called earlier. She wants to know if you're free to have lunch this weekend."

"It's not Thanksgiving."

"There's that brilliant mind I'm always bragging about." Her bracelet tinkles.

I want a clearer look at the charms and clasp and design. Its fragility. "So why does she want to have lunch?"

"Probably because she's your grandmother."

"Did she just learn this?"

"Beatriz."

"What?" I ask, and find I mean it. "What do you want from me here? What does she?"

Mom pauses, taking a good look at me. "I thought you'd been feeling better," she says. It's so fucking unfair that I want to rip the bracelet right off her wrist. "Are things with you and Santiago okay?"

It's funny she asks this at the precise moment in time when maybe we are actually somewhat okay. I didn't know how he'd take the news about me and Dustin, or me and Bryce for that matter, but he was kind. Furthering the point, neither of us has mentioned the kiss since it almost happened.

Still, I rub at my face. I spend hours every day getting the lines precise and the blending flawless. And right now, I want to peel it off and lay it on the table and ask my mom if I suddenly look happier. To sincerely understand if her comprehension of my mental well-being is as simple as me dressing one way or not sitting alone at lunch. For the smallest of seconds, I'm tempted to ask if she knows what a neurotransmitter is, but even I know when I'm crossing a line.

Shockingly, I like funerals. I've been to my fair share. Attended my dad's a few weeks before I was born. Then Santiago's abuela, Bryce's dad, Bryce. I don't remember the first two, but I guess I count them. Some part of me was there, and that's more than I can say of myself at Bryce's.

If I started crying at school, people would stare. There's a code to the world, one you see clearly after you've soaked yourself in enough grief that it clings to your clothes, your hair, your bones. There are times you cry, times you don't. Follow the script. Don't make it weird. Don't come back until we can't smell it on you. If it lingers, we will pretend not to notice.

I threw up at Bryce's funeral. It wouldn't have been so bad if it was in a trash can, but I didn't make it that far. Watching someone in choir robes mop up a puddle of my insides was the closest I came to checking back in to myself. That day, I was somewhere else. A place where the script didn't exist. Where I could throw up in a church lobby and no one would ask me why. What a privilege it is, I realized in the months after, to ache so publicly.

But there were still repercussions. The way mom is looking at me right now, like she's never stopped worrying that the next funeral I attend will be my own. I just wish her belief in the odds wasn't so contingent on me eating a fucking Caesar salad with a woman unfortunate enough to have been handed the role of my ancestor.

"I can do Sunday," I say. "At noon."

Mom smiles brightly. She heard the words exactly as I meant her to, like that is the only time I'm free this weekend. Like I have other things to do. A life to live.

The week tumbles by, and when Sunday arrives, I find myself sitting across from Eileen at a small bistro she chose a town over from Greensville. She offered to pick me up, but I imagined sitting in a car with her for thirty minutes and insisted I could just meet her.

Everything I assumed about my grandparents growing up had prepared me for their disdain when we finally met. Sure, they'd been paying for my and Mom's livelihoods for years, but I knew the lengths people go to alleviate themselves even momentarily from gnawing guilt.

Still, in her pearls that are probably real and little lilac cardigan that matches her purse, she smiles at me. Under my trench coat, I'm in a black baby-doll dress that doesn't reach my fingertips and thick spiderweb stockings on top of fleece-lined tights. The design complements the arachnid buckle on my platform loafers. When I walked through the bistro doors fifteen minutes ago, all Eileen did was tell me I look pretty and ask if I'm growing my hair out. It's getting long enough that the strands are beginning to fold over.

"So, Beatriz, have you heard back from schools yet?" Eileen sips her lemonade, then frowns at the light pink lipstick that clings to the glass.

"Not yet," I say. "Probably next month. Or April."

"Your mom tells me that you get excellent grades. A near-perfect GPA," she says. "Sounds like you have a good chance of getting into some impressive colleges."

I watch a dot of condensation trail down my untouched lemonade. "Maybe." I filled out the forms and wrote the essays, but if any of those schools want more than proof of intelligence, I won't have to worry about sinking four years and thousands of dollars just for the sake of pleasing my mom.

"Well, I wanted to discuss something I've already talked about with your mother." Eileen fluffs out her napkin, fiddling with it on her lap for a suspicious amount of time. "Your grandfather and I would like to help pay for your higher education."

"Oh."

"We don't expect to have any sway in your decision, and you don't even need to tell us before you commit to somewhere. It's just—" Her voice breaks off and when she lifts her head, tears glisten in her eyes. "We never got to see Andrew go to university."

My throat goes dry enough that when I swallow, it burns. My father's name is an occasion that requires pause. In the absence of words, though, the thoughts swarm.

I am being handed a future he never got. I am being handed a future, period. "I—thank you."

She nods, then fusses in her purse for a tissue and mirror. As she wipes under her eyes, she notices her patchy lipstick.

"I could recommend a brand that won't transfer so much," I say as she starts to reapply. "The formula is pretty matte, but you could coat it with a gloss if you want a different finish. The gloss will still transfer, but the base will stay better than the one you're using now."

Eileen slowly drops the hand holding the mirror and scans my face. "You know a lot about makeup, don't you?"

"I guess." A shyness I didn't think myself capable of anymore overtakes me.

She tucks her things away, placing her purse back on the empty chair beside her. "Have you ever considered pursuing a career in that?"

Yes. "Sometimes."

Eileen hums at this. But before the topic can continue toward dangerous honesty about my real aspirations, our food arrives. Twin sandwiches on beds of crisp lettuce. The bread is dry and my tomatoes are so soft that they plop out after the first bite, but it's a good meal. The remaining conversation is easy, simple things like Eileen's plans to redo their living room, whether I'd like to see their home in New Hampshire sometime, how my mom is doing. We hug when we're ready to leave, and I thank her for today.

Carefully, Eileen reaches for my hand and gives it a quick squeeze. "No, thank *you.*" Her gaze sweeps over my head. "I can really see your hair color now. You look so much like him."

In the car, I text Santiago.

Want to come over and shave my head?

"What if I cut you?"

Santiago shakes behind me, gripping my electric razor so tightly that his knuckles have gone white.

Lottie is curled up in my lap, but I set her on the ground. She'll leap away when the razor starts screaming anyway. "There's a protective shield."

With his free hand, he ghosts his fingers over the ends of my hair. "Do you ever forget it's this short?"

"It's not like hair has nerve endings." I twist around in the chair, flicking his where it brushes his shoulders. "No phantom limbs."

"I know *that.*"

"All right, then let's get this show on the road."

When I spin back around, I realize I am indeed waiting for the sensation of my hair whipping behind me and then settling. And when my eyes meet Santiago's in the mirror, for a second, I expect to see him joined by another face.

Bryce and I were both blond, his hair favoring the strawberry variety and mine the dirty. Once, during a particularly mischievous tween afternoon when his bad ideas had finally begun their transition from childhood curiosity gone wrong to utter chaos, he thought it would be fun to welcome Santiago into our club. Candace and Phil had just started dating, something I could've guessed from Candace's renewed liveliness even if I hadn't noticed her renewed bleached roots. So we were bored, reckless, supervised by a lovestruck adult, and had easy access to supplies. It was a recipe for a good story and bad hair. And I was always willing to do whatever would keep Bryce happy.

Fortunately for Santiago, Candace wandered into the unlocked bathroom as we were still unspooling tin foil and promptly shut us down. He'd been a willing and enthusiastic participant, but had we been successful, he'd also have likely been bald.

The irony of that being the desired outcome this time isn't entirely lost on me.

Santiago clicks the on button and flinches at the noise. After a deep breath, he places a hand on the back of my neck and glides the blade over a portion of my head.

He gasps as the hair showers down onto me and the floor. But his hand doesn't move.

"I know I asked for this, but your shock at not maiming me is mildly concerning," I say, dusting a few hairs off my nose.

"If I thought I'd make you look horrible, I wouldn't have agreed."

"You're suddenly quite confident."

"Not in myself," he says. "I don't think there's anything that could keep you from looking pretty."

The spot where his hand still holds me warms. I watch his face in the mirror for something—a wink, a smile, a joke in his eyes. But he's just focused on me. On not hurting me.

Gently, his touch shifts, tilting my head so when I look at my reflection in the mirror, I see myself from a slightly different angle.

chapter thirty-four

SANTIAGO

When people think of winter, at least in California, they usually think of December and January, all the holiday cheer and romanticized snow. Teetering on the edge of February has me wishing that was true here, my feet tired of their trained response to clomp down on the mats outside the main hall to free ice from my boots. I'm shaking off the last bit when Whitney pushes past me, her all-white ensemble a celebration of the exact weather I'm currently cursing.

"Hey!" I call, catching the closing door and following her down the stuffy hall. "How have you been? We haven't talked in a minute." Bea is particularly skilled at avoiding people, and in her presence, I've adopted the talent.

Whitney glares over her shoulder. "Seriously?"

And I thought the air outside was cold.

"Wait." Miraculously, she does, turning around with an iron-clad grip on her books, completely still against the wave of moving bodies surrounding us. "Are you mad at me? I'm sorry for being weird on Valentine's Day, I was just—"

Whitney runs her tongue over her teeth. "You're sorry for how you acted toward *me* on Valentine's Day?"

It takes me a second. "Is this about Olive?"

"They asked for Beatriz's permission," she states, then gives me a look when I don't catch on. "I didn't even know about the date until I came home from Valentine's dinner to them crying."

Guilt slices me in the gut. "They were crying?"

"Santiago, they've been in love with you since we were kids. Of course they cried."

"I thought I ended things amicably," I try. "It was just one date."

"Let me ask you just one thing, then."

"Okay."

"Did you ever feel a connection? Or did you only go to prove a point?"

"That's two things," I say to buy myself time. Whitney's eyes go venomous with impatience. "I don't know!" I wish I was a better liar right now, but I know what happens when I become one. "I thought maybe there could be something between us and I wanted to give it a shot."

Whitney shakes her head at me, seeing straight through my bullshit even better than Bea would. "They asked for Beatriz's permission," she repeats.

"And?"

"And Beatriz gave it." We both know what she means.

"You can't be mad at me for not liking your sibling."

"No, I can't," she agrees, then her eyes snag on my chest, and she laughs without humor. "But I can be mad at you for using them."

I tuck my escaped key back under my sweater and watch Whitney march off, finding Dustin and Abby at the end of the hall by their shared locker. I could be one of them, have a normal senior year where dating drama and petty fighting occupied most of my thoughts.

But I tried that life, and found that the only way I managed to live it was by being someone else. And here, in a town where everyone knows my losses, there's no opportunity to be anyone or anything more.

chapter thirty-five

I have a dream where Santiago gives me a hickey. I remember very little of the straightforward plot beyond that. I don't dream much these days by way of not sleeping much, so I guess beggars can't be choosers.

The second I picked him up for school, I felt like he could see it on my face. I should've just let him ride that ridiculous bike even if the snow is persevering into March.

We're in PE now, attempting to keep Hula-Hoops spinning around our waists for thirty seconds. I could list at least eleven activities that would be more nourishing to my physical health.

"Okay, this is bullshit." His hoop clatters to his feet. "How are you doing that so well?"

"Superior athleticism."

"Big talk from the girl who still hasn't beaten me at the mile."

I ignore his taunts and pick up speed. This is such a pointless activity. I wish it wasn't making me so happy. "I couldn't crush your ego like that."

"Because you've always given such concern to my ego."

And then my mind does it—it flashes to the dream. For a second I feel like I'm there again. His mouth, gentle and warm. My body, relaxed and content.

I wonder if he sees it on my face, but he isn't looking directly at me. His eyes are just off target.

"What are you doing?" I tug at the collar of my PE shirt where it hangs loose beneath my unzipped hoodie.

"Just admiring my work," he says softly.

I clamp my hand over my neck.

"It looks good, right?" He steps around me, appraising. "It's growing in pretty even."

Right. My haircut.

"You did great," I say, and turn so he won't see me blush.

We're doing partner work in English, so Santiago and I are tucked in a corner. Hunched over my packet on the rhetorical triangle, I look up to find him staring.

"Are you okay?" he asks, chewing on a pen. "You seem distracted today."

"Distracted by doing our assignment?" I lift my papers. "Your pen is going to burst in your mouth. Ink isn't great for the digestive system."

"Then it can be your turn to take care of me."

Memories of his cold touch on my feverish face, these ones real.

He taps his pen against my arm. "Where have you been all day?"

"Ew." I wipe away the saliva.

"Your mind keeps going somewhere else." He sets his chew toy down. "Would you like company over there?"

I'm a good liar. I could lie. "I had a weird dream." Or I could say that.

He nods me on.

"That's it."

"Okay, what was it about?"

"Doesn't matter."

"So it was *really* weird." He cracks his knuckles. I'm glad the classroom is busy with noise. "Like, plot holes galore, or like, *I didn't think my brain was capable of reaching this level of fucked up?*"

I give it a second. "Neither?"

"Hm." He tilts his head. "Well, consider my curiosity piqued, but I won't pry."

"Good." I go back to reading.

"Oh," he says, reading me instead. "I was in the dream."

"Yes." The word plops out of my mouth.

Santi clicks his tongue. "Do I have to be the awkward one who insists you elaborate on your definition of *weird* now?"

"Is someone else volunteering to do it?"

"I could probably convince Dustin." He nods to where Dustin's working with Abby across the room. "He owes me for stacking all the potato sacks yesterday while he and Courtney were fighting on the phone."

"Again," I note. He hums in agreement. "I feel bad for them."

"Same," he says. "But can we put a pin in that? We're getting sidetracked."

"This is such a lovely sidetrack, though. Other people's complicated relationships are way more fun to talk about than my own."

Fuck. Santiago catches the slip. "Weird dream." He ticks off on his fingers. "Me. Complicated relationships."

The funny thing about all of this is how easy it used to be to shut up and keep to myself. Years of work are down the drain because of him.

"Holy shit." Slowly, he grows a smile. "Did you have a sex dream about me?"

"Shh!" I hush him, smacking his arm. Luckily, the chatter in the room is steady enough that no one overheard.

Santi ducks into a whisper. "How good was the dream?"

"I wonder what it feels like to be friends with people who respect boundaries." I try to focus my eyes on our classwork.

"Oh cool, we're finally friends."

"I'm taking it back."

"You can't take back your sex dream, though."

"It wasn't a *sex* dream," I correct. "All you did was give me a hickey."

He frowns. "That's boring. Hickeys are tacky."

"Bitter you've never gotten one, huh?"

"Yup," he says, and shakes his head wistfully. "Only given them in dreams."

I groan into my notebook.

"It's fine. I'm hot, I get it. You don't need to be embarrassed."

I lift my head. "Olive has terrible taste."

"Apparently you do too."

I flip through my notes to busy my hands. After a minute of mediocre annotating, I glance back at him.

His full lips twitch as he reads, softly mouthing along. At a certain point, I know I'm practically ogling, but I can't seem to stop. Finally, he notices.

"Done with the Logos section? I still have a few paragraphs to go."

I blink at him. "You're just taking the dream thing in stride?"

He scribbles in the margins of his packet. Among the doodles, I spot a trio of keys. "It was just a dream, right?"

"Right," I confirm. So neither of us is going to mention the almost-kiss.

"Cool." He clears his throat. "Still down to come over Saturday to peer-review our essays? I'll make sure to finish the readings by then."

I nod and try to get back to work. But the words swim and stay hazy.

Dreams don't reveal our deepest desires. I think they're mostly random. Which is why when I do manage to sleep, I try to forget them.

Dreams of Bryce yelling at me. Dreams of Whitney and me actually crashing. Dreams where Mom can't hear me screaming for her. Dreams where it's Santiago in the coffin instead of Bryce. Where it's me instead of Bryce.

They're just dreams. I can lie to myself well enough.

chapter thirty-six

SANTIAGO

At work, I try to keep my mind occupied in whatever ways I can, even indulging in some ritualistic behavior just for the reprieve from my thoughts, bringing groceries out to cars, cleaning the same aisle three times and then a fourth for reasons, meticulously looking over the potentially expired apple shipment from this week, already bruised upon arrival and veering into inedible territory now.

Dustin joins me, poking at the sensitive green skin of one of the health-code violations. "Thank god we just got some fresh red ones." I'm too focused on using one of the apple's discolorations as a Rorschach test to reply. He shoulders me. "You good?"

I'm in the same position I put Bea in a few days ago, but I don't have the willpower to make Dustin work for the confession. "What does it mean if someone has a weird dream about you?"

He stops putting on his gloves. "Does this someone favor the color black?"

"I never said it was Beatriz."

"Name one other person in your life that would tell you they had a weird dream about you," Dustin says while scooping up rotten fruit. "Quickly."

"She didn't tell me outright, okay?"

Dustin gives me a look. "The two of you are really something."

Now would maybe be a good time to mention that I know he slept with Bea—if such a time exists—but I have no idea how to say it without sounding like I'm jealous of him. Which I guess I technically am, but not in the way he or anyone else would probably assume.

While I was being a terrible person in California, doing so well at lying about and escaping my old life that I'd managed to lie about and escape my old friendships too, Dustin was here showing her the smallest kindness. He knows her in a way I don't and never will, and I wish I could pry open whatever knowledge came with their intimacy without crossing the boundaries required to ask for a play-by-play.

His phone rings, but he doesn't stop with the apple cleanup.

"Spam?" I ask, though he hasn't checked to know.

"Close enough," he mumbles.

"Courtney?" I follow him to the back room, where he ties up the bag and trashes it along with his gloves.

"I just don't have time for her today." It takes effort to keep up with him as he marches back to the apples. "Do you know why she's mad at me now?" He lifts and drops a fresh crate onto the display. "She's mad that I partnered with Whitney instead of Rick for a history project. He scoffs as he lifts another crate. "*Whitney*! Who is her friend, supposedly, not to mention gay. But nope, I must have an ulterior motive for picking the girl with a perfect GPA over Rick, who I haven't even spoken to since Beatriz decked him." Dustin's panting by the time he finishes his rant. He drops the second crate and an apple tumbles out, falling and cracking open on the ground.

I pick up the flayed carcass, my hands immediately sticky with juice. He stares at it, and his breathing slows down. "I'll get the mop," I say.

"It's my mess," he replies.

We make our way back to the employee room for the mop I overused earlier. He carries it while I handle the small bucket.

"I'm sorry about Courtney," I say. He dips the mop in the water, painting the floor clean. "It sounds like she's pretty hard on you."

He shrugs. "If it was just about her insecurities, I could work with that. But the way she talks to me, always accusing me of doing something wrong . . . it makes me feel like shit."

"Do you want a hug?"

Dustin stops mopping. "Why?"

"Because you're having a rough time," I say. "And you might need one."

It's the right answer, apparently, because Dustin all but collapses into my arms. Eric and I weren't really huggers, and touching Bea has become a field of land mines, so I sink into the intimacy for a moment. Bryce and I used to hug so tightly, I thought our skin might meld together.

Dustin exhales against me and then pulls away, turning his face to the side where the light only emphasizes the shininess of his eyes.

"So are we going to finish the conversation about you and Beatriz?" he asks as he swipes at his nose.

"Nah. Forget I brought it up."

He laughs. "Like I said, the two of you are really something."

We're a lot of things, actually. And if anyone asked me to list them, I wouldn't know where to start, or stop.

When Bea comes over the next day, I let her inside and immediately flop onto my bed. "All right, let me see your paper first so I can determine just how much worse mine is."

She drops her bag on the floor, her chunky boots already abandoned in the foyer. "You think my failed material is any better than yours?"

"Obviously." Mrs. Ridley didn't give a single person a passing grade on our trolley-problem essays, hence all the ethos, Logos, and pathos readings this week. We've at least got the chance to peer-review, edit, and resubmit for a better score.

The trolley problem is fairly well-known. You're operating a lever that controls two tracks a trolley could take. On one is a single person you love, and on the other are five strangers. Which track do you make the trolley plow over? Who do you kill?

Even if Mrs. Ridley hadn't carefully outlined all the issues with my paper, I'd know where I went wrong. We were supposed to defend our decision, but I couldn't make one, so I decided to do nothing.

Whatever track the trolley was already on, I'd let it proceed that way. Not because it followed the path of fate, allowing what would've happened in my absence to be fulfilled by the universe, but because by the time I made it to my concluding paragraph, I'd already torn all the cuticles on both my hands, rubbed a hole through the toe of my sock, and come close to crying enough times that typing an incoherent two-sentence conclusion choosing inaction felt like the only thing that would keep me breathing.

"Have at it," Bea says, startling me. "I'm gonna use the bathroom."

Her backpack is a nightmare, with enough squished papers on the bottom you'd think something was nesting in there. Luckily, this paper is an easy find, clinging to the cover of her English notebook for dear life.

I skim, mostly because Bea uses words that belong in thesauruses rather than a seventeen-year-old's vocabulary and this entire prompt is still making me queasy. But there's a shift in tone at the end, noticeable even without the big red circle around it from Mrs. Ridley's pen.

Playing God is for the politicians, not me. Realizing you're responsible for someone's preventable death is suffocating enough that the trolley may as well crush me instead. I'd become a penny on the tracks before I'd choose who lives and who dies.

Mrs. Ridley draws arrows to earlier points Bea made, directing her to what stances she thinks she could've defended better. It's all so chaotic, the lines and demands and enforced morals, all of it masking the panic permeating from Bea's words. I can practically see her standing before the switch, the world gone frantic around her, before she steps on the tracks herself.

And me, wandering away from it all, letting the screams swallow me whole.

chapter thirty-seven

BEATRIZ

"I hate this place," I groan as Santiago and I enter the local mall. The air outside was biting at my tights-covered legs where they peek out of my long skirt's slit. Now, my platform loafers glisten with melted snow beside a pair of weatherworn Docs.

Santiago opens his mouth, and I lift my hand to stop him. "Whatever sarcastic joke you were going to make about me being not like other girls can remain unsaid."

He grins. I have the oddest desire to pet him, to stick my hands in his hair and slide my fingers over his scalp.

I flinch and turn away, focusing my eyes on the nearest kiosk of jewelry.

"These look very your style," Santiago says, flicking a gold chain covered in hearts. I make a face. "Kidding. I know you're a silver girl."

As he walks onward, I run my fingers over my gunmetal earrings. Then graze the key under my shirt. Bryce's, and golden.

"So where exactly are we going?" Santi's eyes dance across the massive building. We had to drive almost an hour to get here. Calling it local is generous, but generosity is required when there are no actual malls in Greensville.

"Annie's Gifts and Jewelry," I recite. "My mom said to pick out a nice frame."

She has to work tomorrow night during the "celebration of Bryce's life" that Candace is throwing for what would've been his eighteenth birthday, so she's making up for it by framing a cute picture she found of their family at Candace and Phil's wedding. Bryce was the best man and Whitney was the maid of honor, the two of them comically overdressed for a pair of eleven-year-olds. Olive begged to wear a suit like Bryce and opted for ring bearer over flower girl, but their jacket is tied around their waist in the photo, the buttons on their sleeve cuffs undone.

No one is looking at the camera. Candace's gentle smile of patience for her kids is as bright and white as her sensible gown. Phil watches her with enough admiration and devotion that I ache a little every time I glance at the photo. The kids look like kids in every shot from that day, dozens of goofy, far-off grins followed by adolescent scowling after the posing took more than five minutes. But this is the only picture where Phil and Candace look like kids too.

"Oh, bless me, is that really you two?"

Santiago and I spin around to see the most random blast from the past: our fifth-grade teacher, Mrs. Heather. She's aged, as we all have. Time is shown on her in wrinkles and sun spots, while on us, it's mainly height and hair length.

Her pale skin glows under the mall's fluorescent lighting as she walks over. "Is that really Santiago Espinosa and Beatrice Dougherty?"

"Sort of," Santiago murmurs.

"I haven't seen you kids in years," she coos. I'm surprised she even recognized us. "Oh gosh, look at how you two have grown."

We smile politely. I wait for Santiago to speak.

"I'm sure you're used to seeing your students get older. You've taught so many classes over the years," he says. And in a place like this, running into them is inevitable.

She sighs deeply. I've heard the sigh a million times. Sometimes they mean it. Sometimes they just need a second to let the sadness wash over them, to pull it back to the surface and remember what once was shocking and heartbreaking and tragic but is now just a memory. A thing you think about around the holidays or when someone tells a certain story. *How sad*, they'll sigh. Because when it isn't your tragedy, what else is there to do? What else is there to say?

"I wish that were true," Mrs. Heather says, voice wobbling more than her ankles in her kitten heels. "But you two know more than I do just how devastating it is that we don't see Bryce walking around here anymore." She tsks, shaking her head. Her graying curls, sealed with hairspray, barely move.

"Yeah," Santiago says. Because, again, what else is there.

"He would be so happy, though, seeing the two of you smiling like this. Enjoying your lives." Her eyes go glassy. "It's good to see you pushing forward, moving on. You can't let the sad things hold you back, nope. Have to live every single day with a positive attitude, that's what I always say." Softly, almost to herself, she adds, "I wish I could have reminded him of that."

"Definitely would've saved his life," I say. Santiago glares at me while Mrs. Heather smiles. "They should put you on national news. We'd have depression and suicide solved by dinner."

Her smile drops. "I'll let you get on with your afternoon." She pulls her purse to her chest and teeters away, her heels too loud and plastic on these floors.

I head off to find the fucking store. I don't wait to see if Santiago is following.

He catches up as I storm into the gift shop.

I lift the closest frame without looking at it. "This one's fine."

Santiago pulls it from my hand, slowly turning it over. It's covered in soccer balls. "Bryce hated soccer. He just pretended to like it that one time to impress my cousin." Santiago bumps my shoulder lightly. I soften, the smallest touch enough to remind me that I'm not alone here, the briefest anecdote enough to remind me that Bryce was a person outside of what strangers think they knew about him and his pain.

Carefully, Santiago returns my selection. "Do you want to talk about it?"

"We're buying our dead best friend's family a present for what should be his eighteenth birthday. What's there to say?"

He rubs at his chest, and I see the faint outline of a key under his shirt. I haven't asked him about it since the day he used it to take care of me. "Go sit somewhere, I can find a frame. Consider it my penance. You've dealt with those speeches way more than I have."

"Santiago."

"Bea," he pleads, inviting me in on the hurt he felt hearing those words too. Someone deciding one moment of our joy was evidence that we've moved on. As if waking up every morning still breathing, older than he'll ever be, isn't enough to make me sick with guilt. "Let me do something for my friend."

Santi finds me outside the store five minutes later, a beautiful, sunset-orange frame in his hands. When he passes it to me, our fingers brush, and instead of pulling away, I embrace the moment and his palm. Then we're holding hands. And we leave the mall like that, not having to talk about it further.

chapter thirty-eight

SANTIAGO

I used to relish days at Bryce's house, welcoming every time I got to feel like I had real adults in my life who would behave the way I expected parents to. Candace was a stickler for manners and chores, never allowing Bryce and me to get away with the shenanigans that Abuelo often indulged us in and Magda was often entertained by. Even Bryce's dad was more structured than anyone in my home, always asking me, Bea, and Bryce to help rake leaves, shovel snow, or pick weeds, depending on the season.

Bryce's house obviously doesn't elicit the same feelings anymore, case in point when Candace opens the door to the home I've only been in once—the night of Whitney's party—and sours at the sight of me and Bea.

"Hi, Mrs. Ocampo," I say, because calling her by her first name has always been a rebellious act Bea and I save for private conversations and our own heads. Though I never quite got used to referring to her as an Ocampo instead of a Dawson, like Bryce and his dad. It's funny that my adolescent memories still tag her as

Bryce's Mom more than anything else when I see so much of her in Whitney these days.

"So sweet with the formalities," Candace says without offering a casual substitute or acknowledging Bea. "Is your grandfather well?"

"Yeah, he's actually celebrating his friend's ninetieth birthday at the center tonight, or he would've been here."

Candace's jaw tightens just a fraction. Bryce barely made it past fifteen, and someone out there is celebrating a life six times as long. It's a privilege, really, to live long enough to not recognize your baby pictures in the mirror.

We ditch our shoes by the front door, and I realize that no one did the same at Whitney's party. I imagine she was too fucked up to care at the time. I don't envy whatever that cleanup looked like.

Candace leads us through the foyer and into the living room. "And your father? How is his music and all of that?" she asks over her shoulder, waving at someone we pass.

"He's good," I say, though the last text I got from him was over a week ago and nothing more than a blurry selfie of him and his bandmates. In the dim light and flurry of movement, it almost looked like a photo of me.

Bea lightly touches my hand before reaching into her bag to retrieve the wrapped frame. Magda, always one for arts and crafts between hectic shifts like the one keeping her from this party, packaged it nicely in crisp wrapping paper and a perfect bow. "This is from my mom."

Candace takes the gift carefully, eyes glazing straight over Bea. "I'll be sure to give her a call."

Bea nods awkwardly. I realize this is the first conversation of theirs I've witnessed since the funeral. Even then, it was just

Candace telling someone to clean up Bea's vomit before I was rightfully accosted and then wrongfully disappeared.

"The house looks really nice," Bea says, an unfamiliar modulation to her voice but one clearly lacking sarcasm.

Candace's smile is tight-lipped. "Thank you for taking the time to be here." It's formal, even for her, and she heads for the center of the room without further comment.

I watch the air go back into Bea's lungs.

"I didn't realize things were so tense between the two of you," I admit.

Bea blinks. Today her eyebrows are bright orange, though there isn't a hint of color on the rest of her. "She's allowed to speak to me however she wants. Especially today."

Before I can respond, Candace taps a knife to a champagne flute in front of the fireplace. "If you'd all indulge me, I'd like to take a moment to acknowledge the incredible young man we are here to celebrate tonight." The last of the chatter in the house quiets, and Bea and I have to move forward as stray guests enter from the other rooms.

"Bryce was our shining, joyful boy," Candace says, admirably stable. "He was such a brilliant mind. You all know how much he loved the stars. I'm convinced he would've been the first astronaut to reach Mars if he—" She catches herself, but the unspoken words are worse than if she'd just continued the sentence. The crowd shifts uncomfortably at this moment of polished and polite grief suddenly gone unkempt.

Candace clears her throat and coats her face with a grin. "Well, thank you all for coming to celebrate him. I know he is smiling down on each and every one of you."

"Yeah, I'm sure he's loving this, Mom," Whitney moans. Bea

and I both startle as we register her beside us. She and Bea share a small smile, almost by accident, but look back to Candace as everyone joins her in lifting their drinks.

Olive also appears, hands gripping four flutes of sparkling gold liquid. "Here."

"Champagne?" Bea asks, sniffing.

"Apple cider," Olive corrects. Whitney shrugs, taking a small sip. Bea slaps her hand away, nodding toward Candace.

"To our boy, Bryce. I'll never understand losing him." Candace lifts her glass impossibly higher. "Cheers."

"Cheers," Bea, Whitney, Olive, and I say at the same time, and we down our drinks.

"Well, we said we'd be here for the toast, and that's over, so." Olive loosely drops their glass onto a side table, and I have to rush over to catch it before it crashes to the floor. When I turn around, Whitney is gone too.

Bea carefully places her glass down beside Olive's. "I'd also like to run and hide."

"I'll take Olive, you take Whitney?" I offer, and am surprised when she nods without argument. Maybe we both have apologies to give tonight.

Finding Olive again is quick. I think about the first place I'd go if I was drowning in thoughts of Bryce during a party here, then grab my shoes and try the first place I did go under those circumstances.

"Hey." I sit down on the frozen lounge chair next to Olive's. "Are you okay?"

They turn toward me, eyes bordered by clumpy, tear-streaked mascara. "It's just a lot in there."

The festivities are cheerful in the same way some candy is nauseatingly sweet. It's not like tonight requires a TED Talk on mental health, but the evening feels devoid of any acknowledgement of Bryce's cause of death.

Growing up, Bryce's birthdays were epic. For his eighth birthday, we drove to a massive laser-tag place where Magda forged Pa's signature so I could play. On his ninth birthday, his dad took me, Bea, and Bryce to a traveling circus with a petting zoo, where Bryce made sure we said hello to every single animal, naming them all as we went. By his tenth birthday, his dad was in the final stretches of his life, so we decorated the house with balloons and streamers and Silly String. Bea helped Bryce's dad draw a cake on the back of his shiny, bald head, and it was the first and only time I saw Bryce cry tears of joy.

The next year, we had an all-night movie marathon that felt oddly like this party. Lights stayed off for our viewing experience, but the halls were lined with sweet candles that masked the scent of death clinging to the walls, or at least tried to.

Given that history, it feels odd to ask, "Are Bryce's birthdays normally like this?"

Olive wipes their nose with their sweater sleeve. "The first year, we had a dinner that was just us and visited the cemetery. Last year, she invited our whole family though, including people from my dad's side who only saw Bryce at the wedding." They messily brush their bangs off their face. "It feels weird having all those people in there."

"Yeah." I rub my chilled hands together. I hardly recognized most of the guests, which is rare in this town. "Candace probably just doesn't want to be alone."

Olive laughs, and it sounds so much like Whitney, I almost do a double take. "No, she doesn't want any of us to be sad."

"Isn't that a good thing?"

"She doesn't want any of us to be sad, ever," they clarify. "Did you know we've never done anything like this for Bryce's dad? Not even when Bryce was alive."

Bryce, smiling, laughing, joking. A boy who was never allowed to be sad, which didn't make his sadness disappear—it just made it invisible.

Olive takes a deep breath, then gets up from their chair. "We should go back inside."

I follow them, but before we reenter, I place a hand on their shoulder. "We're good, right? Whitney said—"

"Whitney says a lot of things," they interrupt, nudging me off. "If she's upset with you, I doubt it really has to do with me. You and I are fine."

They step inside before I can reply, or pretend to fully believe them.

chapter thirty-nine

BEATRIZ

I swore I saw Candace downstairs five seconds ago, but she appears to have spawned in the upstairs hallway. With her palm pressed to a portrait of six-year-old Bryce, she hasn't yet noticed me.

"He hated this photo," she says, disproving my assumption.

I swallow and join her. I struggle to make eye contact with Bryce, so I focus on his hair instead. So bright and bouncy. So unlike the greasy, unwashed strands that marked his final year. "Everyone hates their baby photos."

"He hated a lot of things near the end."

My jaw locks and I press my teeth together hard enough that the tears can't fully spring forth.

Candace drops her hand and sighs. "Enjoy the party." I watch her make her way back to the festivities below, her smile growing with each step until it almost looks real. It reminds me of Bryce enough that I'm momentarily transfixed. But my feelings are easier to ignore when I remember what I'm here for.

I knock lightly on Whitney's door. She doesn't respond. "You should turn your volume down if you want to hide."

Her video pauses and I hear her toss her phone. "Just come in."

My hand finds the light switch easily, as it always did. I close the familiar door behind me. "This isn't very hostly of you."

"Bite me," she says from her bed. Her fancy earrings are discarded on the floor alongside her tiny cardigan. She's lying in a camisole and flared out skirt, socks rolled down to her ankles. Her hair looks mussed.

Clearing my throat, I perch on her desk.

She sits up so her skirt is less revealing. "Is this where I thank you for checking in on me?"

"No, but you can call us even for banning me from your birthday."

She scoffs. "You showed up anyway."

"Never could resist a good party."

And then we're just sitting in her room. Not fighting, but not friends. Not anything else either.

"Where's your better half?" Her voice is artificially sweet as she flops back onto her pillows.

It takes all my self-control not to say he's in a grave. "Santiago's looking for Olive." I swear I see a flash of disappointment pass her face. I guess I'd want Santiago for comfort over me too. "It feels pointless to ask if you're okay."

"Then don't," she snaps. A beat passes before she shyly pats the bed beside her.

I've learned and keep to my side. The chunk of space between us is so big, it's almost comical. I turn my head to look at her. She's already looking at me.

"Are you and Santiago really not—?" Her question trails off. This again.

I open my mouth to lie, but a knock interrupts us.

"What's the secret phrase?" Whitney shouts.

Santiago's lips squeeze through the cracked door. "Bryce would've despised that massive collage of him downstairs."

Whitney smiles. "You may enter."

He swings the door open fully, revealing Olive behind him. "I brought company."

"Oh good, we're starting our own *Breakfast Club*," I deadpan.

Olive crawls into the space between me and Whitney while Santi sits below Whitney's feet.

"Let the meeting of the only people who know what Bryce actually would have wanted for his birthday celebration commence," Olive says, clapping twice. I can't help but smile.

"He'd be eighteen today, so he'd want to buy a lotto ticket," Whitney starts.

My smile drops. I didn't think we were really going to discuss it.

"And he'd totally go get a piercing! But before he went home, he'd pull it out and hide the jewelry in one of those shoe pockets he always carved into his soles," Olive adds.

"I'd rag on him for being up for the draft now," Santiago says, mock saluting. I sort of hate him for playing along.

"The ego he'd have over being eighteen before you." Whitney points her toe at me. My birthday is a couple weeks away. I'll be older than my dad soon, and I've been evicting that thought from my mind every time it tries to move in. I've already been betraying Bryce for years as it is.

"He'd go buy an R-rated movie ticket," Olive continues, giggling. "But then take me to see whatever new animated kids' movie was showing."

Whitney and Santiago laugh along, then they all turn to me. Everyone expects me to like this game.

The Bryce they're talking about is happy. He loves his schemes and goofy plans. He makes summer bucket lists and memorizes the stars. He includes his little stepsibling in everything, even when Whitney doesn't want them involved. He teases me about my birthday, for being slightly younger, but is already figuring out what to get me.

I can't do this.

"I need to go to the bathroom."

Whitney's face falls.

"Bea, wait—" Santiago starts, but I'm already gone.

This house may not be the one Bryce grew up in, but it was also second nature to me once. I make it to the bathroom with ease. I lock the door behind me just in time to sink to the floor.

The air is tight in my chest, each breath as poisonous and unhelpful as the last. I feel like someone is squeezing my insides, and even if I know I will be fine, the ever-present fear that this could actually kill me still comes rushing to the surface.

Bryce should be here, celebrating his birthday in all those ways everyone wishes he could. He'd make inappropriate comments about dating me as a younger woman, but he'd want a cake that was laughably childish—maybe something with clowns or an elaborate frosting volcano adorned with plastic dinosaurs. He'd ask us to go somewhere like the cheap, preteen-riddled arcade attached to the one movie theatre in town or the indoor mini-golf place east of here that has only ten holes and smells like rubber, just so he could feel like a kid again for a bit. But after, we would get those lotto tickets and piercings. He'd ask me to take pictures of him, Santi, and Whitney with their new matching earrings before doing what Olive said and yanking them out so Candace would never know.

He'd wear something warm that flattered the fire in his hair, and he would show up five minutes late for the family dinner Candace made for him, but he'd give her that winning smile and she'd let him off the hook because that's her son. That's her baby boy. That's her kid who's an adult now, and wow, we can't believe he made it through everything to get here.

The last birthday he had on this planet, he spent with me and a tin of sprinkled cupcakes I overbaked. A few people stopped by our table at lunch to take some, but no one stuck around long enough to sing him "Happy Birthday." Candace said their dinner was family only, so I didn't attend, and he later told me she made the exact type of salmon he always reminded her he hated. He didn't say anything this time, just swallowed down every dry bite.

Someone is crying. It's heavy and raspy and wet and. Oh. It's me.

It's me and I can't get myself to stop and the sobs rack my body so much that I have to plant one hand on the ground and another on my chest just to keep from tipping over. Beneath my palm, my heart slams with an unsteady violence.

I crawl toward the sink and fumble around until I hit the faucet and get the water running. I'm still crying, and somehow I'm doing this too.

Scooping cold water into my hand, I splash it over my head.

The cold shocks my spine as it slips down my neck. There's very little hair to intercept it. In and out. In and out. In and out.

The air is smoother. My lungs aren't collapsing.

I'm on the floor. I'm breathing. I'm alive.

Fuck, I'm alive.

I stumble my way to standing and lean against the wall until I'm sure I won't fall over. My cheeks are wet, but my makeup hasn't budged. I'm not surprised. I got good at it for a reason.

"Bea?" Santi's muffled behind the door. "Whitney told me I should give you a minute, but I'm here if you want company."

I flush the toilet and run the sink as I blot my face. I should probably actually change my pad, but I can't be gone any longer. I dry my hands and hair on Whitney's towel. At least the water won't show on my black clothes.

When I swing the door open, Santiago steps back.

"What's up?"

He squints at me. "You good?"

"Fine."

Please let me lie to you. I do it every day.

"Okay," he says. It's a familiar feeling, being grateful for getting what I asked for and disappointed for not getting what I want. "Candace is calling everyone for cake."

I take a deep breath under the guise of annoyance. "If she makes us sing to Bryce, I will start doing my own screamo rendition." My voice comes out surprisingly steady.

"I'll do your calc homework for a week if you grace us with that."

I shut off the bathroom light and glide past him. My heart flutters treacherously from the second of proximity, or maybe it's the anxiety lingering. I don't know which I'd prefer. "I have a higher grade than you. That isn't motivation."

He rolls his eyes but smiles. I wish I didn't love making him smile so much. "Just for that, I'm telling Candace you want to give a speech."

Thankfully, Candace doesn't make us sing for Bryce. A pity, because I would actually love to scream.

I glance around our little group. We're silent compared to the rest of the party. Olive picks at frosting with the tip of their fork. Whitney ate her slice already and has moved on to texting Abby. I can see the screen from here. Santiago mashed his piece, leaving him with a plate of blue-and-brown goo. If I were outside of myself, I'd see me holding a slice with one bite of frosting taken out of it, just enough to dye my tongue.

I wonder how much of a say we really have in our loneliness. Solitude in crowded rooms isn't as poetic as it sounds. Most of the time, it's just inescapable. But this solitude is layered. We're all alone here, but we're alone together.

chapter forty

SANTIAGO

Miraculously, after three years of existing without seasonal changes more tangible than a twenty-degree increase or decrease, I survive a Vermont winter. The snow thaws, the April air warms, and I have no excuse not to ride my bike around town other than the small smile Bea gives me every morning when she sees me emerging from my house. Which is to say the bike hasn't left the garage, and I need someone to smack me over the head with one of the dozens of newspapers cluttering our foyer since Abuelo refuses to cancel his subscriptions.

Equally as astonishing is how Olive and I manage to fall back into our own rhythm after Bryce's birthday, with today being no exception as they lean over their physics homework on the stool I usually sit on when working the register.

"You know my parents aren't paying you to use this place as a tutoring center, right?" Abby asks as she glides a mop under our quickly raised feet.

"I can help you with your homework too," I offer.

Abby leans on the mop handle. "What makes you think I need help?"

"That's her way of saying Whitney already helps her," Olive notes without looking up, blanching when they do. "I'm kidding! I've seen your report card." They nod to the bulletin board at the front of the store boasting free wood, babysitting services, an open mic night at the library, and Abby's and Dustin's report cards, both impressive in their own right.

"I like it when you're snippy," Abby says to Olive, then turns to me. "I don't actually mind, I'm just obligated to give you a hard time."

It's a casual enough comment that I could leave it be, but I've always been the type to pick at my scabs even when I know nothing but bleeding will come from it. I thought after Bryce's birthday, both Ocampo siblings were cool with me again. "Why?"

Abby shrugs, face impartial, then goes back to mopping, only pausing to answer her phone when it dings. The beam on her face tells me whatever she just received is from Whitney, whether it's good news or bad news or a selfie or something as benign as Whitney sharing what she's eating for a snack. I know because I've seen it a million times this year, a public declaration of something that I think is still meant to be private. But I recognize it in a different sense, having seen it just this morning on another face as I walked out my front door.

chapter forty-one

Mom thinks she wakes me up for my eighteenth birthday with breakfast in bed. Of course, I've been up for hours. Even back when I slept regularly, my dreams were intolerable around my birthday. One year, I dreamt my dad showed up to my party. He hadn't died, just faked it, and he was here to apologize. But when I opened my mouth to forgive him, all I could do was scream.

Since Bryce died, I know they'll just be about him.

I blow out the single lit candle atop the stack of syrup-soaked pancakes. "Gracias, Mami." Today is about her too.

Mom sighs. "You didn't make a wish."

"I'm just fast."

She rolls her eyes. "You can try again with your real cake tomorrow." I'm glad she doesn't sound too guilty about working tonight. "There's a surprise downstairs for you." Then she leaves me to eat and get ready for my big day. Sixteen and seventeen fell respectively on a Saturday and Sunday. But I have to go to school for eighteen.

My makeup isn't any more special than usual. Thick black eyeliner with an extra stem curving down from the wing. Smoke it out with black shadow. Gray blush and contour. Pencil in my brows straight, no arch or tail. The liner is bold enough, it would get too busy otherwise. Dark blue lipstick that looks black unless I'm standing in the sunlight, with a touch of silver glitter on my Cupid's bow and inner corners.

Spiked choker. Silver hoops increasing in size down my ears. Matching silver rings in my face. Black leather cuff, right wrist. Long, black, lace smock dress, platform boots with all the buckles.

I go downstairs to the kitchen. Before finishing my lipstick, I ate every last bite of the sticky, sweet breakfast. It made me feel like a good daughter.

"Surprise!" Santiago springs up from behind the counter.

I shout and nearly drop my plate.

Santiago laughs, unfazed. "Happy birthday, Bumble-bea."

"Does eighteen come with new nicknames?" I deadpan over the sound of my racing heart.

"As your elder, I am delighted to inform you that it does." He tries to hand me a sparkling pink tiara I've seen in the decoration aisle of the grocery store. "For you."

I place my plate in the sink. "There's no way in hell I'm wearing that."

"Then it's a good thing we're not in hell." He steps up to me. His hair is still damp from the shower. Carefully, he slides the tiara onto my head. Shivers erupt down my spine, but I hold myself completely still. I feel his cool breath on my cheek as he turns my chin slightly to make sure the band is secured behind my ear. Finally, he smiles, deep enough that his eyes crinkle just so at the corners. "Perfect."

Dizzily, I step back, giving him enough time to grab his phone and snap a photo.

"Hey!"

He flashes the blurry shot at me. My eyes look like full moons and my lips are scowling in a dark smear across my face. The hilarity of my expression and outfit and tiara all combined isn't lost on me.

"For the photo album," he whispers, winking as he glides to the foyer.

My heart hasn't calmed. My hands sweat, my breath shakes. I don't know how to handle feeling these things when they aren't caused by something bad. It would almost be easier if I hated this all.

I do take off the tiara before we walk into school. Santiago pretends to pout, but it's clear he's surprised I even indulged him for the whole car ride.

When I was little, Mom would bake enough cupcakes for my entire class. I'd always have something like balloons or a sash or a funky felt hat in the shape of a cake waiting for me, courtesy of Santiago and Bryce. For the past two years, Whitney's left me cards in my locker. I try not to look or feel deflated when I open it today and nothing tumbles out.

"So I was thinking you could come over to my house for dinner?" Santiago says. He leans against our row of lockers, twirling a pen around his long fingers. After this morning, it's enough to make eye contact difficult.

I tug my history textbook out of my backpack. "Why?"

He stays focused on the pen. "I don't know. It's almost like it's your birthday or something."

I swat his hand so he drops his makeshift toy. He gives me an annoyed look that endears me to him all over again.

"Fine," I say. "Only because my mom is working. But no surprises. I hate surprises."

"I was a surprise." He picks up the pen.

"To me in the fall or to your parents?"

He lightly flicks my chin with the dirty pen. "You're lucky it's your birthday."

The rest of the day goes by slowly and unceremoniously. Olive wishes me a happy birthday in PE and their friends start chorusing the sentiment until I wave them off so our whole class doesn't catch on. The caf serves potato wedges, which Santiago says is a sign since they're my "favorite." We get our revised trolley-problem papers back, but there isn't a grade on mine. Only a note written on the last page to see Ridley after school.

When class ends, I tell Santiago to wait for me by my car, then approach Ridley.

"You wanted to talk to me?" I ask, dropping into the seat beside her desk.

She takes off her glasses. "Yes. I was surprised to see you didn't make any revisions to your paper, even after Santiago left very helpful suggestions. You laid the groundwork for some convincing arguments but threw them all away in the end for a decision that wouldn't even stop the trolley from killing anyone."

"I made a choice, and I stand by it."

"Are you sure?"

"What do you mean?" I hand over my paper. "I chose myself."

"You did in the final paragraph." She flips through the essay. "But the rest of your paper isn't in agreement. You acknowledge a Logos argument, knowing you'd be legally liable if someone got hurt due to your involvement. You acknowledge the ethics and morals of prioritizing certain lives over others. You took great clinical care to look at the problem from every possible angle, but it was only in your conclusion that you seemed to take an actual stance, just without any evidence."

"I have to provide evidence when it comes to my personal choices?"

A smile flickers over her face. I don't speak in class unless I'm called on. "You know you have a nearly perfect grade, right?"

I nod, not needing to perform any false modesty. I've always been good at school. Freshman year was the only time I really struggled with it. Doing Bryce's homework and my own took up a lot of time, but he would've failed otherwise. People would've known there was something wrong if I hadn't stepped in.

"If you don't revise this paper or at least explain to me why you don't think you need to, that perfection won't hold."

Dropping the plus after my A wouldn't end me. I could get up and leave.

"The trolley problem isn't real," I say instead. "It's for people who've never actually been in that type of situation. They get to imagine themselves as a tragic hero—either for saving someone they love and taking on the burden of being responsible for others' deaths, or for saving strangers knowing they sacrificed someone they love to do it." I'm not trying to play this card. It isn't even a card, just the truth. "Death isn't hypothetical to me."

Ridley nods at this, then picks up a pen and scribbles something. She hands my essay back. "Thank you, Beatriz."

On my way to meet Santiago at my car, I check it. She crossed out her previous note, replacing it with a *100* and a new comment.

I lost my sister when I was your age. I'd pick the tracks too.

We stop at the grocery store to pick up stuff for Señor Espinosa. I twirl a tin of tomato soup with my finger while Santiago scours the canned corn. His quick hands adjust them with almost imperceptible results as he looks, a nervous tic on his lips. I don't comment on it.

Dustin and Abby's mom walks by on her way to restock the dairy items. I notice their dad at the register.

"Guess Dustin isn't working today," I say.

"Disappointed?" His eyes stay on the corn, but he's smirking.

"I could ask you the same thing."

Now he faces me. "You seem awfully sure that I can't have platonic feelings for the hot people in my life."

"Not sure how platonic it is to refer to them as hot."

"Very platonic," he says, and finally picks a can. It clunks into his shopping basket. "If you're jealous I have other friends, though . . ."

"I think bullying me on my birthday is illegal." I push the tomato tin back where I found it. Santiago shifts it as we pass. "And I think I'm good on the friend front."

"Because the perfect one you already have is enough?" He bats his long lashes. I don't encourage him with a response, but I know my smile undercuts the effort.

Santi and I load our arms with groceries so we won't have to take a second trip up his front yard. Several cars were parked a few houses down, more so than usual for a random weekday.

He unlocks the door as it hits me. One of those cars was Whitney's.

"Surprise!" voices shout as a flash attacks my eyes. I drop the groceries, the can of corn Santiago so carefully selected bursting onto the porch.

Whitney, Olive, Dustin, Abby, and Señor Espinosa stand in the living room. I look from them to the foyer, where Mom crouches with a camera, evidently not at work.

Santiago sets down his bags to pick up everything that fell out of mine. I should be helping or at least saying something. Every word dies on my tongue, anger and gratitude and guilt and betrayal all lodged in my throat. The flash's afterimage is impossible to ignore. The next thing I know, I'm down the hall and slamming Santiago's bedroom door behind me.

Seconds later, it reopens. "If it helps, it wasn't my idea."

"This is your house."

"And your mom is a very persuasive woman."

The only reason I don't scrub my face in frustration is knowing I'd have to walk around without coverage for the rest of the night. "A warning would've been nice." I drop onto Santiago's bed.

He joins me. "If you want to bail, I've got a window."

The look on Mom's face when she snapped that photo lingers. "I can't."

His fingers trace a star on my knee. Through the fabric of my dress, I feel the warmth of his touch. "It's your birthday. You can do whatever you want."

I can't, actually. Once upon a time, I liked birthday parties. They were a rare opportunity for me to celebrate existing instead of rue it. If I could do whatever I want, I'd be her again.

"He'd have made me wear that felt cake hat all day," I say. Santiago's hand stalls. "Now I'm older than him." I let the pronoun substitute two names.

"Why does it sound like you're apologizing for that?" he asks.

I sigh, the ever-present weight on my chest not lifting. It and my key feel heavier today.

"We should go back out there," I whisper. His eyes search my face for something. Then, gently, he nods. His hand leaves my knee, and I wish, not for the first time, that he stayed.

We all pretend I didn't run away from this party at first, and dinner goes fine. I suffer through the pre-cake song made tolerable only by Santiago singing comically louder than everyone else and holding *Bea* for the length it takes the rest of them to sing my full name. Then Mom claps her hands and leads us into the Espinosa living room for presents.

Whitney gets me a new travel makeup bag decorated with little black cats. Olive gifts me a small clay cat they made and painted to look like Lottie. I hold it sacredly, and Santiago promises to keep it safe on his desk until I leave. Dustin and Abby give me a mug with a black cat on it. There's a theme.

The makeup brushes Mom asked me to order on her behalf are waiting for me at home. Señor Espinosa jokes that hosting and cooking dinner was his gift. Then we all turn to Santiago.

"I feel like I should've gone first." His cheeks redden as he passes me a small, rectangular bundle of purple tissue paper.

I carefully peel back the present's skin.

"You got her a gift card?" Whitney's voice trails off, a mix of judgment and amusement. It heightens and unburdens the tension in the room all at once.

"Oh, well, yeah." Santi scratches the back of his neck. "Well, I know you're low on your go-to liquid eyeliner but that you wanted to try that old brand you used to love's updated formula since it doesn't have that shimmer effect you sometimes dislike about your current one." His words stumble over one another, eyes trained on the plastic in my lap. "You said you didn't want to buy both but also didn't want to buy a whole new liner that you'd never use again if it sucked, so I thought this way, there's less risk involved. You might still end up with one you don't like as much, but you can at least try them out without worrying you wasted your money."

"So I'd just be wasting your money," I say, almost too seriously.

He laughs nervously. "It's not a waste if it's for you."

"Thank you." I try to pour more into the statement. Something to express this feeling I don't think they've invented words for yet, at least not in any language I know. Actually, that's the closest I can think of: knowing. I feel known.

I recognize there are other people in the room, but I forget about them until Mom claps again. She suggests a movie, but everyone needs to go do homework. In their shoes, I would've brought up the excuse hours ago.

"Happy birthday," Whitney whispers in my ear as she hugs me goodbye. For a second, I wonder why she's squirming, but then I feel the contours of a card pressed against my chest. I wave off Olive, Abby, and Dustin from the porch as they follow her.

"Guess that makes four of us," Señor Espinosa says, rubbing his hands together. "What're we watching?"

We put on some old sci-fi movie from the '80s at Señor Espinosa's suggestion. He and Mom sit on the plush chairs while Santiago and I take the couch. By the time we're twenty minutes into the movie—most of which I zoned out for—I realize two things: I am lying against Santiago, and he is shaking.

He sits with his back against one armrest, body tilted so his chest is facing the TV and his legs hang over the side of the sofa. I sit with my back against his chest, my legs bent so they barely fit across the rest of the cushions. I didn't register how long his knee's been bouncing, letting it blend in with the rest of my sensory input as my thoughts drifted.

In the dark, I twist my head around. There's a moment before he moves his gaze to me when I notice his eyes had been darting all around the room.

"You good?" I whisper.

"Yeah," he whispers back, our faces inches apart. His breath is cold and minty.

The bouncing stops but starts up again five minutes later. Before I can ask about it, he sits up.

"Sorry," Santiago says at full volume. "I'm gonna use the bathroom."

"Want us to pause it?" Mom asks.

He waves the suggestion away. "Nah, I'll be back in a second."

Mom and Señor Espinosa focus back on the screen, but I watch Santiago's shadow. Instead of turning into the bathroom, he walks to the end of the hall and slips out the back door.

"Actually, I have to use the bathroom too," I say, already scooching off the sofa.

"Honey, this is the best part!" Mom whines.

"No te preocupes, Magdalena." Señor Espinosa groans as he

stretches for the remote and pauses the movie. "Necesitamos más palomitas."

Mom helps Señor Espinosa out of his chair and into the kitchen, leaving me unnoticed.

When I step outside, Santiago is crouched against the back wall of the house, head tilted back and eyes tightly shut.

"I know my mom makes bad jokes during movies, but are they really this painful?"

It earns me the smallest smile, another gift rather than a genuine reaction.

Minding my dress, I drop into the space beside him and tap my socked feet together.

He exhales. "I just need a minute."

"You can have as many as you need."

Frustration flickers over his face. "You should go back inside and enjoy your birthday."

"Do you actually want to be alone?" A beat, and he shakes his head. "Talk to me."

He shuts his eyes slowly, less tense than before. "It's the TV."

"What about it?"

"You know how when you're in a dark room watching TV and then move your eyes, the light trails across your vision?"

I stare at the back porch light, then whisk my eyes away quickly. It arcs across my line of sight like a shooting star. "Yeah."

He takes a deep breath and I pull his hand into both of mine, returning us to my knee like earlier. "Sometimes, when that light thing happens, I need to do it again. The same way. And it's not that hard, but it just happens, again and again and again. Even if I don't mean to, when I look at the screen and move my eyes the littlest bit, especially to read the captions, it creates that effect. But then I always have to do it again." He hesitates. "Or it feels like something bad will happen."

"Okay."

His eyes peek open. "Okay?"

I nod. I've known him for as long as I've known anything. This confession doesn't surprise me. He sighs, head falling onto my shoulder.

"My dad keeps taking forever to text me back," he says quietly. "And earlier, your comment about Bryce." Grief spirals aren't foreign to me. "Doing these things makes me feel like I have some control. I know it's not real, and yet."

"And yet."

"I don't like this," he moans.

"What part of it?" I ask, adjusting my posture.

Laughing without humor, he looks up. "All of it. Being like this. Talking about it."

"We don't have to talk about it if it's making it worse."

"No, it's not . . ." He trails off, frustrated. "I don't want to put this on you. After Bryce . . . I don't want to add to it."

I let my head fall to the side, resting atop his so we're stacked. "I get panic attacks sometimes." I pause, feel for any shift in his body. He doesn't move. "You're not adding anything that isn't already here. At least not anything burdensome."

"I mean, I'm literally making you carry the weight of my head right now," he jokes, running his free hand over the lace cuffs of my sleeves.

"You're carrying the weight of mine too."

And then he pulls our hands into his lap and we watch the stars until the credits roll inside. It's the best birthday I've had in years.

★ ★ ★

At home, I open the card from Whitney. Her message is brief this time.

Happy birthday, Bea
I hope it's a good one. You deserve it.
Love,
Whitney

chapter forty-two

SANTIAGO

It's a slow weekend shift, most of the rush already having come and gone during the morning when Abby and Dustin were working. It's just me and Dustin now. Courtney stopped by earlier but didn't say a single word to Dustin as she purchased a gallon of milk from me and asked about my plans for prom next month. It's been quiet since.

I'm reorganizing the till for the fourth time when all of a sudden, the lights go out.

"What the hell?"

"Santiago?" Dustin calls from somewhere in the shadows. Slowly, my eyes adjust until I can make out shapes, including his walking down the nearest aisle.

"I thought the Brexlers went easy on their Easter display this year?" When I was doing homework at Bea's last week, I noticed far fewer light-up bunnies than usual.

"Let me go check the breaker." The words are just out of his mouth when the lights come back and his phone starts ringing. He goes to check anyway, returning as he hangs up. "That was my dad. Said half of town lost power 'cause of some downed lines up north. Should be fixed by late morning, but we can close up for the rest of the night. Our backup generators will hold."

"Damn." I lock the register and pull out my cell to call the center. "Hi, Kim, it's Santiago. Is my grandfather there?" Kim takes a moment to track him down, so I carry my phone with me while Dustin and I grab our stuff from the staff room.

"Santi." Abuelo's voice startles me by the time we're done. "Billy just told me he heard half the town's power is out?"

The grapevine in this place. "Yeah, I'm leaving the store now. Are you good at the center? How's the hospital?"

"Todo bien," he says. "We still have power here, but we might wait for the streetlights to come back on before heading home." I hear Billy shout something about the dangers of driving in complete darkness. "My chauffeur is taking precautions."

I relax, unaware I'd been tense. Abuelo in a car on a dark road late at night is my worst fear. "Good plan. I'll be careful getting home. Tell Billy to call me if anything changes. Love you."

"Will do," Abuelo says. "Te quiero."

Dustin offers me a ride since I walked earlier, taking advantage of one of the warmer days we've had in a while. He smacks my hand when I change the radio station for the third time, but before I can do it a fourth, my phone starts ringing.

"Tell Beatriz I say hi," Dustin says smugly.

"You don't know it's Bea." He gives me a look. "Just watch the road." I answer the call. "Hey, did y'all lose power too?"

Bea sniffles. "Yeah, we did."

I immediately sit up. "Are you okay?" Dustin glances over.

She clears her throat. "Do you think I could come to your house?"

"Yeah, yeah, of course. I'm on my way home now. Want to meet there?"

"Okay," she says shakily.

"Bea, what's going on?"

"I lied," she says. "About no longer being afraid of the dark."

Bea is waiting on my porch when Dustin drops me off, a full face of makeup dripping down her cheeks even as she gives him a cursory wave. I jog over and immediately wrap her in a hug.

She laughs wetly into my hair. "This is so embarrassing."

"Guess the new eyeliner isn't waterproof," I say. She laughs harder, which was the goal. "Come on, let's go inside."

The power is out here too, but Abuelo keeps himself well stocked, so we light enough candles to brighten the living room and kitchen.

Bea settles onto the sofa, keeping her limbs tucked close to her chest as I place the small flames around. When I'm done, I join her, maintaining a safe one-cushion distance between us.

"Thanks," she whispers.

I mess with a strand of my hair. "When I showed up on Halloween, you said you weren't scared anymore."

She shrugs. "I didn't want help."

"Does Magda know?"

"That I'm still scared of the dark? Doubtful," she says. "But she definitely doesn't know that I'm here right now."

"Why not?"

Bea blows out an exhausted breath. "She worries about me enough as it is. Childhood phobias are something I can and should be able to manage. Plus, night shifts at the hospital pay well. I don't want her missing those on my behalf."

"You watch the stars though," I say carefully.

She works her lip between her teeth, smearing dark purple onto them. "I can almost ignore the fear if I know my mom's home and light is just a flipped switch away. On nights like this, though, I can't handle it. I know I'm not entirely alone when I'm watching the stars, because he . . ." I don't make her finish the sentence. "But not having an escape from the darkness scares me."

"Well, you're welcome to stay as long as you'd like," I tell her. Slowly, she uncurls her limbs a little. "Do you want to clean that up?" I wave at my own face. "You can take a shower, but the water will be cold, so you'll probably want to be quick."

She presses a finger under her eye, and it comes back streaked with eyeliner. "Water and three-in-one soap isn't going to remove this much makeup."

"I'm insulted you think so little of me." I get up and grab a candle, waiting for her to follow me into the bathroom. I open the shower and dazzle my free hand. "Ta-da."

She leans past me, unbearably close, and reads the bottles. Tea-tree shampoo, frizz control conditioner, lavender soap, and gentle face wash sit on the small nook. "Congrats on the bare minimum." She pats my cheek, surely depositing blots of her black tears onto me.

"Yeah, well. It's all yours." I hand her a clean spare towel. "Don't use too much of my conditioner."

She makes a face.

"Let me bring you a few more candles." I run to grab them, a change of clothes, and a jar of coconut oil from the kitchen. I set the candles on the counter first, then hand her the supplies. She lifts the jar, a question on her face. "To remove your makeup," I explain. "I heard it's good for that."

I wait in my room, trying not to listen to the rhythmic sound of water running from all the way down the hall. After an agonizing seven minutes of this, my phone beeps with a text.

Pa: hey tito I know the anniversary just passed I hope you're doing ok

The message reads quick, no punctuation to lessen the blows between words. It wasn't the anniversary, it was Bryce's birthday, that was weeks ago, and no, I'm not okay.

"Where should I hang this?" Bea magically appears in the doorway wearing my pajamas, raccoon eyes and water droplets clinging to her spiky hair. She lifts the wet towel.

"Hook behind the door works."

She drifts back down the shadowed hall, and before I follow, I type.

Santiago: Thanks, Pa <3

In the bathroom, Bea is already rubbing coconut oil off one eye. When she removes the bundle of toilet paper, her skin is clean, the tissue the opposite. "This stuff is actually pretty good for your brows and lashes, too. Come here."

I take a cautious step forward as she washes her hands and scoops up fresh oil with the back of a long nail. She focuses just above my gaze as she spreads the coconut oil on my brows. It means I get to stare right at her bare face, tongue peeking out and piercings reflecting the candle flames.

"Okay, close your eyes," she says.

I don't want to. I want to stay in this stolen moment, one I can write off as easily as anything else, even though the longer I refuse, the guiltier I become.

Her gaze drops to mine. "I said you can close."

"Yeah," I say numbly. Her eyes are so dark that I can't tell where her pupils end and her irises begin.

Tenderly, she reaches up to brush a strand of my hair from my face—the same strand I was toying with earlier—then tucks it behind my ear. "Close your eyes," she repeats, but this time it sounds like a plea, like confirmation that she feels this too. It's the guiltiest and most relieved I've ever been.

I close my eyes.

chapter forty-three

My phone sits idly in my lap, the battery crawling closer to death every time I unlock it. I could call Mom and let her know where I am. But then I'd have to let her know why I came.

Santiago returns from changing in the bathroom. "I didn't realize how cold it still gets at night without heat." I smile as he yanks open a dresser drawer and puts a second pair of socks on his feet. He used to tease Bryce when he got cold, now it's his tolerance that's weak. "Remind me to never let my abuelo do laundry day with all the blankets ever again." The stalled washer and dryer are full to the brim with them, all soaked.

"Maybe we should build a fire."

"You remember how to make one?" he asks. I shake my head. "Yeah, that was always Whitney's forte." In the middle of tugging at a frayed thread on his sweater, he freezes. "Wait." He jogs out of the room, adorably cozy, and comes frolicking back with a thick, crocheted bundle. "Abuelo always keeps this under his bed. My abuela made it." He drapes the blanket over my shoulder.

My fingers clutch the intricate webbing. "What about you?"

He shrugs, and his floppy sleeves bounce as he drops onto the bed beside me. "I can handle it."

I don't doubt that. But I sidle closer, lifting one side of the blanket so it hugs him too. We're much too tall for this, the fit awkward and imperfect.

"Do you think about your abuela a lot?" I ask, feeling suddenly childish and silly. Maybe it's because this reminds me of the sleepovers we were only allowed to have as young kids. Candace deemed it inappropriate for me to join after we hit our preteens. There's a sad humor to her thinking that would be a roadblock to any and all sex under her roof.

Santiago adjusts the blanket. "Sometimes? I don't remember her much. It's sort of like missing my mom, you know? Except she's out there somewhere. Meanwhile, my abuela . . ."

I swallow and think of my dad. A stranger I've missed my entire life.

It's late and the only light in the room is warm candle flame, so the hard words come easy. "Do you believe in anything? Like, bigger than this." I let my hand fall open to the ceiling.

"In a way," he says, watching me. "Sometimes my OCD feels like a god. Play by the rules, prevent the awful stuff from happening. It's not really a religion, and I'm not sure how much of *me* really believes it, but it's there." His jaw ticks. It's the first time he's named his illness with me. "What about you?"

"I don't know. I wish on stars still," I admit in a whisper. "Like Bryce taught us to." Find the biggest and brightest. Put your all into it.

"Believing in the stars isn't so bad." Santi smiles, his face close enough to blur in my vision.

I look down, shaking my head. "It's not the stars I believe in." He bestowed them with the magic, with the ability to comfort me under the yawning abyss of the night sky. Without him, they'd just be chemicals, an assortment of atoms. I suppose I think of his body the same way. Maybe even this life.

Santi reaches across me to tug the edge of the blanket tighter over my far shoulder. In response, I melt against his side and let the lines between our bodies fade like the hazy edges of a shadow. I am so exhausted, so starved for something unidentifiable. He feeds and fuels the hunger in equal measure.

His warmth begins to bleed into mine. The chill at my core, bone-deep, starts to thaw. I feel protected and, even if only for a moment, at peace.

For the first time in years, I open my eyes and see Mom standing above me while actually waking me up.

"This is cozy," Mom says. I follow her gaze to the lump beside me.

Serenely, Santi yawns and stretches one arm above his head. The other is currently trapped under my body.

I jolt up, shocking him fully awake.

"Seño—I mean Magda," he says to Mom. His hands fumble to pull his shirt down from where it rode up in his sleep. I'm glad Mom being here gives me an excuse to already be blushing. "I—this is not what it looks like."

Mom's hands stay planted on her hips. "It looks like my daughter spent the night at someone's home without asking or even telling me she was leaving the house."

"It's *Santiago*," I say, reading the sexual implication.

"Ouch," Santiago stage-whispers. Neither of us laughs. "Conversation for another day."

I shift to the other end of the bed to put distance between us. "We slept toge—*I mean* in the same bed—on accident." I sound flustered enough I could be Santiago. I'm so used to precision, especially with Mom. But his loose way with words must be rubbing off on me. "I was going to drive home when the power came back, but I guess we crashed."

"You didn't mean to sleep over," she says. "But you're in pajamas."

Pointing out that they're Santiago's probably won't help, so I surrender a little. "I didn't want to be home alone. In the dark."

Mom presses a hand to her temple. "Santiago, can I speak to my daughter for a minute?"

"Sure," he says. We all wait. "Oh, you mean—yeah, I can go." He scrambles out of his own bed, closing the door quickly behind him.

Mom sits on the empty slice of mattress Santiago had been occupying. "Abejita, do we need to have another talk? Sobre los pájaros y las abejas?"

Well there goes all the innocence of my childhood nickname. "We really don't." She didn't want me raised on the same abstinence-only education that she was, so I'm well acquainted with conversations about the importance of consent, protection, and abortion access.

"Because nothing happened or . . ."

I swallow. "Both."

She nods, looking at her hands. I know it isn't disappointment in *me* radiating off her. She wishes I would've told her the first time I had sex. I'm older now than she was when she had me. I was younger then, though. "Do you want to talk about that time?" She pauses before layering the question. "*Those* times?"

I've been honest all morning, so I give myself permission to lie now. "I'm good."

She clears her throat and stands. "Well, um, I was just giving Señor Espinosa a ride back from the center. He spent the night since Billy didn't want to risk the streets in the dark. Are you okay driving yourself home? I need to get out of these clothes."

I nod, surprised at how quickly we've dropped this.

Mom kisses the top of my head, and I feel her smile at the way my hair tickles her mouth. "I'm glad you have a friend again," she whispers.

I blink as she leaves, listening to her and Señor Espinosa in the hall. Eventually, the front door closes and I hear the TV turn on in the living room.

Santiago pokes his head back in. "Coffee?"

His abuelo keeps the good, Colombian kind. I stick out my hands.

He enters with two mugs, passing me one and slurping from the other. I can tell by the smell that his is cocoa.

"So, does Magda hate me now?"

"No." I blow on my drink. "I told her you're a very generous lover."

He rolls his eyes and takes a long sip.

"What did your abuelo have to say?"

"He asked if we were safe."

I choke, spitting coffee back into my mug.

"Cute," Santiago notes. I shake my head and set the cup down, wiping my face with the hem of his borrowed shirt. "I think I might have actually disappointed him when I said nothing happened."

The almost-kiss flashes in my mind. Both our keys are hanging loose over our clothes.

"He's not machista like that," I defend, then stretch. "Ugh, I should get home." I look down at my outfit. "You want these back now, or . . . ?"

"You could wash the coffee saliva off first if you're feeling nice."

I'm tempted to strip and hand it back to him just for the bit. "I'll run it under the sink. Just for you."

He smiles into his mug as I gather my stuff. "You treat me so well."

★ ★ ★

I've dreaded many days this year, but today was unexpected. Given the routine nature of my pain, it's at least refreshing to be surprised. The worst part is how nice everyone is being about it. That is until passing period when Santiago slams my locker shut.

"Oh, I'm sorry, was that in your way?" I deadpan, and try to pull it back open.

He knocks my hands aside. "You're *valedictorian?*"

My mouth curls into a smile against my will. "Sort of." They won't know for sure until spring finals, but class rankings were announced today. With senioritis on the rise, I doubt they'll change. "It's not actually official. It doesn't mean anything."

"Shut your smart face up." He grabs me and spins us around, just enough that my feet pop off the ground. "You're valedictorian!"

I'm giggling. I can't believe I'm giggling. I don't giggle. "*Stop.*" I laugh.

"I'm vague associates with a genius." He sets me down. "Classmates with the next Einstein."

I push him away. "There are like a hundred kids in our class. All I had to do was get mildly better grades than them."

"That's just as impressive as discovering gravity, in my eyes."

I squint. "That was Newton, not Einstein."

He grins. He already knew that. "See? You *are* a genius."

"And *you* are insufferable," I say with far too much affection in my voice.

He lets me finish gathering my stuff as we walk toward calc. On our way there, more people congratulate me on the announcement.

"Wow, she's smart *and* popular." He fans his face, swooning. "I might have to start having sexy dreams about you."

"I think I might sit with Rick at lunch."

"Don't forget to ask him to prom. It's fast approaching."

We snag desks at the back of the room since we're too deep into the school year for teachers to give a shit about their original seating charts. Maggie Oliver, ranked third in class, congratulates me from the front row, joined by a few others. I wish at least one person would scowl at me, even just in jealousy. I haven't seen Whitney yet. She ranked second.

"Speaking of prom," Santiago continues, twirling his pen. "What are our plans?"

"You may have just won the prize for the most lackluster promposal Greensville has ever seen." I flip open my notebook and slice a thin line down the pad of my finger. "Fuck."

He points his pen at me. "That's what you get for being sarcastic." Then he drops his pen, beckoning for my hand. For some reason, I give it to him. He turns my finger over, staring intently at the beading blood. My skin warms. "I think you'll live."

I snatch it back and press the wound into my sleeve. "Should've applied to schools for premed."

He rolls his eyes. "I just assumed we'd go to prom together."

"How romantic," I say thoughtlessly. There's a second where

I think he won't let me get away with it. Then he just opens his notebook. "I guess I can pencil in a pity friend date."

"Between accepting your Nobel Prize and inventing a new law of thermodynamics, presumably," he says, and I nod to confirm. "So does the valedictorian thing mean you're giving a speech at graduation?"

"Probably not once they see my current draft. And before you ask, no, you can't read it."

Our conversation is bisected by Will Sanders and Courtney passing to take their seats. "If you don't thank me with my own special paragraph, I will leave the ceremony," Santiago says.

"Promise?"

He grins, shaking his head. "So, just to confirm, yes to prom, no to reading your speech, and maybe to mentioning me in it?"

"You got two out of three right," I say, then face forward as class begins.

I get my first college-app response right after dropping Santiago off at home. When the email notification dings, the sound amplified in my empty car, I pull over and open the message with numb hands.

Beatriz Andrea Dougherty, we're pleased to—

I click off my phone.

This is a good thing, objectively. It's an immense privilege. Eileen and Neil will help pay. I can get a quality education and find something I'm decent at that'll give me a stable future.

Bryce wanted college. My dad was set to go to community. Mom thought about nursing school. Futures cut short, and mine has just begun.

"This is a good thing," I repeat aloud to myself, even as my eyes begin to well with tears.

★ ★ ★

I don't tell Mom. Only a few of her coworkers have kids my age and she doesn't talk regularly enough with Candace to know acceptances have started rolling out. As long as Señor Espinosa keeps his mouth shut about Santiago getting into several California state schools, I'm fine. To balance it out, I tell her I'm going to prom with Santiago. It's a pleasant surprise for us both.

It's also how I end up in the thrift store on a Saturday afternoon, squeezing my boobs into a dress made for someone several cup sizes smaller.

"This is not going to fit."

"The tag said it was your size!" she shouts unnecessarily through the flimsy curtain preventing the entire store from witnessing my half-naked body.

I squirm against the garment. "Yeah, and clothes targeted toward women are known for their consistent sizing and universal fitting."

"Fair point. Hand it over."

I tug the fabric down my hips and pass it through the curtain. Mom trades me another dress for it.

"What about this one?" Her disembodied hand waves it like a flag. It's bright orange.

"Mom."

A sigh. "I tried."

I scoff and turn to the remaining dresses. The first three are all duds. A deep navy floor-length with straps too thin to give me the chest support I need. A gray cocktail that was clearly made with someone much shorter than me in mind. A black-and-white floral print that hangs too loose on my frame. All that remains is a puddle of black sequins I found on the floor by one of the racks.

With nothing to lose after already ending up in the distinctly sour mood manifested by trying on ill-fitting clothing, I attempt to make sense of this dress. It's a skin-hugging long-sleeve. If holding it up against my body while looking in the mirror is a fair visual to go off of, it should hit me at just the right length to accommodate heels.

I slide into it. Even reaching at an awkward angle, the zipper glides up my back with ease. I take a deep breath and look in the mirror.

The material embraces my body. When I move, I look like I'm covered in scales, the light reflecting a deep iridescent shimmer off every sequin. It was made for me.

"Do you have the last one on?" Mom asks.

I run my hands down my second skin, tilting my head as I observe myself. I try to smile but startle at the visual.

I'm going to prom. I get to wear a pretty dress and dance with a pretty boy and be happy. I get to experience something that symbolizes growing up and preparing to say goodbye to this chapter of my life. And hello to the rest of it.

I yank the zipper down before my breathing gets too tight. Within several pounding heartbeats, I get myself out of the dress, and by the next few, I'm back in the one I arrived in.

I hang everything up. But I leave this one as I found it. A puddle on the floor, one I can't see myself in.

"It didn't feel right," I tell Mom when I step out. As we exit the store, I can't help but turn around for one last look.

★ ★ ★

At home, I find an old black slip dress. I cut up a lace skirt I never wear and add it to the dress' hem so it skims my ankles. In the mirror, I observe the jagged edges where the fabrics meet. Mom offered to sew it for me since I never picked up the skill, but I needed to do this myself.

The top is a little tight, crushing my boobs and pinching my hips. The waist billows slightly around my rib cage and stomach. With heels, I look a bit goofy. No one will glance at me twice other than to judge. It's perfect in a different way.

chapter forty-four

SANTIAGO

The day of prom, I step out of my room messing with my tie, wearing the same poorly fitting suit from Halloween. I didn't try it on again until this morning, despite Dustin's warnings that he had to get his suit tailored three times. "Abuelo, can you help me with this?"

"He can't, but I can."

I drop the tie.

Pa sits on the sofa with Abuelo, the two of them holding matching mugs steaming enough to make this look like a dream.

I run, nearly tripping on my feet, and tackle him in a hug before he can even fully rise from the sofa.

Pa's arms wrap around me. "Hey, Tito."

I pull back and take a look at him, trying to note the changes that've developed over the months we've been apart, the new snake tattoo winding around his wrist and the silver ring that drips from his earlobe. His face is rough with stubble and signs of aging I hadn't noticed before, the wear and tear of days on the road showing around his eyes and chapped mouth. If I shoved myself into a time machine, poured cheap beer, semi-habitual smoking, and '80s indie rock in, then set the dial for about two decades, I think he'd be the result.

"What are you doing here? I thought you were still traveling with that folk singer."

He clicks his tongue. "Like I would miss my son's prom." He waves away the rising memories of him missing Thanksgiving, Noche Buena, Christmas, and New Year's/my birthday. "Besides, I had to be here to give you this." He reaches behind the sofa for a garment bag.

I gape at it. "Pa, you didn't."

"Try it on!" He passes me the hanger, then drops to a whisper. "Check the pocket later."

The suit fits me perfectly, a sleek black cut that I pair with the gray thrift-store undershirt I'd already dipped into my work savings for. Pa drives us over to Bea's house, making a crack at Bea being the one driving us to prom instead of me, and I watch Abuelo's scowl in the side mirror deepen.

Magda lets us in and has her own sweet reunion with Pa, the two of them sharing an uncomfortable amount of things in common when it comes to their parental origins.

"Bea is just finishing her makeup," Magda says, then turns to Pa. "Original Santiago, would you mind carrying in a box for me from the garage? I'm looking for some old cameras to take pics of the kids."

I excuse myself to use the bathroom while they handle that, but I really just need to wipe off my sweaty hands. In the mirror, I fiddle with my slicked-back hair and tighten my tie knot. As I reach for the handle, I hear talking.

"Tell Eileen thank you for the suit," Abuelo's voice carries from the foyer. "And thank *you* for having the idea. I can't believe Santiago took credit." It takes me a moment to make the connection that I'm not the Santiago being talked about.

"It's fine," Magda says. "Santi looked so happy. That's all that matters."

I glance down at my clothes, then pull off the jacket and check the tag. I don't recognize the brand, but a quick Google search on my phone says it's expensive, the type of expensive Pa wouldn't even know where to buy. Lying must be hereditary.

I remember his earlier comment about the pocket and dig in, finding precisely what I guessed I would. A single condom nestled deep within. Weirdly, this is probably the most responsible thing Pa's ever done for me. It's not even expired.

"Santi!" Magda calls, this time meaning me. I shove the condom away, pull myself together, and give the mirror one more scan, trying not to see my dad there.

When I return, Magda, Pa, and Abuelo all look at me, then up the stairs.

Bea stands above us all in a long, black, silk dress, lace brushing the tops of her spiked heels. She descends with a confidence that I'd question if I hadn't seen her navigate months of iced-over ground in platforms, or if I wasn't so distracted by her face. Black is smudged around her eyes in a gradient shadow, her brows are lightly drawn, her face sparkles with piercings, and her lips pout with a dark wine-colored gloss. The makeup is a variation of her normal style, so she doesn't appear that different than usual.

It nearly bowls me over.

"Hey," I say.

"Hey." Her mouth breaks into a smile that matches my own,

and I don't even care that our families are watching this entire exchange, I'm so overcome.

Magda poses us on the stairs. "Santi, put your hands on her waist."

I do as I'm told, but as Magda reloads her film, I lean into Bea. "Is this okay?" I ask, my lips brushing her ear as her minimal hair tickles my cheek.

She places her hands over mine, securing them around her. I wonder if her key is burning against her chest right now too. "Yes."

After Magda takes dozens of photos on dozens of cameras, we are set free. Prom is where it always is in this town, the nicest hotel between us and Bennington. The drive there goes by as quickly as my heartbeat, with stilted and restrained conversation occupying the wedge of space I'm suddenly hyperaware of between us. Every few seconds, one of us catches the other staring, but we do nothing about it other than grin.

When we park and get out, I think the silence will coat the entire evening. But Bea reaches a hand over, stopping me, before carefully using one finger to brush back a strand of hair that escaped my gel sealant. In her heels, she is an inch or so taller than me.

"You look good," she says softly.

I swallow. "So do you."

I offer her my hand, and she takes it.

Prom Committee picked *The Starry Night* as our theme, likely because it was the theme four years ago and the decorations were still around. My theory is supported by the mostly torn paper stars hanging from the ceiling and faded paint on the large van Gogh replica sitting behind the snack table.

"Hey!" Dustin shouts as Bea and I enter. Courtney trails behind him, her tight red dress and heels slowing her down. "You guys made it!"

"Unfortunately," Bea says, but she's leaning into me as she does.

"You two make a cute couple," Courtney notes when she finally reaches us. "Who would've thought?"

"We're not together," Bea corrects.

"So you're not each other's dates?" Courtney tilts her head unnaturally.

Bea doesn't respond, but she doesn't let go of my hand either.

"Oh, before I forget," Dustin interjects, then produces a plastic card from his brown jacket pocket. "Don't know how you guys plan to spend the evening, but my folks rented a couple rooms for us to hang out in after prom is over. I think they mostly wanted to keep us from driving drunk or going somewhere like Rick's after-party." He pauses to glance toward the dance floor where Rick is grinding with a girl I don't recognize at this angle, a crowd of guys from the basketball team surrounding them.

Bea takes the card between her clawed fingers. "They're not worried you're going to use it for more cliché reasons?"

Courtney latches onto Dustin's side. "That's not a problem for us."

I don't know what that means, and if Bea's face is any indication, neither does she. But a slow song comes on and the couple leaves us, most of the attendees also moving to the dance floor.

"Shall we?" Bea asks.

"You *want* to dance?"

"No, but I figure if we get it out of the way early enough, no one will bother us about it later." Over her shoulder, I see Whitney and Abby swaying with a group of other girls. The two of them are holding hands, wearing matching corsages.

Bea and I find ourselves on the outskirts of the crowd, and despite the earlier awkwardness, my hands meet her waist and hers meet my neck with a comfortable ease.

"This is nice," I say, embarrassed by my strained voice and racing heart beating between our chests.

Her fingernails lightly graze the back of my neck, where goose bumps quickly rise. "I don't hate it. Your dancing has at least improved since middle school."

"Please don't mention that pity slow dance," I groan as my grip on her waist dares to lower itself, gliding across the deep silk. Tommy Larkin asked Whitney to the sixth-grade dance before I could, so Bea and Bryce took turns dancing with me so I wouldn't feel like such a third wheel. I got a slow dance with each, though Bryce and I cut it short when people began staring.

We shake with her laughter. "Hey, you were the second-best partner I had that night."

Both our bodies stiffen, the allusion to Bryce like cold water over the moment. She pulls back slightly, my flesh chilled where her warm touch was moments before.

I'm the worst friend in the entire world. "Do you think he would've spent tonight busting out moves from those etiquette classes Candace made him take?" I ask, loosening my hold on her like I'm yanking my own teeth out, choosing to be a better friend to Bryce than her right now.

Her expression is unreadable, even to me. "I don't like playing these games."

"What games?"

"Thinking about what he'd do or think if he were still here." Her dark eyes are trained on the ground, but she keeps swaying with me.

"Why?"

"Because it's not real?" She pulls away fully. "He isn't here. He's never going to be here again."

"Obviously I know that," I defend. "It just—I don't know, it makes it easier sometimes."

"Of course you'd think it's easier to pretend." She works her jaw and blinks rapidly, eyes going shiny. "You do realize that if he *were* here, I'd be dancing with him."

"Maybe," I say, mentally rearranging that image in several different ways. "Maybe not."

I was good at badminton for a reason. I can return a hard hit with equal power.

"Why?" Bea asks, leaving it open for an array of possibilities— both in question and answer.

She walks out of the hall with purpose, lifting the hem of her dress so it doesn't slow her down, though I doubt anything could right now.

I'm going after her when my phone dings in my jacket pocket. I pull it out and read Pa's text.

> hey tito I didn't want to spoil your night with a big goodbye
> but I'm heading to ny to meet with an agent for the band
> have fun talk soon

I laugh, squeezing my phone so I don't throw it to the floor because of course, *of course* none of it was for me, the trip or the suit or the effort. I've always been a footnote in other people's lives, and here I am, still pretending otherwise.

Turning as the song changes, I find Abby and Whitney again, dancing with Courtney and Dustin and other familiar faces, all of them people I grew up with and should know intimately, not just by name. Instead, they blend in with one another, all of them capable of a life that feels beyond me now.

Wouldn't it be enough to just have a simple, normal prom? Dance with some classmates, get tipsy on spiked punch, hang out in a hotel room for a bit, then get a ride home or crash here with ten other knocked-out teens? Tomorrow, I could upload pictures to Instagram and text some to my parents and finish up my homework. Graduate, go to college, have a normal life. I could just have a normal life. No one would be dead or dying or inevitably becoming one of the two.

"Fuck."

I look down at my hand. I was snapping until my thumb slipped, nail slicing against the pad of my pointer finger, leaving an angry red line in its wake. I'll be fine—I didn't even break skin—but things don't have to be deadly to hurt.

chapter forty-five

Dustin did me the second favor of our weird pseudo-friendship when he handed the room key to me instead of Santiago. It takes a few tries to find the right door. Eventually I get it and slip inside, leaving the lights off.

I fall backward onto the bed. Mom told me to never touch the filthy top sheets in a hotel. But I can't get myself to move.

Bryce and I didn't go to Homecoming in ninth grade. As enticing as the night always sounded, we loved Halloween and wanted a final year of trick-or-treating before we became real teens. It felt like a pale imitation of our childhood, though. No Santiago trying to guess what candy each house would have, no Whitney organizing our route by efficiency, no Olive begging to come along. I felt old and embarrassed at the ripe age of fourteen, like my happiness had already peaked without me even realizing it.

Maybe if I tried harder to make that Halloween fun. Maybe if I said something when Bryce and I walked up to that first house and saw the entire yard decorated with headstones, the first of which said YOUR DAD in blocky writing, a bad version of a bad joke, instead of pretending I didn't see the hurt in his eyes. I wonder if he saw any in mine.

There's a knock on the door. It startles me enough to pause my impending spiral.

"Bea?"

I sit up. "Yeah."

The electronic key-reader beeps green, and Santiago steps inside. "Dustin gave me another card."

He approaches the bed, dropping down beside me. Our knees kiss. "I'm sorry for bringing up Bryce like that." Looking at Santiago is like staring down a freshly kicked puppy. Sometimes being mad at him feels like both the problem and the solution. Right now, it just feels exhausting.

"I did it first." The urge to scrub a hand down my caked face is almost unfightable. "I'm sorry for making it weird."

"It already is, though, isn't it?"

I scan his face. He's determined. He's made up his mind. We're doing this.

"It isn't," I say honestly. "But it should be."

"We should feel bad," he says.

You don't? I almost ask. I'd love to know what it's like to exist in skin made of something other than guilt and regret. But the pinch in his brows says he would too.

Dangerously, I reach a hand up to smooth away the frustration. "We do feel bad."

Slowly, just as dangerously, he snakes a hand around my wrist. I still my fingers. "Sometimes I don't," he admits.

I'm not meant to be doing this, whatever the two of us have been doing. I fucked up the plan with Bryce. I fucked up the plan with Whitney. But I was supposed to stick to this one. I risked everything to do so.

And then he showed up again.

"Bea, I don't know where we go from here."

Me neither. This wasn't supposed to happen. Not again.

His free hand forms a fist in his lap. "I'm—I think I'm in lo—"

I place my free hand on his arm to silence him.

I glance at his mouth, then back to his eyes. But it isn't enough. I don't get to pretend like this just happened. "Can I kiss you?"

"Yes." He responds so quickly, his answer may as well have been a part of the question.

We crane our necks forward, the rest of our bodies holding their own stiff lines. Our hands and chests and legs know what we're betraying right now. But our mouths have run out of things to say to avoid this, so they do the only thing that's left.

His lips catch mine, the barest whisper of a touch. We retreated on New Year's, and we do it again this time. But only so I can look at him, lift a hand to smooth his furrowed brow a second time. That small touch is enough.

My hand burrows deep in his hair instead of just grazing one strand, my restraint shattering into neediness as I pull him closer. His hands brace my face, holding me like something precious enough to require a firm grip, refusing to let me fall and shatter.

Kissing him doesn't feel like fireworks or jackhammers in my chest. Nothing about this reminds me of roller coasters or the adrenaline rush of that first jump into the lake after a long winter. I don't even get butterflies.

Instead, kissing him is a sigh. It's coming up for air, catching a drop of rain on your tongue, earnest singing, effortless brush-strokes. It's the final puzzle piece, a trust fall where we're both falling and catching and trusting. There isn't a name for this—I can only think in metaphors.

Achingly slow, he kisses me and I kiss him. And somewhere caught between a daze and a moment of clarity, we separate just enough to fit words between us.

"Beatriz." My name on his tongue is a question on my pulsing lips.

I hold his eyes with my own, close enough that he blurs. For the briefest second, I don't recognize him. Then, softly, I kiss him back, whispering his name into the act.

More questions come from both ends. And following each one, faithfully trailing our betrayal, is a *yes*.

I don't wake up because I don't fall asleep.

His head rests on my chest and his arms wrap around my body. Long shadows pour over his face, but his small, content smile shines bright enough to be seen even in the dimmed room.

Carefully, I untangle myself from him and close the bathroom door behind me.

My clothes are still on the floor outside. I stand naked in front of the mirror, a key over my heart.

The endorphins and moment have passed. All that's left is hollowness.

Disgust meets me in my reflection. Disgust with myself for allowing this to happen again. With myself for not stopping it. With myself for wanting to leave this place with his hand in mine and see where we end up.

With myself, with myself, with myself.

How could I be so selfish? It isn't enough to be breathing, to be alive and living and waking up every day while Bryce—God, what is *wrong* with me?

I'm on the floor and the air won't come into my lungs and I can't wake Santiago or he'll help me and even gasping for oxygen as my heart pounds on the walls of my chest, even choking on the distant fear that I will die right here and right now, at least one brick from the fortress I spent all those years building stays stubbornly put.

Unbidden, though, I note the coolness of the tile on my cheek and unbalance of only one long earring still dangling from my right ear. The feel of smeared lipstick on my chin. The stickiness of my sweaty body.

The air comes easier. I remember who I am. I remember what I'm meant to be doing.

Someone else takes over.

I pee. I wash my hands and splash my face. I wipe away the smeared lipstick. I remove the single earring and grip it in my palm. Not too tightly, though the urge is there.

Quietly, I open the bathroom door. Santiago doesn't rouse.

I put my underwear, bra, and dress back on. I sit on the floor for my heels.

I check myself in the mirror over the dresser. If I go into the bathroom again, I might not come out. In the dark, I decide I am fine.

I don't look for Santiago's reflection behind me.

The opening door screeches, but he still sleeps soundly. I wish he didn't feel so safe with me. I wish he'd wake up and yell.

I breathe easier with every step I take away from the room, but I don't get far.

"Don't make him wake up alone."

I spin around. Whitney stands at the end of the hall, petals falling from her corsage onto the floor, an ice bucket dangling in her other hand.

I forget how to speak for a second. "I was just going for a walk."

"At this hour?" She stares at my clutch. I forgot I even grabbed it.

"Let me go. Please."

She shakes her head, laughing sadly. "He deserves better than this."

"Why do you think I'm leaving?" I ask. She blinks. I swallow. "I made a mistake. I'm leaving before it goes any further."

"Sex wasn't far enough?"

It's a question hidden in another. My appearance answers at least one of them.

"It's not that simple," I say. It's pointless. We both know it is.

She laughs again, glancing at the closed doors around us like they're in on the joke. "Well, you're nothing if not consistent."

"This was different," I say, trying to convince us both. "It can't go anywhere, this—it can't mean anything. He'll hate me for it tomorrow, but eventually he'll be glad I walked away."

"Trust me, he won't be," she says, which means whatever I say next will be a cop-out. "How long are you going to do this? What's even the point? Because if it's about punishing yourself, you're so far beyond that by now."

"You don't get it," I say, though it feels like a lie. Because if she knew, maybe she would. But no one knows. Not the whole truth. "You never got it, you never—"

"*God*, Bea, I lost him too!" she shouts, dropping the bucket and storming closer. I'm stunned into silence. "You don't have ownership over this grief! You don't get to isolate yourself and make us the villains for it and keep saying it's in the name of Bryce's memory or whatever! I'm so fucking tired of it and it's exactly why—" She stops herself short of me, panting.

"Just say it." I don't want her mercy. I don't want her to coddle me now.

"It's exactly why I was relieved when you broke up with me," she says.

And then it's all out there. The thing neither of us ever touched. The thing that, even amid our jokes and barbs about each other's hair and clothes and friends and lifestyles, we still deemed too fragile to toss around.

I can't decide if it hurts more or less to see the regret already clouding her eyes. "Bea—"

"Don't," I warn. A single hand raised between us. "I'm sorry I was such a burden to you." Devoid of my usual sarcasm, the statement falls flat to our feet. And then, because I can't help but gut her back, "But don't tell me you ever considered us together enough to break up. You and Santiago aren't Bryce. Neither of you could *ever* be him. You were just bad attempts at filling his void."

The air leaves her. If I weren't so attuned to her every breath, I'd think she was angry instead of hurt. "*Fuck* you."

We both spin as a door creaks open behind me.

"Sounds like you already did," Santiago says.

chapter forty-six

SANTIAGO

Beatriz chases me down the hall past Whitney, who can't even look me in the eye. My loose tie and unhidden key flap against my chest, my hastily put-on clothing hanging limp around my rigid body. I'm sure my face is covered in Bea's makeup.

I burst out of the emergency door to the courtyard, completely unconcerned with setting off a fire alarm. All our classmates are probably awake anyway, having fun, normal nights, so I'm pretty disappointed when we aren't blasted with sound. I don't want to be the only one with a pounding head.

"Santi!" Bea shouts, stumbling through the door after me.

I whirl around. "I don't even—what am I supposed to say to you right now?"

"Let me explain," she tries, so desperate to keep me from running. Like she didn't just flat-out explain to Whitney that she was leaving me and was done with this—whatever this was. An impulse or punishment or mistake or cheap replacement. All of the above.

"What explanation could you possibly give to make this okay

right now?" I say, choking on the words, hating how deeply my voice portrays my hurt.

"I was going to talk to you," she says, but neither of us believes her, and a not insignificant part of me is sure I deserve this after how I ignored her for all those years.

"About which part?" I ask, wanting to draw the full truth out of one of us for once. "You and Whitney? Me and you? Any of it?" When the silence stretches on long enough that the only thing that could break it is a lie, I have my answer.

I start to leave again, but she grabs my hand and urges me to face her. "You can't be mad at me for dating someone else." It's the cruelest, lowest fucking blow she could've picked right now, and we both know it.

"Oh, we're pretending like that's what I'm mad about?" I spit back, like I'm not the expert at pretending.

I hate that I'm crying, that I'm trying to be angry and stand my ground when all I want is to fall to the floor and sob and scream. I want to be a kid again. I haven't been one for a long time.

"I—" She gasps like a fish out of water. "It's complicated. No— no, actually this was simple. It was wrong, and it shouldn't have happened."

"Why?" I ask, tears gliding down my cheeks.

"Because he's dead!" she shouts, and the night swallows her words before they can echo. The second they're said, they're gone. "He died! I wasn't supposed to be—I wasn't supposed to be—"

"Happy?" I ask, furious. "Having fun? Feeling anything but loneliness?" She looks away, face wet in the moonlight. "You hate Whitney so much, and for what? Showing you that maybe your life didn't begin and end with his?"

Bea steps back like I slapped her. "What the fuck is wrong with you?"

"Me?" I throw my arms up. "What the fuck is wrong with all of us?" My chest feels sliced straight through. "What did we all do to each other?"

"You left us!" she shouts. "That's what *you* did. You let a pointless fight with Bryce be the end of your friendship! One stupid, ridiculous fight over *whatever*, and you abandoned him and me, you selfish fucki—"

"The fight was about *you*!"

Everything goes dead silent.

"What?"

I hate it, but I want her to hurt, not because she lied and hid things from me, not because she and Whitney got together while Bryce rotted in the ground, not even because an hour ago she took my virginity and now we're arguing in the cold over entirely different things.

But because a part of me has always hated myself for the exact same reason a small part of me now hates her. My heart has been made of glass for three years now, a single crack splitting its way up the organ, and with this final confession, the whole thing will shatter. If I thought I was crying before, I don't know what I'm doing now.

"No, no, you fought about—about something random. You—he said it didn't matter," Bea says, like she's trying to convince me of something she wasn't even part of, or at least didn't think she was part of.

"Bryce and I fought because I wanted him to give you the key to my house. I wanted you to have it so you wouldn't be so alone with me gone, and he—he accused me of trying to win you over, trying to take the one person he still had left." I shut my eyes against the memory—feel choked by it and the loose key around my neck in equal measure—but it's been repressed too long and bursts behind my lids with an almost satisfying pain. Bryce's face, pink and as bright as his hair, eyes livid, mouth remorseless. "I didn't understand because he had so many people who loved him, but he didn't see it that way. He said I always thought his life was so perfect, that I was jealous and probably happy that his dad died so he'd finally be miserable like me. I didn't realize what he was confessing." The knife twists in my gut, like it has a million times whenever I recount the conversation. "His last words to me were telling me to never talk to you again."

"What—I—No." She shakes her head, trying to push the confession away, but she can't stop herself from remembering. "You said you were told to leave me alone." Our conversation in the supply closet, my careful bending of the truth, of who I'd been listening to. "Why didn't you tell me?"

It kills me, even now, even after hearing the way she talked about me to Whitney, how pathetically and sincerely I love her. But I couldn't protect her from this forever, and I couldn't let it fester in me for the rest of my life.

"Why do you think, Bea?" And then I walk away again, and this time, she lets me.

chapter forty-seven

BEATRIZ

I get home. I think I drove. I had to have driven. My keys are still in my hand, but I don't remember the drive. I only realize I'm home when Mom walks through the door, smiling and then gasping and then running toward me.

"What's wrong?" She cups my face in her hands. When she pulls them away, they're wet with makeup. Or tears. I'm crying. I'm melting.

"Why don't you ever talk about Dad?" I ask from somewhere miles away.

"What? Honey, what happened?"

"Because you never talk about him," I say. "Even when we're with Eileen and Neil, you don't bring him up. No pictures of him on the walls, no photo albums dedicated to his memories. It's like he's just *gone*. Forever."

She crouches before me, hands on my thighs. I'm on the table. I'm sitting on the coffee table. It groans but doesn't give.

"I tried, I tried so hard, I promise I tried. I told myself it would be fine, I could handle it, I could *fix* him. Why couldn't I?" I pause and look at her. "Getting pregnant was the worst thing that ever happened to you, and then Dad died, but I fixed that. I was a good daughter, I *fixed* it. Your life was hard because of me, but I got good grades, I behaved, I didn't cause a fuss, I applied to fucking college." Tears fall down my face, but I'm not crying, not in any real way. The tears are just slipping out like my words. "I was so easy, you always said I was easy."

"Beatriz." Her voice is glass.

"What was I supposed to do, Mom?"

She wraps her arms around me.

I try to push her off, screaming and feral in my anger. It's like I'm not in my body anymore. I'm watching from outside of myself.

"You think you're such a good mom for being concerned after!" The accusation rips out of me, arms flailing against her. "You—I needed someone then, I always needed—he, *he* needed someone."

"I know, baby, I know."

I keep fighting, a wild animal. I shove, I scream. But she's my mom—of course she's strong enough to hold me. And I'm so tired. I'm so tired that I let her.

We fall to the ground in a heap. I feel nothing.

"I didn't want to ruin it all," I cry, sobs racking my body. "I wanted to fix it, I thought I could fix it."

She holds my head closer, pulling me in. I've outgrown her. I can't believe I was ever part of her, inside and now out. A tumor beyond fulguration or ablation.

"I'm sorry," she says, and the apology vibrates through my back for my chest to absorb.

Bryce is dead. He's dead.

He's dead and he's been dead and I know that, it's all I think about, so why, why does it *still* feel like this? Like I'm being told for the first time, like someone shoved their hand through my skin and gripped my heart and squeezed. He's been dead for what feels like minutes and also my whole life, and yet I still can't believe it. He's dead.

chapter forty-eight

SANTIAGO

Here's how it happened.

In my memories, I see the scene in third person, a removed party outside of my own body and role. It's a few weeks before I'm set to move away, and I want to make a trade in Bryce's yard as we're gathering the last of the dead summer leaves. In the middle of the raking, I pull out what was meant to be a gift, and give Bryce my key to Bea's house. I explain that he can give Bea his key to my house, and I can take her key to his house, not knowing he wouldn't even make it another year there. Bea loved Abuelo, and I wanted her to have access to an extended family even without me, so it only felt right to transfer the keys around. Bryce and Bea were dating—it made sense for him to have the key to her house instead of mine. And though I never would have admitted it, maybe my biggest motivation was that I loved being around Bryce more than anything in the world—I'd miss it like breathing—and I wanted to bring a key to his home all the way across the country.

I wasn't nervous for the conversation because Bryce is my best friend, but when the words leave my mouth casually, they enter his ears callously.

Bryce and I never fought before, which sounds like a lie when you're talking about a friendship as long as ours. Though I'm thoroughly a liar now, I was honest back then. Maybe that's why I wasn't prepared for his anger.

He cast my actions in a new light, accusations battering me in a way only my own intrusive thoughts had before. Every bad thing I ever considered about myself spewed out of him in new flavors. I was selfish, I was senseless, I was so focused on my own existence that I hadn't stopped to consider anyone else's pain, I thought his life was so perfect. I was jealous of my best friend and wanted to steal something we'd always shared: Bea.

The memory is so worn now that I can't recall most of the words verbatim, my own self-loathing doing a poor restoration job. But the end is perfectly preserved, crystal clear in both intention and intensity. Bryce was glad I was leaving, and he didn't want me to talk to him ever again. Or to Bea. I should just leave them alone.

I kept one of those promises, but I'm not sure it counts for anything anymore.

Dust clings to my shoes as I walk home from the hotel, backdropped by dawn. I didn't even check out properly, just left after waking, and my lack of self-preservation right now scares me, a test arriving when I hear the first car of the day. My thumb twitches but stays down.

Gravel crunches as the car slows behind me anyway, and I

turn, shielding my eyes from the sun to watch as one window rolls down, exposing a familiar face.

"You know how to drive?" I ask.

Olive leans over. "Got my Junior Driver's License last week." The door unlocks.

I get inside, a little too exhausted to care about the legality, and yank at my tie, already a loose leash around my throat. "I'm surprised you're up this early."

"I'm visiting Bryce."

"Oh."

"My dad and Candace hate the cemetery, but Whitney goes a lot. I don't normally join her."

Half of me would be content never talking about Bryce again if it meant I stopped feeling this way, but I already know how that'd fail. The other half wonders if I'm even capable of forming a single thought that doesn't connect back to him somehow; if I'm so stained by this loss that its color will bleed into everything I touch for the rest of my life. I think I loved him too much to ever wash my hands of it. "You don't like going?"

"I didn't like the reminder that he's gone," they admit. "Something changed my mind though. Recently." Their gaze flashes to me quick enough that I could let it go, but I'm so tired of secrets—keeping and being kept from them.

"Is that *something* me?"

"Sort of." I let them have a moment to consider how they want to say this. "When I told you at Bryce's birthday that I wasn't hurt by how you handled our date, I was lying. I knew you didn't like me, but I wanted to make it work. Me and you. My childhood crush. It was like I was owed it, after everything."

"I'm flattered, but—"

They hold up their hand, so I shut my mouth.

"Grief tricks you. All the death and finality—I wanted it to mean something. I made all these promises to myself about how I wouldn't waste my life. I wouldn't fight with my sister or parents or Candace, or spend hours in my room alone anymore. I'd travel the world, I'd write books, I'd make every moment count and I'd never spend them being afraid or angry or sad."

"What happened?"

"Life." They laugh, flicking their turn signal. "When Bryce died, my entire existence boiled down to a *before* and an *after*. I thought the after had to be unrecognizable from the before. Someone I loved was dead, from suicide of all things. There was no way the world could just continue on." Olive blinks away tears. "Whitney and I bickered the morning of the funeral. A week later, I snapped at Candace for asking me to do chores when I was watching a show. I ignored my dad when he needed help in the yard that whole summer."

I think of that promise to Bryce again, how easy keeping it seemed in the early aftermath of his death, a way to honor him that required nothing more than betraying my only living best friend from afar. Then I came back here and saw her, and suddenly the difficulty mounted.

"One day I woke up and the after was my life now," Olive continues. "Which meant that it came with everything life has to offer, fear and anger and sadness included. I could try to live a better life, but it was always going to be a *life*. They're inherently imperfect. I think that's kind of the point."

We reach a stop sign and they pause, leaning back, hands easy in their lap. "Realizing you weren't going to like me back reminded me that just because my brother died doesn't mean I won't still have my heart broken a million other ways. That's the price for the good stuff, you know?"

I don't get it, how they could have worked this out while the rest of us have been fighting for scraps of anything even akin to coping. I spent years playing make believe about my dead best friend being alive, and in some weird attempt at atonement, treated my living best friend like she was dead to me. Bea pushed away everyone who tried to help bind her wounds just so she could exhibit some control over ripping them fresh every day. I thought Whitney had it all figured out, but a heartbroken girl in a prom dress immediately comes to mind, her limp hair sagging alongside her mouth.

"What if the good stuff is covered in the bad?" I ask, realizing that my greatest moments of happiness this year were always wrapped up in something that had touched my grief. Because I am my grief always, even on the good days.

Olive shrugs. "I don't know. Our grief might all be the same, but it's still different."

We reach my street and they unlock the doors before they've even properly stopped the car. I go to unbuckle my seat belt, but pause. "I shouldn't have led you on by saying yes to that date. I'm really sorry."

They smile, and it looks sincere. "I've been through worse."

I crawl into bed, suit and dust and all, and scratch my forehead. The urge to scratch it again the same way, in the same spot, rises to the surface so naturally, it's like breathing. And the same burn that would fill my chest if I stopped breathing fills my head when I don't do it.

I'm taunting the universe, and I will be punished for it. Olive is going to wreck their car on the way to the cemetery. Abuelo is going to have a heart attack while I'm at work. Bea is going to step wrong going down the stairs and break her neck on the fall. Pa isn't going to look both ways as he crosses a bar's parking lot, and he'll be mowed down by a drunk driver.

They wash over me, vivid and horrid, and my entire body itches. But I don't scratch.

I shut my eyes and tuck my hands under my back, painfully aware that I'm here and I'm alive and this is real, and I do not run from it.

chapter forty-nine

BEATRIZ

Mom hasn't left me alone since I came home from prom. She happens to clean the hall when I shower. She needs my help cooking dinner. She calls off work because she's tired. I've decided this treatment is fair. It reminds me of right after Bryce died. But there's something different this time, something I'm still absorbing.

In my lowest moment, when the world felt like it was crumbling down on me again, I came home. I put myself in front of someone who loves me.

I don't know what to do with this.

The closest thing Mom gives me to alone time is letting me stay inside to do homework while she tends to the front yard's weeds. We have Monday off for teachers' conferences, so I can defer reality for one more day.

A knock at the door startles Lottie as I pet her while doing calc proofs. Mom must've accidentally locked herself out.

But I find Dustin standing on my porch instead. With his

hands tucked in his back pockets, he smiles easily at me. "Hey. Your mom said you're studying. Mind if I come inside?"

"Santiago isn't here," I say.

"I know."

"Oh." I stare at Dustin for a beat. He maintains his smile. "Right, sorry. Uh, come on in."

I'm aware he's seen me naked, but seeing me without makeup right now feels more intimate. When I sit back down on the couch, he joins me.

I tolerate the silence for ten seconds. "I don't mean to be rude, but why exactly are you here?"

He wipes his palms on his jeans. "Courtney and I broke up yesterday." I wait for him to go on. He doesn't.

"I'm . . . sorry?"

"Thanks," he says, amused by my attempt. "It needed to happen before we made each other as miserable in college as we have in high school." My face must show surprise, though I don't feel it. "I don't mean to be blunt or overstep here, but I wanted to ask about what happened between the two of us last year."

I should've seen this coming. Many lessons have been thrown at me this year. The most oddly specific one that I've been hit with over and over again is that sleeping with someone and trying to pretend you didn't only works for so long. "Okay."

He takes a deep breath. "I'm not asking because I'm expecting anything here, I promise. Ending things with Courtney after so long just has me thinking about a lot of stuff, and I never understood why you picked *me*."

I know what he's asking. "You weren't the first one after Bryce."

"Really?"

I nod, somewhat relieved to know Whitney never told him about us. "But you . . ." The words are so hard to get out. "I half lied to Santiago about why I did it when I told him about it."

"I wasn't sure if he knew," he says. "What was the half lie?"

"I told him I did it because I wanted the whole school to know."

He blows out a breath. "I guess I sorta fucked that up for you, huh?"

"Yeah, if only you'd been more of a gossip."

"I'll work on it."

We share a smile. "But that wasn't the only reason," I go on. The moment turns serious again. "I think . . . I don't know, I think I wanted to prove something to myself. That it didn't all start and end with him."

Dustin nods at this. "I don't know what the four of you had together, but it seemed pretty special."

"We were just kids," I say. It's an excuse, a dismissal, and a plea.

"We still are," he says softly.

"I'm sorry about Courtney," I repeat, meaning it more this time.

"Thanks. You're the only other person I've ever been with," he admits, needlessly embarrassed. "I haven't even kissed anyone but the two of you. And I always wondered if I did something wrong by not talking to you about what happened afterward. But then Courtney wanted me back and . . . it was a cycle, I think? If she wanted me, I was wanted. If she didn't, I felt like no one would. You sort of challenged that for me, until I realized it was a one-time thing."

"It wasn't really about you," I offer, and his eyes say he under-stands this too. Just as much as picking him wasn't about him, not pursuing him after wasn't either. "I'm sorry for involving you."

"I was a willing participant," he says, grinning a little.

"You're a good person," I add, because I know what it feels like to classify yourself as the problem. His grin deepens into something sweeter, and I'm glad that he doesn't thank me again.

We're graduating soon. Though Dustin and I have never been close, it sinks in my stomach that we won't be in school together anymore. Whitney, Olive, Abby. Courtney and Rick. All those familiar faces, for better or for worse. This was never going to be my life forever.

Dustin slaps his hands on his thighs. "Well, I should probably get out of your hair." He pauses and looks at my freshly shaved head. Mom helped me last night. "Sorry."

I laugh. "I'll walk you out."

I think that'll be it for our conversation, but he turns around at the door. "I don't know what happened with you and Santiago at prom, but I heard yelling. Are you okay?"

I wonder how many times someone has to get asked that question before they give an honest answer. For me, it's whatever number this time is. "Not really. But I'm trying to be."

He nods. "That's what counts."

Dustin and Mom exchange pleasantries as he walks past her to his car. Once he's driven away, Mom approaches, but before she gets the words out of her mouth, I speak.

"I need to go talk to someone."

I've been standing outside of Candace's house for ten minutes now. It's the first time I've left my home without makeup in years.

I know Whitney isn't here because she and Abby are cramming in their final Good Samaritan hours helping with the teachers' conferences. Olive is with them because they may be the only Greensville student in existence who plans to finish their hours before senior year. And Phil's at work, his car absent from the driveway. This has to happen now.

My feet just haven't gotten the memo.

I jolt when the front door opens. My heart pounding in my chest, I watch Candace make her way down the front yard double-fisting trash bags. I'm convinced she hasn't noticed me until she looks up and doesn't flinch.

"I was going to let you come inside at your own pace, but Whitney forgot to take this out earlier, and it's stinking up my kitchen." Candace lets the bags drop in a noisy thump. "She isn't home." The way she says it tells me she knows what we were to each other once upon a time.

I borrow Dustin's boldness. "I'm actually here to see you."

"Oh."

"Yeah." I swallow, but my throat stays dry.

It's been haunting me for almost three years now. I didn't want to accept anything about Bryce's death. The role I played in it, the fog of life that followed. The gnawing in my chest I struggle to believe I'll ever escape.

I never understood one thing, though. And now is the only time I think I'll ever be brave enough to ask.

"Why have you never confronted me about knowing Bryce was depressed?" I ask. "You told my mom that I was."

A week after his death. Mom sobbing in the living room while I sat motionless on the couch before her. Questions I didn't have answers to pouring out with her tears. But Bryce was dead. Why the fuck did anything as trivial as my feelings matter?

And then there was Candace, driving away from our house to go plan her son's funeral, a copy of the letter I never got to read for myself folded neatly in her pocket. I only know what it said about me, which was enough.

Candace picks up the bags and walks past me. I watch as she drops them in the bins and wipes her hands together. "We don't have to do this." It's both a warning and a request, her voice tender on the edge of raw.

"Yes we do," I say. My voice is splitting at the seams too, but I can't walk away now.

She sighs and pulls off her glasses. Wiping the lenses with the bottom of her silk blouse, she considers the sky instead of me. I wonder if, without the thick glass clearing her vision, she could almost pretend I'm him.

"His letter wasn't for anyone but us." Her tone is bored, but tension underlies the words. She's forcing the monotony to keep the tears at bay. I'm familiar with the strategy. "Your mother needed to know that you were struggling too. The rest of it—"

"You could've told people. Blamed me."

She shakes her head. "If you wanted everyone to know, you could've told them yourself."

"This isn't about me."

"Isn't it?" she says.

I find the the courage to say what we both know I'm getting at. "You should hate me."

"You were a child."

"That's not a denial."

She exhales in frustration. "This is a ridiculous conversation. Go home, Beatriz." She turns to leave.

"I could've stopped it."

I tried to yell, but it came out too quiet. Candace freezes in place all the same.

"I could've done more," I go on. "Been stronger or supported him better or just *talked* to someone. And if I had, he would still be here."

When she turns slowly, I brace myself for a slap or lecture or both. Since the day I heard the news, I have waited for this. I have been punishing myself for almost three years, and finally—*finally*—someone will give me what I deserve.

My eyes shut as she marches toward me. But when the strike doesn't hit, I open them slowly.

Candace is not a woman who shows much emotion. Even at Bryce's funeral, she hardly shed a tear. But her blue eyes are stained pink now. Her thin lips tremble.

"The first time I properly read that letter and realized that both of you had been feeling so . . ." She struggles to name it. "I wished it had been you instead."

It's the worst thing anyone has ever said to me. Too many nights I've spent echoing the same thought over and over, bouncing it against the walls of my skull until it becomes a mind-numbing plea.

I wish it had been me. I wish it had been me. It should have been me.

But Candace isn't looking at me with the disdain I see in the mirror every day.

"You were a child," she says again. Her throat bobs painfully, like her words are glass shards. "And I wished you had died." She plants her hands on her hips and bends forward for a moment, sick with guilt. "Every time I saw you, I felt it. *God*, I still feel it sometimes."

I don't even realize I'm choking on tears until I cough violently, desperate for air. And then I'm on the ground, hands and knees and it's pouring out of me.

Candace places one hand on my back while I sob. She doesn't comfort me beyond that touch. It may be the greatest kindness anyone has ever shown me.

"I don't hate you," she says. And for the third, and final time, "You were a child."

Mom's pictures of us don't just hurt to look at because Bryce is alive in them. They hurt because we were children. Even up until the end, children. I was sleeping with my boyfriend constantly, awake all night doing double the homework, riddled with guilt over existing, crying silently in the shower, trying everything in my power—except asking for help—to keep a kid alive, and I failed.

For the first time in my life, I consider the possibility that it wasn't something I, another kid, could have succeeded at.

I open my eyes, and Candace is standing at a distance again. I'm glad she didn't try to hug me.

"When Bryce's father was sick, he had doctors and a whole support system. I think—I didn't understand it, but Bryce probably needed that too," she says, voice cracking. "Maybe so do you."

"I don't think I can forgive myself."

"I don't think I can forgive myself either," she says. "But I do forgive you."

I want her to tell me Bryce does too. For everything. Living without him, not following him to the grave, thinking I was enough to save him. For Whitney and Santiago.

But she doesn't know how he would feel—none of us do. Which means I can't decide that he hates me either.

I watch Candace walk up the driveway. I wonder if, when she goes inside, she pretends for a second. If she ever calls his name from the foyer and lets herself believe that he will respond.

Maybe it's harder in a new house, when things have changed and you've grown. Maybe it's easier. Maybe it's both, and neither.

chapter fifty

SANTIAGO

We have Monday off school, so I agree to work a shift. I'm pushing my bike out of the garage when an unfamiliar car pulls up. If I couldn't hear The Georgias through the busted speakers, I'd be surprised when Pa jumps out of the front seat. Or maybe the past few days have just left me a little numb.

"Santi!" He jogs up the yard, a card loose in his hands. "I'm glad I caught you."

"What are you doing here? What happened with that agent?" I ask as he collides into me, a hug and a tackle combined.

"Forget about that guy." He pulls back, smiling with his arms still around me. "Happy graduation."

The unsigned card finds its way into my hands, a stinging paper cut erupting between my pointer and middle finger from the transaction. "School isn't out for a few more weeks," I say. "I haven't graduated yet."

"I know, I know, remember, I asked about that at prom?" I don't remember, but maybe he's confusing a conversation with

Abuelo. "I was just stopping by before heading back West. You know that girl Angie we used to run with a few years ago?"

I spot a bead of blood and pinch the cut between my fingers. It could be helping, could be hurting. "Uh, sure."

"Well, she told me to wish you a happy graduation, but, more importantly, she hooked us up with this sick venue looking for a regular act. If we impress them, the band might snag it." A limp hand motions to the card. The paper is dampened from my sweat. "Before I leave, I thought we could take a couple photos if you already have your cap and gown." He laughs to himself, so pleased with the idea.

"So, you're not coming to the ceremony." One opportunity to the next, none of them flexible enough to fit in fatherhood.

"It's not that simple," he almost whines, and I have to remind myself we aren't both teenagers. "I can't just drop everything to come. And you know what those things are like, sitting in the sun for hours just for one moment of cheering." He reaches out to pat my cheek. "I cheer for you every day, Tito."

Now it's my turn to laugh. "How would you know?"

"What?"

"How would you know what a graduation ceremony is like?" I tick off on my fingers, spreading around the dot of blood. "You missed my preschool graduation because you slept in after a late show. You missed my elementary school graduation because you were touring. You missed my middle school graduation because The Arrow Hearts were playing in Jersey and the tickets were *too cheap* to miss the chance to network." My hands drop. "Should I even bother inviting you to my college one? Have you even asked me about college?"

"You're not being fair," he barks. "I have a life outside of you."

"*So do I.*" The words fall out of my mouth, a child spitting up their alphabet soup.

His arms wrap around his gut, infantilizing him. "I was never fit for this."

I want to be empathetic, put myself in his shoes and think about what I would do if two years from now I was handed a baby. "That's not my problem," I say, because I couldn't when I *was* that baby.

Tears well in his eyes, and guilt rises to the surface, my third-oldest friend. "I should probably go," he says. All I do is nod.

He pulls me in for another hug. And just this once, I let myself melt into it, playing a game where I can pretend to have a life I don't, a dad I don't. In this life, he's crying because he's proud that his son grew up all right, not because he's relieved.

I've been on a plane four times in my life. Before taking off, they give that little safety speech where they emphasize that if the plane is going down or oxygen runs out and those bright yellow masks drop from the ceiling, you're to take care of yourself first. I get it, obviously, because an unconscious parent can't exactly assist their child. It makes sense to prioritize yourself in the short term, because your kid is the long-term goal.

None of those planes ever fell from the sky, but my world has been crashing for years now with my father strapped in right beside me. I've watched him struggle with his mask for my entire life while I choked, gasping for anything even remotely close to a breath of fresh air.

He has to take care of himself first. I don't have to like it, even if I get it from his point of view. Still, for once in my life, I wish he'd glance my way and remember he was always meant to come back for me. Instead, I watch him drive away and take a deep breath for myself.

My classmates come in and out of the store for day-off snacks with their friends, the few fellow seniors incapable of talking about anything that isn't prom.

I play the game, the one Bea hates, and ask if Bryce hadn't died, would we be among them? The three of us each grabbing something sweet, savory, and salty to share over a movie at Bea's house. The two of them a couple, me the yearning third wheel. Who would I even be yearning for? Would anything have changed if nothing had?

Movement at the end of the nearest aisle catches my attention, and I see Whitney and Abby making their way out of the break room with arms full of food kept back there for employees, likely bringing it to the school for the conferences. Even though it's only been two days since I saw her at prom, Whitney looks so different. When she catches my eye from across the store, I wonder if she's thinking the same thing about me.

She makes a beeline for the exit, but Abby doesn't immediately follow. Instead, she walks up to me at the register, waving a hand for the key to the cash drawer.

"I'm taking a cut of your paycheck for this," Abby says as we swap places. "Hurry if you want to catch her."

I fold my hands together. "Thank you."

I chase Whitney out of the store.

"I didn't know!" I shout, long before I catch up. She turns around and watches me for a second, out of breath from the quick dash. "I'm sorry."

"What are you apologizing for?"

I walk across the lot so our conversation won't be projected to all of our lingering classmates glancing over at my outburst. "I didn't know you and Bea had been together."

Lips pursed, she tilts her head. "So, you're apologizing for not knowing something that both of us kept a secret from you? That's what you feel bad about?"

"No . . . ," I say slowly. "I guess not."

Bitter laughter puffs out of her. "Whatever apology you give her is going to be better than this, I can at least count on that." The false amusement slips away. "All year you tried so hard to be there for her. She pushed you away, insulted you, basically refused to acknowledge that you were friends, and what did you do? You kept trying, no matter what." Her jaw tightens. "And then there's me."

A chill creeps up my spine. Unanswered texts, ignored invitations, ditching her and her group at lunch to sit with Bea. "I—you have friends."

"Wow," she sighs. "Fuck you, Santiago."

Whitney's anger all year, her annoyance at my and Bea's closeness. Finding out she and Bea were a couple seemingly connected those dots. I thought it all added up to jealousy toward me.

"She never made room for my pain," Whitney whimpers. "It was always about *her* grief, about isolating herself from everyone and everything, and I couldn't do it anymore. Olive lost a brother too, but Bryce was something else to them. He was *my* best friend, even if you two were his." She motions to me. "Then you came back and you reached out to me first and I was so relieved, because here it was. *Finally*, someone who's going to get it."

My mouth opens and closes. "I thought you had things all figured out," I say. "You didn't seem like you needed us."

She shakes her head, radiating disappointment. "You two, of all people, should've known better."

I didn't understand how she could do both: lose him and be happy. But me and Bea at the mall comes to mind. Me and Bea in general, actually.

Me and Dustin laughing while cleaning. Me and Abuelo cooking. Magda showing me photos, welcoming me back into her home. Olive crafting that little bird. Abby, excited to show me her nails every week. Even Pa, with his spontaneous visits and attempts at parentage.

Olive said it best, life comes with both.

"Can I give you a hug?" I ask.

Whitney should yell at me, but she nods instead. I pull her in, wrapping my arms fully and tightly around her.

"I'm so sorry," I say, finally knowing what for.

Whitney relaxes into me, resting her body so completely that she'd fall right over if I let go.

chapter fifty-one

BEATRIZ

When I get home from talking to Candace, he's waiting on my porch, still wearing his work clothes.

"Hey," I say.

"Hey," Santi replies.

We go inside only to stop halfway up to my room. The photo above the stairs gives me pause. Bryce and me months after Santiago left, grinning faces squished together. His smile doesn't reach his eyes.

Mom hung it up a few weeks after he died. It might be the last picture of the two of us. When I sit down on the step below it, Santiago does the same without question.

"I knew Bryce wanted to die," I say, every syllable laced with enough pain to knock me over if I wasn't already on the ground.

"But—" Santiago's face goes pale. "We were all surprised." Even after what he told me Bryce said during their fight, even after being on the receiving end of Bryce self-destructively pushing away someone who loved him, he believes this. Or maybe pretending is still easier.

These are the same stairs Bryce used to slide down in a sleeping bag, little-boy bones too bouncy to ever break on the descent. Bryce, who used to sit at the bottom step while I finished getting ready for school back when it didn't take me as long as it does now. Bryce, who always wondered what was below the ancient carpeting, convinced we'd find something magical in the mundane. Bryce, who clings to my life, even in death.

I shake my head. Exhuming this is dangerous, but it's been rotting in me for far too long. "The first time he—" A crack in my voice cuts me off. I push through the shards of it. "The first time he told me he wanted to die, the way he talked about it seemed so . . . peaceful. Like it was some temporary escape. Just a pause from the world that's always been so loud and hard." Passive and blameless. I didn't want to have a dead dad, and I didn't want to be a burden to my mom, this thing that ruined her life.

I ball my hands into painful fists, sharp nails meeting tender palms. I came into this world guilty and desperate for absolution. Look where that got me.

"When?" Santiago asks.

"A bit after his dad died," I reply, the words just as hard to say as I'm sure they are to hear. Bryce was only eleven then.

"That—but I was still here." Santi's eyes blink furiously. "He didn't—I never—why wouldn't he tell me?"

I shrug. "He thought I'd get it, and I thought I did." I didn't want Mom to worry. Bryce didn't want Candace to worry. The best-kept secrets are the ones with mutually assured destruction.

But the destruction came anyway. Secrets burst open, Bryce

gone. A lifetime of worrying about him would've been better than this. Anything would've been.

"Is this what you were just talking to Candace about?" His voice sounds so removed from his body. "When I showed up, your mom said you were over there."

"In a way," I reply, shocked that I don't carry the same detachment in mine. "But she knew. His letter—Bryce mentioned me in his letter." Santiago stares at me, processing. "He said he was sorry for lying."

"About what?" he asks, afraid.

My hands shake. "That last year he was alive . . . it was different. I'd started doing all his homework for him so he wouldn't fall behind. I dropped PE almost immediately because I was too exhausted to participate and thought it'd tank my GPA. That's why I'm taking it now." Mom would have worried, so I covered my tracks. Buried the evidence of my struggling. It's ironic though, that I get even less sleep now. "I could feel that his sadness was different, and still—" I clear my throat. "He told me not to worry, that he was just stressed about school and stuff with his family. I don't know why I believed him," I say. He knew before I did, that it wasn't the same for me.

Santiago's hand finds mine. "You said you thought you understood it."

It's a question. "I did. And then he died." How fucked is that, realizing I never wanted to die right after he decided that he did. Except that's not the full truth. "And then the accident."

Santi's grip relaxes but doesn't disappear. "What accident?"

I take a deep breath. This should be the easier part. "Whitney and I started hooking up the summer between sophomore and junior year." To his credit, he tries to hide his reaction to this pivot. He does a good enough job that I struggle to place his emotions. "My mom and I dropped off food for their family around the anniversary. She and Candace got talking, and Whitney invited me upstairs." As ridiculous as it sounds, I don't know which of us kissed the other first. It happened and then I left and then she went to visit her mom in the Philippines as dry season turned to wet season, and I thought that was that. "It went from there."

The invitations to hang out came after, though by then I'd already resigned myself to a punishing life of solitude. I justified indulging her—going for ice cream, riding our bikes up and down the blocks between our houses, watching movies in her room—because in a way, I owed her. At least that's what I told myself.

We didn't talk about it, which was fine in the bubble of summer. But as the months changed, so did we. Suddenly, the invitations weren't about the two of us. I was being welcomed into a world I hadn't asked to be included in, Abby texting me about her birthday party, Olive popping into Whitney's room to chat with us, Courtney requesting to follow the private Instagram I hadn't posted on in years.

School was starting and Whitney didn't understand why I hated sitting with her and her friends; meanwhile her friends barely understood why Whitney wanted me to join them. Even then, when our relationship should've been so transparent, it still seemed to be all about Bryce. Which it was, but also wasn't.

Whitney and I went out of town to pick up some books for the new school year, me behind the wheel as we drove down the long road. It wasn't raining or snowing, the early fall day unusually clear. And so when the sun shone on her in the passenger seat,

I granted myself one second to look and feel what I'd been feeling for months, knowing it was inevitably heading toward an end.

What I saw was a beautiful girl with an exterior that shimmered like a glacier, simultaneously stunning and icy and hard, but breakable. What I didn't see was the car veering into our lane.

I cranked the wheel toward the side of the road and the car was spinning and Whitney was screaming and the *only* thing in my mind was: I don't want to die.

I couldn't take it back.

I started seeing things too clearly. Every plan I'd made had grounded me. Watch a movie with Mom tonight, try a new brand of oat milk the next time I stop by the grocery store, take Lottie to the vet this weekend, study with Whitney. I thought I'd been drifting away, detached from the world by my grief. But life managed to weigh me down little by little every day until I felt like an old birthday balloon sinking to the ground long after the party had ended. Or maybe I was the child it once belonged to, swatting at it, begging it to float again.

Part of me did want to float away. Sometimes I still do.

Santiago doesn't interrupt, absorbing years of secrets I've kept even from myself. I hardly register the words leaving my mouth, my internal dialogue suddenly external. It's quiet for so long before he speaks.

"So, how did things end with you and Whitney?"

I'm not proud of it. "Well, we didn't actually crash. But a week later, I told her I didn't want to do it anymore. I didn't speak to her until Bryce's birthday, months later. By then she seemed happier."

"Was that a punishment? Letting her go?"

I've managed the entire thing without crying, but my throat tightens now.

He nods.

"I don't know what to do with all of this," I admit. "Me and my pain and guilt. I'm scared this'll always be me. But I'm also scared to be anyone else."

For years, the grief clouded my life. I could only see as far as it let me, and that was either forever without someone I loved or tomorrow. At some point, I learned to wade through the fog. Kept finding a reason to push the expiration date back, even if just to see the sun set and stars emerge one more time.

"It's not your fault," Santiago says, and maybe one day I'll believe him.

I miss Bryce. He was hilarious and bossy and a liar and creative and fun and selfish and wonderful. I think of him often but not honestly. I think of him the way he wanted the world to see him— joyous and okay—rather than the way he was: a kid who needed help.

I wish he was here.

"Me too," Santi says. I spoke aloud again.

"I really wish he was here," I repeat, this time on purpose.

chapter fifty-two

SANTIAGO

When I wake up, it's a few hours later and I'm alone in Bea's bed. I prop myself up on one elbow, leaning over to find Lottie on the floor, pawing at one of my discarded socks. Apologetically, I take it from her and slip it back on before crawling through the open window.

The sun is setting, bathing Bea's face gold while she casts a long shadow that matches her clothes. It's tricky to navigate my way over, survival instinct riddling my body with every move, and I feel a shard of terror that the reason she finds it so easy to come up here is because she doesn't fear the ground the way I do. Her earlier confession may have me looking for signs in every act, a new obsession to mull over. But when she scoots aside to make space for me, she keeps a steady hand planted on the roof and a cautious eye on the edge.

"I didn't hear you get up," I say, brushing dirt off my hands as I settle. After talking, we both knocked out.

She tugs her knees closer to her chest. "I was quiet. And you're a heavy sleeper."

We remember prom at the same time—I see it in the way her posture stiffens. It's a day of honesty and I already played my part with Pa and Whitney, but I know where this next conversation has to lead us, no matter how daunting the task.

Carefully, I hook a finger through the cord around my neck and the key emerges, twinkling in the last sparks of sunlight. "I shouldn't have told you about the fight the way I did."

She pulls the chain out from under her shirt, revealing her key. "We both had bad timing."

I shake my head, and the movement drops the key from my fingertip, landing back onto my hollow chest. "I knew you would blame yourself, and I never wanted that for you. I doubt he would either."

She rubs at her unpainted eyes. "Why *me*? Why fight over me, of all things? He wasn't the jealous type, and you and I never—" Prom flashes through both of our minds again, our mouths and bodies behaving in the least platonic ways imaginable. "There was nothing like that between us, right?"

"Right," I say honestly, because even if I thought Bea was pretty back then, it wasn't in the way I do now. "But I don't think it was about him believing anything was going on." For so long, I was angry that Bryce—my best friend and probably, if I'm being honest with myself, the first person I ever loved—distrusted my intentions enough that he thought my friendship with Bea was motivated by romance. That's too simple a solution though, one that absolves and indicts all of us in a clean sweep. Bryce was wrongfully jealous. Bea and I never so much as entertained a romantic or sexual thought about each other when he was alive. Now, Bea and I are proving him right. Bryce's suspicions came true. It would all be so much neater if it boiled down to these things.

But Whitney was jealous of me and Bea, and not for any of the assumed reasons. I forgot how easy it is to pretend that love has a hierarchy in type, but romance isn't the end-all be-all.

"Bryce told you what he was feeling," I say. "Maybe he wanted me to see it for myself." The rest of the conversation steps forward, shadowing the parts I often highlighted. Bryce angry that I wanted Bea, but not him, to have access to Abuelo, Bryce angry that I implied Bea losing me would hurt more than him losing me, Bryce angry because I was leaving and he couldn't stop me, but he could yell at me and tell me to go instead, snatching back control.

Isn't that what we've all been yearning for, control over what the world throws our way, a coauthoring position in the narrative of our lives?

No one ever told us specifically how Bryce died, so on the worst days, I let myself wonder about it. Did it hurt? Was he scared? Did he want to take it back, in those final moments? Did he realize, as he slipped away, that he'd pressed stop when all he really wanted was a pause?

Or did the same sick relief I feel when I complete a ritual—some arbitrary action that I've convinced myself is the solution to escaping death and tragedy—wash over him? Did the permanency not matter, because in that moment, his pain felt so overwhelming that it wrongly convinced him this was the only cure?

I've been running from death my whole life. It's inevitable, and one day I'll have to embrace the reality that I cannot control it, but it's not a cure for anything.

"I get why you ignored me now," Bea says, startling me. She

rests her cheek on her knees so she can watch my face as she forgives me. "Honoring his final wish."

"I left you to deal with it on your own." Whatever resentment I feel for my parents, both of them, twists its way back to me; that genetic predisposition to run that I thought I could escape. The irony of it all would be laughable if not for my life's corrosion.

"If it's any consolation, I doubt I would've accepted the help, had you offered it," she admits. "I didn't think I deserved to live, least of all have a friend. After a while, sending a message, knowing you weren't going to respond, was its own form of punishment."

"Not replying was too." I won't let the OCD take all the credit, but for too long, I've tried to draw stark lines between it and me, as if it wouldn't bleed into facets of my identity, especially those related to grief. "You're still allowed to hate me for it."

She scoots closer, picks up my hand, and just holds it there for a second, like she's feeling the weight of it. "What if we forgive each other?"

The sun has set, orange sky melting into dark night, and the stars begin to emerge. I've used so many metaphors and labels and feelings to describe her and us. And here we are again, mirrors and liars and, I think above all else, forgiveness. "Is that where we go from here?"

"Maybe. I just don't want to hurt you," she says like a confession. "And I'm scared that's all I'm good for with people." We've both had Bryce's death hanging over us for so many years, each taking responsibility without verbalizing the claim.

"You're worth more than your mistakes. Why do you think I hang out with you?"

She shrugs. "Clearly a ploy to get me to sleep with you."

I snort. "Clearly."

"Don't forget to thank your dad for that condom."

My snort turns into a full-blown laugh, one we share heartily between us, and it's a moment we both desperately need amid everything else. Eventually our laughter subsides, but it remains ringing in my ears and sounds an awful lot like crying, the way it echoes.

"I should apologize for leaving," she says. "I panicked." It doesn't sound like an excuse.

"Did kinda suck waking up alone to the sound of you and Whitney arguing about whether or not I deserved to be ditched after having sex for the first time. Can I ask you something though?" She nods without hesitation. "Was it an apology, or way of paying me back or something?" My jaw tightens as I hear the longing in my voice show all my cards, a hand full of hearts. "You said that's how you justified you and Whitney."

She takes a deep breath, and though it hurts to see her have to consider this, I'm glad she's actually taking the time to parse through her emotions and actions.

Finally, her shoulders lose their tension. "You weren't a mistake," she says, and I immediately believe her. "Or an apology or payment. It happened because I wanted it to." The last statement comes out like a confession, guilt battling with desire on her face. "You can still hate me for it too."

"You're my best friend and I love you," I say, and she looks up at me from below my chin. I watch with awe as her pupils grow the longer we let the words sit in the air. "How about that's where we go from here?"

She shifts her hand from around my waist to cup the side of my face. "I love you too."

The kiss is quick, and then we're back to watching the stars. It isn't a goodbye or punctuation to this conversation or whatever we're becoming, it's a promise of more to come. It's the best kiss in the world, and anyone else would've blinked and missed it.

chapter fifty-three

A few days later, I'm waiting in the kitchen when Mom comes downstairs to start making breakfast. I expect her to startle, but she just sighs in relief.

"You weren't in your room," she says.

Now I startle. "You checked?"

She nods, and we both ignore my surprise.

"I was up early." I know I need to tell her about the insomnia and the roof. I know, sometime soon, I need to tell her about a lot. This is the first step of that.

I slide my phone across the counter, open to a photo album of screenshots. They're college acceptances. Almost everywhere I applied, I got in.

"Oh my god!" she yells. Lottie jumps off my lap and scrambles into the living room. Mom throws her arms around me. "Abejita, this is amazing!"

"It is," I tell her. "But I'm not going."

Her smile doesn't falter, eyes still glued to the screen as she pulls back. "To which one? You've got plenty of choices."

"To any of them."

She freezes. "Beatriz—"

"There's a great makeup school in LA," I say quickly. "They have scholarships, and I can get an apartment with roommates using money from Eileen and Neil if their offer still applies. I'll work while getting my certification and pay it all back." And there's always community college.

"I don't think you know what this means." Mom waves my phone. "Going to any of these schools could change your life."

"How?" I allow the word take up all the space in the room it wants.

"Connections, career opportunities, a degree! You could really make something of yourself." She leans on the counter, lets it hold her frustration and weight. "You don't have to give up makeup, but you don't have to give this up either."

Guilt claws its way up my throat. Wanting a future for myself when Bryce is gone still feels so unfair. After talking to Candace and Santiago, though, I considered a new angle. Maybe the unfairness lies in Bryce being dead, not in me being alive.

She bites her lip so hard at my silence that I expect her to draw blood. "I just want the world for you."

I'm older than my mom was when I was born. For years, I've blamed myself for robbing her of a future other than this. Then blamed her for not seeing that blame and the way it made living feel a bit like a crime. Now, I don't think it's anyone's fault. We're all just trying our best.

"I don't want the world," I say. "I just want to be happy."

She rubs at her forehead. I admire the wrinkles there. "We'll need to talk more about this plan. You, me, and your grandparents," she says. "But your happiness is the most important thing. I won't stand in the way of that."

I am disappointing her. She loves me. They coexist.

"I also have to ask you three things," I say.

"Okay."

One. "I'd like to find a therapist or psychologist, and maybe a psychiatrist."

She nods, the tiniest smile on her lips. She suggested this years ago when Candace first told her about me and my pain. I refused the help then. "That seems reasonable."

Two. "Can you tell me more about Dad?" I let my voice crack on the words. So much of my life has been about avoiding questions like this one, scared they might gut me. Visible wounds and unhidden bleeding were antithetical to my purpose here. And though I don't want to be sliced open anymore, not really, I'd like to see what happens when I don't wear such protective gloves with my own desires. Pain is part of being alive. "I want to know him in whatever way I still can."

At first all she can manage is another nod. "Yes. Yes, of course."

Three. "Your bracelet." She blinks as her hand reaches for it. I touch my own key. I always thought I needed my mom to show me what she'd lost after my dad died. I want the opposite now. "I'd also like to know about the person who gave it to you."

chapter fifty-four

SANTIAGO

I consider texting first, but get the feeling that it's only so I don't have to hear his hurt again. Sitting on my bed, I press my phone to my ear and listen to it ring.

"Santiago?" Eric's voice is a cocktail of relief and confusion.

"Hey," I say. "Figured it was about time I called you back."

"Are you serious?" The only time I ever really saw Eric angry was during badminton games, a hilarious character trait when I really think about it, but that anger was always gone by the end of the match, a temporary, adrenaline-fueled emotion. "It's been fucking months, dude."

"I know." I scrub a hand over my face. "It's been a lot, moving back here."

"Yeah, I bet," he says flatly, but still with more sympathy than I probably deserve.

When Pa does stuff like send me that photo album and pop in and out of my life, does he think he's doing the right thing? When he puts his and his friends' dreams above my and Abuelo's needs, is he also just trying to survive living a life he didn't plan for? Bea said it's complicated, whether I'm "allowed" to be mad at him and my mom, but she didn't say no.

Eric clears his throat. "Lunch is ending soon and I left my backpack with everyone." A toilet flushes in the background.

"Are you in the bathroom?" I try not to laugh, but my failure is rewarded by Eric joining in.

"The no-phones-during-lunch policy is still alive and well," he says, and for a brief moment, it's like I didn't leave, he didn't find out I was lying about my friendships and losses, and we're just two guys who hang sometimes.

"I'm sorry I dodged your calls," I rush out, trying not to take up more of his time. "Thank you for reaching out so much, even after I lied."

Sounds crackle over the speaker, like Eric is shifting around. Our school bathrooms weren't exactly built for private conversations. "I looked into your friend's death after we saw that initial post. I didn't know it'd been suicide. I'm really sorry."

My legs bounce up and down, feet tapping repeatedly on the carpet. "Yeah, me too."

The bell rings loudly enough that I might as well be there with him. "Shit. I really have to go. But I hope you're doing all right."

It's not the thing you say when you plan on speaking again, but I knew walking into this call that I had to be okay with that possibility.

I put a hand on my knee in the middle of my rhythm, leaving it on an odd number of bounces. It hurts, but I stop running in place.

"Thanks," I say over the rush of intrusive thoughts. "I hope you do all right too."

★ ★ ★

After dinner, Abuelo and I sit on the porch, enjoying one of those rare Vermont days in late spring where the sun hangs longer in the sky, keeping the air warm and comfortable even as evening approaches. A group of kids ride their bikes down the street, giggling and screaming as they wobble on wheels. Trailing behind them is a trio of adults who wave at Abuelo and me as they pass. I think I recognize them, but don't know their names. We wave back anyway.

"I'm glad I got this year here." I sip on my lemonade, watching a bird glide from one neighbor's tree to another. "I didn't get a proper goodbye last time. I think I'm finally getting some closure."

"I don't think such things exist."

The bird flies off. "What do you mean?"

Abuelo's glass pings as he sets it on the ground below his chair, his shaky hands and the awkward angle depriving him the privilege of gentleness. "You don't get to be my age without saying quite a few goodbyes. When I first started losing friends at the center, I couldn't help but wish I'd said something different the last time I saw them. So many *See you tomorrow*s and *Hasta luego*s. So few *Goodbye, te quiero. Thank you*s. But you can't protect yourself from grief and loss with a couple nice words." He leans back into his chair, resting his weathered hands on his soft stomach, so content in his body and home. "Still, I'm going to try."

"What are you talking about?"

"We both know I'm getting old. It's the whole reason you're here. And we both know your father is not going to drop his dreams to come take care of me when you leave for school."

I pick at the dry skin on my palm. "So, maybe I defer a year and stick around until—"

"Until what, mijo?" His hands, tissue-paper soft and just as frail, envelop mine like cheap gift wrapping. "I'm not going to get better, because I'm not sick. I'm just old." With my hands still enclosed in his, he gives them a small squeeze. "I'm going to die one day, Santi. Probably not today or tomorrow, but I will die. I need you to realize this."

I try to pull away, but his grip is firm. "Trust me, I know." Without my hands to pick at, something to touch or focus on, I feel my heart rate spike. "Sometimes all I think about is death and the people I love dying. I can't escape it."

"No," he says with a rueful smile. "You can't."

In a blink, it's not just my hands he's holding, but all of me. I've fallen into his lap, bent over his chair with my head pressed to his chest. Despite his words, I try to freeze time. I capture this moment—the feel of his arms, his heartbeat harmonizing with mine, a hand on the back of my head, tender words covering up my sobs—I encase it safely in amber. I do, I do.

I can't.

In another blink, we aren't hugging. Hours have passed. I'm doing homework on the sofa and Abuelo's humming along to the radio in the other room, making tea. Steam floats toward me, hot and fragrant enough to make my eyes water.

He's here. It's not a forever statement; it's not something I can preserve.

But he is here. I take a deep breath.

The end of high school feels like a slow crawl, the days long and painful in their monotony. I still try to relish every moment of it, remember that growing up is a privilege I shouldn't take for granted, even when it feels like an insurmountable task. Even when I'd rather do anything but calculus homework now that I've accepted UCSB's offer into their engineering program, complete with generous financial aid. Even when looking over Olive's practice physics final is giving me flashbacks to my cram sessions last year with people I will likely never speak to again.

It's also a privilege to scribble a bright red *100%* on the top of the packet.

"Really?" Olive snatches it and flips through.

"The pen doesn't lie." I stand, cracking my back. "But the tutor does need to get going." I promised Abuelo I'd help him clear out Pa's old room for Billy to start moving stuff in. Neither of them wants to grow older alone, and they don't have to.

Olive walks me out to my bike, hugging their test. "I couldn't have made it through this year without you."

"You would've been fine," I say. "Smarts run in your family."

I pause for them to refute this, remind me that they and Bryce never shared any DNA or take a dig at Whitney, but all they do is bite their lower lip and roll the papers into a tube that they shove into their back pocket.

"I actually have something to give you, sort of as a thank-you. And an apology." Nervousness plays out on their face, similar to on Valentine's Day, and for a second, I'm worried I'll have to tell them outright about Bea and me, though most of the school has already noticed us holding hands around the halls. Bea rolls her eyes at the attention, but she never loosens her grip.

Olive digs into their front pocket, then unearths a ghost.

I freeze. "Where did you find that?"

Olive hands me a silver key hanging on a chain, just as shiny as the day I last saw it. "It was—" Their voice snaps off, requiring what feels like a full minute to recover. "Bryce had it on him the day he died."

I turn the key to my house over in my palm, in denial even as I feel the texture of its truth. "He threw it during our fight."

Olive swallows. "He must have gone back for it."

I see it so clearly, it feels like my own memory. Bryce sprawled out on the ground, mining through the overgrown grass and disregarded twigs littering the trees bordering their property, dirt wriggling under his nails and leaves clinging to his denim knees.

"Candace was so quick to start donating most of his stuff. I knew if I took something big, she'd notice. But he was always good at hiding things."

"Where?" I ask, because even Bea didn't know he'd kept the key.

They glance down at their feet, then back to me. Bryce's ridiculous shoe pockets, where he kept his prize possessions in his sole, so that every step he took could be fueled by the things he loved.

Bryce—my best friend, my greatest loss—didn't die hating me. He carried me with him until the end.

This should rocket through me, but the discovery lands softly, like it was something I always knew and was just trying to prove to myself. I didn't hate him after that fight—I could never. I should've known better than to believe his bluff.

I hold the key like a precious piece of glass, though if I dropped it, I'm sure I'd be the one to break.

"I'm sorry for not giving it to you sooner," Olive says shakily. "I missed him, and I always wanted to be a part of your group, but I knew how much this meant to you both, and even if I still don't know what you were fighting about, I should have—"

"You should keep it."

"What?"

Part of me screams as I place the key back into Olive's hands, fifteen-year-old me clawing in desperation, begging for this evidence of our friendship, this piece of Bryce I thought I lost. I never want to let it out of my sight in case I ever doubt that we were more than our lowest moment, but we were more than this too.

"I want you to have it," I say, and decide not to speak for Bryce's wishes. Olive closes their fingers around the key. "Promise me you'll use it, though," I request. "My abuelo would like the company next year."

Olive smiles, and in it, I see Bryce.

chapter fifty-five

The end is nigh. My classmates empty their lockers. Teachers put on movies and let us talk through them. College T-shirts clutter the halls. Santiago enlisted Mom to help him craft one for my cosmetology school and didn't stop smiling the entire day I wore it.

I feel it best when I walk campus in the morning or take Lottie on a stroll. I have known this place and been known by it, for better or worse. The familiarity that was an undercurrent to my days is palpable now. I wonder who I will be without it. For the first time, I believe that the world is bigger than this. It's liberating and terrifying.

Santi sits with Dustin, Abby, Olive, and their friends instead of with me at lunch today. Because I want him to, and more importantly, because he wants to. Being my friend—or boyfriend or whatever, we're figuring it out—shouldn't come at the expense of having friends, plural. I know I'm welcome. I've sat with them a few times. But I've got other plans.

I'm contently eating my cafeteria potato wedges, remembering that being alone doesn't always have to mean feeling lonely, when Whitney saunters around the building.

"I wasn't sure you'd come," I admit, making space for her in the sliver of grass that isn't damp. She toes the space with her loafer before joining me on the ground.

"Congrats on makeup school," she says. Pulling her backpack into her lap, she begins to unpack her lunch.

"Eh, it's no Dartmouth prelaw."

"Says the valedictorian. Speech or not."

I told Jefferys I'd accept the honor of valedictorian but didn't want to give a graduation speech. So the opportunity went to the salutatorian. Who just so happens to be Whitney.

"I couldn't come up with anything inspiring," I say.

She scoffs through a smile. "Well, at least you'll have plenty of options to match the cap and gowns." I know she'd been pulling for something other than black, but tradition won out. "Planning on trying a new aesthetic in LA?"

"It started as a way to get people to leave me alone. Or dress like a perpetual funeral. But I think I like it."

"You *think?*"

"I don't know," I admit. "I guess I get to figure that out now." All these years on pause, I didn't consider who I would be on the other side of what I thought would be the rest of my life. And here I am, on the precipice of so much change, still processing what it means to want again. To have a future and acknowledge it as something I plan on reaching.

"Well, it suits you. For now."

I take a hard pivot. "I'm really sorry."

She twirls her fork in a circle, pausing to chew. "Apologize to yourself. You're the one missing out on flattering colors. Would it kill you to wear a nice hazel every once in a while?" She rolls her eyes. Like the most offensive thing I've ever done to her is not maximize use of my ideal color palette.

"We can talk fashion later," I laugh. "But this isn't an apology for my wardrobe."

She takes a shy bite. "It should be."

I don't want to tease our way out of this. "What you said after prom was right. I hurt people who were kind to me so I could keep punishing myself."

She's quiet for a beat. "You didn't have anyone to talk to, did you?"

I'm confused. "About Bryce?"

"Yeah," she says, the guilt on her face foreshadowing her next words. "When he was alive."

I focus on the trees in the distance just past the school's fence. Firm and tall. Still swaying in the breeze, still vulnerable to crashing. "I didn't talk to anyone about a lot of stuff. I wanted to focus on him, and I thought I could do it on my own." I'm scared of what I need to say next. "I'm sorry if I put you in a similar position." Bryce didn't mean for me to sideline my life to keep his going. Even now, I can't blame him for the role I took on. But imagining I did this to Whitney makes me wish I could be angrier at him than I am.

Her shoulders slump beside mine. "We handle our grief differently."

"Yeah, you handle it with grace and honor, and I bury myself in it."

"Don't," she snaps. "I hate when people say that about me."

"What?"

"*You handle grief with such grace . . . ,*" she mutters. "Just because

I wasn't sobbing in the halls or hiding away from the world in my bedroom doesn't mean that my grief wasn't just as world-ending. I had a miserable enough family to worry about without—" Her hands shake in her lap, always ready to fix things. I don't reach for them.

"I mean, you slept with me," I note. "So you clearly fucked up in some respects." We share a layered laugh. "Do you ever worry you're incapable of loving someone that isn't tied to him?" I can't imagine having to explain Bryce to someone who never knew him. The task sounds akin to describing a color that doesn't exist. Words would always fail. "Look at all of our track records, mine especially."

She sighs. "I figure I'm going to be tied to him for the rest of my life. Whether the person I love is or isn't is sort of beyond the point." She lightly touches her pinkie to mine, where both of our hands rest on the ground between us. "But you and I weren't about him. Not for me, at least."

"What was it about, then?"

"Maybe just having something good among all the bad. Even if it was built to fail, it was good for a while."

I almost don't ask, but it's just the two of us out here. "Do you have that with Abby? Something good?"

Her hand slips away, and it's okay because she's smiling in that soft way she rarely does. "Yeah, we have that together." I think of Mom and the girlfriend she's promised to introduce me to. Everything after the loss hurts, but it isn't all bad.

"I'm happy for you," I say with an embarrassing amount of conviction.

She clears her throat. "What about you and Santiago?"

My exhale is long and deep. "I don't know if I deserve it," I admit. A good thing. Happiness. Breathing.

"I don't think that's how it works. Bryce was supposed to be my maid of honor alongside Olive, neither of them even maids," Whitney laughs, but underneath it, the sadness remains. "I don't think I or they deserved to lose that. So who gets to decide what we deserve to gain?"

I nod, holding back tears. I don't know if the blame will ever truly fade. "Would you hate me for it?" Loving someone besides him, besides her.

"It was hard seeing you with him, feeling like neither of you needed me. But I'd never hate you for living your life."

I play that awful game. I wonder where we'd be right now if Bryce were alive.

We'd be preparing for a night at Bryce and Whitney's house, where we'd watch some terrible sci-fi film Bryce fell in love with over the weekend and just had to subject the rest of us to. Or we'd go to the indie bookstore out of town after school, laughing at the goofy titles of self-help books. We'd be sitting at a lunch table, maybe even with Olive if Whitney allowed it, and despite our pasts, we'd never have to think of the word *grief* ever again.

Or.

Santiago would still be in LA. Whitney would be hanging out with Abby and Courtney like she'd started doing at the beginning of freshman year when Bryce was still around. Bryce and I would both be suffering, both trying to fix it in ways that were never going to work. I'd be sobbing silently into my pillow after finishing both of our homework assignments, and he'd be endlessly staring at the ceiling in his room, dry-eyed.

Or.

We'd grow up and grow apart. We'd get the chance to find good things with good people, and it wouldn't all begin and end here.

The next best life doesn't exist. There's just this one.

"Thank you." I could leave it to interpretation, but I've learned some things are better said explicitly. "For being my friend when I wouldn't fully let myself be yours."

She smiles at me without the walls she's had to build around herself. I built mine in makeup and dark colors and apathy. Santiago built his in jokes and pretending and running away.

Whitney was far more discreet. She built hers in social status, in big parties and being loved by the world. Because she couldn't feel her brother's love anymore.

"I'm glad I did it," she says.

The bell rings, so we collect our trash and stand up. I do something I haven't done in years and hug her tightly and unapologetically. The way she grips me back denies my worst fears. This isn't a goodbye.

I'm proven right a few weeks later.

Whitney is already waiting with the spare graduation cap when Santiago and I get out of my car. She does a slow scan of my outfit. Black skirt, fishnets, black mesh long-sleeve with a tank over it. Chains galore and my usual makeup, though I went for purple eyeliner today instead of black. She shakes her head, laughing to herself as Santiago greets her with a hug. Like we didn't all have dinner together last night. "At least you've got some color."

Santi's brow furrows, so I clue him in. "Whitney has thoughts on me looking like *this*."

"Like what?" he asks, arm still hooked over Whitney's shoulders. "Gorgeous? Stunning? *Bea*-utiful?" Whitney and I both groan, but my heart warms.

"We get it." Whitney nudges him but doesn't pull away. "You two slept together."

Santi blushes. "Takes one to know one."

"Hey, I just realized that we can compare notes!" she says, delighted.

"*Okay.*" I step between them. "That's enough of that."

Whitney winks at Santi and walks away to answer her phone. I recognize her ringtone for Abby. "We'll talk later."

Years have passed since I've been here, so I don't know if this constitutes as busy. But scattered across the cemetery are people, some in groups, some alone. In their grasps are flowers and photos and one another's hands. Even the plaques with no one standing by them are decorated with signs of life.

I used to come here with Bryce, especially during the last year of his life. He'd trace the lines of his father's headstone, looking like he had half a mind to dig a hole, crawl in, and join him. I thought I understood that. The burning desire to slip out of a world where you lost someone too soon. Though part of me does get it now, I see it differently.

I want a life without pain and loss and grief and heartbreak and guilt. Bryce didn't want a life with those things. Semantics, I know. But the difference remains.

He deserved more time.

Santiago blocks the sun and view as he leans over me. One hand rests under my jaw and the other softly sweeps my cheekbone until it catches an eyelash. He presents it to me with a small smile. "You want to make a wish?" I ask him.

He blows it away without a thought. I wrap my hand around his wrist and pull it close, if for nothing other than to feel his heartbeat. It doesn't perfectly match my own, but it doesn't need to.

"I'm glad you came back," I say.

He swallows. "I'm glad you stayed." And I know exactly what he means. Because I am too.

We give Olive time on their own. When Whitney returns, we talk about graduating tomorrow. We talk about summer plans. We talk about staying in touch, finding time to visit. Santi and me to New Hampshire. Whitney to California. All of us back here. It's casual, but we know the value in the words.

Olive waves when they're ready for company, and then the three of us join hands.

I almost came alone because I thought this was something I should do by myself. That line of thinking may have always been my problem, or at least part of it. *Should* versus *want to*. Again with the semantics.

But I meant what I told Mom. I don't want the world, I want to be happy. At least sometimes. I don't know if I'd actually like to reach a day where losing someone I loved doesn't make me sad. The bitter truth is that my grief will probably always be a little earth-shattering, and I think that might be okay. Feelings aren't mutually exclusive.

I cannot have that dream life with a living father, a living Bryce. I cannot have a life without pain and loss and grief and heartbreak and guilt.

I can, however, have this life. A smile on my face in a cemetery, hands held by good people on a good day, the sun still the brightest star in the sky.

acknowledgments

As always, thank you to my absolute dream agent, Thao Le, for consistently championing me and my books. So much appreciation for the entire Sandra Dijkstra Literary team, especially Jennifer Kim and Andrea Cavallaro.

Thank you to Rachel Diebel for three whole books together! It's an unreal joy and honor to work with you, and there's no one I'd have trusted more with this story. Plus, I needed all of the SoCal humbling.

Thank you to everyone at Macmillan and Feiwel and Friends for their work on my books, including but not limited to: Jean Feiwel, Avia Perez, Kelly Markus, Jie Yang, Kim Waymer, Kelsey Marrujo, Natalia Becerra, Liz Szabla, Rich Deas, Anna Roberto, Holly West, Kat Brzozowski, Dawn Ryan, Emily Settle, Foyinsi Adegbonmire, and Brittany Groves. Thank you Taylor Pitts for copyediting and Kerry Johnson for proofreading. Abby Granata and Ursula Cordova, I cannot put into words how much I love this cover you've both blessed me with.

Thank you to readers new and old for being here. It means the world.

Thank you to my therapist for helping me process much of what inspired this book.

d.a.c.u.—aka Christina, Chloe, Tashie, and Zoe—you are godsends in publishing and life.

Bubs, our friendship is the great love.

There are too many of you to list every time, so thank you to all my family and friends for your endless support and keeping me grounded. A chunk of this first draft was written on your sofa, Abuela.

To every late loved one, thank you for blessing me with whatever time we had together. Who you were in life made even the deepest pits of my grief well worth the pain.

Dan and Bree, I love you both. We've got Nobel Prizes to win.

Dad, I love you, you're the best. I will always know what being believed in feels like because of you. Mwuah mwuah.

Mom, I love you, I miss you. Thank you for everything, but especially the small things. I don't think you ever knew what a life vest a sandwich or brownie or car ride or movie together could be. I hope to see you again someday. Besitos.

Fourteen-year-old Racquel who slapped on some dark makeup and played pretend in her room, thank you for the seed that grew into Beatriz and this story. These characters have been a campfire and a blanket and a safe space for me to examine what you weren't ready to at fourteen. Eleven years later, our dream book is out in the world, and we're still here. Cheers to every version of this story we've written—there have been a lot, but I have to immortalize *The Lost Acquaintances of a Fallen Star* in print for old times' sake—and to every version of ourselves we've been and will become. I promise to continue meeting myself on the other side of every bad day.